CHILDHOOD, BOYHOOD, AND YOUTH

Leo Tolstoy

Childhood, Boyhood, and Youth

Translated with an Introduction
by Michael Scammell

THE MODERN LIBRARY

NEW YORK

2002 Modern Library Paperback Edition
Biographical note copyright © 1994 by Random House, Inc.
Introduction copyright © 2002 by Michael Scammell

LIBRARY OF CONGRESS CATALOGING-IN-PUBLICATION DATA
Tolstoy, Leo, graf, 1828–1910.
[Detstvo, otrochestvo i iunost'. English]
Childhood, boyhood, and youth : a novel/Leo Tolstoy; translated, with an
introduction, by Michael Scammell.
p.   cm.
ISBN 0-375-75944-1
I. Scammell, Michael. II. Title.
PG3366.D5   2002
891.73'3—dc21   2001057937

Modern Library website address:
www.modernlibrary.com

Printed in the United States of America

2 4 6 8 9 7 5 3 1

LEO TOLSTOY

Count Lev (Leo) Nikolayevich Tolstoy was born on August 28, 1828, at Yasnaya Polyana (Bright Glade), his family's estate located 130 miles southwest of Moscow. He was the fourth of five children born to Count Nikolay Ilyich Tolstoy and Marya Nikolayevna Tolstoya (née Princess Volkonskaya, who died when Tolstoy was barely two). He enjoyed a privileged childhood typical of his elevated social class (his patrician family was older and prouder than the tsar's). Early on, the boy showed a gift for languages as well as a fondness for literature— including fairy tales, the poems of Pushkin, and the Bible, especially the Old Testament story of Joseph. Orphaned at the age of nine by the death of his father, Tolstoy and his brothers and sister were first cared for by a devoutly religious aunt. When she died in 1841 the family went to live with their father's only surviving sister in the provincial city of Kazan. Tolstoy was educated by French and German tutors until he enrolled at Kazan University in 1844. There he studied law and Oriental languages and developed a keen interest in moral philosophy and the writings of Rousseau. A notably unsuccessful student who led a dissolute life, Tolstoy abandoned his studies in 1847 without earning a degree and returned to Yasnaya Polyana to claim the property (along with 350 serfs and their families) that was his birthright.

After several aimless years of debauchery and gambling in Moscow and St. Petersburg, Tolstoy journeyed to the Caucasus in 1851 to join his older brother Nikolay, an army lieutenant participating in the Caucasian campaign. The following year Tolstoy officially enlisted in the military, and in 1854 he became a commissioned officer in the artillery, serving first on the Danube and later in the Crimean War. Although his sexual escapades and profligate gambling during this period shocked even his fellow soldiers, it was while in the army that Tolstoy began his literary apprenticeship. Greatly influenced by the works of Rousseau, Sterne, and Dickens, Tolstoy wrote *Childhood,* his first novel. Published pseudonymously in September 1852 in *The Contemporary,* a St. Petersburg journal, the book received highly favorable reviews—earning the praise of Turgenev—and overnight established Tolstoy as a major writer. Over the next years he contributed several novels and short stories (about military life) to *The Contemporary*— including *Boyhood* (1854), *Three Sebastopol Sketches* (1855–1856), "Two Hussars" (1856), and *Youth* (1857).

In 1856 Tolstoy left the army and went to live in St. Petersburg, where he was much in demand in fashionable salons. He quickly discovered, however, that he disliked the life of a literary celebrity (he often quarreled with fellow writers, especially Turgenev) and soon departed on his first trip to western Europe. Upon returning to Russia, he produced the story "Three Deaths" and a short novel, *Family Happiness,* both published in 1859. Afterward, Tolstoy decided to abandon literature in favor of more "useful" pursuits. He retired to Yasnaya Polyana to manage his estate and established a school there for the education of children of his serfs. In 1860 he again traveled abroad in order to observe European (especially German) educational systems; he later published *Yasnaya Polyana,* a journal expounding his theories on pedagogy. The following year he was appointed an arbiter of the peace to settle disputes between newly emancipated serfs and their former masters. But in July 1862 the police raided the school at Yasnaya Polyana for evidence of subversive activity. The search elicited an indignant protest from Tolstoy directly to Alexander II, who officially exonerated him.

That same summer, at the age of thirty-four, Tolstoy fell in love with eighteen-year-old Sofya Andreyevna Bers, who was living with her parents on a nearby estate. (As a girl she had reverently memorized whole passages of *Childhood.*) The two were married on September 23, 1862, in a church inside the Kremlin walls. The early years of the marriage were largely joyful (thirteen children were born of the union) and coincided with the period of Tolstoy's great novels. In 1863 he not only published *The Cossacks,* but began work on *War and Peace,* his great epic novel that came out in 1869.

Then, on March 18, 1873, inspired by the opening of a fragmentary tale by Pushkin, Tolstoy started writing *Anna Karenina.* Originally titled *Two Marriages,* the book underwent multiple revisions and was serialized to great popular and critical acclaim between 1875 and 1877.

It was during the torment of writing *Anna Karenina* that Tolstoy experienced the spiritual crisis that recast the rest of his life. Haunted by the inevitability of death, he underwent a "conversion" to the ideals of human life and conduct that he found in the teachings of Christ. *A Confession* (1882), which was banned in Russia, marked this change in his life and works. Afterward, he became an extreme rationalist and moralist, and in a series of pamphlets published during his remaining years Tolstoy rejected both church and state, denounced private ownership of property, and advocated celibacy, even in marriage. In 1897 he even went so far as to denounce his own novels, as well as many other classics, including Shakespeare's *Hamlet* and Beethoven's Ninth Symphony, for being morally irresponsible, elitist, and corrupting. His teachings earned him numerous followers in Russia ("We have two tsars, Nicholas II and Leo Tolstoy," a journalist wrote) and abroad (most notably, Mahatma Gandhi) but also many opponents, and in 1902 he was excommunicated by the Russian holy synod. Prompted by Turgenev's deathbed entreaty ("My friend, return to literature!"), Tolstoy did produce several more short stories and novels—including the ongoing series *Stories for the People,* "The Death of Ivan Ilyich" (1886), *The Kreutzer Sonata* (1889), "Master and Man" (1895), *Resurrection*

(1899), and *Hadji Murad* (published posthumously)—as well as a play, *The Power of Darkness* (1886).

Tolstoy's controversial views produced a great strain on his marriage, and his relationship with his wife deteriorated. "Until the day I die she will be a stone around my neck," he wrote. "I must learn not to drown with this stone around my neck." Finally, on the morning of October 28, 1910, Tolstoy fled by railroad from Yasnaya Polyana headed for a monastery in search of peace and solitude. However, illness forced Tolstoy off the train at Astapovo; he was given refuge in the stationmaster's house and died there on November 7. His body was buried two days later in a forest at Yasnaya Polyana.

Contents

Biographical Note   v

Introduction *by Michael Scammell*   xv

A Note on the Translation   xxiii

I: CHILDHOOD

I. Karl Ivanich, the Tutor   3

II. *Maman*   9

III. Papa   12

IV. Classes   17

V. The Holy Fool   21

VI. Preparations for the Hunt   26

VII. The Hunt   29

VIII. Playing   34

IX. Something Like First Love   36

X. What Kind of Man Was My Father?   38

XI. In the Study and Drawing Room   41

XII. Grisha   45

XIII. Natalya Savishna   48

XIV. Parting   52

XV. Childhood   57

XVI. VERSES   60

XVII. PRINCESS KORNAKOV   66

XVIII. PRINCE IVAN IVANICH   70

XIX. THE IVINS   75

XX. THE GUESTS ARRIVE   82

XXI. BEFORE THE MAZURKA   87

XXII. THE MAZURKA   91

XXIII. AFTER THE MAZURKA   94

XXIV. IN BED   98

XXV. A LETTER   100

XXVI. WHAT AWAITED US IN THE COUNTRY   105

XXVII. GRIEF   108

XXVIII. MY LAST SORROWFUL REMINISCENCES   113

II: BOYHOOD

I. THE JOURNEY TO MOSCOW   125

II. THE THUNDERSTORM   132

III. A NEW VIEW OF THINGS   137

IV. IN MOSCOW   142

V. MY ELDER BROTHER   144

VI. MASHA   148

VII. BUCKSHOT   151

VIII. KARL IVANICH'S STORY   155

IX. THE FOREGOING CONTINUED   159

X. CONTINUED   163

XI. A BAD MARK   166

XII. THE KEY   171

XIII. THE DECEIVER   174

XIV. ECLIPSE   176

XV. DAYDREAMS   179

XVI. IT WILL ALL COME OUT IN THE WASH   183

XVII. HATRED   188

XVIII. THE MAIDS' ROOM   191

XIX. BOYHOOD   196

XX. VOLODYA   200

XXI. KATYENKA AND LYUBOCHKA   203

XXII. PAPA   205

XXIII. GRANDMOTHER   208

XXIV. ME   211

XXV. VOLODYA'S FRIENDS   213

XXVI. DISCUSSIONS   216

XXVII. THE BEGINNING OF A FRIENDSHIP   221

III: YOUTH

I. WHAT I CONSIDER THE BEGINNING OF MY YOUTH   227

II. SPRING   229

III. DAYDREAMS   233

IV. OUR FAMILY CIRCLE   237

V. RULES   242

VI. CONFESSION   245

VII. A TRIP TO THE MONASTERY   247

VIII. A SECOND CONFESSION   251

IX. How I Prepared for the Examinations 254

X. The History Examination 257

XI. The Mathematics Examination 262

XII. The Latin Examination 266

XIII. I Am Grown-up 270

XIV. What Volodya and Dubkov Were Doing 275

XV. My Success Is Celebrated 279

XVI. A Quarrel 283

XVII. I Prepare to Make Some Calls 288

XVIII. The Valakhins 292

XIX. The Kornakovs 297

XX. The Ivins 300

XXI. Prince Ivan Ivanich 304

XXII. A Heart-to-Heart Talk with My Friend 307

XXIII. The Nekhlyudovs 312

XXIV. Love 317

XXV. I Become Better Acquainted 322

XXVI. I Am Seen to My Best Advantage 326

XXVII. Dmitri 330

XXVIII. In the Country 335

XXIX. Our Relations with the Girls 340

XXX. My Occupations 345

XXXI. *Comme il faut* 349

XXXII. Youth 353

XXXIII. The Neighbors 359

XXXIV. Father's Marriage 364

XXXV. How We Took the News 368

XXXVI. University   373

XXXVII. Affairs of the Heart   378

XXXVIII. Society   381

XXXIX. A Drinking Party   384

XL. Friendship with the Nekhlyudovs   389

XLI. Friendship with Nekhlyudov   393

XLII. Our Stepmother   398

XLIII. New Companions   404

XLIV. Zukhin and Semyonov   411

XLV. I Fail   417

Introduction

Michael Scammell

Leo Tolstoy is best known for the two great novels that crowned his mature career, *War and Peace* and *Anna Karenina*. Many readers may also be familiar with the stories and novellas of his late period: "The Death of Ivan Ilyich," *Resurrection,* and *Hadji Murad.* Much less familiar, however, are the early works he wrote before attaining international fame, including a first "novel" that displayed much of the psychological penetration, moral fervor, and vivid characterization for which he is so admired. The work in question, *Childhood, Boyhood, and Youth,* deserves to have the term *novel* in quotes not for any shortcomings of style or characterization (despite the fact that it was Tolstoy's first published work), but rather because of its almost ostentatious absence of conventional "plot." It was an early example of Tolstoy's notorious disregard for form, which he underlined by never quite finishing his original plan for the work.

Tolstoy began it in 1851, at the age of twenty-three, while serving as a cadet in the Russian army in the Caucasus. He was completely unknown at the time and was taking an active part (so active that he almost got himself killed at one point) in one of Russia's innumerable campaigns to subdue Chechnya. His original plan was to write a novel in four parts covering "Childhood, Boyhood, Adolescence, and Youth," and it was intended to be in the form of letters to a friend, an idea inspired in part by the epistolary novels of the eighteenth century, and more particularly by Laurence Sterne's *A Sentimental Journey,* a book that Tolstoy had studied from cover to cover and even started to translate into Russian.

This was not Tolstoy's first effort at writing. He had drafted plans for several literary ventures, including a history of twenty-four hours in his life that in many ways anticipated Joyce. The latter was not irrelevant to the new work, either, since most of Part One covers little more than two and a half days in the life of the first-person narrator. Having completed the first part, Tolstoy sent it to the famous poet Nikolai Nekrasov, who was then editing Russia's leading liberal journal of the day, *The Contemporary.* He accompanied it with a humble note begging to be informed if it was worth printing, adding that the editor's decision would answer the question of whether he would keep writing or "burn everything I have begun." Nekrasov not only considered the manuscript worth printing, but he wrote to his still unknown correspondent (Tolstoy had signed himself with the initials of his first name and patronymic, L.N.) that he was extremely impressed by the "simplicity and reality" of its subject matter and hoped to be able to publish the sequel when it was ready, for its author undoubtedly had talent.

Misled by the first-person autobiographical form of the narrative, Nekrasov printed it as *The Story of My Childhood,* thus arousing the ire of the superficially humble but in fact extremely proud *Count* Leo Tolstoy. Replete though the story was with genuinely autobiographical detail, Tolstoy had manipulated the facts and combined or altered actual characters to create a "universal" portrait of childhood that would go well beyond the experience of a single individual. He informed Nekrasov of this fact in no uncertain terms in a letter that he then judged too wrathful to send (but nevertheless saved for posterity), and replaced it with a milder and more politic version.

The reviews in the main literary magazines of the day went far to mollify the author's hurt pride. One prescient critic stated that if this was the unknown author's first work, "Russian literature is to be congratulated on the appearance of a new and remarkable talent." Turgenev, then Russia's leading novelist, sent warm greetings and sincere praise to the unknown young author via Nekrasov, and even Dostoevsky, in distant Siberian exile, took note of the remarkable story he had just read in *The Contemporary.*

Tolstoy's originality was apparent from the outset. His starting point was the conviction that "nobody before me had ever felt or expressed the poetry of that age" (that is, childhood), and he set out to communicate that poetry via the intense emotions, confusions, and fears attendant upon a young boy growing up in a loving but not entirely happy family circle. The freshness of his approach was linked with his energetic repudiation of the excesses of the romantics and the "sentimental school" in Russian literature that had preceded him. "What garbage are those tears that resemble pearls and eyes that sparkle like diamonds," he wrote in a preface that remained unpublished. "I have never seen lips of coral, but lips the color of brick; nor turquoise eyes, but eyes the color of laundry blueing." Such blunt honesty and reductive imagery were essential components of Tolstoy's aesthetic, which demanded "truth to life" as a condition of all art worth the name.

He also insisted on emotional honesty. When the boyish hero and narrator of *Childhood*, Nikolenka (Nikolai), tries to recollect the way his mother had looked before she died, for example, he confesses that he cannot remember her general appearance. Yet what he does remember conveys an unforgettable impression of the figure of a beloved mother. The young boy "sees"—the verb is important—in his mind's eye "her nut-brown eyes, always with the same expression of kindness and love in them, the birthmark on her neck, a fraction below the spot where there were some tiny curly hairs, her white embroidered collar, and the thin tender hand that had so often caressed me and that I had so often kissed." Such details might be considered just what a very young child *would* see and remember of a dead mother, but the secret of Tolstoy's success as an artist lies not just in his physical descriptions but in the combination of the physical with the psychological: the mother's eyes are not just nut-brown, but filled with kindness and love; her hand is not just thin, but tender and caressing.

It is possible that Tolstoy learned his sensitivity to gesture and his tender sensibility from Sterne, but he also owed a great deal to *David Copperfield*, which he read during this period; Dickens offered the idea that childhood holds the key to the mysteries of a person's behavior. But Tolstoy went beyond both Sterne and Dickens in making the workings of memory an essential part of his method. As is often the case with artists of genius, he was ahead of his time. Not only Joyce but Proust, too, was to explore in exhaustive detail the role of "emotion recollected in tranquility," and childhood was a perfect subject for such an exercise.

Another indispensable element of Tolstoy's talent was his determination to expose the bogus and the false, and the contradictions inherent in human beings and their works. As he wrote in his unpublished preface, "I have never met a man who was all bad, all pride, all good, or all intelligence." And he added with a touch of perverseness: "I can see stupidity in even the most intelligent book, and intelligent things in the conversation of even the greatest fool alive." In fact he did not suffer fools gladly, especially of his own class. But he was unusual among his Russian contemporaries in being prepared to take his readers into the servants' quarters and paint sympathetic portraits of tutors, stewards, and housekeepers (again following Dickens). Above all he revered family values and the intimacies of the family circle, writing, in *Boyhood*, of "those mysterious wordless relations that reveal themselves in an imperceptible smile, a gesture, or a glance between people who live constantly together."

It was two years before Tolstoy felt ready to send *Boyhood* to *The Contemporary*, and it proved every bit as successful with the reading public as its predecessor. Covering the years until the moment when Nikolai enters the university, it has the distinction of being written partly in the present tense, an evidently unconscious expression of Tolstoy's thrust for immediacy, though he seems not to have planned it that way. But with all the continuing freshness and delicacy of its prose, the reader becomes increasingly aware of another feature of Tolstoy's style: his proclivity for philosophical digressions and moralizing. Many of these are attractive and quite striking: "It seems to me that the human mind in each individual follows the same path in its development as that of whole generations" or "happiness does not depend on external causes but on our attitude to them." But as the narrative of *Boyhood* progresses, they begin to take up more space and at times come to seem almost intrusive.

After the completion of *Boyhood,* Tolstoy applied his creative talents to other genres. In 1855–56 he published *The Sebastopol Sketches,* three stories of Russian soldiers in action in the Crimean War that anticipated some of the battle scenes in *War and Peace,* and his first short story, "Two Hussars." He was evidently tiring of his original project, for it was not until 1857 that the third part, *Youth,* finally appeared in print, and the fourth part, *Adulthood,* was never written.

On the one hand, Tolstoy seems simply to have run out of steam, but on the other, he was having genuine problems with form. In his initial acceptance letter, Nekrasov had written of *Childhood* that "if, as is to be expected, the sequel contains more animation and action, it will be a fine novel." By "animation and action" Nekrasov seems to have meant plot, but a plausible plot for the novel was precisely what eluded Tolstoy. It was to prove a lifelong problem, notably in *War and Peace* but also in his "tightest" work, *Anna Karenina.* Henry James, a vigorous proponent of the tightly knit, artistically shaped novel, dismissed Tolstoy's mature masterpieces as "loose and baggy monsters, with their queer elements of the accidental and the arbitrary," and found much sympathy for his views among fellow practitioners and critics of his era, particularly as realism in the novel ceded ground to modernism.

Tolstoy undoubtedly had a problem with tying up loose ends, but the "meandering and seemingly ungoverned design" of his major works, as George Steiner once put it, was not entirely accidental, for Tolstoy's disdain for the conventions of literature extended to what he regarded as the artificial constraints of plot and suspense as well. Such disdain was part and parcel of his hectic impatience with the conventions and vanities of social life in general, and of a piece with his desire to dig down to the bedrock of human nature and study it untrammeled by rules and regulations. Furthermore, Tolstoy wanted to leave room for moral digressions, exhortations to spiritual betterment, and philosophical observations that would underpin the psychological realism and truth to observed life that he strove for: everything else should be sacrificed to that end.

It cannot be said that Tolstoy (whatever the strictures of Henry James) was naïve about his art. He revised over and over again with enormous care, even when writing *Childhood,* and was so sure of his grasp of human psychology, and so secure in his realism, that his prose comes to seem as transparent as a pane of glass through which we, his readers, are free to observe the teeming life on the other side. Matthew Arnold expressed this thought when he wrote (of *Anna Karenina,* though it could apply to most of Tolstoy's major works) that the novel should be taken "not . . . as a work of art" but rather as "a piece of life." It was an absurd statement in some ways, but Tolstoy would have understood and been pleased by it. He wanted nothing better than for the reader to stroll through his stories unconstrained by the exigencies of plot or incident, and to encounter characters who are far too vivid and interesting for it to matter whether something outwardly dramatic happens to them, or their problems are neatly resolved in the end.

Such is quintessentially the experience of the reader of *Childhood, Boyhood, and Youth,* who gets to know the heart and mind of the young boy Nikolenka from the very inside, is gradually introduced to his tutors, his siblings, and his family circle, then gets to watch him grow up, widen his circle, make friends, and fashion a social life, all the while observing his emotional problems, his moral dilemmas, his successes, and his failures. In effect it is Tolstoy's version of the bildungsroman, except that he can't be bothered to fashion it into a proper story with a climax and a denouement.

The novel ends when Nikolenka experiences a typical burst of repentance over some bad behavior and vows for the umpteenth time to reform his life, promising on behalf of himself (and Tolstoy) that he will report on the results in the next installment of his saga, which will be devoted to "the second and happier half of my youth." There never was a fourth and final installment, for "happiness," as Tolstoy remarked at the start of *Anna Karenina* ("All happy families are alike, but each unhappy family is unhappy in its own way"), is generally uninteresting; and so there is no conclusion per se. Tolstoy leaves the reader hanging, just as in real life we see individuals or groups of people for the last time without knowing it will be so, and without the benefit of closure. But it doesn't matter, because the journey Tolstoy takes us on has been so delightful, the characters on the other side of the glass so fascinating, and the lives we have seen so vivid and instructive that we are more than content to have come as far as this.

———

MICHAEL SCAMMELL is the author of *Solzhenitsyn: A Biography,* and has translated many works of fiction and nonfiction from Russian, including Dostoevsky's *Crime and Punishment,* and *The Gift* and *The Defense,* by Nabokov. He teaches nonfiction writing and translation at Columbia University, and is working on a biography of Arthur Koestler.

A Note on the Translation

Nearly four decades have elapsed since I completed this translation of Tolstoy's first novel. Given the passage of time, it would be surprising if I didn't find things I would do differently now—choosing different words, different cadences, different syntax in some cases. But the real surprise to me is how little I would change. Tolstoy's prose is not difficult to translate. His Russian was heavily influenced by French, a language that he learned, as we see in *Childhood,* virtually from the cradle. And he was surrounded during his early years by people for whom French was the preferred medium of polite conversation, a convention he satirized in the opening pages of *War and Peace* by writing the dialogue all in French.

Tolstoy's syntax is Latinate, akin to Turgenev's but wholly different from the quintessentially Russian syntax of his illustrious contemporaries Gogol and Dostoevsky. Tolstoy also strives for the utmost simplicity and transparency, and some of the awkwardness of his long phrases arises from precisely this fanatical search for the right word and the right image, no matter what the cost in rhythm and euphony. In my translation I tried to recapture that awkwardness, hewing to the doctrine of "the servile path" instilled in me by the author of that doctrine, Vladimir Nabokov, whose work I had translated earlier (and Nabokov had an enormous admiration for Tolstoy). It may be fanciful on my part, but I think that my youth also had something to do with it: adhering as strictly as possible to the original was both a cover for timidity and a hedge against criticism, not to speak of a by-product of inexperience.

The text from which this translation was made was published by the State Publishing House, Khudozhestvennaya Literatura, Moscow, in 1955, which reproduced the text that appears in volumes one and two of the ninety-volume Jubilee Edition of Tolstoy's complete works in Russian.

M.S.

I: CHILDHOOD

I

KARL IVANICH, THE TUTOR

At 7 A.M. on August 12, 18—, on exactly the third day after my tenth birthday, when I had received such wonderful presents, Karl Ivanich woke me up with a fly swatter—made of wrapping paper on the end of a stick—with which he was swatting a fly immediately over my head. He did this so awkwardly that he jogged the picture of my guardian angel which was hanging on the oaken headboard of my bed, and the dead fly fell directly on my head. I thrust my nose out from under the quilt, steadied the still-swaying picture with my hand, brushed the dead fly onto the floor, and cast a sleepy but irate glance at Karl Ivanich. But he, dressed in his brightly colored, quilted dressing gown, which was gathered at the waist with a belt of the same material, and wearing a red knitted skullcap with a tassel, and soft goatskin slippers on his feet, continued to patrol the walls, taking aim at the flies and swatting them.

"Just because I'm small," I thought, "why does he have to bother me? Why doesn't he swat the flies by Volodya's bed? There are heaps of them there! No, Volodya's older than me; and I'm the youngest of all: that's why he tortures the life out of me. All he thinks about the whole time," I whispered to myself, "is how to be unpleasant to me. He knows very well that he woke me up and frightened me, but he makes out he didn't notice . . . what a nasty man! And his dressing gown and cap and tassel—they're all nasty!"

While I was thus mentally expressing my displeasure with Karl Ivanich, he went to his bed, looked at the watch hanging over it in a beaded and embroidered leather slipper, hung the fly swatter on a nail and turned to us in what was clearly an excellent frame of mind.

"Auf, Kinder, auf! . . . s'ist Zeit. Die Mutter ist schon im Saal," he cried in his kind, German voice; then he came to me, sat at the foot of the bed, and took a snuffbox from his pocket. I pretended to be sleeping. First Karl Ivanich took a pinch of snuff, wiped his nose and snapped his fingers, and only then did he turn his attention to me. Smilingly he began to tickle my heels. *"Nun, nun, Faulenzer!"* he said.

Afraid as I was of the tickling, I nonetheless refrained from jumping up in bed and did not answer him, merely thrusting my head farther under the pillows, kicking my legs as hard as I could and making every effort not to laugh.

How kind he is and how he loves us, and yet I was able to think so badly of him!

I was annoyed both with myself and with Karl Ivanich; I felt like laughing and crying at the same time. My nerves were on edge.

"Ach, lassen Sie, Karl Ivanich!" I cried with tears in my eyes, thrusting my head out from under the pillows.

Karl Ivanich was taken aback. He left my feet alone and began asking me what the matter was and had I perhaps had a bad dream. . . . His kind, German face and the concern with which he tried to divine the reason for my tears caused them to flow even faster: I felt ashamed and could not understand how a moment before I had been capable of not loving Karl Ivanich and of finding his dressing gown, cap, and tassel nasty. Now, on the contrary, they all seemed extraordinarily nice to me and even the tassel seemed clear proof of his kindness. I told him I was crying because I had had a bad dream—to the effect that *maman* had died and was being taken away to be buried. All this I invented because I had not the slightest recollection of what I had dreamed that night; but when Karl Ivanich, touched by my story, began to comfort me and soothe me, I began to feel that I really had dreamed that terrible dream and my tears now flowed for an entirely different reason.

When Karl Ivanich had left me and I sat up in bed and started pulling my socks onto my little legs, my tears abated a bit, but I was still plagued by gloomy thoughts about the dream I had invented. Our manservant Nikolai came in. He was a tiny tidy little man, always serious, proper and deferential and a great friend of Karl Ivanich. He was carrying our clothes and footwear: boots for Volodya, while I still had to wear those hateful shoes with ribbons on them. I would have been ashamed to cry in his presence. Furthermore, morning sunshine was pouring merrily in through the windows and Volodya, making fun of Marya Ivanovna (our sister's governess), laughed so merrily and heartily as he stood over the washstand that even the serious Nikolai, standing there with a towel over his shoulder, soap in one hand and basin in the other, said with a smile:

"That'll do, Vladimir Petrovich; please get on with your washing."

I cheered up completely.

"Sind Sie bald fertig?" came Karl Ivanich's voice from the classroom.

His voice was stern and no longer held that kindness that had moved me to tears. Karl Ivanich was a completely different man in the classroom: he was a schoolmaster. I washed and dressed myself promptly and with hairbrush still in hand, smoothing my wet hair as I went, answered his summons.

Karl Ivanich, glasses on nose, book in hand, was sitting in his usual place between the door and the window. To the left of the door were two shelves: one was ours, the children's; the other was Karl Ivanich's *own*. Ours contained all sorts of books—school and nonschool: some were standing, others lay flat. Only two large volumes, *Histoire des voyages,* in red bindings, were leaning sedately against the wall; then came long ones, fat ones, big ones, small ones—covers without books and books without covers; everything got squeezed and pushed in there just before playtime, when we were told to straighten out the library, as the shelf was loudly termed by Karl Ivanich. The collection of books on his *own* shelf, though not as large as ours, was even more heterogeneous. I can remember three of them: a German brochure on the manuring of cabbage—without a binding; one volume of a history of the Seven Years' War—in parchment that was burned at one corner; and a complete course of hydrostatics. Karl Ivanich used to spend the greater part of his time reading and even ruined his eyes with it; but he never read anything apart from these books and the magazine *Northern Bee*.

Among the objects lying on Karl Ivanich's shelf there was one that reminds me of him most of all. This was a cardboard disk mounted on a wooden column in which the disk moved by means of little pegs. The disk had a picture pasted on it representing a caricature of some lady or other and a barber. Karl Ivanich was very good at pasting things and had invented this disk himself, in order to protect his eyes from strong light.

I can see his long figure before me now in his quilted dressing gown and red cap, his thin gray hair peeping out from underneath. He sits beside a small table on which stands the disk with the barber on it, casting a shadow on his face; in one hand he is holding a book, while the other rests on the arm of his chair; beside him are his watch, with a picture of a hunter on the dial, his checked handkerchief, his round black snuffbox, a green eyeglass case, and snuffers on a tray. All this lies so sedately and neatly in its place that from this good order alone one may conclude that Karl Ivanich has a clear conscience and a heart at rest.

Sometimes, when you were tired of running about downstairs in the salon, you would creep upstairs on tiptoe and into the classroom and look—and there would be Karl Ivanich, sitting all alone in his chair and reading one of his favorite books, with an expression of calm gravity on his face. Sometimes I would catch him at moments when he was not reading: his glasses would have slipped down his big aquiline nose, his blue half-closed eyes would have some special expression in them, and his lips would be sadly smiling. It would be quiet in the room; all you could hear would be his regular breathing and the ticking of the hunter watch.

Sometimes he did not notice me and I would stand at the door and think. Poor, poor old man! There are lots of us, we can play and it's fun for us, but he—he's all alone and nobody is nice to him. He's telling the truth when he says he's an orphan. And his life has been so terrible! I remember him telling it to Nikolai—it's terrible to be in his position! And you felt so sorry for him that sometimes you went up to him, took his hand, and said: "*Lieber* Karl Ivanich!" He used to like it when I said that to him. He would always caress me and you could see he was touched.

Maps used to hang on another wall; they were all almost in pieces, but they had been skillfully stuck together by Karl Ivanich. In the middle of the third wall was the door that led downstairs, to one side of which hung two rulers: one, all scored, was ours; the other, newish-looking, was his *own*, used more for encouragement than for drawing lines. On the other side of the door was a blackboard on which a series of circles indicated our major misdemeanors, while our minor ones were marked by little crosses. To the left of the blackboard was the corner in which we were made to kneel down.

How well I remember that corner! I remember the flap on the stove and the airhole in the flap, and also the noise it used to make when you lifted it up. Sometimes you would kneel and kneel there in the corner, so that your knees and back would ache and you thought: Karl Ivanich has forgotten about me. It must be quite nice for him to sit there in that soft armchair and read about hydrostatics—but what about me?—and in order to remind him of your presence you would begin gently to open and close the flap or would start picking plaster from the wall; but if a piece that was too big suddenly fell on the floor with a bang, truly the fright alone was worse than any punishment. But when you looked round at Karl Ivanich, he would be sitting there, book in hand, as though noticing nothing at all.

There was a table standing in the middle of the room, covered with torn black oilcloth through which, in many places, one could see the edges, all cut about with penknives. Around the table were several stools, unpainted but polished by long use. The fourth wall contained three windows. The view from them was as follows: directly below the window was a road whose every pothole, every pebble, and every rut were long familiar and dear to me; beyond the road was an avenue of pollarded lime trees through which, in places, could be glimpsed a wicket fence; across the avenue one could see the meadow, with a barn on one side of it and woods on the other; deep in the woods could be seen the gamekeeper's hut. From the window on the right one could see part of the terrace where the grown-ups normally sat before dinner. Sometimes, while Karl Ivanich was correcting your dictation, when you looked out there, you could see Mama's dark head and somebody else's back and you would hear the distant sounds of talking and laughter. Then you would feel so discontented not to be able to be there that you would think: When will I ever be grown up and have no more lessons and be able to spend all my time sitting with my loved ones and not over these exercises? Discontent would change to sadness and you grew so preoccupied, God knows why or wherefore, that you did not even hear when Karl Ivanich grumbled about your mistakes.

Karl Ivanich took off his dressing gown, put on a blue frock coat with padded pleated shoulders, straightened his tie before the mirror, and led us downstairs—to say good morning to Mama.

II

MAMAN

Mama was sitting in the drawing room pouring tea; with one hand she held the teapot, with the other the tap of the samovar—from which water was flowing over the top of the teapot and onto the tray. But although she was staring straight at it, she did not notice it, nor the fact that we had entered.

So many memories of the past start up when your imagination endeavors to resurrect the features of a beloved one that through these memories, as through tears, you see them only vaguely. These are memory's tears. When I try to recollect Mama, the way she was at that time, I can see only her nut-brown eyes, always with that same expression of kindness and love in them, the birthmark on her neck a fraction below the spot where there were some tiny curly hairs, her white embroidered collar, and the thin tender hand that had so often caressed me and that I had so often kissed; but her general appearance eludes me.

An English piano stood to the left of the couch; my dark-skinned little sister, Lyubochka, sat at the piano, her pink little fingers, just washed in cold water, running with noticeable difficulty over some *études* by Clementi. She was clever. She used to go about in a short little unbleached linen dress and white lace-edged knickers, and she could manage the octaves only in arpeggio. Beside her and half turned away sat Marya Ivanovna, wearing a bonnet with pink ribbons on it and a blue fur-trimmed jacket, and her red angry face took on an even sterner expression at the appearance of Karl Ivanich. She gave him a ferocious look, without answering his greeting, and went on tapping her foot and counting: *"Un, deux, trois; un, deux, trois"* even louder and more imperiously than before.

Karl Ivanich, as usual paying not the slightest attention to this, went straight to my mother's hand and greeted her in German. My mother remembered herself, gave a shake of her head, as though wishing thereby to drive away sad thoughts, offered her hand to Karl Ivanich, and kissed his wrinkled temple at the same time as he kissed her hand:

"Ich danke, lieber Karl Ivanich," and still talking in German she asked:

"Did the children sleep well?"

Karl Ivanich was deaf in one ear and now, because of the noise from the piano, did not hear a thing. He bent closer to the couch, resting one hand on the table while standing one one leg, and with a smile that seemed to me then the height of delicacy, raised his cap and said:

"With your permission, Natalya Nikolayevna?"

In order not to catch cold with his bare head, Karl Ivanich never took off his red cap, but each time he entered the drawing room he asked permission for this.

"Put it back on, Karl Ivanich. . . . I asked you have the children slept well?" said *maman,* moving closer and speaking quite loudly.

But once again he heard nothing, covering his bald pate with his cap and smiling even more sweetly.

"Stop that for a moment, Mimi," said *maman* to Marya Ivanovna with a smile. "We can't hear a thing."

When mother smiled, no matter how nice her face had been before, it became incomparably nicer and everything around seemed to brighten up as well. If, at difficult moments of my life, I were able even fleetingly to see this smile, I would not know the meaning of sorrow. It seems to me that what people call the beauty of a face is constituted by its smile: if a smile adds glory to a face, then that face is beautiful; if it does not change it, it is ordinary; and if it spoils it, it is ugly.

When she had greeted me, *maman* took my head in both her hands and bent it backwards, then she looked at me closely and said:

"Have you been crying today?"

I did not reply. She kissed my eyes and asked in German:

"What were you crying for?"

When speaking affectionately to us she always used this language, which she knew to perfection.

"I cried in my sleep, *maman*," I said, recalling my invented dream in all its detail and shuddering involuntarily at the thought of it.

Karl Ivanich confirmed my words, but kept silent about the dream. Having talked a little more about the weather—a conversation in which Mimi also participated—*maman* placed six lumps of sugar on the tray for some of the senior servants, stood up and went over to the embroidering frame that stood by the window.

"Well, go to your papa now, children, and tell him to be sure to come and see me before he goes to the barn."

The music, counting, and ferocious glances began again and we went to see Papa. Passing through a room that still retained the name, given to it in grandfather's time, of footmen's room, we entered the study.

III

PAPA

He was standing by his writing table, pointing to some envelopes and papers and piles of money and explaining something heatedly and excitedly to his steward Yakov Mikhailov, who was standing there in his usual spot, between the door and the barometer, with his arms behind his back, twiddling his fingers furiously in all directions.

The more excited Papa grew the faster went the fingers, and vice versa: when Papa fell silent, the fingers stopped too; but when Yakov himself began to speak, his fingers became most terribly agitated and jumped about all over the place. It seemed to me one might have guessed Yakov's most secret thoughts from their motions; but his face was always calm, expressing simultaneously a consciousness both of his own worth and of his subservience to my father, much as to say: I'm right, but then you're the boss!

When he saw us Papa merely said: "Wait just a moment," and nodded at the door for one of us to close it.

"My God, dear fellow! What's up with you today, Yakov?" he continued, speaking to the steward, and shrugged one shoulder (this was a habit of his). "This envelope with eight hundred rubles in it ..."

Yakov drew the abacus closer, marked off eight hundred, and gazed into space, waiting to hear what came next.

". . . is for expenses on the estate while I'm away. Understand? For the mill you're due a thousand rubles . . . right or wrong? On mortgages you're due to get eight thousand back again; for the hay, which you calculated you could sell two thousand tons of—let's say at one ruble fifty a ton—you'll get three thousand; so how much money will you have altogether? Twelve thousand. . . . Right or wrong?"

"Right sir, exactly," said Yakov.

But I noticed from the speed with which his fingers moved that he wanted to object to something; Papa interrupted him:

"Well, send ten thousand of this money to the Council, for the Petrovsky estate. And now for the money on hand," Papa went on (Yakov scrambled the beads on the abacus and marked up twenty-one thousand). "Bring it to me and see you enter it up this very day in your expenditure account. (Yakov scrambled the beads and turned the abacus over, thus indicating, probably, that the twenty-one thousand would go the same way.) And please deliver this envelope with the money in it."

I was standing close to the table and looked at the inscription. It had written on it: "To Karl Ivanovich Mauer."

Noticing, probably, that I had read something that did not concern me, Papa placed a hand on my shoulder and gently pointed me away from the table. I did not know whether this was a caress or a reminder, but just in case I kissed his large sinewy hand as it rested on my shoulder.

"Yes sir," said Yakov. "And what would you like me to do with the Khabarovka money?"

Khabarovka was the village belonging to *maman*.

"Leave it where it is and don't use it under any circumstances without my permission."

Yakov was silent for several seconds; then his fingers suddenly began to twirl at an even greater rate, and exchanging the expression of obedient stupidity with which he usually listened to the master's orders for his natural expression of rascally acumen, he moved the abacus closer again and began to speak:

"Allow me to report, Pyotr Aleksandrich, that, have it your own way, but we won't be able to pay the Council on time. You said," he went on, spacing his words, "that we're due to get money for the mortgages, the mill and the hay (Adding these items up, he marked them on the abacus). . . . And I'm afraid of us being a bit out in our reckoning," he added after a short pause, casting a knowing glance at Papa.

"Why?"

"Well, you see: about the mill. The miller's already been to see me twice to ask for a postponement and swore by the Lord Jesus Christ that he hadn't any money . . . he's here even now, actually: wouldn't you perhaps like to talk to him yourself?"

"What does he say?" asked Papa, indicating with his head that he did not wish to speak to the miller.

"Oh, the usual. He says there's been nothing to grind and that whatever cash he had he put back into his dam. But then, if we dismiss him, sir, what good will that do us? You mentioned the mortgages just now, but I believe I already told you once that our money's stuck there and we won't get it back in a hurry. The other day I sent a load of flour to Ivan Afanasyevich and a note about this business: but there again he replied that he'd be glad to make an effort for Your Worship, but there's nothing he can do about it, and that, the way things look, you'll be lucky to get your settlement even in two months. As far as the hay you mentioned is concerned—well, suppose we even sell three thousand worth—"

He marked up three thousand on the abacus and was silent for a moment, looking from the abacus to Papa and back again, with the expression:

"You can see for yourself how little that is! And there again, we'll lose on the hay if we sell it now, you yourself know that . . ."

It was clear he still had a big reserve of arguments; that must have been why Papa interrupted him.

"I won't change my arrangements," he said. "But if there's really going to be a delay in getting hold of this money, it can't be helped: take what you need from the Khabarovka money."

"Yes sir."

It was evident from Yakov's expression and fingers that this last order afforded him great satisfaction.

Yakov was a serf and an extremely zealous and devoted man. Like all good stewards he was miserly in the extreme on behalf of his master and had the strangest notions as to what was in his master's interests. He was perpetually concerned to augment his master's property at the expense of that of his mistress, and tried always to show that it was essential to use all the income from her estates to pay for things at Petrovsky (the village on the estate where we lived). At this moment he was exultant because he had completely succeeded in this.

When he had greeted us Papa said we had been kicking our heels long enough in the country, that we were no longer small and that it was time for us to have a proper schooling.

"You already know, I believe, that tonight I am going to Moscow and am taking you with me," he said. "You will live with your grandmother, while *maman* will stay here with the girls. And remember, her only consolation will be to hear that you are studying well and satisfying your teachers."

Although we had noticed that preparations had been going on for several days already and thus had been expecting something out of the ordinary, this news dumfounded us. Volodya blushed and in a quavering voice passed on Mother's request.

So that's what my dream forboded! I thought. Please God let there be nothing worse, at least.

I felt very, very sorry for Mama and at the same time I was overjoyed at the thought that we were like grown-ups now.

If we're going this evening that means there won't be any classes; how wonderful! I thought. I feel sorry for Karl Ivanich, though. I expect they're dismissing him, because otherwise there wouldn't be an envelope for him. . . . It would be far better to have classes for ever than to go away and leave Mama and hurt poor Karl Ivanich. He's so unhappy as it is!

These thoughts flashed through my mind; I did not move from the spot but stared fixedly at the black ribbons on my shoes.

Having exchanged a few words with Karl Ivanich about the barometer going down, and having ordered Yakov not to feed the dogs, since he wanted to go out after dinner and listen to the young hounds before his departure, Papa, contrary to my expectations, sent us to class, consoling us, however, with a promise to take us hunting.

On the way upstairs I ran out onto the terrace. Lying by the doors in the sun with her eyes screwed up was Papa's favorite hound, Milka.

"Milka, dear," I said, stroking her and kissing her nose, "we're going away today. Good-by! We'll never see one another again."

IV

CLASSES

Karl Ivanich was in an extremely bad mood. This was evident from his lowering brows and from the way he flung his coat into the wardrobe, angrily tightened his belt and forcefully, with his nail, marked the place to which we were supposed to know the text by heart. Volodya had learned it fairly well, but I was so upset that I could do absolutely nothing at all. I looked at the book of dialogues long and foolishly, but the tears that filled my eyes whenever I thought of our imminent separation prevented me from reading; and when the time came for me to say them to Karl Ivanich, who listened to me with a frown on his face (this was a bad omen), I had just reached the place where one man says: *"Wo kommen Sie her?"* and the other replies: *"Ich komme vom Kaffee-Hause,"* when I could hold the tears back no longer and sobbed so much that I was completely unable to say: *"Haben Sie die Zeitung nicht gelesen?"* When we came to copying, my tears falling on the paper made so many blots that it looked as if I had written in water on wrapping paper.

Karl Ivanich lost his temper, made me kneel in the corner, insisted that this was stubbornness and a Punch and Judy show (his favorite expression), threatened me with his ruler, and demanded that I apologize, while I was unable to utter a word for my tears. Finally, probably because he realized that he was being unjust, he went into Nikolai's room and slammed the door behind him.

The conversation in Nikolai's room was audible from the classroom.

"Have you heard that the children are going to Moscow, Nikolai?"

"Why, of course, yes."

Evidently Nikolai must have started to get up because Karl Ivanich said: "Don't get up, Nikolai," and then closed the door. I left my corner and went to the door to listen.

"No matter how good you are to people or how devoted you are to them, it seems you can't expect any gratitude, eh, Nikolai?" said Karl Ivanich with warmth.

Nikolai, who was sitting by the window mending some boots, nodded his head affirmatively.

"I've lived in this house twelve years and I can say before God," went on Karl Ivanich, raising his eyes and snuffbox to the ceiling, "that I have loved them and devoted myself to them more than if they'd been my very own children. Do you remember, Nikolai, when Volodya had that fever, do you remember how I sat by his bed for nine days without closing my eyes? Yes! Then I was nice kind Karl Ivanich, then I was needed. But now," he added with an ironical smile, "*now the children have grown up—they have to have a proper schooling.* As if to say they didn't get a proper one here, Nikolai, eh?"

"I don't see how you could do any better," said Nikolai, laying down his awl and stretching his thread with both hands.

"Yes, I'm no longer needed so I have to be driven out. But where are their promises, where their gratitude? I love and revere Natalya Nikolayevna, Nikolai," he said, placing one hand on his breast, "but what is she? Her opinions in this house count for no more than this"—at this point he threw a piece of leather down on the floor with an expressive gesture. "I know who's behind all this and the reason I'm no longer needed: it's because I don't flatter and spoil them the way *some people* do. I'm accustomed to telling the truth always and in front of everyone," he said proudly. "Good luck to them! They won't get rich just because I'm not there and I, God willing, can find a crust of bread for myself … isn't that so, Nikolai?"

Nikolai raised his head and looked at Karl Ivanich as though wishing to make certain that he really could find a crust of bread for himself—but said nothing.

Karl Ivanich went on a long time and said a great deal more in the same vein: he recounted how his services had been more appreciated by the family of some general, with whom he had lived before (it hurt me to hear this), and talked of Saxony, his parents, his friend the tailor Schönheit, and so on and so forth.

I sympathized with his sorrow and it hurt me to think that father and Karl Ivanich, both of whom I loved about the same, did not understand one another. I went back to my corner, sat on my haunches, and wondered how to restore harmony between them.

When he had returned to the classroom, Karl Ivanich ordered me to get up and take out my notebook in preparation for a dictation. When everything was ready, he sank majestically into his armchair and in a voice that seemed to rise from the depths, began to dictate as follows: *"Von al-len Lei-den-schaf-ten die grausamste ist . . . haben Sie geschrieben?"* At this point he stopped, slowly took a pinch of snuff and continued with new vigor: *"die grausamste ist die Un-dank-bar-keit. . . . Ein grosses U."* Waiting for him to continue after I had written the last word, I looked up at him.

"Punctum," he said with a faint smile and signaled to us to hand in our notebooks.

He read this dictum, expressing his heartfelt opinion, several times and with different intonations, with an expression of the greatest satisfaction on his face; then he gave us a history lesson and sat down by the window. His face was no longer gloomy as before; it expressed the satisfaction of a man who has fittingly revenged an insult.

It was a quarter to one, but Karl Ivanich, it seemed, had not the slightest intention of letting us go: every now and then he started a new lesson. Boredom and hunger increased in equal measure. With great impatience I kept track of all the signs pointing to the imminence of dinner. First the maid went in with a raffia mop to wash the plates, then came the sound of crockery rattling in the buffet, the table was opened out and chairs placed around it, Mimi, Lyubochka, and Katyenka (Katyenka was Mimi's twelve-year-old daughter) came in from the garden. But there was no sign of Foka—Foka, the butler, who always came to announce that dinner was ready. Only then would it be possible to abandon one's books, ignoring Karl Ivanich, and run downstairs.

Now came the sound of footsteps on the stairs; but it was not Foka! I had studied his walk and I always recognized the way his boots squeaked. The door opened to reveal a figure who was a complete stranger to me.

V

THE HOLY FOOL

The man who came into the room was about fifty, with a pale pock-marked oblong face, long gray hair, and a sparse gingery beard. He was so tall that in order to get through the door he was obliged not only to bow his head but to bend his whole body. He was attired in a ragged something or other that looked like a caftan or a cassock; in his hand he held an enormous staff. Once inside the room he pounded the staff on the floor with all his might, wrinkled his brows, opened his mouth inordinately wide, and roared with the most terrible and unnatural laughter. He was blind in one eye and the white pupil in this eye constantly rolled about, endowing his in any case ugly face with a still more repulsive expression.

"Aha! I've caught you!" he cried, running up to Volodya with short little steps, seizing him by the head and starting to examine his crown carefully. Then, with a completely serious face, he moved away from him, went up to the table and began to blow under the oilcloth and make the sign of the cross over it. "O-oh dear! O-oh, how sad! . . . poor things . . . flying away," he said in a voice trembling with tears, looking at Volodya tenderly, and used his sleeve to wipe away the genuine tears that were falling.

His voice was rough and hoarse, his gestures hasty and spasmodic, his speech nonsensical and incoherent (he never used pronouns), but his intonation was so touching and his hideous yellow face at times assumed such a sincerely sorrowful expression that, listening to him, one could not help but experience a feeling compounded of pity, fear, and sadness all at the same time.

This was the holy fool and pilgrim, Grisha.

Where was he from? Who were his parents? What had caused him to choose this life of pilgrimage he led? Nobody knew these things. I only know that from fifteen onward he had become known as a holy fool who, winter and summer, went about barefoot, visited monasteries, presented holy images to those he took a liking to, and spoke in riddles, which some people interpreted as prophesies; also, that nobody had ever known him any different, that he visited his grandmother from time to time, and that some people alleged he was the unfortunate son of rich parents and a pure soul while others said he was simply a peasant and vagabond.

At last the long-awaited and punctual Foka arrived and we went downstairs. Grisha, still sobbing and talking all sorts of nonsense, followed us down, banging his prop on the stairs. Papa and *maman* were walking up and down the drawing room arm in arm, quietly discussing something. Marya Ivanovna, or Mimi, was sitting sedately in one of the armchairs that met with the couch to form a symmetrical right angle, giving instructions in a stern but muted voice to the girls sitting at her side. The moment Karl Ivanich entered the room she glanced at him and immediately turned away, her face taking on an expression that seemed to say: I am not aware of you, Karl Ivanich. We could see from the girls' eyes that they were anxious to give us some extremely important news as soon as possible; but it would have been breaking Mimi's rules to jump up from their seats and approach us. First we had to go up to her and say: *"Bonjour, Mimi,"* and scrape our feet on the floor and only then could we all start talking together.

What an intolerable creature that Mimi was! You could never say anything in her presence: everything was improper in her opinion. Furthermore, she was perpetually nagging us: *"Parlez donc français,"* at which, just to spite her, we felt more than ever like speaking Russian.

At dinner, too, just as you'd got a taste for something and wanted not to be interrupted, she'd be sure to say: *"Mangez donc avec du pain"* or *"Comment ce que vous tenez votre fourchette?"* And what business is it of hers! you'd think. Let her take care of her girls; we have Karl Ivanich for that sort of thing. I fully shared his hatred for *some people*.

"Ask Mama to let us go hunting," whispered Katyenka, catching me by the jacket when the grown-ups had gone ahead into the dining room.

"All right, we'll do our best."

Grisha ate in the dining room, but at a separate little table of his own; he did not lift his eyes from his plate, sighed from time to time, made frightful faces and talked apparently to himself: "What a pity! . . . flown away . . . the pigeon will fly to heaven . . . oh, the gravestone's laid!" and so on.

Maman had been distraught all day; the presence, words, and actions of Grisha made things worse.

"Oh yes, I almost forgot, there was something I wanted to ask you," she said, handing Father a plate of soup.

"What was it?"

"Please have those frightful dogs of yours locked up; they almost bit poor Grisha when he came through the yard. They might attack the children in the same way."

Hearing his name mentioned, Grisha turned to the table, began to show them the tattered ends of his clothing and babbled, with his mouth full:

"Wanted to bite to death . . . God wouldn't allow. A sin to set dogs on people, a great sin! Don't beat, master, why beat? God'll forgive . . . not necessary."

"What's he saying?" asked Papa, surveying him sternly and intently. "I don't understand a word of it."

"I do," replied *maman*. "He told me that some huntsman purposely set his dogs onto him, so he says: 'Wanted to bite to death, but God wouldn't allow,' and he's begging you not to punish the man."

"Oh, so that's it!" said Papa. "Well, how does he know I have any intention of punishing the huntsman?" and then went on in French: "You know I don't care much for these people in general, but this one bothers me in particular and ought to be . . ."

"Oh, please don't say that, my friend," *maman* interrupted him, as though frightened of something. "How can you know?"

"I think I've had occasion enough to get to know this breed by now—so many of them come to you—and they're all of a feather. Always the same old story . . . "

It was evident that Mama was of a totally different opinion on this score and did not wish to argue.

"Pass me a pie, please," she said. "What are they like today, good?"

"No, it makes me angry," Papa went on, picking up a pie but holding it so far away from her that *maman* could not reach it. "No, it makes me angry to see clever well-educated people being taken in."

And he banged his fork on the table.

"I asked you to pass me a pie," she repeated, holding her hand out.

"And they're doing the right thing," went on Papa, still withholding his hand, "when they put such people under lock and key. All they do," he added smilingly, seeing that Mama was not enjoying this conversation unduly, "is upset the nerves of certain persons whose nerves are weak enough as it is," and he handed her the pie.

"I have only one thing to say to that: it's difficult to believe that a man who, in spite of his sixty years, walks about winter and summer barefoot, wears chains weighing seventy pounds under his clothes, without ever taking them off, and has more than once refused a quiet life with room and board—it's difficult to believe that such a man would do all that merely out of laziness.

"And as far as prophesying is concerned," she went on with a sigh, after a brief pause, "*je suis payée pour y croire;* I believe I told you how Kiryusha prophesied the end of poor Papa, right to the very day and hour."

"Oh, look what you've done to me now!" said Papa, smiling and putting a hand to the side of his mouth where Mimi was sitting. (Whenever he did this I always listened extra-carefully in the expectation of hearing something funny.) "Why did you mention his feet? I looked at them and now I've completely lost my appetite."

Dinner was coming to an end. Lyubochka and Katyenka winked at us constantly, wriggled in their seats, and generally betrayed strong symptoms of anxiety. This winking signified: "Why don't you ask them to let us go hunting?" I nudged Volodya with my elbow, Volodya nudged me and then finally made up his mind: beginning in a shy voice and then continuing fairly firmly and loudly, he explained that since we were due to leave today, we would like the girls to come to the hunt with us in the brake. After a short consultation among the grown-ups the question was decided in our favor and—what was even better—*maman* said that she would come too.

VI

PREPARATIONS FOR THE HUNT

During dessert Yakov was summoned and given orders to prepare the brake, dogs, and saddle horses; the orders were given in the greatest possible detail and with each horse named by name. Volodya's horse was lame; Papa ordered a hunter to be saddled for him. The word *hunter* sounded somewhat strange to Mama's ears: she thought a hunter was bound to be something in the nature of a wild beast and would bolt with Volodya and kill him. Despite the reassurances of Papa and Volodya, who said with remarkable heroism that it was nothing and that he even liked it when a horse bolted, poor *maman* continued to assert that she would be miserable throughout the whole trip.

Dinner ended; the grown-ups went into the study to drink coffee and we ran into the garden to talk and scuff our feet along the footpaths, which were covered with fallen yellow leaves. We talked about Volodya riding a hunter, about how Lyubochka ought to be ashamed of running more quietly than Katyenka, about how much we would like to see Grisha's chains, and so on. But about the fact that we were going to separate not a word was said. Our conversation was interrupted by the rattle of the approaching carriage which had a serf-boy perched on each of its springs. Behind the carriage came the hunts-men with the dogs and behind the huntsmen—Ignat, the coachman, riding Volodya's hunter and leading my ancient pony by the bridle. At first we all rushed to the fence to get a better view of these interest-ing things; then, squealing and stamping our feet, we ran upstairs to get dressed, and to dress so that we looked as much as possible like the huntsmen. One of the main ways of doing this was to tuck our pants into our boots. Without a moment's pause we set about doing this, hurrying to finish as quickly as we could, and ran out onto the porch to have fun looking at the horses and dogs and talking to the huntsmen.

It was a hot day. White puffs of cloud with fantastic shapes had begun to appear on the horizon since morning; then a slight breeze had begun to chase them closer and closer, so that from time to time they covered the sun. But no matter how many clouds came or how black they looked, they were clearly not destined to gather into a storm and at the last moment spoil our pleasure. By late afternoon they started to disperse again: some of them turned pale, faded, and fled to the horizon; others, immediately overhead, turned into trans-parent, white scales; only one large black cloud stayed in the east. Karl Ivanich always knew where each cloud was going; he announced that this cloud was on its way to Maslovka, that there would be no rain, and that the weather would be perfect.

Foka, despite his declining years, ran extremely nimbly and quickly down the stairs, cried out "Ready!" and, placing his legs wide apart, stood firmly in the middle of the porch, midway between the thresh-old and the spot where the coachman was supposed to stop the brake, in the attitude of a man who needs no reminding of his duties. The ladies came down and after a short debate as to who should sit where and hold whom (though it seemed completely unnecessary to me to hold onto anyone), settled themselves in their seats, opened their para-sols, and set off. As the brake moved off, *maman* pointed to the hunter and asked the coachman in a quavering voice:

"Is that the horse for Volodya?"

And when the coachman replied in the affirmative, she gave a wave of her hand and turned away. I was terribly impatient: I climbed onto my pony, looked between its ears, and made various evolutions about the yard.

"Please don't step on the dogs," said one of the huntsmen to me.

"Don't worry: this isn't my first time," I replied haughtily.

Volodya mounted his hunter, though, despite his firmness of character, not without certain misgivings, and several times asked as he stroked her:

"Is she quiet?"

But he looked very well on a horse—just like a grown-up. His tightly trousered thighs sat so well on the saddle that I felt envious of him, particularly since, as far as I could judge from my shadow, I looked nowhere near as handsome myself.

Now we could hear Papa's steps on the stairs; one of the kennelmen rounded up the dogs that had strayed away; the huntsmen called the borzois to them and began to mount. A groom brought Papa's horse to the porch; the dogs in Papa's pack, who had formerly lain around the horse in various picturesque poses, rushed to greet him. Running out joyfully after them came Milka in her beaded collar and rattling her collar clip. She always greeted the kennel dogs when she came out: with some she played, with others she exchanged sniffs and growls, and with a few she looked for fleas.

Papa mounted his horse and we set off.

VII

The Hunt

The chief huntsman, who was nicknamed Turka, rode ahead of everyone on his smoke-gray hook-nosed pony, wearing a shaggy cap and
with a hunting horn across his back and a knife at his belt. Judging by
this man's sullen and ferocious exterior one would have thought he
was heading for a fight to the death rather than a hunt. A rippling, motley tangle of dogs ran at his pony's heels, all of them still on the leash.
It was pitiful to see the fate that overtook any unfortunate hound that
took it into her head to lag behind. First she had to make a tremendous
effort to drag her leashmate back and then, when she had achieved
this, one of the kennelmen who rode behind would inevitably flick her
with his hunting whip and say: "Back in the pack!" When we had got
beyond the main gate, Papa ordered us and the huntsmen to ride along
the road, while he turned off into a field of rye.

The harvest was in full swing. The vast gleaming-yellow field was
bounded on one side only by a tall bluish-looking forest, which
seemed to me at that time a most remote and mysterious place, beyond
which was either the end of the world or the beginning of new, unin-
habited countries. The whole field was full of haystacks and people.

Here and there in the tall dense rye, in a cleared patch, one could see the bent back of a reaper, the wave of the ears as they were grasped between the reaper's fingers, or the figure of a woman in the shade bent over a cradle, and sheaves of rye strewn over the cornflower-dotted stubble. In another direction, peasants wearing only their shirts were standing on carts and building haystacks, filling the dry scorching-hot field with dust. When he saw Papa in the distance the village headman, who was wearing boots and a cloth coat slung over his shoulders and holding a tally in his hand, removed his felt hat, wiped his red hair and beard with a towel, and yelled something at the women who were reaping. The bay pony that Papa rode walked with an easy skittish gait, occasionally lowering her head to her chest, pulling at the reins and flicking off with her thick tail the flies and botflies that greedily fastened onto her. Two borzois with their tails curved up in a stiff sickle, lifting their legs high, pranced daintily over the high stubble behind the pony; Milka would run ahead and then, twisting her head round, wait for a tidbit. The hum of voices, the stamping of the horses and carts, the jolly whistling of quail, the buzzing of the insects hovering in motionless swarms in the air, the smell of wormwood, straw, and horse sweat, the thousands of different hues and shadows poured out by the burning sun over the bright-yellow stubble, the blue depths of the forest and the lilac-and-white clouds, and the white gossamer threads that floated through the air or settled on the stubble—all this I saw, heard, and felt.

When we reached Kalinovo woods we found the brake already there and also, most unexpectedly, another cart drawn by a single horse, with a footman sitting inside it. A samovar peeped out from under some straw and a tub that looked like an ice-cream container and several other inviting-looking packages and boxes. There was no mistaking it: a picnic in the open air, with fruit and ice cream. At the sight of the cart we gave vent to noisy expressions of delight, for a picnic in the woods on the grass, and in general at a spot where nobody had ever had a picnic before, was considered a great treat.

Turka came up to the copse, halted, listened carefully to Papa's detailed instructions on how to position his men and where to emerge (though he never took any notice of these instructions and always did things in his own way), unleashed the dogs, unhurriedly fastened the leashes to his saddle straps, mounted his horse and, whistling as he went, disappeared among the young birch trees. The freed hounds expressed their delight at first by wagging their tails; then they shook themselves, steadied themselves, and set off at a gentle trot in different directions, sniffing at the ground and wagging their tails.

"Do you have a handkerchief?" asked Papa.

I took one from my pocket and showed it to him.

"Right, well use it to take this gray dog . . ."

"Zhiran?" I said with the air of an expert.

"Yes, and run down the road. When you get to a clearing, stop there and wait, and mind you don't come back without a hare!"

I wrapped my handkerchief around Zhiran's shaggy neck and dashed headlong toward the appointed spot. Papa laughed and called after me:

"Hurry, hurry, or you'll be late."

Zhiran kept stopping, cocking his ears and listening to the hallooing of the huntsmen. I lacked the strength to drag him along and so I began to cry: "Tally-ho! Tally-ho!" at him. Then he tugged away so strongly that I could scarcely hold him and more than once fell down before reaching my place. Having picked out a shady level spot at the foot of a tall oak tree, I lay on the grass, seated Zhiran beside me, and settled down to wait. As usual in such situations, my imagination far outstripped reality: I was just imagining that I was coursing my third hare when I heard the first hound giving tongue in the woods. Turka's voice rang louder and more excitedly through the trees; the hound was baying and her voice sounded more and more frequently; it was joined by a second, deeper voice, then a third and a fourth. . . . These voices now died away and now interrupted one another. The sounds gradually grew louder and more continuous and at last merged into one clangorous swelling roar. *The thicket was filled with sound and the hounds were in full cry.*

When I heard this I froze at my post. I riveted my eyes on the spot where the trees ended and grinned idiotically. The sweat poured off me and although the drops tickled me as they ran down my chin, I did not wipe them off. It seemed to me that there could never be a moment more crucial than this. A position of such tension was too unnatural to last long. The barking of the hounds now gradually moved farther away; no hare appeared. I began to look around me. Zhiran did the same: at first he had tugged at his lead and whined, but then he lay down beside me, rested his muzzle on my knee, and calmed down again.

Around the uncovered roots of the oak tree under which I sat and over the dry gray earth, between the withered oak leaves, acorns, dead, moss-covered branches, greenish-yellow moss and occasional thin green blades of grass that had managed to struggle through, there swarmed an army of ants. One after the other they hurried along the well-worn little paths they had beaten out: some with burdens, others without. I picked up a dead branch and blocked the way with it. It had to be seen the way some of them, scorning danger, crept under it, while others crawled over the top; but a few, especially those with burdens, were completely nonplused and did not know what to do: they stopped and looked for a way round or went back, or else they crawled along the branch to my hand and were prepared, I believe, to go up inside the sleeve of my jacket. I was distracted from these interesting observations by a butterfly with yellow wings which hovered extremely enticingly just in front of me. As soon as I transferred my attention to it, it flew a couple of yards away, hovered over the almost-faded white bloom of a wild clover, and settled on it. I do not know whether it was basking in the sunshine or extracting honey from the flower, but it was obvious it was enjoying itself. From time to time it fluttered its wings and clung closer to the flower and at last became quite still. I leaned my head on my hands and gazed at it with pleasure.

Suddenly Zhiran whined and tugged at his leash so hard that I almost rolled over. I looked around. With one ear flattened and the other raised, a hare raced by along the edge of the wood. The blood rushed to my head and at that moment I forgot everything: I uttered a frantic cry, released the dog, and broke into a run. But no sooner had I done this than I began to regret it: the hare squatted on its haunches, took one leap, and I never saw it again.

And what was my shame when the baying hounds, who had flushed the hare out from the edge of the trees, were followed into the clearing by Turka, who appeared from behind some bushes! He realized my mistake (which had consisted in my *not being able to wait*) and, looking at me contemptuously, merely said: "Oh, master!" But you have to know how he said it! I would have felt better if he had hung me on his saddle, like a hare.

I stood for a long time afterward on the same spot, deep in despair; I did not call my dog, but merely repeated over and over again, slapping my thigh:

"Oh dear, what have I done!"

I heard the hounds dash farther, heard the cries of Tally-ho on the far side of the thicket, heard them take the hare away, and heard Turka call the dogs in with his enormous hunting horn—but still I did not move from the spot. . . .

VIII

Playing

The hunt ended. A rug was spread in the shade of some young birches and the whole company sat on it in a circle. Gavrilo the butler, having flattened the green juicy grass around him, wiped the plates and took from the little boxes peaches and plums wrapped up in leaves. The sun filtered through the green branches of the young birch trees, covering both the patterned rug, my legs, and even Gavrilo's perspiring bald head with shimmering circles of light. A light breeze fluttering through the foliage of the trees, through my hair and over my sweating face, refreshed me considerably.

When we had been given our share of ice cream and fruit there was nothing more to do on the rug, and despite the slanting rays of the burning sun, we got up and went off to play.

"Well, what shall we play?" said Lyubochka, squinting in the sunlight and dancing over the grass. "Let's play Robinson."

"No . . . it's dull," said Volodya, flopping down lazily on the grass and chewing some stalks. "We're always playing Robinson! If you must do something, let's build a hut."

Volodya was obviously putting on airs: he was probably proud of the fact that he had come on a hunting horse and was pretending to be very tired. And also pretending, perhaps, that he already had too much common sense and too little power of imagination fully to enjoy playing at Robinson. This game consisted of acting out scenes from *Swiss Family Robinson,* which we had read not long before in French.

"Oh, please . . . why won't you do us a favor?" the girls cajoled him. "You can be Charles or Ernest or the father—anything you like," said Katyenka, trying to pull him up by the sleeve of his jacket.

"Really, I don't want to—it's dull!" said Volodya, stretching himself and at the same time smiling complacently.

"It would've been better to stay at home if nobody wants to play," declared Lyubochka tearfully.

She was a terrible crybaby.

"Oh, all right, only please don't cry: I can't stand it!"

Volodya's condescension afforded us very little pleasure; on the contrary, his bored weary look destroyed the whole magic of the game. When we sat on the ground, pretending we were going fishing, and rowed with all our might, Volodya sat with his arms folded in a pose that had nothing at all in common with a fisherman. I mentioned this to him; but he replied that no matter how much we waved our arms about, we wouldn't gain or lose very much, and in any case we wouldn't get very far. I was forced to agree with him. When I pretended to be going hunting with a stick over my shoulder and set off for the trees, Volodya lay on his back, put his hands behind his head, and told me to pretend that he was going too. Words and actions such as these, cooling our enthusiasm for the game, were extremely unpleasant, the more so since it was impossible not to agree privately that Volodya was only acting sensibly.

I myself knew that a stick not only couldn't kill birds, but couldn't even shoot at all. It was a game. If you looked at it that way, you couldn't even ride on chairs; yet Volodya himself, I believe, remembered how on long winter evenings we had covered the armchair with scarves, making a carriage of it, while one of us had mounted as driver, the other as footman, the three girls in the middle, with three chairs for horses—and we had set off on our travels. And what a variety of adventures we had had on the way! And how gaily and quickly the winter evenings had passed! . . . If you considered things rationally, there would be no playing at all. And without playing, what would remain?

IX

SOMETHING LIKE FIRST LOVE

Imagining that she was tearing some sort of American fruit down from a tree, Lyubochka tore off a leaf with a worm of enormous dimensions on it, threw it to the ground in terror, raised her hands aloft and leaped back, as though frightened lest something should squirt out of it. Our game came to a halt; we all fell to the ground, heads together, to look at this rarity.

I was looking over Katyenka's shoulder; she tried to pick up the worm on a leaf she had placed in its path.

I have noticed that many girls have a habit of shrugging their shoulders when wearing an open-necked dress, in order to make it stay in place. I still remember that Mimi used to get incensed by this gesture and say: *"C'est un geste de femme de chambre."* As she bent over the worm, Katyenka made that very gesture and at the same time the breeze lifted the kerchief from her white little neck. Her shoulder, as she made the gesture, was no more than an inch from my lips. I was no longer looking at the worm, I stared and stared and kissed Katyenka's shoulder with all my might. She did not turn around, but I noticed her neck and ears turn red. Volodya, without raising his head, said derisively:

"Why so tender?"

But there were tears in my eyes.

I did not take my eyes off Katyenka. I had long been used to her fresh, fair little face and had always been fond of it; but now I began to look at it more closely and I loved it even more. When we came back to the grown-ups Papa announced, to our great delight, that at Mama's request our journey was to be postponed to the following day.

We rode home with the carriage. Volodya and I, wishing to outdo one another in the art of riding and bravery, capered around it. My shadow was longer than before and, looking at it, I supposed I had the appearance of a fairly handsome rider; but the feeling of self-satisfaction I experienced was soon dissipated by the following circumstance. Hoping to impress all the occupants of the carriage once and for all, I fell behind a bit, then spurred my pony on with my whip and heels, adopted a relaxed elegant posture, and intended to race past them like a whirlwind on the side where Katyenka was sitting. The only thing was I did not know whether to gallop past silently or to let out a yell. But that hateful pony, when it came level with the horses in harness, despite all my efforts, stopped so suddenly that I was propelled out of the saddle onto the pony's neck and almost flew to the ground.

X

What Kind of Man Was My Father?

He was a man of the eighteenth century and had that elusive character—common to young men of that century—made up of chivalry, resourcefulness, self-assurance, courtesy, and a disposition to revelry. He regarded men of the present century with contempt, this view being the result as much of inborn pride as of secret chagrin that in our time he could have neither the influence nor the success he had had in his own. His two principal passions in life were cards and women; he had won several millions in the course of his lifetime and had had relations with incalculable numbers of women of all classes.

A tall well-proportioned figure, a strange way of walking with tiny steps, a habit of shrugging his shoulders, little eyes that were always smiling, a large aquiline nose, irregular lips that met somehow awkwardly but pleasantly, an impediment in his speech, a lisp, and a completely bald head: that was my father's appearance that had not only enabled him to pass for and be a man *à bonnes fortunes,* but that made him liked by everyone without exception—by men of all conditions and classes, and especially by those whom he desired to like him.

He knew how to take the upper hand in any relationship. Never having been a man of *very high society,* he yet always mixed with people of this class and in such a way that he was respected. He knew that ultimate limit of hauteur and self-assurance which would raise him in the eyes of society without constituting an insult to others. He was original, but not always, and employed originality as a means which in some cases was a substitute for breeding or wealth. Nothing on earth could evoke surprise in him: no matter how brilliant the occasion, he always seemed born to it. He was so skillful at suppressing and concealing from others that dark side of life, filled with petty irritations and upsets, which is so familiar to us all, that it was impossible not to envy him. He was a connoisseur of all the things that can afford man comfort or pleasure, and he knew how to make use of them. His pet hobby was brilliant connections, which he had formed partly through my mother's family and partly through the companions of his youth, though he was secretly angry at the latter for having gone so far in rank, while he would now always remain a retired lieutenant of the guards. Like all ex-military men he was incapable of dressing fashionably, but on the other hand his dress was original and elegant. Very loose and light clothes always, impeccable linen, large turned-back cuffs and collars. . . . All this, however, suited his great height, his powerful build, his bald head, and his calm confident gestures. He was susceptible and even tearful. Often when reading aloud, when he came to a pathetic spot, his voice would start to tremble, tears would show in his eyes, and he would put the book down in disgruntlement. He loved music and would sing, accompanying himself on the piano, some popular songs by a friend of his, or gypsy songs, or pieces from operas; but classical music was not to his taste and, disregarding the general opinion, he used to say quite openly that Beethoven's sonatas bored him stiff and sent him to sleep, and that he himself knew of nothing better than "Don't disturb a young maiden," as sung by Semyonova, or "Not alone," as sung by Tanyusha the gypsy girl. His nature was such that he needed an audience for his good deeds. And he considered good only what other people thought was good. God knows whether he had any moral convictions or not. His life was so full of distractions of one kind and another that he never had time to formulate any, and then he was so happy in life that he saw no necessity for it.

In old age he evolved a consistent outlook on life and also unalterable rules—but solely on an empirical basis: those acts and way of life that had afforded him happiness and satisfaction he considered good, and he thought that everyone should always be the same. He used to talk extremely persuasively and this ability, I feel, increased the flexibility of his rules: he was quite capable of interpreting the same action as either a charming prank or a despicable meanness.

XI

IN THE STUDY AND DRAWING ROOM

It was already dusk when we reached home. *Maman* seated herself at the piano while we children brought paper, pencil, and paints and settled ourselves at the round table to draw. The only paint I had was blue; but in spite of this I undertook to draw the hunt. Having with great gusto depicted a blue boy astride a blue horse with blue dogs, I was a little uncertain as to whether I could draw a blue hare, and I ran to Papa in his study to seek advice. Papa was reading something and in answer to my question: "Are there such things as blue hares?" he said, without raising his head: "There are, my friend, there are." Returning to the round table I drew a blue hare and then found it necessary to make a blue bush out of it. But the bush did not please me either: I made a tree out of it, and then a haystack, and then a cloud, and in the end I had made such a mess of the whole paper with the blue paint that I tore it up discontentedly and went off to daydream in the Voltaire armchair.

Maman was playing the second concerto by her teacher, Field. I daydreamed, and light bright transparent memories arose in my imagination. She played Beethoven's *Pathétique* sonata and I thought of something sad, heavy and gloomy. *Maman* often played these two pieces and that is why I remember so well the feelings they evoked in me. These feelings resembled memories; but memories of what? It seemed one could remember things that had never been.

Opposite me was the door to the study and I saw Yakov go in together with some other men who were bearded and wore caftans. The door immediately closed behind them. Well, business has begun! I thought. It seemed to me that nothing in the world could be more important than those affairs that were dealt with in the study; and I was confirmed in this view by the fact that all who approached its door usually did so whispering and on tiptoe. From inside came the sound of Papa's loud voice and the smell of cigar smoke, which, I don't know why, always attracted me very much. Half-asleep, I was suddenly struck by the very familiar squeak of boots coming through the footmen's room. Karl Ivanich, on tiptoe but with a face that was gloomy and resolute, with some sort of notes in his hand, went up to the door and knocked quietly. He was admitted and the door banged shut again.

I hope nothing terrible has happened, I thought. Karl Ivanich is angry: he's ready for anything. . . .

I dozed off again.

Nothing terrible had happened, however; an hour later I was awakened by the same squeaking of boots. Using his handkerchief to wipe away some tears that I noticed on his cheeks, Karl Ivanich emerged from the door and went upstairs, muttering something under his breath. Papa followed him out and came into the drawing room.

"Do you know what I've just decided?" he said in a cheerful voice, laying his hand on Mama's shoulder.

"What, my friend?"

"I'm taking Karl Ivanich along with the children. There's room in the carriage. They've got used to him now and he, it seems, is also attached to them; and seven hundred rubles a year makes no difference at all, *et puis au fond c'est un très bon diable.*"

I could not make out why Papa was calling Karl Ivanich names.

"I'm very glad," said *maman*, "both for the children and for him. He's a wonderful old man."

"If only you had seen how touched he was when I told him to keep the five hundred rubles as a present . . . but the funniest thing of all was the bill he brought me. It's worth seeing," he added with a smile, handing her the piece of paper with Karl Ivanich's handwriting on it. "It's priceless!"

Here are the contents of the paper:

> *Two fishingrods to childrens . . . 70 copeck.*
> *Colorred paper, golded frame, paste and press for boks (presents) . . .*
> *6 rubles 55 copeck.*
> *Book and boe, presents to childrens . . . 8 rubles 16 copeck.*
> *Trousers to Nikolai . . . 4 rubles.*
> *A gold watch promised by Pyotr Aleksantrovich from Moscow cost*
> *140 ruble.*
> *The sum total owing to Karl Mauer except his salarie: 159 ruble*
> *79 copeck.*

Reading this note, in which Karl Ivanich demanded to be paid for all the money he had spent on presents and even for a present that had been promised to him, anyone would think that Karl Ivanich was nothing but an unfeeling mercenary egoist—and anyone would be wrong.

Having gone into the study with the pieces of paper in his hand and a ready-prepared speech in his head, he had intended to give Papa an eloquent exposition of all the injustices he had suffered in our house; but when he began to speak in that same pathetic voice and with those same tender modulations that he usually used when dictating to us, the one to be most affected by his eloquence was himself, so that when he got to the point where he was saying: "No matter how sorry I am to part with the children," he broke down completely, his voice trembled, and he was obliged to take his checked handkerchief from his pocket.

"Yes, Pyotr Aleksandrich," he said tearfully (this part was completely missing from his prepared speech), "I'm so used to the children that I don't know what I shall do without them. I'd rather work for you for nothing," he added, brushing the tears away with one hand and holding out his piece of paper with the other.

That Karl Ivanich was speaking sincerely at that moment I can confirm, because I know his kind heart; but how his piece of paper could be reconciled with his words remains a mystery to me.

"Although you would be sorry, I would be even sorrier to part with you," said Papa, slapping him on the shoulder. "I've changed my mind."

Not long before supper Grisha came in. From the moment he entered our house he had not ceased to sigh and weep, which, in the opinion of those who believed in his prophetic power, foreboded some calamity for our household. He began to say good night and said that he would proceed farther the next day. I winked at Volodya and went out through the door.

"What?"

"If you want to have a look at Grisha's chains, let's go upstairs now to the servants' quarters. Grisha sleeps in the second room—we can easily sit in the box room and from there we'll see everything."

"Wonderful! Wait here and I'll call the girls."

The girls came running out and we set off upstairs. Having decided, though not without difficulty, who should be first to go into the dark box room, we settled ourselves down to wait.

XII

GRISHA

We were all terrified by the darkness; we pressed up close to one another and said nothing. Grisha came in almost immediately after us, walking quietly. In one hand he held his staff, in the other a tallow candle in a brass candlestick. We held our breath.

"Oh Lord Jesus Christ! Holy Mother of God! To the Father, Son and Holy Ghost . . . " he repeated, sucking in air and employing various intonations and abbreviations peculiar only to those who use these words often.

When he had placed his staff in the corner with a prayer and inspected his bed, he began to undress. Having undone his old black girdle, he slowly took off his tattered nankeen smock, folded it carefully and hung it on the back of a chair. His face no longer expressed, as it usually did, hastiness and stupidity; on the contrary, it was calm, thoughtful and even majestic. His movements were slow and premeditated.

Clad only in his underclothes, he sank down quietly onto the bed, made the sign of the cross over it on all sides and with evident difficulty—since he frowned—adjusted the chains under his shirt. After sitting there for a while and carefully examining the several holes in his underwear, he got up, raised the candle till it was level with the icon case, on which stood several icons, saying a prayer as he did so, crossed himself as he faced them and turned the candle upside down. It went out with a splutter.

An almost full moon shone through the windows, which looked out onto the forest. On one side the tall white figure of the holy fool was illuminated by the moon's pale silvery rays; on the other it cast a black shadow which, together with the shadows of the window frames, fell on the floor and wall and even reached up to the ceiling. Outside, the watchman banged on his sheet of iron.

Folding his enormous arms across his chest, lowering his head, and without ceasing to sigh heavily, Grisha stood silently before the icons, then sank with difficulty onto his knees and began to pray.

At first he quietly recited some well-known prayers, merely stressing certain words; then he repeated them, but more loudly this time and with more animation. He began to repeat his phrases, having obvious difficulties with the Old Slavonic vocabulary. His words were incoherent but moving. He prayed for all his benefactors (as he called the people who took him in), including my mother and us, prayed for himself, begged God to forgive him his grievous sins, repeated several times: "God have mercy on my enemies!," got up gruntingly from his knees, fell to the ground once more, repeating the same words over and over again, and then finally got up again, despite the heaviness of his chains, which gave out a sharp hard sound as they banged against the floor.

Volodya pinched me extremely painfully on the leg, but I did not even look around; I merely rubbed the place with my hand and continued to follow all Grisha's movements and words with a feeling of childish wonder, pity, and reverence. Instead of the fun and laughter I had counted on when I entered the box room, I experienced a palpitation and sinking of the heart.

Grisha remained for a long time in this position of religious ecstasy, improvising prayers. At times he would say several times in succession: "The Lord have mercy," but with mounting force and emphasis; at others he would say: "Forgive me, Lord, teach me what to do . . . teach me what to do, oh Lord!"—and with such an expression as though he expected an immediate answer to his pleas; sometimes one could hear only a pitiful sobbing. . . . He got to his knees, folded his arms, and fell silent.

Carefully I put my head around the door, not daring to breathe. Grisha did not stir; heavy sighs escaped from his breast; in the clouded pupil of his blind eye, which was illumined by the moon, there stood a tear.

"Thy will be done!" he exclaimed suddenly with an inimitable expression on his face, then fell supine on the floor and burst into tears like a child.

Much water has flowed under the bridge since then, many recollections of the past have lost all meaning for me and have turned into distant dreams, and even the pilgrim Grisha has long since completed his last pilgrimage; but the impression he made on me and the feelings he evoked will never fade from my memory.

Oh, great Christian, Grisha! Your faith was so firm that you experienced the nearness of God, your love was so great that the words came forth fully formed from your lips—you did not measure them with your reason. . . . And what mighty praise you offered to His splendor when, failing to find words, you fell to the ground in tears! . . .

The feelings of emotion with which I listened to Grisha could not last long, first because my curiosity had been satisfied and second because my legs had gone to sleep from sitting in the same place; also, I wanted to join in the general whispering and fidgeting that was going on behind me in the dark box room. Someone took hold of my hand and whispered: "Whose hand is this?" It was completely dark in the box room, but from the mere feel of it and the voice that whispered right by my very ear, I immediately recognized Katyenka.

Completely unconsciously I grasped her arm, in its short little sleeve, by the elbow, and pressed my lips to it. Katyenka must have been taken aback by this action and snatched her arm away: in doing so she knocked against a broken chair that stood in the box room. Grisha lifted his head, looked around him quietly, and with a prayer on his lips began to make the sign of the cross in all the corners. Noisily and whispering among ourselves, we ran out of the box room.

XIII

Natalya Savishna

Midway through the last century a gay plump red-cheeked lass named *Natashka* used to run barefoot about the village of Khabarovka in a grubby dress. At the request of her father, the clarinetist Savva, and in return for his services, my grandfather took her "into service"—as one of my grandmother's maids. The maid Natashka was notable in this post for her humble nature and zeal. When my mother was born and a nurse became necessary, this duty was entrusted to Natashka. In this sphere too she earned praise and reward for her diligence, loyalty, and attachment to her young mistress. But the powdered head and buckled stockings of the jaunty young footman, Foka, who came into frequent contact with Natashka by virtue of his duties, captivated her rudg but loving heart. She even made up her mind to go to Grandfather herself and ask his permission to marry Foka. Grandfather took her wish for ingratitude, grew wrathful, and banished poor Natashka to the cow-sheds of a distant village for punishment. Six months later, however, owing to the fact that no one was capable of replacing her, Natashka was brought back to the house in her former capacity. Upon returning from exile in her grubby dress, she went to Grandfather's study, fell at his feet, and begged him to restore her to his former favor and affections and to forget the folly to which she had succumbed and which she swore would return no more. And in truth she kept her word.

From that time onward *Natashka* became Natalya Savishna and donned a bonnet; the whole fund of love that remained in her was transferred to her young mistress.

When she was replaced at Mama's side by a governess, she received the keys of the pantry, and the linen and provisions for the entire household were given into her care. She performed these new duties with the same love and zeal. She lived entirely for the master's interests; she saw waste, spoilage, and plunder in everything and applied all her energies to combating this.

When *maman* married, she wished to reward Natalya Savishna for her twenty years of labor and devotion, so she summoned her into her presence, expressed all her love and gratitude to her in the most flattering possible terms, and handed her a sheet of paper bearing Natalya Savishna's release from serfdom, informing her in the meantime that irrespective of whether she continued to serve in our house or not, she would always receive an annual pension of three hundred rubles. Natalya Savishna heard all this out in silence, then took the document, looked at it balefully, muttered something through clenched teeth, and ran out of the room, banging the door behind her. A few moments later, unable to understand the cause of such behavior, *maman* went to Natalya Savishna's room. She was sitting on a chest with tears in her eyes, twiddling her handkerchief in fingers and staring at the floor, where lay the torn-up shreds of her release.

"What's the matter, my dear Natalya Savishna?" asked *maman*, taking her by the hand.

"Nothing, ma'am," she replied. "I suppose you must hate me for something if you're driving me out of the house.... Well, all right, I'll go."

She tore her hand away and, scarcely able to hold back the tears, attempted to leave the room. *Maman* held her back, embraced her, and they both burst into tears.

Ever since I can remember I remember Natalya Savishna, her love and affection; but only now do I value them—then it never even entered my head what a rare and wonderful creature this old woman was. She not only never spoke, but never even thought, it seemed, of herself: her whole life was one of love and self-sacrifice. I was so used to her selfless tender love for us that I never even imagined it could ever have been otherwise; and I was not in the least grateful to her and never even thought to ask myself such questions as was she happy, or was she content.

Sometimes, under the pretext that it was an absolute necessity, you'd run into her room after lessons, settle yourself down somewhere and begin to think aloud, not in the least put out by her presence. She was always busy with something: either she would be knitting stockings, or digging in the chests with which her room was filled, or else making laundry lists, and listening to any rubbish I happened to be saying, such as: "When I'm a general I'll marry a glorious beauty, buy myself a bay horse, build myself a house of glass and pay for Karl Ivanich's family to come from Saxony," and so on, and then she'd say: "Yes, master, yes." Usually, when I got up to go away, she would open a blue chest, on the underneath of whose lid—as far as I remember—there were pasted a colored portrait of some hussar or other, a label from a hair-oil jar, and a drawing by Volodya; take out some incense from the trunk, light it, wave it about, and say:

"This, master, is Ochakov incense. When your late grandfather—God rest his soul—fought against the Turks, he brought this back with him." And then she would add with a sigh: "This is the last bit left."

The chests that filled her room contained absolutely everything. No matter what anybody required, they always said: "You must try Natalya Savishna." And indeed, after rummaging about a bit, she would find the desired article and say: "It's a good job I put that away." In those chests there were thousands of such articles, about which nobody in the house, except Natalya Savishna, knew or cared.

Once I became angry at her. This is how it happened. Pouring myself some kvas at dinner one day, I upset the jug and spilled it on the tablecloth.

"Tell Natalya Savishna to come and admire her favorite," said *maman.*

Natalya Savishna came in and, catching sight of the pool I had made, shook her head; then *maman* whispered something in her ear and with a threatening look in my direction she went out again.

After dinner I was skipping along in an excellent mood, making for the salon, when all of a sudden Natalya Savishna jumped out from behind a door, holding the tablecloth in her hand, caught hold of me, and despite desperate resistance on my part began to rub the wet part all over my face, saying: "Don't wet the tablecloth, don't wet the tablecloth!" I was so insulted by this that I howled with rage.

"What!" I said to myself, marching up and down the salon and choking with tears. "Natalya Savishna, mere *Natalya,* being familiar with *me,* and then hitting me in the face with a wet tablecloth as if I were a peasant boy. No, it's horrible!"

When Natalya Savishna saw that I was crying she immediately ran away, while I continued to march up and down and ponder how I could get even with that impudent *Natalya* for the insult I had borne.

A few minutes later Natalya Savishna returned, came up to me and began to plead with me:

"Enough, master, don't cry ... forgive me, I'm a fool ... I'm sorry ... please forgive me, my dear ... here."

She took a twist of red paper out of her pocket in which there were two toffees and a fig, and with a trembling hand offered it to me. I could not bring myself to look into the kind old woman's face; I accepted the present and turned away and the tears flowed even more freely—no longer from rage but from love and shame.

XIV

PARTING

On the day following the events I have just described, at twelve midday, a barouche and phaeton stood by the front porch. Nikolai was dressed for the road; that is, his trousers were tucked into his boots and his old coat was tightly belted with a sash. He was standing in the phaeton and packing topcoats and cushions under the seat; when it seemed too high to him, he sat on the cushions and bounced up and down in order to flatten them.

"Do me a very great favor, Nikolai Dmitrich. Can you find room for the master's *portmantle* in there?" said Papa's valet pantingly, thrusting his head out of the barouche. "It's only small . . . "

"You should have said something before, Mikhei Ivanich," replied Nikolai rapidly and with annoyance, throwing some bundle onto the floor of the phaeton with all his might. "I swear to God my head's going round as it is, and now you come along with your *portmantle*." He pushed his cap back as he added this and wiped large drops of sweat from his sunburned forehead.

House serfs wearing overalls, caftans, and shirts, though capless; women wearing rough dresses with striped kerchiefs and carrying children in their arms; and barefoot urchins stood around the porch looking at the carriages and talking among themselves. One of the drivers, a hunchbacked old man wearing a winter cap and cloth coat, was holding the barouche's pole in his hands, wiggling it about and thoughtfully watching its movement; the other driver—a handsome young man clad in only a white shirt with red calico panels under the armpits and a conical black felt hat, which he knocked first over one ear and then the other as he scratched his blond curls—placed his jacket on the driver's box, threw the reins up after it, and flicked his plaited whip as he looked first at his boots and then at the coachmen who were greasing the phaeton. One of them was straining to hold up the running board, while the other bent over the wheel and carefully greased the axle and bearing—and even, in order not to waste what was left on the brush, greased it from underneath as well. The jaded post horses with coats of various colors stood by the railings and flicked flies away with their tails. Some of them, spreading their shaggy swollen feet apart, narrowed their eyes and dozed; others scratched one another in boredom, or else nibbled at the leaves and stalks of the tough dark-green ferns that grew beside the porch. Several hounds were there; some lay in the sun, panting heavily, while others in the shade walked under the barouche and phaeton and licked the tallow off the axles. A kind of dusty mist filled the air, the horizon was grayish-violet; but there was not a single cloud in the sky. A strong west wind raised columns of dust from the lanes and fields, bent the tops of the tall lindens and birches in our garden and carried the falling yellow leaves far away. I sat by the window and waited impatiently for all the preparations to be over.

When everyone had gathered about the round table in the drawing room in order to spend a few last minutes together, it did not even enter my head what a sad moment lay before us. The most trivial thoughts wandered through my mind. I asked myself such questions as: Which driver is going in the barouche and which in the phaeton? Who's going with Papa and who with Karl Ivanich? And why do they have to wrap me up in this scarf and padded topcoat? I'm no baby, I shan't freeze. I wish they'd put an end to this and let us get in and go.

"Who shall I give the list of the children's linen to?" said Natalya

Savishna, coming in with a list in her hand, with tears in her eyes, speaking to *maman*.

"Give it to Nikolai, and then come and say good-by to the children."

The old woman wanted to say something but suddenly stopped, covered her face with her handkerchief, and with a wave of her hand left the room. I felt a tiny tug at my heart when I saw this gesture; but impatience to be off was stronger than this feeling and I continued to listen with complete indifference as Papa and Mama talked. They were talking of things that clearly interested neither of them: what needed to be bought for the house, what to say to Princess Sophie and Madame Julie, whether the road would be good or not.

Foka came in, halted on the threshold and in the same voice that he used to announce "Dinner is ready" announced: "The horses are ready." I noticed that *maman* started and turned pale at this news, as though it had caught her by surprise.

Foka was ordered to close all the doors in the room. This amused me no end, as though we were all hiding from someone.

When everyone sat down, Foka also perched on the edge of a chair; but no sooner had he done so than the door squeaked and everyone looked round. Natalya Savishna hurried into the room and without raising her eyes squeezed onto the same chair with Foka. I can see Foka's bald head and wrinkled impassive face now, and that kind bent figure in the bonnet with the gray hair peeping out from underneath. They are huddled together on a single chair and neither of them is comfortable.

I continued to be light-hearted and restless. The ten seconds we had been sitting with closed doors seemed like a whole hour to me. At last everyone stood up, crossed themselves and one another, and began to say good-by. Papa embraced *maman* and kissed her several times.

"Enough, my dear," said Papa, "we're not parting forever, you know."

"I still can't help feeling sad!" said *maman* in a tearfully quavering voice.

When I heard that voice and saw her trembling lips and her eyes full of tears, I forgot everything and became so sad and uncomfortable and frightened that I felt it was better to run away than to have to say good-by to her. At that moment I realized that in embracing Father she was also bidding farewell to us.

She had kissed and crossed Volodya so many times that, supposing my turn to be next, I pushed my way forward; but she blessed him again and again and still pressed him to her bosom. At last I embraced her and clung to her and cried and cried, thinking of nothing but my own grief.

When we went out to sit in the hall the tiresome house servants came to us to say good-by. Their "Kiss your hand, sir" and loud kisses on the shoulder, and the smell of tallow in their hair aroused a feeling in me that is most akin to chagrin in people who are easily irritated. Under the influence of this feeling, it was with extraordinary coldness that I kissed Natalya Savishna's bonnet when she came, in tears, to bid me farewell.

It is strange that I can see all the servants' faces as if it were now and could draw them all in the minutest detail, yet *maman*'s face and attitude quite elude my memory: perhaps because, during this whole time, I could not once bring myself to look at her. It seemed to me that if I did, her grief and mine were bound to swell to impossible limits.

I was first to rush into the barouche and settle myself on the back seat. I could not see anything over the raised canopy, but some kind of instinct told me that *maman* was still there.

Shall I look at her once more or not? . . . Well, for the last time! I said to myself and thrust my head out on the porch side. At that moment *maman*, with the same idea in mind, came up on the other side of the barouche and called me by name. Hearing her voice behind me, I turned around, but so quickly that we banged our heads together; she smiled ruefully and kissed me long and hard for the last time.

When we were several yards away I decided to look back at her. The wind was lifting the blue scarf tied around her head; with lowered head and face buried in her hands, she was slowly ascending the steps of the porch. Foka supported her.

Papa sat next to me and said nothing, while I choked on my tears and felt such a pressure in my throat that I feared I should suffocate. . . . When we turned onto the main road we caught sight of a white handkerchief being waved by someone on the balcony. I started to wave mine back and this action soothed me somewhat. I continued to cry, but the thought that these tears gave proof of my sensitivity afforded me satisfaction and comfort.

When we had gone about half a mile I made myself more comfortable and with stubborn interest started to watch the object that was nearest my eyes—the hindquarters of the horse running on my side. I watched how this skewbald flicked her tail, how she banged her legs together, how the driver's plaited whip reached over her and how her legs started to gallop in unison; I watched the way her breech band was covered with foam near the tail. I began to look around me: at the rippling fields of ripe rye, at the dark fields that were fallow, on which I glimpsed here and there a plow, a peasant or a mare and foal, and at the mileposts, and I even glanced up at the driver's box to see who was driving us; and before the tears had even dried on my face my thoughts were far away from the mother I had just left, perhaps forever. But each recollection returned my thoughts to her. I recalled the mushroom I had found yesterday in the birch avenue, I recalled that Lyubochka and Katyenka had quarreled over who should pick it, and I recalled how they had wept at our departure.

How sorry I felt for them! And for Natalya Savishna, and for the birch trees, and for Foka! Even nasty Mimi—I felt sorry for her too. I was sorry for everything, everything! And what about poor *maman?* And the tears again welled up in my eyes; but not for long.

XV

CHILDHOOD

Oh happy, happy time of childhood, never to be recalled! How could one fail to love and cherish one's memories of it? These memories refresh and elevate my soul and are for me the source of all my best pleasures.

Sometimes, when you were tired of running about, you'd sit down on a high armchair at the tea table; it would be late already, you'd long since finished your sugared milk and your eyes were beginning to close, but you did not move an inch, you sat and listened. And how could one fail to listen when *maman* was talking to someone and her voice sounded so inviting and sweet? Those sounds alone spoke volumes to my heart! With sleep-drugged eyes I gaze intently at her face and suddenly she has become ever so tiny and small—her face no bigger than a button; but I can still see it all quite clearly: I see her glance at me and smile. I like to see her so tiny. I screw my eyes up still more and she becomes no bigger than the little me that I sometimes see in somebody else's pupils—but I've moved and the spell is broken; I narrow my eyes and twist about, trying at all costs to renew it, but in vain.

I get up, clamber back into the chair feet first and make myself cozy in it.

"You'll fall asleep again, Nikolyenka," says *maman;* "you'd better go upstairs."

"I don't want to go to bed, Mama," you say, and indistinct sweet dreams invade your imagination, healthy childish sleep seals your lids, and a moment later you slip into oblivion and sleep until you are waked. Then, through your sleep, you feel somebody's tender hand touching you; from the feel alone you recognize it and, still asleep, you involuntarily grasp this hand and press it tightly to your lips.

Everyone's gone away now; only one candle still burns in the drawing room; *maman* has said she will wake me herself; this is she perching on the armchair where I'm asleep, she has stroked my hair with her wonderful tender hand and that sweet familiar voice sounds just above my ear:

"Get up, my darling: it's time to go to bed."

No one is there to constrain her with looks of indifference: she is not afraid to pour out all her tenderness and love. I do not stir, but I kiss her hand even harder.

"Get up, my angel."

With her other hand she takes me by the neck and her fingers move swiftly and tickle me. In the room it is quiet and almost dark; my nerves have been excited by the tickling and by being woken up; Mama is sitting right beside me; she touches me; I am conscious of her scent and voice. All this induces me to jump up, twine my arms about her neck, press my head to her breast, and say breathlessly:

"Oh my dear, dear Mama, how I love you!"

She smiles her sorrowful enchanting smile, takes my head in both her hands, kisses my forehead, and sets me on her knee.

"So you love me very much, do you?" She is silent for a moment and then says: "Make sure you always love me and don't ever forget me. If your Mama's no longer there, you won't forget her, will you? You won't forget her, Nikolyenka?"

She kissed me even more tenderly than before.

"Don't! Don't say that, Mama darling!" I exclaim, kissing her knees, and tears pour in torrents from my eyes—tears of love and rapture.

And then, afterward, when you were already upstairs and kneeling before the icons in your little quilted dressing gown, what a wonderful

feeling it would be to say: "God bless Daddy and God bless Mummy."
Repeating those prayers, which my childish lips had first lisped after
my mother, my love for her and my love for God somehow strangely
merged into a single feeling.

After prayers you would roll yourself up in your little quilt; your
heart would feel light and bright and joyful; dreams put other dreams
to flight—but what were they? They were fleeting, but filled with pure
love and hopes for radiant happiness. Sometimes you'd remember Karl
Ivanich and his bitter fate—the only man I knew to be unhappy—and
such would be the pity of it and so strong would your love for him
grow that tears would fill your eyes and you'd think: May God make
him happy and may I be permitted to help him, to help ease his grief;
I'm ready to sacrifice everything for his sake. Then you'd push your favorite china toy—a hare or a little dog—into the corner of your
feather pillow and admire the way it lay there so nicely, warmly, and
cozily. Again you'd pray for God to make everyone happy, for everyone
to be content and for there to be nice weather for going out the next
day; then you'd turn on your other side, your thoughts and dreams
would get all tangled up and confused and you'd drop quietly, peacefully off to sleep, your face still wet with tears.

Will they ever return, that freshness, that innocence, that need for
love and strength of faith that one possessed in childhood? What time
could ever be better than the time when the two greatest virtues—
innocent gaiety and a boundless appetite for love—were one's sole in-
centives in life?

Where are those ardent prayers? Where the supreme gift—those
tears of tender emotion? One's guardian angel would fly down, wipe
away those tears with a smile and waft sweet dreams into that un-
spoiled, childish imagination.

Can life have left such harsh marks on my heart that those tears and
joys are gone forever? Do only memories remain?

XVI

Verses

Almost a month after we moved to Moscow I was sitting at a large table upstairs in Grandmother's house and writing; across from me sat the drawing master, who was correcting a charcoal drawing of a Turk's head with a turban. Volodya stood behind the drawing master, craning his neck in an effort to look over his shoulder. This Turk's head was Volodya's first effort in charcoal and was destined that very day, on her name day, to be offered up to Grandmother.

"Aren't you going to shade it in here?" said Volodya to the master, standing on tiptoe and pointing to the Turk's neck.

"No, it's not necessary," said the teacher, putting the crayons and crayon holder away in a drawer, "it's excellent now, so don't touch it any more. Well, and what about you, Nikolyenka," he added, getting up and continuing to look at the Turk out of the corner of his eye. "Tell us your secret now. What are you going to give to Grandmother? Really, I think the best would be another drawing. Good day, gentlemen," he said, taking his hat and chit and going out.

At that moment I too thought a drawing would have been better than what I was laboring over. When we had been told that Grandmother's name day would be soon and that we should prepare some presents, it had occurred to me to write some verses for that occasion and I had immediately picked out two lines that rhymed, hoping I would be able to find the rest equally quickly. I have not the faintest idea how such a strange idea, for a child, could have occurred to me, but I remember that it pleased me very much and that to all questions about it I replied that I would definitely be giving something to Grandmother, but would tell no one what it was to consist of.

To my surprise, however, it turned out that apart from the two lines that came to me in the heat of inspiration, I was unable, despite all my efforts, to compose any more. I began reading the poetry in our books; but neither Dmitriev nor Derzhavin helped me at all—on the contrary, they convinced me still more of my incapability. Knowing that Karl Ivanich liked to copy verses, I began going through his papers on the sly and among a number of German poems found one in Russian that must have come from his own pen.

To Mme. L. Petrovsky. June 3, 1828.

> *Remember near,*
> *Remember far,*
> *Remember I*
> *From this day fourth and allways,*
> *Remember to my grave,*
> *How faythful I can love.*
> KARL MAUER

This composition, inscribed in a handsome rounded hand on a thin sheet of notepaper, appealed to me by virtue of the touching sentiments with which it was imbued; I immediately learned it off by heart and decided to take it for a model. Things went much easier now. By the time the name day came around a congratulatory address of twelve lines was ready and I sat at my desk in the classroom and copied them out onto vellum.

Two sheets of vellum had already been spoiled ... not because I had decided to change anything: my verses seemed excellent to me; but from the third line the ends of the lines seemed to slope upward more and more, so that even from a distance you could see that they were crookedly written and were no good at all.

The third sheet was just as crooked as the preceding ones, but I decided not to copy it out any more. In my poem I congratulated Grandmother, wished her long life and good health and concluded thus:

> To comfort you we shall endeavor
> and love you like our own dear mother.

It was not bad at all, I thought, but that last line somehow offended my ear in some strange way.

"And love . . . you . . . like . . . our own . . . dear . . . mo-ther," I repeated to myself under my breath. "What rhyme could I use instead of mother? Weather? Father? . . . Oh, never mind. It's still better than Karl Ivanich's!"

And I wrote the last line. Then, in the bedroom, I read the whole of my composition through aloud, with feeling and gestures. Some lines had no meter at all, but I did not dwell on these; the last one struck me still more and seemed still worse. I sat on the bed and thought:

Why did I write *like our own dear mother*? She's not here, is she, so there's no need to mention her; it's true I love Grandmother and respect her, but still it's not the same . . . why did I write that, why did I lie? I know it's poetry, but there's still no need.

At that very moment the tailor entered, bringing our new dress coats with him.

"Oh well, so be it!" I said with great impatience; then, still dissatisfied, I thrust the verses under my pillow and ran to try on our Moscow clothes.

Our Moscow clothes turned out to be superb: the brown dress coats had bronze buttons and were made close-fitting—not like they had been made in the country, with room for you to grow—and the black trousers, also narrow, showed off your muscles and fitted over your shoes just right.

At last I'm getting trousers with footstraps on them, and real ones too! I mused, beside myself with joy as I inspected my legs from all angles. Although my new clothes felt very tight and uncomfortable, I concealed this from everyone and said that on the contrary they felt very nice and that if they had any fault at all they were, if anything, a shade on the loose side. After this I stood for a very long time in front of the mirror, brushing my liberally oiled hair; but no matter how much I tried, I was completely unable to flatten down the curls on the crown of my head: as soon as I ceased pressing them down with my brush, in order to test their obedience, they sprang up again and stuck out in all directions, making my face look extremely funny.

Karl Ivanich was dressing in the next room and a blue frock coat and certain other white appurtenances were carried in to him through the classroom. The voice of one of Grandmother's maids sounded at the door that led downstairs and I went out to see what she wanted. She was holding a stiffly starched shirtfront in her hands and told me she had brought it for Karl Ivanich and that she had stayed up all night to get it washed in time. I undertook to deliver the shirtfront and asked if Grandmother was up.

"Good gracious yes, sir. She's already drunk her coffee and the parson's here. My, what a smart young fellow you are!" she added with a smile, inspecting my new clothes.

This remark made me blush; I spun round on one leg, snapped my fingers and gave a skip, hoping by this means to impress upon her that she did not know the half of what a smart young fellow I really was.

When I brought the shirtfront to Karl Ivanich he was no longer in need of it: he had put on another, and, bending before the little mirror that stood on his table, was holding on with both hands to the splendid bow of his tie, testing it to see if his smoothly shaven chin could move easily in and out of it. Having tugged our clothes smoothly into place on all sides and requested Nikolai to do the same for him, he conducted us to see Grandmother. I smile to think how strongly the three of us stank of hair oil as we commenced our descent of the stairs.

Karl Ivanich was holding a little box of his own manufacture, Volodya his drawing, and I my verses; and each of us had a greeting on his tongue with which to accompany his offering of the present. Just as Karl Ivanich opened the door of the salon, the vicar donned his chasuble and the first chords of the service rang out.

Grandmother was already there: bent over double and holding on to the back of a chair, she was standing by the wall and praying devoutly; next to her stood Papa. He turned to look at us and smiled, noticing how we had hastily hidden our prepared presents behind our backs and were trying to make ourselves inconspicuous by stopping just inside the door. The whole surprise effect that we had counted on was completely lost.

When they began to file up to kiss the cross I suddenly felt myself under the painful influence of an overpowering stupefying bashfulness, and sensing that I would never have the nerve to step forward with my present, I hid myself behind Karl Ivanich, who, having congratulated Grandmother in the choicest possible phrases, transferred the little box from his right hand to his left, tendered it to her whose name day it was, and stepped back to make room for Volodya. Grandmother seemed enraptured by the little box with gilt edging and expressed her gratitude in a most affectionate smile. It was clear, however, that she did not know where to put the box, and it was probably for that reason that she invited Papa to note how wonderfully cleverly it had been made.

When he had satisfied his curiosity, Papa passed it on to the parson, who seemed to be extraordinarily impressed with this little knick-knack; he shook his head and looked now at the box and now at the master craftsman who had been able to make such a wonderful thing. Volodya proffered his Turk and also earned the most flattering praise on all sides. Then came my turn: Grandmother turned to me with a smile of encouragement.

Those who have experienced shyness know that this feeling grows in direct proportion to the passage of time, while resolution shrinks in inverse proportion; that is to say: the longer this condition continues, the more overpowering it becomes and the less resolution remains.

My last courage and resolution abandoned me as Karl Ivanich and Volodya offered up their presents, and my shyness reached its uttermost limits: I felt the blood rushing constantly from my heart to my head, felt the color of my face constantly changing and felt huge drops of sweat standing out on my nose and forehead. My ears burned, my whole body trembled and came out in a cold sweat, and I hopped from one foot to the other without moving from the spot.

"Well, show us what you have, Nikolyenka, is it a box or a drawing?" said Papa. There was nothing else to do: with trembling hand I held out the crumpled, fateful sheet of paper; but my voice completely refused to obey me and I stopped mute before Grandmother. I was prevented from recovering myself by the thought that instead of the expected drawing they would read out, in the hearing of all, my completely worthless verses and the words: *like our own dear mother,* which would show clearly that I had never loved her and had now forgotten her. How can I convey my sufferings at the moment when Grandma began to read my composition aloud, when she stopped in the middle of a line, unable to follow it, in order to look at Papa with a smile that to me at that time seemed like mockery, when she pronounced things differently from the way I had intended and when, unable to go on because of her eyesight, she handed the paper to Papa and requested him to read the whole thing through again from the beginning? I thought she was doing this because it sickened her to read such horrible and crookedly written verses and was about to say: "Worthless brat, don't forget your mother . . . take that!" But nothing of the kind took place; on the contrary, when it had all been read through, Grandmother said *"Charmant"* and kissed me on the forehead.

The little box, the drawing, and the verses were placed next to two batiste handkerchieves and a snuffbox with a portrait of *maman* on it, which stood on the folding table attached to the Voltaire armchair that Grandmother always sat in.

"Princess Varvara Ilyinichna Kornakov," announced one of the two enormous footmen who used to ride on the back of Grandmother's carriage.

Grandmother was looking thoughtfully at the portrait set in the tortoiseshell snuffbox and did not reply.

"Shall I ask her to come in, Your Highness?" repeated the footman.

XVII

Princess Kornakov

"Yes, do," said Grandmother, settling herself deeper in her armchair.

The princess was a woman of about forty-five—small, frail, lean, and waspish, with unpleasant gray-green eyes whose expression plainly belied the unnaturally sweet way in which she had composed her mouth. Light-reddish hair peeped out from beneath a velvet hat with an ostrich feather in it; her brows and eyelashes seemed even lighter and redder, in contrast to the unhealthy color of her face. And yet, thanks to her easy movements, tiny hands, and the particular leanness of all her features, her general appearance had something noble and energetic about it.

The princess was very talkative and in her loquaciousness belonged to that class of people who always speak as though they are being contradicted, even when no one says a word: sometimes she would raise her voice and at others she would gradually lower it, but then she would break out again suddenly with renewed vigor and look around at those present, although they were taking no part in the conversation, as though seeking support for herself with this look.

Despite the fact that the princess kissed Grandmother's hand and ceaselessly addressed her as *ma bonne tante,* I remarked that Grandmother was displeased with her: there was something special about the way she raised her eyebrows as she listened to the princess explaining why Prince Mikhailo had been quite unable to come to congratulate Grandmother, despite his tremendous wish to do so; and replying in Russian to the princess's French, she said, emphasizing her words particularly:

"I am very grateful to you, my dear, for your consideration; as for Prince Mikhailo not coming, well, what is there to say? . . . He always has oceans of work; and anyway, what fun is it for him to sit with an old woman?"

And without giving the princess time to refute her words she continued:

"Well, and how are your children, my dear?"

"Oh, one must be thankful, *ma tante;* they're growing, learning, up to all sorts of tricks . . . especially Etienne, the eldest. He's getting such a scamp that we don't get a moment's peace; but on the other hand he's very clever—*un garçon qui promet.* Just imagine, *mon cousin,*" she went on, talking exclusively to Papa, since Grandmother, taking not the slightest interest in the princess' children and wishing to boast of her own grandchildren, was carefully extracting my verses from beneath the little box and unfolding them. "Just imagine, *mon cousin,* what he did the other day . . . "

And bending closer to Papa, the princess began to tell him something with great enthusiasm. When she had finished her story, which I did not hear, she immediately laughed and with an inquiring look at Papa's face said:

"Quite a lad, eh, *mon cousin?* He should have been whipped for it; but the idea of it was so clever and amusing that I forgave him, *mon cousin.*"

And the princess, gazing at Grandmother in silence, went on smiling.

"Do you mean to say you *beat* your children, my dear?" asked Grandmother, raising her eyebrows significantly and putting particular emphasis on the word *beat.*

"Ah, *ma bonne tante,*" replied the princess in a good-natured tone of voice, throwing a quick glance at Papa, "I know your opinion on this score; but allow me to disagree with you on this one thing: no matter how much I've thought and read on this subject, no matter how often I've sought advice, nevertheless experience has convinced me that children have to be governed by fear. You need fear in order to make something out of a child . . . isn't that so, *mon cousin?* And what, *je vous demande un peu,* do children fear more than the birch?"

As she said this she glanced questioningly at us, and I must admit I felt a bit uncomfortable at that moment.

"No matter what you say, a boy's still a child till the age of twelve or fourteen; but with a girl it's a different matter."

What luck, I thought, that I'm not her son.

"Yes, that's all very well, my dear," said Grandmother, folding up my verses and putting them back under the box, as though considering the princess unworthy of hearing such a composition, "that's all very well, but tell me, please, how, after that, can you demand delicacy of feeling from your children?"

And considering this argument irrefutable, Grandmother added, in order to close the conversation:

"However, we can all have our own opinions on that score."

The princess did not reply but merely smiled deferentially, indicating by this that she could forgive these strange prejudices in a person she esteemed so highly.

"Oh yes, introduce me to your young people then," she said, looking at us with an inviting smile.

We stood up and fixed our eyes on the princess's face, having not the slightest idea how to indicate that we had been introduced.

"Kiss the princess's hand," said Papa.

"I beg you to love your old aunt," she said, kissing Volodya's hair. "Although a distant one, I'm counting by friendly relations and not by degrees of kinship," she added, referring primarily to Grandmother. But Grandmother continued to be displeased with her and replied:

"No, my dear, do you think that sort of kinship counts for anything nowadays?"

"This one's going to be a young man about town," said Papa, pointing to Volodya, "and this one a poet," he added as I kissed the princess's lean, tiny little hand, imagining with exceeding clarity a birch rod in this hand, and beneath this rod—a bench, and so on and so forth.

"Which one?" asked the princess, holding me by the hand.

"This little curly one," replied Papa, smiling broadly.

What's he got against my curls . . . is that all he can talk about? I thought and went off into the corner.

I had the strangest notions about handsomeness—I even considered Karl Ivanich the handsomest man in the world; but I was very well aware that I was unattractive myself and in this I was not mistaken; that is why every reference to my appearance was a mortal insult to me.

I remember very well how once at dinner—I was six at the time—they discussed my appearance and *maman* tried to find something attractive about my face: she said I had intelligent eyes and a pleasant smile, but finally, yielding to Father's arguments and the obvious facts, she was forced to admit that I was ugly; and then, when I thanked her for dinner, she patted me on the cheek and said:

"Remember, Nikolyenka, no one will ever love you for your face; therefore you must try to be a good and clever little boy."

These words convinced me not only that I was not handsome, but also that I was bound to be a good and clever little boy.

In spite of this, I was frequently subject to moments of despair: I imagined that there was no happiness on earth for a man with such a wide nose, such thick lips, and such tiny gray eyes as mine; I begged God to perform a miracle—to make me suddenly handsome, and I would give everything I had and everything I might possibly possess in the future in exchange for a handsome face.

XVIII

PRINCE IVAN IVANICH

When the princess had heard the verses and heaped praises upon their composer, Grandmother relented, began to speak French with her, ceased calling her *my dear,* and invited her to return in the evening and bring all her children with her, to which the princess agreed; then, having sat a little longer, she left.

So many guests came that day to congratulate Grandmother that throughout the whole morning there were always several carriages waiting outside at one time.

"Bonjour, chère cousine," said one of the guests, coming into the room and kissing Grandmother's hand.

This was a man of about seventy—tall, wearing a military uniform with big epaulettes and with a large white cross peeping out from under the collar, whose face had a calm open expression to it. The freedom and simplicity of his movements astonished me. Despite the fact that only a semicircle of scant hair remained on the back of his head and that the position of his upper lip showed clearly his lack of teeth, his face was still remarkably handsome.

At the end of the last century, thanks to his noble character, handsome appearance, remarkable bravery, prominent and powerful family, and in particular his luck, Prince Ivan Ivanich had máde a brilliant career at a very early age. He had continued in the service and very soon his ambitions had been so well satisfied that nothing was left to be desired in that respect. From earliest youth he had borne himself as though expecting to occupy that brilliant station in the world in which fate subsequently placed him; thus, although there occurred in his brilliant and somewhat vainglorious life, as in all other lives, setbacks, disappointments, and upsets, he was never once unfaithful to his perpetual calmness of character, nor to his elevated cast of thought, nor to the basic rules of religion and morality, so that he acquired universal esteem not so much on the basis of his brilliant position as on that of his consistency and firmness. He was not very intelligent, but thanks to being in a position that permitted him to look down upon all the petty cares of life, his mode of thought was elevated. He was kind and sensitive, but cold and somewhat haughty in his bearing. This stemmed from the fact that, having been placed in a position where he could be useful to many, he tried by this coldness to guard himself against the ceaseless petitioning and sycophancy of those who only wished to take advantage of his influence. This coldness was softened, however, by the tactful courtesy of a man from *very high society*. He was well educated and well read; but his education had gone no further than what he had acquired in youth, i.e. at the end of the last century. He had read everything written during the eighteenth century in France in the spheres of philosophy and rhetoric and had a thorough knowledge of all the best works of French literature, so that he could and did quote passages from Racine, Corneille, Boileau, Molière, Montaigne, and Fènelon with great pleasure; he had an excellent knowledge of classical mythology, had with profit studied French translations of the ancient monuments of epic poetry, and had a fair knowledge of history, gleaned from Ségur; but he had not the slightest idea of mathematics beyond arithmetic, nor of physics, nor of contemporary literature: in conversation he could maintain a decent silence or utter a few commonplaces about Goethe, Schiller, and Byron, but he never read them. Despite his French-classical education (of which so few examples remain nowadays), his conversation was simple, and this simplicity both concealed his ignorance of certain subjects and revealed his pleasant manners and tolerance. He was the confirmed enemy of any kind of "eccentricity," saying that eccentricity was the subterfuge of people of low breeding. Society was indispensable to him, no matter where he was living; he always lived just as openly whether he was in Moscow or abroad, and on certain days would receive the whole town at his home. Such was his standing there that an invitation card from him would serve as a passport to all the drawing rooms in town, that many young and pretty women were glad to present their rosy little cheeks to him to be kissed, which he did in a seemingly fatherly manner, and that certain apparently very important and respectable people went into indescribable ecstasies when they were permitted to join the prince's party.

For the prince there now remained few such people as Grandmother, who were from the same circle and had the same upbringing and view of things as he did and were of the same age; therefore he particularly treasured his old friendly relations with her and always treated her with great respect.

I could not drink in enough of the prince. The respect that everybody showed him, the big epaulettes, the special delight that Grandmother evinced upon catching sight of him, and the fact that he alone was evidently not afraid of her, spoke to her with absolute freedom, and was even bold enough to call her *ma cousine,* filled me with a respect for him that was equal to, if not greater than, that which I felt for Grandmother. When he was shown my verses, he called me to him and said:

"Who knows, *ma cousine,* perhaps he'll be another Derzhavin." At this he pinched my cheek so painfully that if I did not cry out it was only because I guessed that it was meant affectionately.

The guests departed, Papa and Volodya went out of the room; the prince, Grandmother, and I were left alone in the drawing room.

"Why did our dear Natalya Nikolayevna not come to town?" asked the prince suddenly after a moment's silence.

"Ah! mon cher," replied Grandmother, lowering her voice and placing a hand on the sleeve of his uniform, "she would surely have come if she'd been free to do what she wanted. She writes me that Pierre sug-

gested she come, but that she refused, ostensibly because they have had hardly any money coming in this year; and then she writes: 'Furthermore, there's no reason for me to move the whole household to Moscow this year. Lyubochka's still too small, and as far as the boys are concerned, since they will be living with you I shall feel easier than if they were here with me.' That's all very well," went on Grandmother in a tone of voice showing clearly that she did not find it so very well at all. "It was high time the boys were sent here so they could learn something and get accustomed to society; what kind of education can they get in the country? . . . Why, the elder one will soon be thirteen and the other eleven. . . . Have you noticed, *mon cousin,* they're like complete savages here . . . they don't even know how to enter a room."

"But I don't understand," replied the prince, "why these perpetual complaints about being in difficult circumstances? *He* has a very good fortune and Natasha's Khabarovka, where you and I once used to act in plays, I know like the back of my hand—it's a wonderful estate! And should always bring in an excellent income."

"Let me tell you as a true friend," interrupted Grandmother with a sorrowful expression, "it seems to me that these are all excuses just so that *he* can live here alone and gad around his clubs and dinners and get up to God only knows what; and she suspects nothing. You know what an angel she is—she believes *him* in everything. He assured her that the children ought to be taken off to Moscow while she stayed in the country alone, together with some stupid governess—and she believed him; if he told her to flog the children the way princess Varvara Ilyinichna does hers, I believe she'd agree to that too," said Grandmother, twisting in her armchair with a look of utter contempt on her face. "Yes, my friend," went on Grandmother after a moment's silence, picking up one of her two handkerchiefs in order to wipe away a tear that had appeared, "I often think that *he* is incapable either of appreciating or of understanding her, and in spite of all her goodness and love for him and her efforts to conceal her grief, I know for sure she can never be happy with him; and mark my words, if he doesn't . . ."

Grandmother covered her face with her handkerchief.

"Eh, ma bonne amie," said the prince reprovingly, "I can see you've not grown any wiser—always grieving and lamenting over some imagi-

nary sorrow. Shame on you. I've known *him* a very long time and I know him for a kind attentive and excellent husband and, most important—for a gentleman, *un parfait honnête homme.*"

Having involuntarily overheard a conversation I ought not to have heard, I crept out of the room on tiptoe and in a state of great agitation.

XIX

The Ivins

"Volodya! Volodya! The Ivins!" I shouted, catching sight through the window of three little boys in blue coats with beaver collars; they were just following their dandyish young tutor across the street on their way to our house.

The Ivins were relatives of ours and were almost the same age as we were; soon after our arrival in Moscow we had met and become good friends with them.

The second Ivin—Seryozha—was a dark-skinned, curly-haired boy with a well-defined, turned-up nose, extremely fresh red lips that were rarely able to cover completely his slightly protruding upper row of white teeth, wonderful blue eyes, and an extraordinarily alert expression on his face. He never smiled, but either looked completely serious or else laughed wholeheartedly with his clear, musical and remarkably attractive laughter. His unusual handsomeness had struck me from the very first. I felt irresistibly attracted to him. To see him was enough to make me happy; and at one time all my heart's desires were concentrated on this one wish; whenever I had to pass three or four days without seeing him, I began to pine and felt sad and near to tears. All my dreams, both sleeping and waking, were of him: when I went to bed I hoped I would see him in my dreams; when I closed my eyes I saw him before me and cherished this vision as my greatest delight. I could not have confided this feeling to anyone in the world, so dear was he to me. Perhaps because he got tired of feeling my disturbed gaze fixed constantly upon him, or simply because he felt no liking for me, he was noticeably fonder of playing and talking with Volodya than me. But nevertheless I was content, I desired nothing, demanded nothing, and was ready to sacrifice all for him. Apart from the ardent fascination that he inspired in me, his presence evoked another feeling not a whit less intense—the fear of annoying him: perhaps it was because his face bore a haughty expression, or because, contemptuous of my own appearance, I put too high a value on the attributes of beauty in others, or, what is most likely, since this is a sure sign of love, it was simply that I experienced love and fear of him in equal measure. The first time Seryozha spoke to me I was so confused by such unexpected happiness that I turned pale, blushed, and was unable to answer. He had a very bad habit, whenever he grew thoughtful, of fixing his eyes on one spot and blinking ceaselessly, twitching his nose and eyebrows at the same time. Everyone agreed that this habit spoiled him terribly, but I found it so attractive that I unconsciously started doing the same thing myself, and several days after our first meeting Grandmother asked me whether my eyes were hurting, since I was blinking them like an owl. Not a single word passed between us of this passion of mine; but he sensed his power over me and subconsciously, but tyrannically, used it in our childish relations with one another; and I, no matter how much I wished to tell him all that was in my heart, was too fearful of him ever to take the plunge of frankness; I tried to seem indifferent and submitted to him without a murmur. Sometimes his influence over me seemed harsh and unbearable; but it was not in my power to escape it.

It grieves me to recall this fresh beautiful feeling of disinterested and boundless love that simply died, without ever being expressed or striking an answering chord.

It is strange how, as a child, I tried to be like a grown-up, while, since I ceased to be one, I've often wished I were like one. How many times in my relations with Seryozha did this desire not to be like a child prevent my emotion from pouring out, and force me to pretend. I not only did not dare to kiss him, which I often wanted to do, or take his hand and say I was glad to see him, but I did not dare even to call him Seryozha, but always Sergei: that is how it had been agreed among us. Any expression of sentiment proved that one was a child, and he who permitted himself any was still *a kid*. Though still not having passed through those bitter trials that induce caution and coldness in the personal relations of adults, we deprived ourselves of the pure delights of tender childish affection merely from a strange desire to imitate *grown-ups*.

I met the Ivins when they were no farther than the servants' hall; I greeted them and then dashed headlong to Grandmother: I announced the arrival of the Ivins with as much delight as if this news were certain to render her happiness complete. Then, without taking my eyes off Seryozha, I followed him into the drawing room and watched his every movement. When Grandmother said that he had grown a great deal and fixed her piercing eyes on him, I experienced that same feeling of fear and hope that an artist must feel while awaiting the verdict of a respected judge on his latest work.

With Grandmother's permission their young tutor, Herr Frost, took us down to the garden, sat on a green bench, folded his legs picturesquely, placing between them his cane with a bronze knob on it, and with the air of a man who is extremely satisfied with his actions, lit a cigar.

Herr Frost was a German, but he was a German of a totally different kidney from kind-hearted Karl Ivanich: in the first place he spoke Russian correctly and also—with a bad accent—French, and in general, but particularly among the ladies, enjoyed the reputation of being a very learned man; in the second place he sported a ginger mustache, a large ruby pin in his black silk cravat, whose ends were tucked under his suspenders, and light-blue trousers made of some shimmery material with footstraps at the bottom; in the third place he was young and had a handsome self-satisfied appearance and extraordinarily striking, muscular legs. It was evident that he particularly treasured this last attribute: he considered its effect irresistible as far as persons of the opposite sex were concerned, and it was probably for this reason that he always tried to place his legs in the most prominent possible position and, whether standing or sitting, always to set his calves in motion. This was the type of young Russian German who aspired to be dashing and gallant.

It was very jolly in the garden. Our game of robbers was going beautifully; but one circumstance almost upset everything. Seryozha was the robber: just as he was chasing after the passers-by, he tripped and banged his knee on a tree going at full speed and did it so hard that I thought his knee would be smashed to smithereens. Despite the fact that I was the policeman and it was my duty to catch him, I went up to him and began sympathetically to ask if it hurt. Seryozha grew angry with me: he clenched his fists, stamped his foot, and in a voice that showed clearly how much he had hurt himself, shouted at me:

"Huh, what's this? How can we play after that? Why don't you catch me, eh? Why don't you catch me?" he repeated several times, glancing sideways at Volodya and his older brother, who, in the role of passersby, were skipping along the path; then, suddenly, with a whistle and loud laughter, he dashed off to catch them.

I cannot convey how astonished and captivated I was by this heroic action: despite the terrible pain, he not only did not cry but did not even show that he was hurt, and not for a moment did he forget the game.

Shortly after this, when we were joined by Ilinka Grap and went off upstairs before dinner, Seryozha had occasion to astonish and captivate me still more with his amazing heroism and firmness of character.

Ilinka Grap was the son of a poor foreigner who had once lived at my grandfather's; he was indebted to him for something and now considered it his bounden duty to send his son to us as often as possible. If he supposed that acquaintanceship with us might bring any kind of honor or pleasure to his son, he was completely mistaken, since we not only were not friendly with him, but took notice of him only when we wished to make fun of him. Ilinka Grap was thirteen years old, tall, thin and pale, with a birdlike little face and a good-natured submissive expression. He was very poorly dressed, but on the other hand was so liberal with his hair oil that we always declared that on a hot day the hair oil would melt on his head and run down under his jacket. As I remember him now, I find that he was a very obliging, quiet, and kind-hearted boy; but at that time he seemed such a despicable creature to me that he did not merit either pity or the least shred of thought.

When the game of robbers came to an end we went upstairs and began to romp and show various gymnastic tricks off to one another. Ilinka watched us with a timid smile of wonder and when we asked him to try the same thing refused, saying he was not strong enough. Seryozha was wonderful; he took off his jacket, his face and eyes lit up, and he was constantly laughing and getting up to new tricks: he jumped over three chairs placed next to one another, cartwheeled across the whole room and then stood on his hands on some volumes of Tatishchev's dictionary that he had placed in the middle of the room in the form of a pedestal, doing at the same time such side-splitting things with his legs that it was impossible to resist laughing. After this last trick he thought for a moment, blinked his eyes, and then suddenly, with a completely serious expression, went up to Ilinka and said:

"You try and do it; it's not very difficult, really."

Noticing that he was the object of general attention, Grap blushed and in a barely audible voice assured us that he was completely incapable of doing it.

"Well, what's this then, why won't he show us anything? What a girlie he is . . . he really must stand on his head!"

And Seryozha caught hold of his hand.

"Yes, he must, he must!" we all shouted, crowding round Ilinka; the latter was clearly frightened now and turned pale; we seized him by the arms and dragged him toward the dictionaries.

"Let me go, I can go on my own! You're tearing my jacket!" cried the unfortunate victim. But these desperate cries merely increased our enjoyment; we were choking with laughter; his green jacket split at all the seams.

Volodya and the elder Ivin bent his head down and placed it on the dictionaries; Seryozha and I seized the poor thing's skinny legs, which he was kicking in various directions, rolled his trousers up as far as the knee, and with loud laughter launched them into the air; the younger Ivin held the whole body in balance.

It happened that, after our loud laughter, we all suddenly fell silent and it became so quiet in the room that all we could hear was the heavy breathing of the unfortunate Grap. At that moment I was not at all sure that all this was so funny or jolly.

"Now there's a good lad," said Seryozha, giving him a slap with his hand.

Ilinka was silent and in trying to break free kicked his feet in various directions. With one of these desperate movements he hit Seryozha in the eye with his heel, and it was so painful that Seryozha immediately let go of his leg, put his hands to his eye, from which tears had started involuntarily, and then pushed Ilinka with all his might. Ilinka, who was no longer supported by us, crashed to the floor inertly and was only able to say through his tears:

"Why do you bully me?"

The weeping figure of poor Ilinka with his tear-stained face, ruffled hair, and rolled-up trousers, beneath which we could see the unpolished tops of his boots, astonished us; we were all silent and tried to force a smile.

The first to recover was Seryozha.

"What a sniveling ninny," he said, gently prodding him with his foot. "Can't take a joke? . . . Oh well, come on, get up."

"I always said you were a nasty kid," said Ilinka spitefully and, turning away from us, burst into tears.

"Aha! Kicks people in the eye and then calls them names!" cried Seryozha, picking up a dictionary and brandishing it over the head of the unfortunate Ilinka, who did not think of defending himself but merely covered his head with his hands.

"Take that! And that! . . . Let's leave him if he can't take a joke. . . . Let's go downstairs," said Seryozha with a forced laugh.

I looked at the poor fellow with sympathy; he was lying on the floor, hiding his face in the dictionaries and sobbing so bitterly that it seemed he would die at any moment from the convulsions that racked his whole body.

"Eh, Seryozha," I said, "why did you do that?"

"I like that! . . . I hope I didn't cry today when I almost banged my knee to bits."

Yes, that's true, I thought. Ilinka's nothing but a crybaby; but look at Seryozha—a really fine fellow . . . what a fine fellow he is!

It did not occur to me that the poor boy was probably crying not so much from physical pain as from the thought that five other boys, whom he probably liked, had for no reason at all agreed to hate and persecute him.

I am completely at a loss to explain to myself the cruelty of my actions. How was it I did not go up to him, defend him, and comfort him? What had happened to that feeling of compassion that had made me, on occasion, weep uncontrollably at the sight of a fledgeling jackdaw thrown from its nest or a puppy being carried off to be thrown over the fence, or a chicken in the hands of the cook destined to become soup?

Can it be that this beautiful feeling was stifled in me by my love for Seryozha and a desire to appear in his eyes the same kind of fine fellow as he? How unenviable were this love and desire to seem a fine fellow! They were responsible for the only dark spots on the pages of my childhood reminiscences.

XX

The Guests Arrive

Judging by the extra bustle noticeable in the pantry, by the bright illu-
mination that gave a kind of new festive appearance to all those long-
familiar objects in the drawing room and salon, and judging in
particular by the fact that Prince Ivan Ivanich had not sent his orchestra for nothing, a considerable number of guests was expected that
evening.

At the sound of each carriage going by I ran to the window, put a
hand up between my temple and the window pane and peered out into
the street with impatient curiosity. Out of the darkness that at first
covered everything on the other side of the window, there loomed
vaguely a long-familiar little store opposite us with a lamp burning, a
large house which was across the street at an angle from us, with two
downstairs windows illuminated, and in the middle of the street some
cabby or other with a couple of passengers, or an empty carriage, returning home at a walk. But just then a carriage approached the front
door and I, fully confident that this was the Ivins, who had promised to
come early, ran down to meet them in the front hall. Instead of the
Ivins there appeared, from behind the liveried hand that opened the

carriage door, two persons of the female sex, one large and wearing a blue cape with a sable collar, the other small and completely enveloped in a green shawl, beneath which one could see only her little feet in fur boots. Without paying the slightest heed to my presence in the hall, although I had considered it my duty at the appearance of these two persons to offer them a bow, the little one went silently up to the big one and stopped in front of her. The big one untied the scarf that had covered the little one's entire head, unbuttoned her cape, and when the liveried footman had received these things into his care and removed the small fur boots, there emerged from this cocooned person an enchanting little twelve-year-old girl in a short open-necked muslin frock, white bloomers, and tiny black shoes. Round her white neck was a black velvet ribbon; her little head was a mass of light-brown curls which went so well with her beautiful little face in front and her bare little shoulders behind that I would have believed no one—not even Karl Ivanich—had he told me that they were this curly because they had been rolled up since morning around pieces of the *Moscow Gazette*, and had been scorched with hot iron tongs. It seemed to me she must have been born with this head full of curls.

The most striking feature about her face was the extraordinary size of her prominent half-closed eyes, which provided a strange but pleasant contrast to her tiny mouth. Her lips were together and she looked so serious that the general expression of her face led one not to expect a smile, which made her actual smile seem all the more enchanting.

Trying to remain unnoticed, I slipped through the door into the salon and considered it necessary to pace up and down, pretending that I was preoccupied with something and not at all aware that some guests had arrived. When they had come about halfway down the salon I pretended to recover myself, scraped my feet, and informed them that Grandmother was in the drawing room. Madame Valakhin, whose face I liked very much, mainly because I found it to be extremely similar to her daughter Sonyechka's, favored me with a nod of the head.

Grandmother seemed extremely glad to see Sonyechka: she called her over to her, adjusted on her head a curl that had fallen down onto her forehead, looked at her penetratingly and said: "*Quelle charmante en-*

fant!" Sonyechka smiled, blushed, and looked so sweet that I also blushed looking at her.

"I hope you won't find it dull here, my dear," said Grandmother, lifting her little face by the chin. "I beg you to enjoy yourself and dance as much as possible. We have one lady and two cavaliers here already," she added, turning to Mrs. Valakhin and motioning to me with her hand.

This intimacy was so pleasant for me that I was forced to blush again.

Sensing that my bashfulness was on the increase and having caught the sound of another carriage approaching, I considered it wisest to retire. In the front hall I found Princess Kornakov with her son and an unbelievable number of daughters. The daughters were all identical—the image of the princess and ugly; therefore not one of them caught my attention. While taking off their capes and fox furs they suddenly started talking all at once in their high-pitched little voices and fussed about and laughed over something—probably over the fact that there were so many of them. Etienne was a boy of about fifteen, tall and beefy, with a pallid physiognomy and sunken eyes with blue rings under them and with hands and feet that were enormous for his age; he was clumsy and had a disagreeable irregular voice, but seemed very satisfied with himself and was exactly the way, as it seemed to me with my ideas, that a boy who gets birched might have been.

We stood opposite one another for quite a long time, saying not a word and staring at one another with interest; then, moving closer, we seemed about to kiss one another, but having looked one another in the eye once more, changed our minds for some reason. When all his sisters swept loudly by us in their dresses, I asked him, in order to start the conversation somehow, whether it had not been crowded in the carriage.

"I don't know," he replied carelessly, "you see I never ride inside because the moment I sit down I start feeling sick and Mama knows that. Whenever we go anywhere in the evening I always ride on top, beside the driver—it's much more fun there, you can see everything. Filipp lets me drive and sometimes even gives me the whip. Good for the passers-by, you know, sometimes," he added with an expressive gesture. "It's marvelous!"

"Your Highness," said a footman, coming into the hall, "Filipp would like to know what you did with the whip."

"What? What did I do with it? Gave it back to him, of course."

"He says you didn't give it back."

"Well, I must have hung it on the lamp."

"Filipp says it's not on the lamp either; why do you not say you took it and lost it and now Filipp will have to pay for your mischief-making out of his own money," went on the footman, more and more animated and growing angrier and angrier.

The footman, who appeared to be a venerable but morose man, seemed to be hotly taking Filipp's part and was determined, come what may, to get to the bottom of the matter. Out of an involuntary feeling of delicacy, I moved away as though unaware of anything; but the footmen in the hall behaved quite differently: they moved closer and watched the old servant approvingly.

"Well, if I lost it I lost it," said Etienne, declining any further explanations. "I'll pay him whatever the whip costs. What a scream!" he added, coming up to me and guiding me into the drawing room.

"No, just a minute, master, how will you pay? I know the way you pay: you've been paying Marya Vasilyevna twenty copecks for eight months now, and me too for two years or thereabouts, and Petrushka . . ."

"Be quiet, you!" shouted the young prince, turning white with rage. "I'll tell on you in a minute."

"I'll tell on you, I'll tell on you!" said the footman. "That's bad, Your Highness," he added with special emphasis as we entered the salon, and took the coats to the cloakroom.

"That's the way, that's it!" sounded an approving voice behind us in the hall.

Grandmother had the special gift of applying, in a certain manner in certain cases, the singular and plural pronouns of the second person in order to express her opinion of people. Although she used *thou* and *you* in the opposite way from generally accepted practice, on her lips these nuances took on a completely different meaning. When the young prince went up to her she spoke several words to him using the plural pronoun, and looked at him with an expression of such contempt that if I had been in his shoes I would have lost my head completely. But it was evident that Etienne was a boy of quite a different *stamp:* he not only paid not the slightest attention to Grandmother's reception of him, but seemed even not to notice her person at all, and bowed to everyone present if not gracefully at least with complete ease. Sonyechka took up the whole of my attention: I remember that whenever Volodya, Etienne, and I were talking in the salon at a spot from which Sonyechka was visible and where she could see and hear us, I talked enthusiastically; whenever I happened to come out with what in my opinion was a particularly funny or fine remark, I said it more loudly and looked around in the direction of the door to the drawing room; but when we moved to a different spot from which we could be neither seen nor heard from the drawing room, I kept silent and had no more enthusiasm for the conversation.

The drawing room and salon were slowly filling up with guests; among them, as usual at children's parties, there were several older children who were unwilling to miss an opportunity of dancing and having some fun, but pretended to be doing so solely to please their hostess.

When the Ivins came, instead of the pleasure I usually experienced on meeting Seryozha, I felt a kind of strange dissatisfaction with him because of the fact that he would see, and be seen by, Sonyechka.

XXI

BEFORE THE MAZURKA

"Ha, I see there's going to be some dancing," said Seryozha, coming from the drawing room and taking a pair of new kid gloves from his pocket. "I must put my gloves on."

What shall I do? We don't have any gloves, I thought. I must go upstairs and look for some.

But although I searched all the chests of drawers, I found only our green traveling mittens in one, while in another there was one kid glove that was no good at all to me: in the first place because it was extraordinarily old and dirty and in the second because it was too big for me, but mainly because it was missing the middle finger, which Karl Ivanich must have cut off ages ago to put on an injured hand. I put this remnant on my hand, however, and carefully inspected that place on my middle finger that was always stained with ink.

"If only Natalya Savishna were here: she'd have some gloves, I'm sure. I can't go down like this because what shall I say if they ask me why I'm not dancing? And I can't stay here either because they're bound to miss me. What shall I do?" I said, waving my hands in the air.

"What are you doing here?" said Volodya, running in. "Go and get yourself a partner . . . it's just about to begin."

"Volodya," I said to him, showing him my hand with two fingers stuck into the dirty glove and in a voice expressing a condition close to despair. "Volodya, you didn't even think of this!"

"What?" he said impatiently. "Oh, gloves," he added with complete indifference, noticing my hand. "No, we don't have any; you must ask Grandmother ... see what she says," and without a moment's thought he ran downstairs again.

The coolness with which he reacted to a circumstance that seemed so important to me reassured me and I hurried down to the drawing room, completely forgetting the misshapen glove that I was wearing on my left hand.

Cautiously approaching Grandmother's chair and lightly touching her gown, I said to her in a whisper:

"Grandmother, what shall we do? We don't have any gloves!"

"What, my dear?"

"We don't have any gloves," I repeated, moving closer and closer and placing both hands on the arm of her chair.

"And what's this?" she said, catching hold suddenly of my left hand. *"Voyez, ma chère,"* she went on, turning to Mme. Valakhin, *"voyez comme ce jeune homme s'est fait élégant pour danser avec votre fille."*

Grandmother held me tightly by the hand and looked round seriously but inquiringly at all present, until everyone's curiosity had been satisfied and the laughter became general.

I would have been extremely upset if Seryozha had seen me as I stood there, my face contorted with embarrassment, trying in vain to tear my hand away, but in front of Sonyechka, who laughed so heartily that tears came into her eyes and all her curls bobbed violently up and down around her flushing little face, I did not feel in the least ashamed. I realized that her laughter was too loud and natural to be mocking; on the contrary, the fact that we were laughing together and looking at one another somehow brought us closer together. Although it could have ended disastrously, the episode with the glove had one advantage for me in that it put me at ease in the milieu that always seemed most terrifying to me—the milieu of the drawing room. Now I experienced not the least bashfulness in the salon.

The agonies of those who are bashful proceed from their not knowing what opinion has been formed of them; as soon as this opinion has been clearly expressed—no matter what it is—their agonies cease.

How absolutely charming Sonyechka Valakhin was as she danced the quadrille opposite me with the clumsy young prince! How sweetly she smiled as she gave me her hand in the *chaine*! How sweetly her fair curls bobbed on her little head in time to the music, and how naïvely her tiny little feet did the *jeté-assemblé*! During the fifth figure, when my partner danced away from me to the other side and I, awaiting my cue, prepared to dance a solo, Sonyechka compressed her lips seriously and started to look away. But she feared for me in vain: I boldly executed a *chassé en avant, chassé en arrière,* and *glissade* and as I came close to her I showed her, with a playful gesture, the glove with two fingers sticking out of it. She burst into peals of laughter and her tiny feet pattered over the parquet floor even more sweetly than before. I can still remember how, as we made a circle and all held hands, she bent her little head and without removing her hand from mine rubbed her nose on her glove. I can see all this as if it were before my eyes and I can still hear that quadrille from "The Danube Maiden," to whose strains all this took place.

The time came for the second quadrille, which I was to dance with Sonyechka. Sitting down beside her I felt extraordinarily awkward and had not the faintest idea what to talk to her about. When my silence became too prolonged I began to fear that she would take me for a fool and resolved, come what may, to divest her of any such delusions on that score. *"Vous êtes une habitante de Moscou?"* I said, and after an answer in the affirmative went on: *"Et moi, je n'ai encore jamais fréquenté la capitale,"* counting in particular on the effect of the word *fréquenter.* I felt, however, that although this was a brilliant beginning and fully demonstrated my mastery of the French language, I was not capable of continuing the conversation in the same vein. There was still some time left until our turn to dance would come and in the meantime the silence was renewed: I looked at her anxiously, wanting to know what impression I had made and waiting for her to help. "Where did you find such a funny glove?" she asked suddenly; and this question afforded me great satisfaction and relief. I explained that the glove belonged to Karl Ivanich and even enlarged somewhat ironically on Karl

Ivanich's person, on how comical he was when he took off his red cap and how once, when wearing a green tunic, he had fallen off his horse straight into a puddle, and so forth. The quadrille passed imperceptibly. All this was very fine; but why did I speak so mockingly of Karl Ivanich? Would I have forfeited Sonyechka's good opinion if I had described him with the same love and respect that I really felt for him?

When the quadrille came to an end, Sonyechka said *"Merci"* with such a sweet expression on her face that it seemed as though I really had earned her gratitude. I was in seventh heaven, I was beside myself with joy and was unable even to recognize myself: whence came this boldness, this self-confidence and even impudence? There's not a thing could fluster me now! I thought, strolling light-heartedly about the salon. I'm ready for anything!

Seryozha suggested I dance with him *vis-à-vis.* "All right," I said, "I don't have a partner yet but I'll find one." Surveying the salon with a masterful eye, I observed that all the ladies were booked, with the exception of one tall girl standing by the door of the drawing room. A tall young man was moving toward her with the aim, as I concluded, of inviting her to dance; he was about two paces away from her while I was at the other end of the salon. In the twinkling of an eye, gliding gracefully across the floor, I flew the entire distance separating us, shuffled my feet, and in a firm voice invited her for the *contre-danse.* The tall girl, smiling indulgently, gave me her hand and the young man remained without a partner.

I was so conscious of my power that I did not even notice the young man's chagrin; but later I learned that the young man had asked someone who that boy with the rumpled hair was who had jumped in before him and snapped up his partner from under his very nose.

XXII

The Mazurka

The young man whose partner I had stolen was dancing in the first pair of the mazurka. He jumped up from his seat, holding his partner by the hand, and instead of doing the *pas de Basques,* which Mimi had taught us, simply ran forward; when he reached the corner, he stopped for a moment, swung his feet apart, stamped his heels, turned and with a little skip ran on again.

Since I had no partner for the mazurka, I sat behind Grandmother's chair and watched.

What's he doing? I wondered. That's nothing like what Mimi taught us: she told us that everybody dances the mazurka on their toes, swinging their feet smoothly in a circle; and now it turns out to be completely wrong. Look at the Ivins there, and Etienne, they're all dancing, but none of them is doing the *pas de Basques;* even our Volodya's doing it the new way. Not bad at all!... And look how sweet Sonyechka is! Look at her there... I was enjoying myself immensely.

The mazurka was coming to an end: several elderly gentlemen and ladies were coming up to Grandmother to say good-by and then leaving; footmen, avoiding the dancers, were carefully carrying dishes and things into the back rooms; Grandmother was clearly tired and spoke somewhat reluctantly and very deliberately; the musicians were wearily beginning the same motif for the thirtieth time. The tall girl with whom I had danced noticed me as she was doing one of the figures and with a conspiratorial smile—probably designed to please Grandmother—led Sonyechka and one of the innumerable princesses up to me. *"Rose ou hortie?"* she said to me.

"Oh so you're here!" said Grandmother, turning round in her chair. "Go and dance, my friend, go on."

Although I felt more at that moment like hiding my head under Grandmother's armchair than coming out from behind it, how could I refuse? I stood up and said: *"Rose,"* and looked shyly at Sonyechka. I had hardly had time to recover when a hand in a little white glove materialized in mine and the princess, with a beaming smile, launched into the dance, not suspecting in the least that I was completely in the dark over what to do with my feet.

I knew that *pas de Basques* were inappropriate and improper and might even bring me into total disgrace; but the familiar sounds of the mazurka, acting upon my ear, communicated a certain figure to the acoustic nerves, which in turn transmitted the movement to my feet; and these members, completely involuntarily and to the amazement of all onlookers, began to perform the fatal *pas,* circular and gliding on tiptoe. As long as we went in a straight line I managed to get by somehow, but at the turn I realized that if I did not take the necessary measures I would undoubtedly be out in front. In order to forestall such a calamity I paused for a moment, intending to dance that same *figure* that the young man in the first pair had done so beautifully. But at the very moment I swung my legs apart and was about to do a skip, the princess, hurriedly running around me, looked down at my feet with an expression of blank curiosity and surprise. This look destroyed me. I was so confused that instead of dancing I just stood where I was, trampling the ground in the strangest possible manner, which was neither in time with the music nor like anything at all, and finally came to a complete halt. Everyone was looking at me: some in surprise, some curiously, some with mockery, and some sympathetically; only Grandmother looked completely indifferent.

"Il ne fallait pas danser, si vous ne savez pas!" said Papa's angry voice by my ear; then, pushing me slightly to one side, he took my partner's hand, did an old-fashioned *tour* with her to the noisy plaudits of the onlookers, and returned her to her seat. The mazurka ended immediately.

Lord, why dost thou punish me so terribly?

———

Everyone despises me and always will . . . all roads are closed to me: friendship, love, honor . . . everything's at an end! Why did Volodya make signs to me which everybody saw and which could not possibly help me at all? Why did that hateful princess have to look at my feet? Why did Sonyechka—she's so sweet—but why did she smile then? Why did Papa turn red and catch me by the hand? Is it possible that he too was ashamed of me? Oh, how horrible! If Mama had been here she wouldn't have blushed for her Nikolyenka. . . . And my imagination flew far away after this dear image. I remembered the meadow in front of the house, the tall lime trees in the garden, the clear pond over which the swallows used to twist and turn, the blue sky with transparent clouds standing in it, the fragrant stacks of freshly mown hay; and many more such peaceful radiant memories floated through my disturbed imagination.

XXIII

After the Mazurka

During supper the young man who had danced in the first pair sat at our children's table and paid particular attention to me—a fact that would have flattered my self-esteem no end had I been capable, after what had happened to me, of feeling anything at all. But it seemed that the young man was anxious, come what may, to restore my spirits: he joked with me, called me a fine fellow and as soon as none of the grown-ups were looking poured wine into my glass from various bottles on the table and invariably forced me to drink it up. Just before supper ended, when the butler poured me only a quarter of a glass of champagne from the bottle he held wrapped in a napkin, and the young man insisted on him giving me a full glass and forced me to drink it down in one swallow, I felt a pleasant warmth throughout my whole body and a particular friendliness toward my patron, and burst into loud laughter over something.

Suddenly the strains of a *grossvater* came from the salon and everyone began to get up. My friendship with the young man immediately came to an end: he went to join the grown-ups while I, not daring to follow him, went up to Mme. Valakhin and her daughter and listened inquisitively to what they were saying.

"Just another half-hour," Sonyechka was saying cajolingly.

"No, we really can't, my angel."

"Oh, go on, just for me, please," she said, sidling up to her mother.

"Well, do you think you'll enjoy it if I'm ill tomorrow?" said Mme. Valakhin, incautious enough to smile.

"Ah, you agree then; can we stay?" said Sonyechka, jumping for joy.

"What's to be done with you? Go on and dance, then . . . here's a partner for you," she said, pointing to me.

Sonyechka gave me her hand and we ran into the salon.

The wine I had drunk and the presence and gaiety of Sonyechka made me forget completely my unfortunate adventure during the mazurka. I performed the most amusing tricks with my feet: first, imitating a horse, I moved at a slow trot, lifting my legs high in the air, then, like a ram that is angry with a dog, I pawed at the ground, all the while laughing heartily and not caring in the least what impression I was making on the onlookers. Sonyechka could not stop laughing either; she laughed at the way we whirled round and round, holding on with our hands, she laughed even louder at the sight of an elderly gentleman who, lifting his legs slowly, stepped over a handkerchief, looking as though this was extremely difficult for him to do, and she almost died of laughter when I leaped till I almost touched the ceiling, showing off my agility.

As we were going through Grandmother's study I glanced at myself in the mirror: my face was perspiring, my hair was disheveled, and my curls stuck out more than ever; but the general expression of my face was so cheerful, good-natured and healthy that I was even pleased with it myself.

"If only I were always like I am now," I thought, "I would be attractive in spite of everything."

But when I looked again at the lovely face of my partner, it contained, besides that cheerful healthy carefree expression that pleased me in my own, so much refined and delicate beauty that I became annoyed with myself and realized how stupid it was for *me* even to hope to attract the attention of such an enchanting creature as this.

I could not hope to be loved in return and of course I did not even dream of it: even without that my heart was overflowing with happiness. I did not realize that in exchange for the feeling of love that filled my heart with joy it was possible to demand even greater happiness and to desire more than merely that this feeling should never cease. I felt wonderful as it was. My heart fluttered like a dove's, the blood constantly rushed to it, and I felt close to tears.

When we walked along a corridor past a dark box room under the stairs, I glanced at it and thought: "What happiness it would be if it were possible to spend one's whole life with her in this dark box room! And if no one knew we were there."

"This evening has been very jolly, has it not?" I said in a low trembling voice and quickened my step, frightened not so much by what I had just said as by what I was going to say.

"Yes . . . very!" she replied, turning her head to me with such a frank and kind expression that I ceased to be afraid.

"Especially after supper . . . but if only you knew how sorry I am (I wanted to say *unhappy* but did not dare) that you will be leaving soon and we will never see one another again."

"Why won't we see one another again?" she said, staring fixedly at the toes of her shoes and running her finger along some trellised screens that we were passing just then. "Every Tuesday and Friday Mama and I go to the Tverskoy Boulevard. Don't you ever go for walks?"

"We'll certainly ask for one this Tuesday and if they don't let me go I'll run out on my own—without a cap. I know the way."

"Do you know what?" said Sonyechka suddenly. "I always say *thou* to some boys that come to our place; why don't we use *thou* too? Do you want to?" she added, tossing her head and looking me straight in the eye.

At this moment we were just entering the salon and another lively part of the *grossvater* was beginning.

"Come on," I said, using the second person plural at a moment when the music and noise would drown out my words.

"Say *thou*, not *you*," corrected Sonyechka and laughed.

The *grossvater* ended and I still had not managed to say a single sentence using *thou*, though I constantly invented ones in which this pronoun was repeated several times. I lacked the courage to say it. *Thou this* and *thou that* rang in my ears and produced a kind of intoxication in me. I saw nothing and no one but Sonyechka. I saw them tuck her curls back and in behind the ears, revealing parts of her forehead and temples that I had never seen before; I saw them wrap her up so tightly in a green shawl that only the tip of her nose was visible; I noticed that if her pink little fingers had not made a little opening by her mouth, she would most certainly have suffocated, and I saw her, as she went down the stairs after her mother, turn quickly to nod at us and then disappear through the door.

Volodya, the Ivins, the young prince, and myself, we were all in love with Sonyechka and we followed her with our eyes as we stood there on the stairs. To whom in particular had she nodded her head? I do not know; but at that moment I was firmly convinced it was me.

Saying good-by to the Ivins, I spoke to Seryozha very casually and even coldly and shook his hand. If he realized that from this day forth he had lost my love and his power over me, he probably regretted it, though he tried to seem completely indifferent.

For the first time in my life I had been unfaithful in love and for the first time I experienced the sweetness of that feeling. I was overjoyed to be exchanging an exhausted feeling of habitual devotion for a fresh feeling of love, full of mystery and the unknown. Furthermore, to fall out of love and in love again at the same time means to love twice as strongly as before.

XXIV

In Bed

How could I have loved Seryozha so deeply and for so long, I wondered, lying in bed. No, he never understood me, he was incapable of valuing my love and didn't deserve it . . . but Sonyechka? How lovely she is! "Say thou, say thou . . ."

I jumped up on all fours, vividly imagining her face, covered my head with the quilt, pulled it under me on all sides until there were no gaps left, lay down again, feeling a pleasant warmth about me, and plunged into sweet reveries and memories. Fixing an unmoving stare on the quilt lining, I saw her as clearly as I had an hour before; I mentally conversed with her and this conversation, although it made no sense whatever, afforded me indescribable delight, because *thou, thine* and *thee* figured in it the whole time.

These dreams were so vivid that I was unable to sleep for my delicious agitation and I wanted to share my overflowing happiness with someone.

"Darling!" I said, almost aloud, turning abruptly onto my other side. "Volodya! Are you asleep?"

"No," he replied in a sleepy voice. "Why?"

"I'm in love, Volodya! Really in love—with Sonyechka."

"Well, so what?" he replied, stretching himself.

"Oh, Volodya! You can't imagine what's happening to me. . . . I was lying here just now, wrapped up in my quilt, and I saw her so clearly and talked with her—it was simply amazing. And do you know what else? When I lie and think of her I get all sad, goodness knows why, and I feel ever so much like crying."

Volodya stirred.

"There's just one thing I'd like," I went on, "and that's to be with her always and always to see her and nothing else. Are you in love with her too? Tell me the truth, Volodya."

It's strange that I wanted everyone to be in love with Sonyechka and to tell me this.

"What's it got to do with you?" said Volodya, turning to face me.

"You don't want to sleep, you were pretending!" I cried, noticing from his shining eyes that he had not the least thought of sleep, and I threw off my quilt. "Let's talk about her instead. She's lovely, isn't she? . . . So lovely that if she said to me: 'Nikolyenka, jump out of the window or hurl yourself into the fire!' well, I swear I'd do it at once," I said, "and with pleasure. Oh, how lovely she is!" I added, seeing her vividly before me, and in order to get the full benefit of this picture I turned abruptly onto my other side and thrust my head under the pillows. "I feel terribly much like crying, Volodya."

"You fool!" he said with a smile and then paused for a moment. "I feel quite different from you: I think that if I could I'd like to sit next to her first and talk to her . . ."

"Ah! So you're in love too?" I interrupted him.

"Then," continued Volodya, smiling tenderly, "then I'd kiss her on the fingers, the eyes, the lips, the nose, the feet . . ."

"Nonsense!" I cried from under the pillows.

"You don't understand," said Volodya contemptuously.

"Oh yes I do, but you don't and you're talking nonsense," I said through my tears.

"Well, there's nothing to cry about. You're a proper little girl!"

XXV

A LETTER

On April sixteenth, almost six months after the day I have just described, Father came upstairs to see us during classes and announced that we would be returning to the country that same evening. I felt a sudden contraction in my heart at this news and my thoughts immediately flew to Mama.

The cause of such a sudden departure was the following letter:

Petrovsky,
April 12.

At ten this evening I received your kind letter of April 3 and as always I am replying immediately. Fyodor brought it from town yesterday, but since it was late he gave it to Mimi this morning. And Mimi, on the grounds that I was unwell and upset, kept it the whole day. I actually did have a mild fever and to tell you the truth, I have been unwell and have stayed in bed for four days now.

Please don't be alarmed, dear friend: I feel quite well and if Ivan Vasilyevich allows me, I'll get up tomorrow, I think.

On Friday last week I went for a spin with the children; but right where you come out onto the main road, by that bridge that has always terrified me, the horses got stuck in the mud. It was a beautiful day, so I decided to make my own way to the main road on foot, while they pulled the carriage out. By the time I came to the chapel I was very tired and sat down to rest, but since it took them about half an hour to collect enough people to pull the carriage out, I began to get cold, especially my feet, since I was only wearing thin-soled bootees and the water had gone right through them. After dinner I came over hot and cold but took my normal indoor walk, and after tea I sat down with Lyubochka to play a duet. (You won't recognize her; she's made such progress!) But imagine my surprise when I noticed that I could not keep time. Several times I attempted to count, but everything in my head got terribly mixed up and I felt a queer noise in my ears. I counted: one, two, three, and then suddenly: eight, fifteen, and the main thing was that I saw I was wrong and could not get it right under any circumstances. Finally Mimi came to my assistance and almost forcibly put me to bed. So there, my friend, is a detailed report of how I took sick and how I was myself to blame. The following day I had a fairly high fever and was visited by kind old Ivan Vasilyich, who is still here with us and who promises to have me up and about again soon. He's a wonderful old man, this Ivan Vasilyich! When I had the fever and was delirious, he sat by my bed the whole night without a wink of sleep and now, since he knows I'm writing, he's sitting with the girls in the sitting room, and I can hear him from the bedroom telling them German fairy tales, and can hear them splitting their sides with laughter as they listen to him.

La belle Flamande, as you call her, has been staying with me for over a week now, because her mother's away somewhere on a visit, and has demonstrated the most sincere affection for me with her ministrations. She also confides her intimate secrets to me. With that beautiful face of hers, that kind heart and her youth, she could turn into a wonderful girl in every respect if she were in good hands; but in the society she has to live in, judging by her stories, she will perish absolutely. It occurred to me that if I did not have so many children of my own, it would be a kindness for me to take her.

Lyubochka wanted to write to you herself, but has torn up three pieces of paper already and says: "I know what a tease Daddy is: if I make even one little mistake he'll go round showing it to everybody." Katyenka is just as sweet as ever, and Mimi just as kind and boring.

Now let me turn to more serious things: you write that your affairs are going badly this winter and that you will be obliged to take some of the Khabarovka money. I even find it strange of you to ask my permission for this. Surely, whatever belongs to me belongs just as much to you?

It is so kind of you, my friend, to conceal the real state of your affairs for fear of grieving me; but I can guess: you have probably lost a great deal, but I'm not in the least grieved by that, I swear; therefore, as long as things can be put right, please think no more of it and don't torment yourself needlessly. I am used not only to not counting on your winnings, but—forgive me—nor on your whole estate either. I am as little pleased by your winnings as I am upset by your losses; the only thing that grieves me is your unfortunate passion for gambling, which deprives me of a part of your affections and forces me to tell you such bitter truths as I am now, yet God knows how much it pains me! I never cease praying to Him for one thing—that He preserve us . . . not from poverty (what is poverty?) but from that horrible situation in which the children's interests, which I am bound to defend, come into conflict with our own. Up till now the Lord has answered my prayer: you have never overstepped any limit beyond which we would be forced either to sacrifice money that belongs not to us but to our children, or to . . . but it's too terrible even to think of, and yet this horrible calamity always menaces us. Yes, this is a heavy cross that the Lord has sent us both to bear!

You write to me also about the children and return to our ancient quarrel: you beg me to agree to send them to boarding school. You know my prejudice against such an education. . . .

I don't know, dear friend, whether you will agree with me or not, but in any case I implore you, out of your love for me, to give me your promise that as long as I am alive and after I am dead, if God sees fit to part us, you will not let this happen.

You write that it is essential for you to go to St. Petersburg on family business. Godspeed, my friend, go, and come back soon. We are all so bored here without you! Spring is superb this year: they've already taken out the balcony door, the path of the orangery was completely dry four days ago, the peach trees are out in full bloom, snow is left in only one or two places, the swallows have arrived, and today Lyubochka brought me the first spring flowers. The doctor says that in three days I'll be quite well again and I'll be able to get some fresh air and bask in the April sunshine. Good-by, dear friend; don't worry, please, either over my illness or over your losses; finish your business soon and come home with the children for the whole summer. I'm making wonderful plans about the way we'll spend it and only you are necessary to make them come true.

The next part of the letter was written in French in coherent but irregular handwriting, on a separate piece of paper. I translate word for word:

Don't believe what I told you about my illness: no one suspects the real degree of its seriousness. All I know is that I shall never leave this bed again. Don't lose a moment, come at once and bring the children. Perhaps I shall still have time to embrace you once more and bless them: that is my last desire. I know what a terrible blow I am dealing you; but it doesn't matter; sooner or later, from me or from others, you would have received it; let us try to bear this misfortune with firmness and trusting in God's mercy. Let us bow to his will.

Don't think that what I am writing is the raving of a sick imagination; on the contrary, my thoughts are extremely clear at this moment and I am completely calm. Don't console yourself in vain with the hope that these are the vague mistaken forebodings of an apprehensive heart. No, I feel and I know— I know because God saw fit to reveal it to me—that I have a very short time to live.

Will my love for you and the children die with me? I have realized that this is impossible. I feel things too strongly just now for me to think that that feeling, without which existence makes no sense to me, could ever be destroyed. My soul cannot exist without love for you: and I know that this will exist forever if only because such a feeling as my love could not have come into being if it were destined ever to come to an end.

I shall not be with you; but I am fully confident that my love will never leave you, and this thought so rejoices my heart that I await my approaching death calmly and without fear.

I am calm, and God knows that I always have and still do look to death as a transition to a better life; but why am I choked by tears? . . . Why deprive the children of their beloved mother? Why inflict such a grievous unsuspected blow on you? Why should I die when your love has made life so infinitely happy for me?

His sacred will be done.

I can write no longer for tears. Perhaps I shall not see you. Thank you, my beloved, for all the happiness you have surrounded me with in this life; when I am there I shall ask God to reward you. Good-by, dear friend; remember, I won't be here, but my love will never leave you wherever you are. Good-by, Volodya, good-by, my angel, good-by, Benjamin—my Nikolyenka.

Is it possible they will forget me one day?!

A note written in French by Mimi had been inserted into the letter. Its contents were as follows:

The melancholy forebodings that she writes of have been more than borne out by the doctor. Yesterday evening she ordered this letter to be taken to the post at once. Thinking that she had perhaps been delirious when she said this, I waited till this morning and then decided to open it. I had only just opened it when Natalya Nikolayevna asked me what I had done with the letter and ordered me to burn it if it had not been sent. She talks about it the whole time and is convinced that it will crush you. Do not postpone your departure for a single moment if you wish to see this angel before she leaves us. Excuse this scribble. I haven't slept for three nights. You know how I love her!

Natalya Savishna, who spent the whole night of the eleventh in Mama's room, told me that when *maman* had written the first part of the letter, she placed it beside her on the bedside table and took a rest.

"I myself," said Natalya Savishna, "I must confess, dozed off in the armchair and the stocking slipped out of my hands. But then in my sleep I heard something—round about one it was—as though she was talking to someone; I opened my eyes and looked: there she was, the darling, sitting on the bed with her hands clasped so, and the tears came streaming out of her eyes. 'So everything is finished?' was all she said and then buried her face in her hands.

"I jumped up and began to ask: 'What's the matter?'

" 'Oh, Natalya Savishna, if only you knew who I have just seen.'

"In spite of all my questions she wouldn't say any more, but just ordered her table to be given her, wrote a little more, ordered the letter to be sealed in her presence and then to be sent immediately. After that things got worse and worse."

XXVI

WHAT AWAITED US IN THE COUNTRY

On April eighteenth we alighted from our traveling carriage at the front door of our Petrovsky home. Leaving Moscow, Papa had been preoccupied, and when Volodya asked him if *maman* was ill, he looked at him sorrowfully and nodded his head. During the journey he was noticeably calmer; but as we approached the house his face became sadder and sadder and when, stepping down from the carriage, he asked the panting Foka, who had just run out: "Where's Natalya Niko-layevna?" his voice was shaking and there were tears in his eyes. The good old man Foka, stealing a sideways glance at us, lowered his eyes and as he opened the door of the hall, turned away and replied:

"Her ladyship hasn't been out of her bedroom for six days now."

Milka, who, as I learned later, had not ceased to whine plaintively since the very first day of *maman's* illness, rushed joyfully to greet my father, jumped up at him, yelped and licked his hand; but he pushed her aside and walked through into the drawing room and thence into the sitting room, from which a door led straight into the bedroom. The closer he came to this room the more noticeable, from the way he moved, became his agitation; going into the sitting room, he walked on tiptoe, hardly daring to breathe, and crossed himself before steeling himself to grip the handle of the closed door. At this moment a disheveled tear-stained Mimi ran in from the corridor. "Oh, Pyotr Aleksandrich!" she said in a whisper, with an expression of genuine despair; then, noticing that Papa was turning the door handle, she added barely audibly: "You can't go in there—you have to go through the maids' room."

Oh, how painfully this worked on my childish imagination, already attuned to grief by terrible forebodings.

We went to the maids' room: in the corridor we bumped into Akim the simpleton, who always used to amuse us with his faces: but at that moment not only did he not seem funny to me, but nothing affected me so painfully as the sight of his vacant and impassive face. In the maids' room two girls who were sitting and working at something stood up and bowed to us with such a melancholy air that I began to be afraid. Walking through Mimi's room next, Papa opened the bedroom door and went in. To the right of the door were two windows, shaded with shawls; Natalya Savishna sat by one of them with glasses on her nose, knitting a stocking. She did not commence to kiss us the way she usually did, but merely stood up and looked at us through her glasses, and the tears streamed from her eyes. I found it very unpleasant that at the first sight of us everyone burst into tears, whereas before they had been completely calm.

Some screens stood to the left of the door and behind the screens a bed, a little table, a small cabinet full of medicine, and a large armchair in which dozed the doctor; beside the bed stood a young and very fair girl of extraordinary beauty, wearing a white morning robe with the sleeves slightly rolled up and placing ice on *maman*'s forehead; *maman* was invisible to me at that moment.

This girl was *la belle Flamande* whom *maman* had written about and who subsequently played such an important role in the life of our whole family. As soon as we entered she took one hand away from *maman*'s head and adjusted the folds of the robe on her chest, then said in a whisper: "Unconscious."

I was full of grief at this moment but I could not help noticing every little detail around me. It was almost dark in the room and hot, and it smelled of mint, *eau de cologne,* camomile, and spirit of ether all together. This smell had such an effect on me that not only when I smell it, but even when I merely recall it, my imagination instantly carries me back to that gloomy stuffy room and resuscitates all the minutest details of that terrifying moment.

Maman's eyes were open, but she saw nothing. . . . Oh, I shall never forget that terrible look! So much suffering was expressed in it! . . .

We were led away.

When I asked Natalya Savishna later about Mama's last moments, this is what she said:

"When you were taken away she tossed and turned for a long time, the darling, as though something were choking her here; then her head slipped off the pillows and she dozed off, as quiet and peaceful as a heavenly angel. I had just gone out to see what had happened to her drink and when I came back she had thrown everything down around her, the poor thing, and was beckoning your papa to go to her; he bent over her, but you could see she didn't have the strength to say what she wanted: she just opened her mouth and then started to groan again: 'My God! Oh, Lord! The children! The children!' I wanted to come and get you, but Ivan Vasilyevich stopped me: 'That'll upset her all the more, better not,' he said. After that she could only lift her hand and let it fall again. And what she meant by it the Lord only knows. I myself think she was blessing you, wherever you were; yes, evidently the Lord didn't grant her (before the final end) to look upon her babes again. Then she raised herself, the darling, put her hands like this and said— in such a voice that I can't bear to recall it: 'Mother of God, do not leave them!' At this point the pain reached to her very heart, you could see from her eyes that she was in terrible agony, the poor thing; she fell back on the pillow, clenched the sheet between her teeth, and the tears, my child, just flowed and flowed."

"And then?" I asked.

Natalya Savishna was unable to say more: she turned away and wept bitterly.

Maman died in terrible pain.

XXVII

GRIEF

Late in the evening of the following day, I felt a desire to look at her once more; overcoming an involuntary feeling of fear, I quietly opened the door and tiptoed into the salon.

In the middle of the room stood the coffin, surrounded by snuffy candles in tall silver candlesticks; in the far corner sat the sexton, reading psalms in a low monotonous voice.

I stopped by the door and started to look; but my eyes were so red with weeping and my nerves so much on edge that I could make nothing out; everything merged somehow strangely together: the light, the brocade, the velvet, the tall candlesticks, the pink lace-embroidered pillow, the wreath, the beribboned bonnet, and something else that was transparent and waxen. I stood on a chair in order to examine her face; but in the place where it had been I was again confronted by that same sallow transparent object. I could not believe that this was her face. I began to gaze at it more closely and little by little began to recognize in it those dear familiar features. I gave a start of horror when I became convinced it was she; but why were her closed eyes so sunken? Why this awful pallor and this blackish spot on one cheek, showing through the transparent skin? Why was the expression of her whole face so stern and cold? Why were her lips so pale and set so beautifully and majestically, expressing such unearthly calm, so that a cold shiver ran down my spine and through my hair as I gazed at them? ...

As I looked I felt an incomprehensible, irresistible force drawing my gaze to that lifeless face. I did not take my eyes from it and my imagination drew pictures for me, blooming with life and happiness. I forgot that the dead body lying before me, which I gazed at senselessly, regarding it as an object having nothing to do with my memories, was *hers.* I imagined her first in one situation, then in another: alive, gay, smiling; then I would suddenly be stunned by some feature in that pale face that happened to catch my eye: I would recall the terrible reality and shudder, but did not cease to look. And again dreams replaced reality and again the consciousness of reality destroyed my dreams. Finally my imagination tired, it ceased deceiving me; my consciousness of reality also disappeared and I fell into a complete trance. I don't know how long I remained in this condition, I don't know what it consisted of; I only know that for a time I lost all consciousness of my existence and experienced a kind of exalted, ineffably sweet, sorrowful feeling of pleasure.

Perhaps, having flown away to a better world, her beautiful soul looked sadly back at the world in which she had left us; she saw my sorrow, took pity on it, and on wings of love, with a heavenly smile of compassion, descended to earth to bless and console me.

The door creaked and a sexton came in to relieve the first one. This noise aroused me and the first thought to come to me was that since I was not weeping and was standing on a chair in a pose that had nothing at all touching about it, perhaps the sexton would take me for an unfeeling boy who had climbed onto a chair out of pity or curiosity: I crossed myself and started to cry.

Recalling my impressions now I find that this moment of self-oblivion was the only one of true grief. Before and after the burial I did not cease to weep and was sad, but now I am ashamed to recall that sadness because it was always mixed with some sort of feeling of self-ishness: at times it was a desire to show that I was more grieved than anybody else, at others a concern about what effect I was having on other people, and at still others a curiosity that forced me to keep watch on Mimi's bonnet and on the faces of those around me. I despised myself for not experiencing an exclusive feeling of sorrow and I tried to conceal all other feelings; because of this my grief was insincere and unnatural. Furthermore, I experienced a kind of pleasure in knowing that I was unhappy and tried to increase this sense of unhappiness, and it was this egotistic feeling, more than anything else, that smothered true sorrow in me.

Having spent the night sleeping soundly and peacefully, as is always the case after great sorrow, I awoke with my tears dried and my nerves calmed. At ten o'clock we were summoned for the funeral service, which was to be held before the carrying out of the body. The room was filled with house serfs and peasants who, all weeping, had come to say farewell to their mistress. During the service I wept decorously, crossed myself and bowed to the ground, but I did not pray in my heart of hearts and was fairly unmoved; I was worried about the fact that the new coat I was wearing was very tight under the armpits, and about how not to soil my trouser knees too much, and I surreptitiously kept watch on everybody else there. Father stood at the head of the coffin; he was as white as a sheet and was clearly having difficulty holding back the tears. His tall figure in its black tail-coat, his pale expressive face, and his always graceful and confident movements as he crossed himself, bowed, brushing the floor with one hand, accepted a candle from the priest or went up to the coffin, were remarkably impressive; and yet, I don't know why, but it was just this ability to seem so impressive at that moment that I disliked in him. Mimi stood leaning against the wall and seemed barely able to remain on her feet; her dress was crumpled and covered with fluff and her bonnet sat askew; her eyes were swollen and red and her head shook; she sobbed ceaselessly in a heartrending voice and constantly covered her face with her handkerchief and hands. It seemed to me that she was doing this in order to hide her face from the others and take a moment's rest from her simulated weeping. I remembered how she had told Father yesterday that *maman*'s death was such a terrible blow to her that she would never recover, that she had now lost everything, that this angel (that's what she called *maman*) had not forgotten her in her last hour and had expressed a desire to provide for her and Katyenka's future indefinitely. She had shed bitter tears as she said this and perhaps her grief was genuine, but it was not pure or unadulterated. Lyubochka, wearing a black crape-edged dress and all wet with tears, kept her head lowered, glancing from time to time at the coffin, and her face expressed nothing but childish terror the whole time. Katyenka stood next to her mother and despite her long face, looked just as rosy as ever. Volodya's frank nature was frank in sorrow too: at times he stood plunged in thought, his still gaze fixed on some object, but at others his mouth would suddenly begin to twitch and he would hastily cross himself and bow. All the outsiders at the funeral were intolerable to me. The condolences they offered Father—that she would be better off there, that she was not made for this world—provoked irritation in me.

What right did they have to speak and weep about her? Some of them referred to us as *orphans*. As if we didn't know without them that that's what they call children without a mother! They were probably pleased to be the first to use it of us, the same as people usually hasten to be the first to address a newly married girl as *madame*.

In the corner of the salon, almost hidden behind the open door of the buffet, knelt a gray-haired and bent old woman. Clasping her hands together and raising her eyes to heaven, she was not weeping but praying. Her soul strove toward God, she begged Him to reunite her with the one she had loved above all others on earth, and she was serenely confident that this would be soon.

That's who truly loved her! I thought, and a feeling of shame came over me.

The funeral service ended; the deceased's face was revealed and everyone present, excepting us, started to go up one after the other and touch their lips to it.

One of the last to go up and bid farewell to the corpse was a young peasant woman carrying a pretty little five-year-old girl whom, God knows why, she had brought along with her. At that moment I unwittingly dropped my wet handkerchief and was about to pick it up; but just as I bent down I was petrified by a terrible piercing scream, which was filled with such horror that, should I live to be a hundred years, I shall never forget it, and even now, when I think of it, a cold shiver runs over my body. I raised my head: that same peasant woman was standing on a stool beside the coffin and having difficulty in holding onto the child who, waving her little arms about and tilting her frightened face back, her bulging eyes riveted on the dead woman's face, was screaming frantically. I uttered a cry that was, I believe, still more terrible than the one that had petrified me, and fled from the room.

Only at that moment did I realize the origin of that strong unpleasant smell which, mixed with the smell of incense, was filling the entire room; and the thought that that face, which a few days beforehand had been full of beauty and tenderness, the face of her whom I had loved most of all in this world, could be a source of horror, seemed to reveal a bitter truth to me for the first time and filled my soul with despair.

XXVIII

MY LAST SORROWFUL REMINISCENCES

Maman was no more, but our life went on in the same old way: we went to bed and got up at the same times and in the same rooms; morning and evening tea, dinner and supper—all were at the usual time; the tables and chairs stood in the same places; nothing in the house or in our way of life changed; only she was not there. . . .

It seemed to me that after such a catastrophe everything was bound to change; our usual way of life seemed to me to be an insult to her memory and was too vivid a reminder of her absence.

On the day before the burial, after dinner, I felt like sleeping and went to Natalya Savishna's room, counting on being able to occupy her bed with its soft feather mattress and warm quilt. When I entered, Natalya Savishna was lying on the bed herself and must have been sleeping; hearing the noise of my footsteps, she raised herself, threw off the woolen scarf that had been covering her head to keep the flies away, straightened her bonnet, and sat on the edge of the bed.

Since I had been used to coming fairly often before to sleep in her room after dinner, she guessed why I had come and said to me as she got up from the bed:

"What? I suppose you've come to take a rest, my child. Lie down."

"What do you mean, Natalya Savishna?" I said, holding her by the hand. "Not at all . . . I just came . . . anyway, you yourself are tired: you lie down instead."

"No, master, I'm already slept out," she said (I knew she hadn't slept for three days and nights). "And anyway, I'm not up to sleeping now," she added with a deep sigh.

I felt like talking to Natalya Savishna about our misfortune; I knew her sincerity and love and for that reason it would be a pleasure to cry in her company.

"Natalya Savishna," I said after a brief pause, seating myself comfortably on the bed, "were you expecting this?"

The old woman looked at me uncomprehendingly and with curiosity, probably not understanding why I had asked her this.

"Who could have expected it?" I repeated.

"Oh, master," she said, throwing a glance of the tenderest compassion at me, "not only did I not expect it, but even now I can't hardly think of it. It's high time an old woman like me laid her bones to rest, yet look what I've lived to see: There was the old master—your grandfather, God rest his soul, Prince Nikolai Mikhailovich, my two brothers, sister Annushka—I buried them all and they were all younger than me, master, and now look: for my sins, I suppose, I've been made to outlive her too. His will be done! The reason He took her was because she was worthy, it's the good ones He needs up there."

This simple thought astonished and pleased me and I moved closer to Natalya Savishna. She folded her arms on her breast and looked upward; her moist sunken eyes expressed great but tranquil sorrow. She was serenely confident that God had not parted her for long from the being on whom, for so many years, the full force of her love had been concentrated.

"Yes, master, it hardly seems any time since I nursed her and swaddled her and she called me *Ours*. She used to come running to me sometimes, throw her arms round me and kiss me and say over and over again: 'Oursy, my beauty, my little turkeychick.' And I'd joke with her and say: 'It's not true, my girl, you don't love me; you see, as soon as you grow up big you'll get married and forget your Oursy.' She'd get thoughtful then. 'No,' she'd say, 'I'd rather not get married if I can't take Oursy with me; I'll never leave Oursy.' But now she has gone, she couldn't last out. And how she loved me, your dead mother! But then who didn't she love, if the truth be told! Yes, master, you must never forget your mama; she was no ordinary person, she was a heavenly angel. When her soul is in the heavenly kingdom she'll still love you and still rejoice over you from there."

"Why do you say, Natalya Savishna, *when* it's in the heavenly kingdom?" I asked. "It's already there, I thought, isn't it?"

"No, master," said Natalya Savishna, lowering her voice and moving closer to me on the bed, "her soul's still here."

And she pointed to the ceiling. She spoke almost in a whisper and with such feeling and conviction that I involuntarily raised my eyes, looked at the cornices, and searched for something.

"Before the souls of the righteous go to heaven, master, they have to undergo forty trials, forty days, and can even stay in their own homes . . ."

She talked for a long time in the same vein and talked with such simplicity and confidence that it was as though she were speaking of the most humdrum things, which she herself had seen and on whose account no one could ever have the slightest shadow of doubt. I listened to her with bated breath and although I did not understand too well what she was saying, I believed her absolutely.

"Yes, master, she's here now, watching us, and perhaps listening to what we are saying," concluded Natalya Savishna.

And lowering her head, she fell silent. She had to have recourse to her handkerchief in order to wipe away the tears that were falling; she got up, looked me straight in the face and said in a voice trembling with agitation:

"The Lord has moved me many rungs closer to Him by this. What is left for me now? Who shall I live for? Who shall I love?"

"Well, don't you love us?" I said reproachfully, barely able to hold back the tears.

"God knows how much I love you, my children, but I've never loved anyone the way I loved her and I can't love anyone that much."

She was unable to say any more; she turned away from me and sobbed loudly.

I had no more thought of sleeping; we sat silently opposite one another and wept.

Foka came into the room. Noticing our condition and probably not wishing to disturb us, he stopped in the doorway, looking at us shyly and in silence.

"What do you want, Foka?" asked Natalya Savishna, wiping her eyes with a handkerchief.

"A pound and a half of currants, four pounds of sugar, and three pounds of rice for the funeral cake, please."

"Right away, right away, my lad," said Natalya Savishna, hurriedly taking a pinch of snuff and going to the chest with rapid little steps. The last traces of the grief produced by our conversation disappeared as she resumed her duties, which she regarded as extremely important.

"Why four pounds?" she said grouchily, taking out the sugar and weighing it on a spring balance. "Three and a half will be enough."

And she took several grains off the scales.

"And what sort of game is this? Only yesterday I let them have eight pounds of rice and now they're asking for more! I don't care what you want, Foka Demidich, I'm not giving you any more rice. That Vanka's glad there's so much confusion in the house: he thinks nobody'll notice. No, I'm not letting anybody take liberties with the master's things. Well, who ever heard of such a thing—eight pounds?"

"How can I help it? He says it's all gone."

"Well, go on, then, take it; here! Let him have it."

I was amazed at the transition from the tender way in which she had spoken to me to grouchiness and petty calculation. Thinking about this afterwards, I realized that in spite of what was happening inside her, she possessed enough presence of mind to keep herself busy with work, while force of habit drew her to her normal occupations. Grief had affected her so powerfully that she did not deem it necessary to conceal the fact that she could also concern herself with peripheral matters; she would not even have understood how such an idea could occur to anyone.

Vanity is the feeling that is most incompatible with genuine sorrow, yet at the same time this feeling is so firmly grafted onto human nature that it is very rarely that even the greatest grief succeeds in driving it out. Vanity in sorrow manifests itself in a desire to seem either deeply grieved, or unhappy, or else firm; and these base desires, which we do not acknowledge but which hardly ever leave us—even in the deepest sorrow—deprive it of depth, merit, and sincerity. But Natalya Savishna was so completely overwhelmed by her distress that not a single desire remained in her and she lived by habit alone.

When she had issued Foka the necessary provisions and reminded him of the pie that had to be prepared for offering to the clergy, she let him go, picked up her knitting, and sat down beside me again.

The conversation turned to the same subject again and once more we shed tears and wiped them away.

My chats with Natalya Savishna were repeated every day: her quiet tears and calm reverent words afforded me pleasure and relief.

But soon we were parted: three days after the funeral the whole household moved to Moscow and I was fated never to see her again.

Only with our arrival did Grandmother learn the news and her grief was extraordinary. We were not allowed in to see her because she was beside herself all week and the doctors feared for her life, the more so since she not only would not take any medicine, but would not talk to anyone, or sleep, or take any kind of food. Sometimes, sitting alone in her room in her armchair, she would suddenly begin to laugh and then to sob without tears; she would go into convulsions and start shouting senseless or terrible things. This was the first powerful grief that had shaken her and it reduced her to despair. She needed to blame someone for her distress and she would utter terrible words, threaten someone with extraordinary vehemence, leap up from her armchair and pace about the room in swift long strides, and then collapse insensible again.

Once I went into her room: she was sitting in her armchair as usual and seemed to be calm; but her look astounded me. Her eyes were wide open and their gaze was dim and vacant: she looked straight at me but must not have seen me. Her lips slowly began to smile and she said in a tender touching voice: "Come here, my friend, come closer, my angel." I thought she was talking to me and moved closer, but she was not looking at me. "Ah, if only you knew, my darling, how much I suffered and how glad I am now that you've come . . ." I realized that she was imagining she saw *maman* and I stopped. "And they told me you were gone," she went on, frowning. "What nonsense! Is it possible that you could die before me?" and she broke into loud hysterical laughter.

Only people who are capable of loving deeply can experience deep sorrow; but that same necessity to love acts for them as an antidote to grief and cures them. Because of this, man's moral nature is more resilient than his physical nature. Grief is never fatal.

After a week Grandmother was able to weep and she began to feel better. Her first thought, when she came to her senses, was for us, and her love for us had increased. We did not leave her chair; she wept quietly, talked of *maman*, and caressed us tenderly.

No one could have thought, witnessing Grandmother's sorrow, that she exaggerated it, and the manifestations of that sorrow were powerful and moving; yet I don't know why, but I had more sympathy for Natalya Savishna, and even now I remain convinced that no one loved *maman* and regretted her end so purely and sincerely as that simple-hearted loving creature.

For me the happy time of childhood ended with the death of my mother and a new era began—the era of boyhood; but since my recollections of Natalya Savishna, whom I never saw again and who had such a powerful and beneficial influence on my future development and on the development of my sensibility, belong to the first era, I will say a few words concerning her death.

After our departure, as I was told later by some people who remained in the country, she was terribly bored for lack of something to do. Although she still had charge of all the chests and did not cease to rummage in them, transferring things, weighing them and distributing them, still she missed the noise and bustle of a gentleman's country house, with the masters actually present, such as she had been used to from childhood. Grief, the change in her way of life, and the absence of things to do soon led to the breaking out of a senile ailment to which she had been prone. Exactly a year after mother died she developed dropsy and took to her bed.

It was hard, I think, for Natalya Savishna to live—and still harder to die—alone in that big empty house at Petrovsky, without friends or relations. Everyone in the house loved and respected Natalya Savishna; but she was friends with no one and was proud of the fact. She held that in her position, as housekeeper, where she enjoyed the full confidence of her employers and was in charge of so many chests full of valuables, friendship with anyone was bound to lead to partiality and criminal indulgence on her part; therefore, or perhaps because she had nothing in common with the other servants, she kept her distance from everyone and said that she had neither kith nor kin in the house and would let no one take liberties with the master's things.

Confiding her feelings to God in heartfelt prayer, she sought and found consolation; but sometimes, in moments of weakness to which we are all prone, when man's greatest consolation is found in the tears and sympathy of a living creature, she would lift her pet pug onto the bed beside her (which would lick her hand, fixing its yellow eyes upon her), talk to it, and weep silently as she fondled it. When the pug began to whine pitifully, she would try to soothe it and say: "Stop it, I know I'm going to die soon without your help."

A month before her death she took some white calico, some white muslin, and some pink ribbons out of her trunk; with the help of her girl assistant she made herself a white dress and bonnet and supervised all the preparations, down to the smallest detail, for her funeral. She also sorted out the master's chests, wrote out an inventory, and handed them over to the steward's wife in perfect order; then she took out two silk dresses, an ancient shawl that Grandmother had once given her, and Grandfather's gold-embroidered uniform that had also been given to her to keep. Thanks to her good care the embroidery and braid were like new and the cloth untouched by moth.

Just before her end she expressed a desire for one of the two dresses—the pink one—to be given to Volodya to make a dressing gown or a quilted jacket, while the other—in a puce check—was to go to me for the same purpose; and the shawl was for Lyubochka. She bequeathed the uniform to whichever of us was first to become an officer. All the rest of her belongings and money, except for forty rubles which she set aside for the burial and remembrance services, she left to her brother. Her brother, who had been freed from serfdom many years before, was living in some distant province and leading a most dissolute sort of life; therefore she had had absolutely nothing to do with him while alive.

When Natalya Savishna's brother arrived to collect his inheritance and the dead woman's whole belongings turned out to amount to twenty-five rubles in bills, he would not believe it and said it was impossible that an old woman, who had lived in a rich house for sixty years and had had everything in her charge, should have lived her whole life so frugally and grudged every penny only to leave nothing in the end. But this was truly the case.

Natalya Savishna suffered for two months with her illness and bore her sufferings with truly Christian fortitude: she did not grumble, she did not complain, but merely invoked the name of God constantly as was her custom. An hour before her death, quietly and joyfully, she made her last confession, took her last communion, and was anointed with oil.

She begged forgiveness of all the house servants for any wrongs she might have done them and begged her confessor, Father Vasily, to inform us that she did not know how to thank us for our kindness and begged our forgiveness if, in her stupidity, she had ever offended us, but "she was never a thief and could say she'd never made a penny at the master's expense." This was the only quality that she esteemed in herself.

Having donned her ready-made robe and bonnet, she reclined on the pillows and talked to the priest right to the very end; she recalled that she had left nothing for the poor, obtained ten rubles and begged him to distribute them in the parish; then she crossed herself, lay back and breathed her last, smiling joyfully and with the Lord's name on her lips.

She relinquished life without regret; she was not afraid of death and accepted it as a good. This is often said, but how rarely it actually happens! Natalya Savishna could afford not to fear death because she died with unshakable faith and after having observed the laws of the Bible. Her whole life was one of pure disinterested love and self-abnegation.

What though her beliefs might have been somewhat more exalted and her life directed to a loftier aim? Surely this pure soul is none the less worthy of love and admiration for that?

She accomplished the best and mightiest deed that is possible in this life—she died without regret or fear.

She was buried, at her own request, not far from the chapel that stands on my mother's grave. The mound under which she lies is over-grown with burdock and nettles and fenced about with black railings, and I never forget to go over to those railings from the chapel and bow to the ground.

Sometimes I stop in silence between the chapel and the black rail-ings. Painful memories awake suddenly in my breast. And then I think: can Providence have joined me to these two beings only to make me eternally grieve for them?

II: BOYHOOD

I

THE JOURNEY TO MOSCOW

Once more two carriages stand at the front entrance of our Petrovsky home; one is a coach, into which Mimi, Katyenka, Lyubochka, and the maid get, with *himself,* the steward Yakov, on the box; the other is the phaeton in which Volodya and I are riding, together with our new manservant, Vasily, who has just been chosen from among the serfs.

Papa, who is to come to Moscow several days later, is standing hatless on the porch and making the sign of the cross over the coach window and the phaeton.

"Well, Christ be with you, off you go!" Yakov and the coachmen (we are taking our own horses) remove their hats and cross themselves. "Hup, hup! Good luck!" The coach body and the phaeton begin to bounce over the uneven road and the birch trees of the big avenue slip past us one after the other. I do not feel at all sad: my mind's eye is fixed not on what I am leaving but on what is ahead of me. In proportion as we retreat from things connected with the painful memories that till now have filled my imagination, these memories lose their force and are quickly replaced by a joyous sense of awareness of life, full of power, freshness, and hope.

Rarely have I spent a few days—I won't say gaily: I still felt somewhat too ashamed to give myself up to gaiety—but so pleasantly and so enjoyably as the four days of our journey. No longer was I confronted by the closed door of Mama's room, which I could never pass without shuddering, or the piano, which we not only did not approach but regarded with a kind of terror, or by mourning clothes (we all wore simple traveling garb), or by all those things which, reminding me so vividly of my irrevocable loss, forced me to be wary of the least manifestation of life for fear of offending *her* memory. Here, on the contrary, ever new and picturesque places and objects arrested and diverted my attention, while spring nature filled my heart with joyous feelings—contentment with the present and bright hopes for the future.

Very early in the morning the pitiless and—as is always the case with people new to their jobs—overzealous Vasily jerks off the blanket and assures us that everything is ready and it is time to go. No matter how you huddle up or bargain or grow angry in order to prolong that sweet morning sleep for at least a quarter of an hour, you can see from his determined face that Vasily is implacable and is prepared to jerk that blanket off twenty times if necessary, so you jump up and run out into the yard to get washed.

The samovar is already bubbling in the passageway and Mitka the postilion boy is blowing on it, red as a lobster; out in the yard it is damp and foggy and it is as though steam were rising from the pungent manure; the bright cheerful rays of the morning sun light up the sky in the east and the thatched roofs of the big open sheds enclosing the yard glint with the dew covering them. Our horses are there underneath, tethered around some feeding troughs, and one can hear their regular champing. A shaggy Fido, who has been taking a quick nap before dawn on a pile of dry manure, stretches himself lazily and with a wag of his tail sets off for the far side of the yard at an easy trot. The bustling landlady opens the squeaking gate, drives the thoughtful cows out into the street, in which one can already hear the stamp and lowing and bleating of a flock of sheep, and exchanges a remark or two with her sleepy neighbor. Filipp, his shirtsleeves rolled up, winds up the pail from the deep well, splashing bright water about, and empties it into an oaken trough, around which the newly awakened ducks rinse themselves in a puddle of spilled water; and I look with pleasure at Filipp's face, with its broad thick beard, and at the thick veins and muscles standing out on his bare powerful arms whenever he makes an effort.

Behind the partition, where Mimi and the girls have slept and through which we conversed last night, movement is heard. Masha, carrying various objects that she tries to hide from our inquisitive gaze with her dress, runs past us more and more often; at last the door is opened and we are invited in to drink tea.

Vasily, in a paroxysm of excessive zeal, is constantly running into the room, carrying out now this and now that, winking at us and doing his level best to cajole Marya Ivanovna into leaving as early as possible. The horses are harnessed and express their impatience by jingling their bells from time to time; trunks, cases, casks, and caskets are packed away again and we take our places. But in the phaeton we keep finding a hump instead of a seat and we cannot make out how it was all packed yesterday and how we are possibly going to sit; there is one walnut tea caddy in particular with a triangular lid, which has been transferred to our carriage and placed under me and provokes me to extreme indignation. But Vasily says that it will squash down and I am obliged to believe him.

The sun has just overtopped a solid white cloud covering the east and the whole area is bathed in a quietly cheerful light. Everything is so beautiful around me and my heart is light and calm. . . . A wide wild ribbon of road winds away in front of us between fields of withered stubble and shrubbery glistening with dew; here and there on the road a gloomy broom shrub can be seen, or a young birch tree with tiny sticky leaves, casting a long motionless shadow over the dried-up clayey ruts and sparse green grass in the road. . . . The monotonous sound of our wheels and bells fails to drown the singing of the sky-larks, which twist and turn low over the road. The smell of motheaten upholstery and dust and a kind of acid smell, peculiar to our phaeton, are submerged in the smells of the morning, and I feel a joyous agitation inside me and a desire to do something—signs of true pleasure.

I did not have time to pray at the inn; but since I have observed more than once that something untoward always happens to me on the days when, for some reason or other, I forget to perform this rite, I try to correct my mistake: I take off my cap, turn to face one corner in the phaeton, say my prayers, and cross myself under my jacket so that no one can see me. But a thousand different things distract my attention and absent-mindedly I repeat the same words of a prayer several times in a row.

Now some slowly moving figures come into view on the footpath that winds alongside the road: these are pilgrims. Their heads are wrapped in dirty scarves, they carry birch-bark knapsacks on their backs, they have dirty torn cloths wound round their legs and heavy bast shoes on their feet. Rhythmically flourishing their sticks and barely troubling to glance at us, they move forward one behind the other with slow heavy steps, and questions come to my mind: where and why are they going? Will their journey last long, and will the long shadows they cast on the road soon meet the shadow of that broom there that they have to walk past? Here is a barouche and four, with post horses, rushing toward us. Two seconds, and faces that were looking at us curiously and welcomingly from a distance of two yards have already flashed past, and somehow it seems strange that these faces have nothing in common with me and that I shall never, perhaps, see them again.

Running along the side of the road now are two shaggy sweating horses, wearing collars and with their traces fastened to breechbands, while behind them, his long legs in big boots dangling down on either side of a horse that has a yoke across its withers and on which a bell tinkles barely audibly, a young driver is riding with his felt hat cocked over one ear and slowly singing a plaintive song. His face and pose express so much lazy carefree contentment that it seems to me it must be the pinnacle of happiness to be a driver, to ride with no load and to sing sorrowful songs. Far away over there, beyond the ravine, a village church with a green roof stands out against the pale-blue sky; over there is a village, the red roof of the squire's house and a green garden. Who lives in that house? Are there children, a father, mother, tutor? Why shouldn't we go there and introduce ourselves to the owners? Here is a long train of enormous carts harnessed to teams of three horses, all well-fed and thick-legged; we have to skirt it on one side. "What are you carrying?" asks Vasily of the first driver, who, having taken his huge feet off the front board and flourished his whip, looks long at us with an intently stupid gaze and only says something in reply when we are too far away to hear him. "What's your cargo?" Vasily says to another cart, on the front of which, beneath some new bast matting, another driver is lying. A blond head with a red face and gingery beard is thrust out for a moment from under the matting, then casts an indifferent contemptuous glance at our phaeton and disappears again—and it occurs to me that these cart drivers probably do not know who we are, or where we come from or where we are going. . . .

Absorbed in diverse observations for about an hour and a half, I do not pay any attention to the crooked numbers depicted on the mileposts. But now the sun is beginning to feel hotter on my head and back, the road is growing dustier, and the triangular lid of the tea caddy is beginning to make me feel very uncomfortable; I change my position several times; I begin to feel hot, uncomfortable, and bored. I concentrate all my attention on the mileposts and on the numbers depicted on them; I make various mathematical calculations concerning the time at which we might possibly reach the next stage. Seven miles makes one third of twenty-one and it's twenty-three miles to Liptsy, therefore we've gone one third and how much? and on so.

"Vasily," I say, noticing that he is beginning to nod on the box, "let me come up onto the box, there's a good fellow." Vasily agrees. We exchange places: he immediately starts snoring and sprawls out so that there is no room left for anybody in the phaeton; while before me, from the height I now command, a most wonderful picture unfolds: our four horses, Neruchinsky, Sexton, the left thill horse, and Apothecary, all of which I have studied down to the last little detail till I know the nuances of quality in each.

"Why is Sexton harnessed on the right today and not on the left, Filipp?" I ask somewhat shyly.

"Sexton?"

"While Neruchinsky's not pulling at all," I say.

"It's impossible to harness Sexton on the left," says Filipp, ignoring my last remark. "He's not the sort of horse you can put on the left. On the left you need a horse that's—well, a real horse, and not a horse like that."

And with these words Filipp leans to the right and, cracking the reins with all his might, starts lashing poor Sexton over the tail and legs in a sort of special way, from below, and in spite of the fact that Sexton pulls with all his might and makes the whole phaeton veer around, Filipp puts an end to this maneuver only when he feels obliged to rest and for some unknown reason to cock his hat on one side, even though up to now it has been sitting on his head extremely well and firmly. I take advantage of such a happy moment to ask Filipp to let me *drive*. First Filipp gives me one rein, then another; finally all six reins and the whip pass into my hands and my happiness is complete. I do everything I can to imitate Filipp and ask him if it is all right. Usually it ends with him being dissatisfied with me: he says that this horse is doing all the pulling while that one does none, then thrusts an elbow in front of my chest and takes the reins away. The heat continues to increase, the mackerel clouds begin to swell up like soap bubbles, higher and higher, and then subside slowly and take on dark-gray shadows. A hand is thrust out of the coach window, holding a bottle and a little package; with amazing agility Vasily leaps off the box of the moving phaeton and brings back kvas and cheesecake.

On steep downward slopes we all get out of the carriages and sometimes run ahead to the bridge, while Vasily and Yakov, braking the wheels, support the coach on either side with their hands, as though they were able to prevent it from turning over. Then, with Mimi's permission, I or Volodya get into the coach, while Lyubochka or Katyenka board the phaeton. The girls enjoy these permutations very much, because they find, quite rightly, that it is much more fun to ride in the phaeton. Sometimes when it is very hot and we are traveling through a copse, we fall behind the coach, pull off some green boughs and make a summerhouse in the phaeton. The moving summerhouse then overtakes the coach at full speed, to the accompaniment of piercing squeals from Lyubochka, who never forgets to do this whenever she particularly enjoys something.

But here is the village in which we are to have dinner and rest. The village smells are already upon us—smoke, tar, and bread, and we hear the sounds of talking, footsteps, and wheels; the bells no longer sound the way they do in open country and huts flash by on either side, with thatched roofs, fretted plank wings, and tiny windows with red and green shutters, in which, here and there, the heads of curious peasant women appear. Here are the village children wearing only shirts; with wide-open eyes and arms akimbo they stand stock-still, or else, their bare feet pattering swiftly through the dust, ignoring the threatening gestures of Filipp, they run after the carriages and try to climb onto the trunks strapped on behind. Ginger-haired innkeepers now run up to the carriages from either side and one after the other try to lure the travelers into their inns with attractive words and gestures. Whoa! The gates screech, rollers slide into place, and we ride into the yard. Four hours of relaxation and freedom!

II

THE THUNDERSTORM

The sun was sinking in the west and its hot slanting rays scorched my neck and cheeks unbearably; it was impossible to touch the burning sides of the phaeton; a dense cloud of dust rose from the road and filled the air. There was not a breath of wind to carry it away. At a constant distance before us the high dusty coach body with its trunks swayed regularly from side to side; beyond it we could see the whip brandished by the driver from time to time, the driver's hat, and Yakov's cap. I did not know what to do with myself: neither Volodya, who with his dust-blackened face was dozing beside me, nor the motions of Filipp's back, nor our phaeton's long shadow, which ran along at an acute angle behind us, afforded me any entertainment. My whole attention was concentrated on the mileposts, which I could see from a long way away, and on the clouds which, though formerly scattered over the horizon, had now acquired sinister black shadows and had gathered into one big lowering mass. Occasionally thunder rumbled in the distance. This last circumstance did most of all to strengthen my impatience to arrive at an inn. Thunderstorms always induced in me an inexpressibly painful sensation of sickness and terror.

We were still six miles from the nearest village when a big violet thundercloud which, without a breath of wind had come up from God knows where, bore down on us at great speed. And now the sun, still not obscured by clouds, illumines its lowering form and the gray stripes reaching out from it to the very horizon. From time to time lightning flashes in the distance and we hear a low rumble, which gradually grows louder, approaches, and changes to intermittent peals of thunder, filling the entire welkin. Vasily stands up on the box and raises the phaeton's canopy; the coachmen put on their coats and at the sound of each thunderclap take off their caps and cross themselves; the horses prick up their ears and dilate their nostrils, as though sniffing at the smell of fresh air which the approaching thundercloud brings with it; and the phaeton travels swiftly over the dusty road. I begin to feel terrified and I can feel the blood circulating faster through my veins. But now the foremost clouds have begun to cover the sun; it has just peeped out for the last time, lighting up one horribly lowering side of the horizon, before disappearing. Everything around us is suddenly transformed and takes on a lowering character. An aspen grove suddenly starts to tremble; its leaves turn to a kind of dull-whitish color which stands out starkly against the violet background of the cloud; they twist and rustle; the tops of some tall birch trees begin to sway and tufts of dry grass whirl across the road. Swifts and white-chested swallows dart about the phaeton and fly right in front of the horses' chests, as though wishing to stop us; rooks with ruffled feathers fly somehow sideways downwind; the edges of the leather apron that we have buttoned down begin to lift up, letting in gusts of damp air, and flap about and bang against the body of the phaeton. Lightning seems to flash inside the very carriage, dazzles the eyes and for an instant illumines the gray cloth and braid and the figure of Volodya huddled in the corner. At this very second, directly overhead, there resounds a majestic roar which, as though climbing higher and higher, wider and wider, in a gigantic spiral, gradually grows in intensity until it changes to a deafening crash that makes you tremble involuntarily and hold your breath.

The wrath of God! How much poetry there is in that folk saying!

The wheels spin faster and faster; I notice from the backs of Vasily and Filipp, who is shaking the reins impatiently, that they too are afraid. The phaeton runs swiftly downhill and drums across a wooden bridge; I am afraid to move a muscle and expect our joint demise from moment to moment.

Whoa! The whippletree has torn out and despite the constant deafening thunderclaps we are obliged to halt on the bridge.

Pressing my head against the side of the phaeton and with a sinking heart that takes my breath away, I look hopelessly at the movements of Filipp's thick black fingers as he fastens the loop and straightens out the traces with painful slowness, pushing the outside horse with his hand and whip handle.

Anxious feelings of sickness and terror have been mounting in me together with the increasing fury of the storm, but when that majestic moment of calm arrives that always precedes the unleashing of a storm, these feelings reach such a pitch that, should this state continue for another quarter of an hour, I am certain I will die of fright. At this very moment there appears suddenly from under the bridge, wearing only a dirty tattered shirt, some sort of human being with a swollen idiotic face, its swaying head cropped and uncovered, its legs bandy and muscleless, and with some sort of red shiny stump instead of a hand which it thrusts straight into the phaeton.

"Ma-a-ster! For the love of Christ, a poor man . . ." sounds a sickly voice, and with every word the beggar crosses himself and bows from the waist.

I cannot express the feeling of cold horror that grips my soul at this moment. A shiver runs over my scalp and my eyes, senseless with terror, are riveted on the beggar. . . .

Vasily, who has charge of alms for the journey, is giving instructions to Filipp on how to secure the whippletree, and only when everything is finished and Filipp, gathering up the reins, has climbed onto the box does he begin to get something from his side pocket. But no sooner have we started than a blinding flash of lightning, which momentarily fills the whole glen with blazing light, causes the horses to stop again and then, without the slightest interval, is accompanied by such a deafening crash of thunder that it seems as though the entire vault of heaven is falling about our ears. The wind grows even stronger: the horses' manes and tails, Vasily's greatcoat and the edges of the apron all point in the same direction and flap desperately under the impact of gusts of ferocious wind. A large drop of water falls heavily onto the leather roof of the phaeton . . . then another, and a third, and a fourth, and suddenly it is as though someone has begun a drum roll overhead and the whole neighborhood echoes with the sound of falling rain. I notice from the way Vasily's elbows are moving that he is undoing his purse; the beggar, continuing to cross himself and bow, is running alongside, close to the wheels, so that he is in danger of being run over. "Give . . . for the love of Chri-i-st." At last a copper coin flies past us and the pitiful creature in his soaking-wet shirt, which clings tightly to his skinny limbs, swaying in the wind, halts perplexedly in the middle of the road and disappears from view.

The slanting rain, driven by a strong wind, pours down in bucket-fuls; whole torrents run off the back of Vasily's frieze-coat and into a pool of cloudy water that has formed on the apron. The dust, which at first rolled up into little pellets, has now turned to liquid mud, pounded by the wheels; the jolts are getting fewer and muddy streams flow along the clayey ruts. The lightning is becoming paler and more diffuse and the peals of thunder no longer stand out so much against the steady drum of the rain.

Now the rain begins to slacken; the thundercloud begins to disintegrate into billowy masses and to gleam brighter where the sun must be, and through the grayish-white edges of the cloud can be glimpsed a patch of azure sky. A moment later a timid ray from the sun gleams in the puddles on the road, in the needles of fine vertical rain, falling as through a sieve, and on the glistening blades of grass in the road. I experience an unutterably blissful feeling of hope in life which quickly supplants my painful feelings of terror. My heart smiles, just as refreshed and gladdened nature smiles. Vasily throws back the collar of his greatcoat, takes off his cap and shakes it; Volodya throws off the apron; I thrust my head out of the phaeton and greedily breathe in the fresh fragrant air. The washed, gleaming body of the coach, with its boxes and trunks, sways along in front of us; the backs of the horses, their breechbands, the reins, and the wheel-rims are all wet and gleam in the sun as though varnished. On one side of the road a boundless field, sown with winter crops and crossed here and there by shallow gullies, gleams wetly green and black and stretches in a shadowy carpet to the very horizon; on the other side an aspen grove, overgrown with young shoots of walnut and bird cherry, stands stockstill, as though overcome with happiness, slowly dropping shining raindrops from its newly washed branches onto last year's withered leaves. On all sides crested skylarks weave and plunge swiftly through the air, singing joyfully; the fussy movements of tiny birds can be heard in the bushes and the sounds of a cuckoo come clearly from the grove. This wonderful forest smell after a spring storm, this smell of birch trees, violets, moldering leaves, fungus, and bird cherry is so enchanting that I cannot stay in the phaeton; I leap from the running board, run to the bushes and, despite the fact that they spatter me with raindrops, tear off the wet branches of a blossoming bird cherry, beat myself on the face with them and inhale deeply their wonderful scent. Paying no heed even to the fact that enormous clods of mud have stuck to my shoes and that my stockings are hopelessly wet, I splash my way through the mud to the window of the coach.

"Lyubochka! Katyenka!" I cry, handing them several branches of bird cherry. "Look how nice it is!"

The girls squeal in consternation; Mimi shouts at me to go away, otherwise I shall certainly be run over.

"Just smell that blossom!" I cry.

III

A New View of Things

Katyenka sat beside me in the phaeton, her pretty little head bowed, and watched the dusty road thoughtfully as it ran away under the wheels. I looked at her silently and was surprised by her unchildlike expression of sadness; this was the first time I had seen such an expression on her pink little face.

"Well, we'll soon be in Moscow," I said. "What do you think, how will it be?"

"I don't know," she replied unwillingly.

"Yes, but still, what do you think: is it bigger than Serpukhov or not?"

"What?"

"Oh, nothing."

But with that intuitive feeling by which one person guesses the thoughts of another and which serves as the guiding thread of a conversation, Katyenka understood that I was hurt by her indifference; she raised her head and turned to look at me:

"Did your papa tell you that we were going to live with Grandmother?"

"Yes. Grandmother wants to live completely together with us."

"Will all of us live there?"

"Of course; we shall live in one half upstairs and you in the other half; and Papa will stay in the wing; and we'll all be dining together downstairs with Grandmother.

"*Maman* says that Grandmother's very grand—is she bad-tempered?"

"No-o! She only seems so at first. She's grand but not at all bad-tempered; on the contrary, she's very kind and jolly. If only you had seen the ball she had on her name day!"

"Even so, I'm afraid of her. Anyway, goodness knows if we'll ..."

Katyenka suddenly fell silent and became thoughtful again.

"Wha-a-t?" I asked with anxiety.

"Oh, nothing."

"No, you said something about 'goodness knows ...'"

"Well, and you talked about the ball at Grandmother's."

"Yes, what a pity you weren't there; there were tons of visitors, a thousand people, music, generals, and I danced.... Katyenka!" I said all of a sudden, stopping in the middle of my description. "You're not listening."

"Yes I am, I'm listening; you said you danced."

"Why are you so dull?"

"I can't always be jolly."

"No, you've been very different since we came back from Moscow. Tell me the truth," I added with a resolute look, turning to face her. "Why have you become so queer?"

"*Am* I queer?" replied Katyenka with warmth, which proved that my remark had touched her. "I'm not at all queer."

"No, you're not the same as you were," I went on. "It used to be obvious before that you were together with us in everything, that you treated us as being in the same family and loved us the way we did you, but now you've become so serious, you're keeping your distance from us ..."

"Not at all ..."

"No, let me finish," I interrupted, already beginning to feel that slight tickle in my nose that always heralded tears; these always came to my eyes whenever I came out with an idea that was close to my heart but had been suppressed for a long time. "You're keeping your distance from us and you talk only to Mimi, as though you don't want to know us."

"But you can't stay the same always; you have to change sometimes," replied Katyenka, who was in the habit of explaining everything by a kind of fatalistic determinism when she did not know what to say.

I remember that once, when she quarreled with Lyubochka, who had called her a *stupid girl,* she replied: "Not everybody can be clever, some have to be stupid"; but I was not satisfied by the answer that one had to change sometimes and I continued to question her:

"Why do you have to?"

"Well, we won't always be living together, you know," replied Katyenka, blushing slightly and gazing intently at Filipp's back.

"Mama could live with your mama because they were friends; but goodness knows whether she'll get on with your grandmother, who, they say, is so bad-tempered. And anyway, besides that, we're bound to part one day: you're rich—you have Petrovsky; but we're poor—Mama doesn't have anything."

You're rich—we're poor: these words and the concept connected with them seemed extremely strange to me. Only beggars and peasants, so far as I knew, could possibly be poor, and it was utterly impossible for my imagination to connect this concept of poverty with the graceful pretty Katyenka. It seemed to me that if, until now, they had always lived with us, Mimi and Katyenka, then they always would live with us and would share everything equally. Any other course was impossible. But now a thousand new and indistinct thoughts concerning their lonely situation swarmed through my head, and I felt so ashamed of the fact that we were rich and they poor that I blushed and could not bring myself to look at Katyenka.

What if we are rich and they are poor? I thought. And how does it follow from this that we're bound to part? Why don't we share everything we have equally? But I realized that it was best not to talk to Katyenka of this and some sort of practical instinct, as opposed to these logical speculations, told me that she was right and that it would have been inappropriate to tell her of my idea.

"Is it really true that you'll leave us?" I said. "How will we live apart?"

"What can we do? It hurts me too. But if it does happen I know what I'll do ..."

"Become an actress ... what rot!" I interjected, knowing that it had always been her favorite dream to be an actress.

"No, I used to say that when I was little ..."

"Then what will you do?"

"I'll go into a nunnery and live there; I'll wear a nice black dress and a velvet bonnet."

Katyenka began to cry.

Has it ever happened to you, reader, that at a particular point in life you notice suddenly that your view of things has completely changed, as though all the objects you had seen till then suddenly turned around to reveal a new and hitherto unknown aspect? A moral transformation of this kind took place within me for the first time during our journey, and this I consider to be the beginning of my boyhood.

For the first time I acquired a clear concept of the fact that we, that is to say our family, were not alone in this world, that not all interests revolved around us, and that there existed other lives, the lives of people who had nothing in common with us, who did not care about us and who had not the slightest idea even that we existed. Without a doubt I had known all this before; but not the way I became aware of it now; I had not been conscious of it, had not felt it.

An idea becomes a conviction only by traveling a certain path, which is often quite unexpected and quite different from the paths which other minds have to follow in order to acquire the same conviction. My path was this conversation with Katyenka, which affected me deeply and forced me to meditate on her future situation. When I looked at the villages and towns through which we passed and in which, in each house, there lived at least one such family as ours, and at the women and children who glanced at our carriage with a moment's curiosity and then disappeared from view forever, and at shopkeepers and peasants who not only did not bow to us, as I was accustomed to seeing them do at Petrovsky, but did not even bother to glance at us, the question occurred to me for the first time: What are they occupied with if they have no time for us? And this question gave rise to others: how and what do they live on, how do they bring up their children, do they send them to school, do they let them out to play, how do they punish them, and so on.

IV

In Moscow

Upon our arrival in Moscow the change in my view of things and people and in my attitude to them became even more pronounced.

At my first meeting with Grandmother, when I saw her gaunt wrinkled face and lusterless eyes, the feelings of servile respect and fear that I had had for her gave way to a feeling of sympathy; and when, laying her face on Lyubochka's head, she burst into tears as though seeing the corpse of her beloved daughter before her, even my feeling of love for her gave way to sympathy. I was embarrassed to see her sorrow at the sight of us; I realized that in ourselves we were nothing in her eyes, that we were dear to her only as a reminder, and I felt that every kiss she planted on my cheeks expressed but one thought: she's gone, she's dead, I shall never see her again!

Papa, who took practically no notice of us at all in Moscow and came to us only at dinnertime, wearing black tails or a frock coat and with a constantly preoccupied face—he, with his great shirt collars worn outside, his dressing gown, village elders, walks to the barn, and hunting, lost a great deal in my eyes. Karl Ivanich, whom Grandmother called a valet and who suddenly, for God knows what reason, took it into his head to cover his respectable and familiar bald pate with a ginger wig meticulously parted not quite in the middle, seemed so strange and ridiculous to me that I was amazed that I had not noticed it before.

Some kind of invisible barrier also grew up between us and the girls; we already had separate secrets; it was as though they flaunted their skirts, which were becoming longer, in front of us, and we our trousers with footstraps at the bottom. And on the first Sunday, Mimi came to dinner in such a sumptuous dress and with such ribbons in her hair that it was at once obvious that we were no longer in the country and that everything would be different now.

V

My Elder Brother

I was only a year and a few months younger than Volodya; we had always grown up, taken lessons, and played together. No distinction was
ever made between elder and younger; but it was precisely at the time
of which I am speaking that I began to realize that Volodya was not the
same as I either in years or interests or capabilities. It seemed to me
even that Volodya was aware of his pre-eminence and took pride in it.
This conviction, though possibly unfounded, provoked my vanity,
which suffered in every clash with him. He was superior to me in
everything: in games, in studies, in quarrels, and in his ability to com-
port himself well, and this put a distance between us and forced me to
undergo moral sufferings that were completely beyond my understanding. If, when Volodya was made pleated Holland shirts for the
first time, I had said straight out that I was extremely upset not to have
some myself, I am sure I would have felt better and it would not have
seemed, every time he straightened his collar, as though he were doing
it solely to annoy me.

The thing that tormented me most was that Volodya, so it seemed
to me, understood me but tried to conceal that he did.

Who has not noted those mysterious wordless relations that reveal themselves in an imperceptible smile, a gesture, or a glance between people who live constantly together: brothers, friends, husband and wife, master and servant, particularly when these people are not entirely frank with one another? How many unspoken desires and thoughts and how much fear of being understood are expressed in a single fortuitous look, when, timidly and uncertainly, your eyes meet!

But perhaps I was deceived in this respect by my excessive sensitivity and penchant for analysis; perhaps Volodya felt none of the things I did. He was ardent, frank, and inconstant in his enthusiasms. Carried away by the most diverse subjects, he would abandon himself to them heart and soul.

One day he suddenly had a craze for painting: he himself started painting, spent all his money and then begged for things from the drawing teacher, Papa, and Grandmother; another time it was a craze for things to decorate his table with, which he collected from all over the house; then it was a craze for novels, which he got secretly and read for whole days and nights.... I involuntarily got drawn into his crazes; but I was too proud to follow in his footsteps and too young and dependent to choose a new path for myself. But there was nothing I envied so much as Volodya's happy and nobly open nature, which manifested itself particularly vividly in the quarrels that took place between us. I used to feel that he was behaving well, but I was unable to emulate him.

Once when his craze for things was at its highest pitch I went up to his table and accidentally smashed a small empty multicolored bottle.

"Who asked you to touch my things?" said Volodya, coming into the room and noticing the disorder I had introduced into the symmetry of the various objects adorning his table. "And where's the little bottle? You must have ..."

"I dropped it accidentally and it broke, so what of it?"

"Do me a favor, *don't dare* touch my things—ever," he said, gathering up the fragments of broken bottle and looking at them regretfully.

"Please *don't order* me around," I replied. "If I broke it, I broke it; what is there to say?"

And I smiled, although I did not in the least feel like smiling.

"Yes, it doesn't matter to you, but it does to me," went on Volodya, giving a shrug of his shoulder, a gesture he had inherited from Papa. "First he breaks it and then he laughs about it; what an unbearable *brat!*"

"I'm a brat and you're grown-up—but stupid."

"I'm not going to start calling names," said Volodya, pushing me away slightly. "Get out."

"Don't push!"

"Get out!"

"I said don't push!"

Volodya took me by the arm and wanted to drag me away from the table; but I was already exasperated to the very limit: I seized the table by one leg and overturned it. "There, take that!"—and all the porcelain and crystal ornaments crashed to the floor with a splintering sound.

"You obnoxious brat!" cried Volodya, trying to save the falling things.

Well, everything's finished between us now, I thought, leaving the room. We've quarreled forever.

We did not say a word to one another until evening; I felt myself in the wrong, was afraid to look at him and was unable to do a thing all day; Volodya, on the other hand, was very good at his lessons and, as always, had talked and laughed with the girls after dinner.

As soon as our teacher ended the class, I left the room: I was too frightened, uncomfortable, and ashamed to remain alone with my brother. After our evening history class I picked up my notebooks and headed for the door. As I walked past Volodya, in spite of the fact that I wanted to go up to him and make friends, I puffed myself up and tried to make my face look angry. At this very moment Volodya lifted his head and with a barely perceptible, good-humoredly mocking smile, looked at me boldly. Our eyes met and I understood that he understood both me and the fact that I understood he understood; but an irresistible impulse forced me to turn away.

"Nikolyenka!" he said in a most simple and not at all pathetic voice. "Don't be angry any more. Forgive me if I offended you."

And he held out his hand.

Something seemed to rise higher and higher inside me and suddenly began to constrict my chest and pluck at my breath; but this continued only for a second: tears appeared in my eyes and I experienced a feeling of relief.

"For-give . . . m-me, Vol . . . dya!" I said, pressing his hand.

Volodya looked at me, however, as though he could not understand why there were tears in my eyes. . . .

VI

MASHA

But not one of the changes that took place in my view of things was as staggering to me personally as that which resulted in my ceasing to regard one of our maids as a servant of the female sex and seeing instead a *woman,* on whom, to a certain extent, my peace of mind and even happiness might depend.

Ever since I can remember I remember Masha being in our house and never, until the incident that completely transformed my view of her and that I am about to relate, had I paid the slightest attention to her. Masha was twenty-five when I was fourteen; she was very pretty; but I am afraid to describe her, I am afraid lest my imagination again pictures to me that bewitching and alluring image that was formed in it at the time of my passion. In order to make no mistake, I will say only that she was extraordinarily white-skinned, magnificently developed, and was a woman; and I was fourteen.

At one of those moments when, homework in hand, you occupy yourself with walking up and down the room, trying to tread only on the cracks between the floorboards, or with singing some foolish air, or wiping ink on the edges of your desk, or pointlessly repeating some saying—in brief, at one of those moments when your mind refuses to work and your imagination comes to the fore and looks for impressions, I left the classroom and with no particular aim in view went down to the landing.

Someone in shoes was going upstairs round the next spiral. Naturally I wanted to know who it was, but suddenly the sound of steps died away and I heard Masha's voice: "Oh, it's you, up to your tricks again; what if Marya Ivanovna comes—that won't do us any good, will it?"

"She won't come," said Volodya's voice in a whisper, and this was immediately followed by a rustling sound, as though Volodya were trying to detain her.

"Ow, where do you think you're putting your hand? Shame on you!" and Masha, her kerchief pulled askew to reveal her plump white neck, ran past me.

I cannot express the degree to which I was astonished by this discovery, but my feeling of astonishment soon yielded to sympathy for Volodya's action: I was no longer surprised by the action itself, but at how he had discovered that it was nice to act that way. And I involuntarily wanted to emulate him.

Sometimes I spent whole hours on the landing, with no particular aim in view, listening with tense concentration for the least little movement above; but I could never steel myself to do what Volodya did, despite the fact that this was what I wanted more than anything in the world. Sometimes, hidden behind the door, I would listen with painful feelings of envy and jealousy to the scufflings going on in the maids' room and would think: What would be my position if I went upstairs like Volodya and wanted to kiss Masha? What would I say with my broad nose and my curls sticking up when she asked me what I wanted? Sometimes I heard Masha say to Volodya: "What I have to put up with! Why are you pestering me; go away, you with your tricks. . . . Why is it master Nikolai never comes and plays the fool . . ." She did not know that at that moment master Nikolai was sitting under the stairs and would have given the whole world merely to be playing Volodya's tricks.

I was bashful by nature, but my bashfulness was increased by the conviction that I was ugly. . . . And I am convinced that nothing has such a striking impact on a man's development as his appearance, and not so much his actual appearance as a conviction that it is either attractive or unattractive.

I was too vain to reconcile myself to my situation and comforted myself, like the fox, by reassuring myself that the grapes were still sour; that is, I tried to despise all the pleasures that were obtainable through a pleasant appearance, that Volodya enjoyed before my eyes and that I envied with all my heart, and bent all my mental and imaginative powers to the task of finding pleasure in proud isolation.

VII

BUCKSHOT

"Good heavens, gunpowder!" exclaimed Mimi, gasping with horror. "What are you doing? Do you want to set fire to the house and kill us all?"

And with an indescribable expression of steadfastness on her face Mimi ordered everyone to stand aside, marched up to the scattered buckshot with long decisive strides and, scorning the danger that could result from a sudden explosion, began to stamp on it with her feet. When, in her opinion, the danger was already over, she summoned Mikhei and ordered him to throw all this *gunpowder* out of reach, or, better still, into the water, and with a proud toss of her bonnet set off for the drawing room. "They're certainly being looked after very well, I must say," she muttered.

When Papa came from the wing and we went with him to see Grandmother, Mimi was already there in the room, sitting by the window, and looked menacingly past the door with a kind of mysteriously official expression on her face. In her hand she was holding something wrapped in several sheets of newspaper. I guessed that this was the buckshot and that Grandmother already knew everything.

Besides Mimi in Grandmother's room there were also the maid, Gasha, who, as was obvious from her flushed angry face, was extremely upset, and Dr. Blumenthal, a tiny pockmarked man who was vainly endeavoring to calm Gasha and making mysterious placatory signs to her with his head and eyes.

Grandmother herself was sitting somewhat sideways and laying out patience, which always signified that she was in an extremely bad mood.

"How do you feel today, *maman?* Did you have a good night's rest?" said Papa, kissing her hand respectfully.

"Excellent, dear man; I believe you are aware that I am always well," replied Grandmother, in a tone of voice suggesting that Papa's question was a most inappropriate and offensive one. "Well, aren't you going to give me a clean handkerchief?" she went on, turning to Gasha.

"I gave you one," replied Gasha, pointing to a snow-white cambric handkerchief lying on the arm of the chair.

"Take this filthy rag away and get me a clean one, my dear."

Gasha went to the chiffonier, pulled out a drawer, and then slammed it shut again so fiercely that the room's windows rattled. Grandmother looked darkly round at us all and continued to watch the maid's movements. When she gave her what seemed to me to be the self-same handkerchief, Grandmother said:

"When are you going to grind me some snuff, my dear?"

"I'll do it when I get the time."

"What did you say?"

"I'll do it today."

"If you don't want to serve me, my dear, you should say so: I would have released you long ago."

"Nobody will be much upset if you do," muttered the maid under her breath.

At this moment the doctor started to wink at her; but she looked at him so angrily and resolutely that he immediately lowered his eyes and began to fiddle with his watch.

"Do you see, my dear," said Grandmother, turning to Papa as Gasha, still grumbling, left the room, "how I am spoken to in my own house?"

"Oh, please, *maman,* I'll grind you some snuff myself," said Papa, who evidently was considerably disconcerted by this unexpected remark.

"No, thank you: she's only so rude because she knows that no one except her knows how to grind snuff the way I like it. Do you know, my dear," went on Grandmother after a moment's silence, "that today your children almost set the house on fire?"

Papa looked at Grandmother with respectful curiosity.

"Yes, look what they were playing with. Show him," she said, turning to Mimi.

Papa took the buckshot from her and was unable to conceal a smile.

"But that's buckshot, *maman,*" he said, "it's not in the least dangerous."

"I'm very grateful to you, my dear, for teaching me what's what, only I'm too old . . ."

"Nerves, nerves!" whispered the doctor.

And Papa immediately turned to us:

"Where did you get this and how dare you meddle with such things?"

"There's no point in asking them; you ought to ask that *valet* of theirs," said Grandmother, enunciating the word *valet* with particular scorn. "Is that what he calls looking after them?"

"*Waldemar* said that Karl Ivanich himself gave him the gunpowder," interjected Mimi.

"There, you see what a fine fellow he is," went on Grandmother, "and where is he, this *valet,* what's his name? Send him in."

"I gave him permission to visit some friends," said Papa.

"That's no excuse; he should always be here. The children are yours, not mine, and I have no right to advise you, because you're cleverer than me," went on Grandmother, "but it seems to me high time you hired a governor for them and not a *valet,* a German peasant. Yes, a stupid peasant who can't teach them anything except bad manners and Tyrolean songs. Is it necessary, I ask you, for children to be able to sing Tyrolean songs? However, *now* there's no one to think of these things and you can do as you like."

The word *now* meant when they do not have a mother, and evoked sorrowful memories in Grandmother's heart—she lowered her eyes to the snuffbox with the portrait on it and became thoughtful.

"I've been thinking of this for a long time," Papa hastened to say, "and I wanted to ask your advice, *maman:* shall I offer the post to St.-Jérôme, who's now giving them private lessons?"

"You couldn't do better, my friend," said Grandmother, her voice no longer sounding so dissatisfied as before. "St.-Jérôme is at least a *gouverneur* who understands how to handle *des enfants de bonne maison,* and not a mere *menin,* a *valet* who's good only for taking them for walks."

"I'll talk to him tomorrow," said Papa.

And indeed, two days after this conversation Karl Ivanich ceded his place to the dandyish young Frenchman.

VIII

KARL IVANICH'S STORY

Late in the evening on the day before Karl Ivanich was destined to leave us forever, he was standing by his bed in his quilted dressing gown and red cap, bending over his case and carefully packing his things.

Karl Ivanich's attitude to us of late had been somehow particularly cool: he had seemed to avoid having any contact with us. And now too, when I came into the room, he stole a sideways glance at me and then renewed his packing. I flopped down onto my bed but Karl Ivanich, who had strictly forbidden this formerly, said nothing, and the thought that he would nevermore scold us or stop us from doing things, that he now had no time for us, reminded me vividly of our impending separation. I felt sad that he no longer loved us and I wanted to let him know of my feelings.

"Let me help you, Karl Ivanich," I said, going up to him.

Karl Ivanich glanced at me and turned away again, but in the momentary glance that he cast at me I read not the indifference by which I had explained his coolness but genuine unadulterated sorrow.

"God sees and knows all and His sacred will rules everything," he said, straightening himself up to his full height and breathing heavily. "Yes, Nikolyenka," he went on, noticing the expression of unfeigned sympathy with which I regarded him, "it is my fate to be unhappy from the day I was born to the grave. I have always been repaid with evil for the good I have done to others and my reward will come not here but up there," he said, pointing upward. "If only you knew my story and everything I have undergone in this life! . . . I have been a cobbler, a soldier, and a deserter; I have been a factory hand and a teacher, and now I am zero! And now, like the Son of God, I have nowhere to lay my head," he concluded, and closing his eyes sank into his armchair.

Noticing that Karl Ivanich was in that sentimental frame of mind in which, paying no attention to whoever was listening, he would utter all his innermost thoughts aloud for his own benefit, I sat on the bed in silence and did not take my eyes from his kind face.

"You're not a child; you're able to understand. I'll tell you my whole story and everything that I've undergone in this life. Sometime you'll remember your old friend who loved you so very much, children!"

Karl Ivanich rested one hand on the small table beside him, took a pinch of snuff, and, rolling his eyes upward, in the regular throaty voice that he normally used for dictation, commenced his narration.

"I vos onhappy shtill in mine mutter's womb. *Das Unglück verfolgte mich schon im Schosse meiner Mutter!*" he repeated with even more feeling.

Since Karl Ivanich subsequently related his story to me several times in the same order, using identical expressions and with a permanently unchanged intonation, I hope to be able to retell it practically word for word, though naturally excluding the incorrectness of his speech, which the reader may judge from the initial phrase. Whether this was truly the story of his life, or perhaps the product of his imagination, a product born of his solitary life in our house and which he himself began to believe as a result of frequent repetition, or whether he was merely embroidering the true facts of his life with fantastic events—I still have not decided. On the one hand he told his story with too much lively feeling and methodical consistency—the chief marks of veracity—for it to be disbelieved; on the other hand there were too many poetic felicities in his story, so that these in themselves elicited doubt.

"Through my veins runs the noble blood of the counts von Sommerblatt! *In meinen Adern fliesst das edle Blut des Grafen von Sommerblatt!* I vas born six veeks after vedding. My mother's husband (I called him Poppa) was a tenant of Count Sommerblatt. He could not forget my mother's shame and did not love me. I had a little brother, Johann, and two sisters; but I was a stranger in my own family! *Ich war ein Fremder in meiner eigenen Familie!* Whenever Johann did something naughty Poppa would say: 'I shan't have a moment's peace with this boy Karl!' and I was scolded and punished. Whenever the sisters quarreled among themselves Poppa would say: 'Karl will never be an obedient boy!' and I was scolded and punished. Only my kind Mama loved me and was tender with me. Often she would say to me: 'Karl, come here to my room!' and she would kiss me in secret. 'Poor, poor Karl!' she would say, 'Nobody loves you, but I wouldn't change you for anyone. There's only one thing your mama asks of you,' she'd say to me, 'study well and always be an honorable man, and God will not leave you! *Trachte nur ein ehrlicher Deutscher zu werden,' sagte sie, 'und der lieber Gott wird dich nicht verlassen!'* And I tried. When I was fourteen and could go to communion, Mama said to Poppa: 'Karl is a big boy now, Gustav, what shall we do with him?' And Poppa said: 'I don't know.' Then Mama said: 'Let's send him to Mr. Schulz in town, let him become a cobbler.' And Poppa said: 'All right,' *und mein Vater sagte 'gut.'* For six years and seven months I lived in town at the cobbler's and my master liked me. He said: 'Karl is a good workman and soon he will be my *Geselle!*' but . . . man proposes, God disposes . . . in seventeen ninety-six conscription was introduced and all who could serve and were between the ages of eighteen and twenty-one had to gather in the town.

"Poppa and my brother Johann came to town and together we went to draw lots to see who should become a *Soldat* and who not become a *Soldat.* Johann drew out a bad number—he had to be a *Soldat;* I drew a good number—I didn't have to be a *Soldat.* And Poppa said: 'I had only one son and now I must part from him! *Ich hatte einen einzigen Sohn und von diesem muss ich mich trennen!'*

"I took him by the hand and said: 'Why did you say that, Poppa? Come with me and I'll tell you something.' And Poppa came. Poppa came and we sat at a little table in a tavern. 'Give us a couple of

Bierkrug,' I said and they brought some. We drank a glass each and brother Johann also had one.

" 'Poppa!' I said, 'Don't say that, don't say you only had one son and you have to part with him; my heart wants to *leap out* when I hear *that*. Brother Johann won't have to serve—I'll go. . . . Nobody needs Karl here so Karl will be a *Soldat.*'

" 'You're an honorable man, Karl Ivanich,' said Poppa to me and kissed me. *'Du bist ein braver Bursche!' sagte mir mein Vater und küsste mich!'*

"And I became a *Soldat!*"

IX

THE FOREGOING CONTINUED

"That was a terrible time, Nikolyenka," went on Karl Ivanich, "that was the time of Napoleon. He wanted to conquer Germany and we defended our fatherland till the last drop of blood! *Und wir verteidigten unser Vaterland bis auf den letzten Tropfen Blut!*

"I was at Ulm! I was at Austerlitz! I was at Wagram! *Ich war bei Wagram!'*

"Surely you didn't fight too?" I asked, looking at him in surprise. "Surely you didn't kill people?"

Karl Ivanich immediately reassured me on that point.

"Once a French grenadier fell behind the others and collapsed in the road. I dashed up with my rifle and was about to bayonet him, *aber der Franzose warf sein Gewehr und rief pardon,* and I let him go!

"At Wagram Napoleon drove us onto an island and surrounded us so that there was no means of escape. For three days and nights we were without food, standing up to our knees in water. That scoundrel Napoleon would neither capture us nor let us go! *Und der Bösewicht Napoleon wollte uns nicht gefangen nehmen und auch nicht freilassen!*

"On the fourth day, thank God, they took us prisoner and led us off to a fortress. I was wearing blue trousers, a uniform jacket made of good-quality cloth, and I had with me fifteen thalers and a silver watch—a present from Poppa. A French *Soldat* took everything away from me. Luckily I had three gold pieces that Mama had sewn into my jersey. Nobody found them.

"I did not want to stay long in the fort and I made up my mind to escape. One day, an important holiday, I said to the sergeant who was looking after us: 'Sergeant, today is an important holiday and I wish to recognize it. Bring me two bottles of Madeira, please, and we'll drink them together.' And the sergeant said: 'All right.' When the sergeant had brought the Madeira and we had each drunk a glass I took him by the hand and said: 'Sergeant, I take it you have a mother and father?' He said: 'Yes, Mr. Mauer . . .' 'My father and mother,' I said, 'haven't seen me for eight years and don't know whether I'm still alive or whether my bones have long since lain in the damp earth. Oh, sergeant, I have two gold pieces which were sewn into my jersey; take them and let me go. Be my benefactor and my mother will pray to God for you all her life.'

"The sergeant drank up a glass of Madeira and replied: 'Mr. Mauer, I like you very much and feel sorry for you, but you are a prisoner and I am a *Soldat!*' I shook him by the hand and said: 'Sergeant!' *Ich drückte ihm die Hand und sagte: 'Herr Sergeant!'*

"And the sergeant said: 'You're a poor man and I won't take your money, but I'll help you. When I go to sleep, buy the soldiers a bucket of liquor and they will fall asleep. I shall not be looking.'

"He was a good man. I bought a bucket of liquor and when the *Soldaten* were drunk I put on my shoes and old overcoat and quietly crept through the door. I went to the ramparts and wanted to jump, but there was water below and I did not wish to spoil my last clothes: I went to the gate.

"A sentry with a rifle was walking *auf und ab* and he looked at me. *'Qui vive?' sagte er auf einmal,* and I remained silent. *'Qui vive?' sagte er zum zweiten Mal,* and I remained silent. *'Qui vive?' sagte er zum dritten Mal* and I ran. I jomped in vater, crawled in other bank, und dashed. *Ich sprang ins Wasser, kletterte auf die andere Seite und machte mich aus dem Staube.*

"All night I fled along the road, but when dawn came I was afraid of being recognized and hid myself in some tall rye. There I knelt down, clasped my hands together, thanked our Heavenly Father for my deliverance and fell into a peaceful sleep. *Ich dankte dem allmächtigen Gott für Seine Barmherzigkeit und mit beruhigtem Gefühl schlief ich ein.*

"I awoke in the evening and went further. Suddenly a large German wagon came up behind me, drawn by two black horses. A well-dressed man was sitting in the wagon, smoking a pipe and looking at me. I walked very slowly so that the wagon would overtake me, but when I went slowly the wagon went slowly, and the man looked at me; I speeded up and the wagon speeded up, and the man was still looking at me. I sat down by the road; the man halted his horses and looked at me. 'Young man,' he said, 'where are you going so late?' I said: 'I'm going to Frankfurt.' 'Get into my wagon, there's plenty of room, and I'll take you. . . . Why have you nothing with you, why are you unshaven and your clothes so muddy?' he said when I got in beside him. 'I'm a poor man,' I said. 'I hope to get work somewhere at a *Fabrik;* and my clothes are muddy because I fell down in the road.' 'You're not telling the truth, young man,' he said, 'the road is dry now.'

"And I remained silent.

" 'Tell me the whole truth,' said the good man. 'Who are you and where do you come from? I like your face and if you're an honest man I'll help you.'

"And I told him everything. He said: 'All right, young man, let's go to my cable factory. I'll give you work, clothes, money, and you can live with me.'

"And I said: 'All right.'

"We came to the cable factory and the good man said to his wife: 'Here's a young man who fought for his country and escaped from prison; he has neither home nor clothes nor food. He will live with us. Give him some clean linen and feed him.'

"I lived at the cable factory for a year and a half and my master loved me so much that he did not want to let me go. And it was fine for me. I was a handsome man then; I was young, tall, with blue eyes, a Roman nose . . . and Madame L—— (I cannot mention her name), my master's wife, was a young and pretty woman. And she fell in love with me.

"When she saw me she said: 'Mr. Mauer, what does your mama call you?' I said: 'Karlchen.'

"And she said: 'Karlchen! Sit down beside me.'

"I sat down beside her and she said: 'Karlchen, kiss me!'

"I kissed *him* and he said: 'Karlchen, I love you so much that I can't stand it any longer,' and he trembled all over."

Here Karl Ivanich paused for a long time, rolling his kind blue eyes upward and slightly nodding his head, and he started to smile the way people smile under the influence of pleasant memories.

"Yes," be began again, straightening up in his armchair and closing the front of his dressing gown, "I've experienced much that is good and much bad in my life; but there is my witness," he said, pointing to an embroidered picture of the Savior hanging over his bed. "No one can say that Karl Ivanich was a dishonorable man! I did not wish to repay the kindness that Mr. L. had shown me with black ingratitude and I decided to run away. In the evening, when everyone had gone to bed, I wrote my master a letter and placed it on the table in my room; then I took my clothes and three thalers and crept quietly out into the street. Nobody saw me and I took to the road."

X

Continued

"I had not seen my mama for ten years and did not know whether she was alive or whether her bones already lay in the damp earth. I went home. When I came to the town I asked where Gustav Mauer, who had been a tenant of Count Sommerblatt's, was living. And they said: 'Count Sommerblatt is dead and Gustav Mauer lives on Main Street now and keeps a brandy shop.' I put on my new vest and fine coat—presents from the factory-owner—combed my hair carefully, and went to see my father at the brandy shop. My sister Marie was sitting in the shop and asked me what I wanted. I said: 'Can I have a glass of brandy?' And she said: '*Vater!* There's a young man here asking for a glass of brandy.' And Papa said: 'Give the young man a glass of brandy.' I sat at a small table, drank my glass of brandy, lit my pipe, and looked at Papa, Marie, and Johann, who had also come into the shop. During the conversation Papa said to me: 'You probably know, young man, where our *armée* is at present.' I said: 'I've come from the *armée* myself and at the moment it's near Vienna.' 'Our son,' said Papa, 'was a *Soldat* and he hasn't written to us for nine years now and we do not know whether he is alive or dead. My wife is always crying over him...' I lit my pipe and said: 'What was your son's name and where did he serve? Perhaps I know him ...' 'His name was Karl Mauer and he served in the Austrian hussars,' said Papa. 'He's a tall and handsome man—like you,' said sister Marie. I said: 'I know your Karl.' 'Amalia!' *sagte auf einmal mein Vater,* 'come here. There's a young man here and he knows our Karl.' *Und mine dear mama* come from back door. I quick recognized *him.* *'You know our Karl?'* he said, then look at me and, all pale, be-gin to trem-ble! ... 'Yes, I've seen him,' I said, and did not dare raise my eyes to look at her. My heart wanted to *leap out.* 'My Karl's alive!' said Mama. 'Thank the Lord! Where is he, my dear Karl? I would die content if only I could see him once more, my beloved son. But God does not desire it, and *he* began to weep. ... *I could not endoor it.* ... 'Mama!' I said, 'I am your Karl!' *Und he fell in my arm. ..."*

Karl Ivanich closed his eyes and his lips trembled.

" *'Mutter!' sagte ich, 'ich bin ihr Sohn, ich bin ihr Karl!' und sie stürzte mir in die Arme,"* he repeated, calming down a little and wiping away the big tears that were rolling down his cheeks.

"But God did not see fit to let me end my days in my homeland. I was fated to be unlucky! *Das Unglück verfolgte mich überall!* ... I lived at home for only three months. One Sunday I was in a café; I had bought a mug of beer and I was smoking my pipe and talking to some friends about *Politik,* about Emperor Franz, Napoleon, the war, and each of us gave his opinion. Next to us sat an unknown gentleman in a gray *Überrock,* who drank his coffee, smoked his pipe, and said nothing. *Er rauchte sein Pfeifchen und schweig still.* When the *Nachtwächter* announced ten o'clock, I took my hat, paid the bill, and went home. In the middle of the night someone knocked on the door. I woke up and said: 'Who's there?' *'Macht auf!'* I said: 'Tell me who's there and I'll open up.' *Ich sagte: 'Sagt, wer ihr seid, und ich werde aufmachen.'* *'Macht auf im Namen des Gesetzes!'* said someone on the other side. And I opened it. Two *Soldaten* with rifles were standing there, and then that unknown man in the gray *Überrock* who had sat next to us in the café came into the room. He was a spy! *Es war ein Spion!* 'Come with me!' said the spy. 'All right,' I said. ... I put on my boots *und Pantalon,* did up my suspenders, and walked about the room. My heart was seething; I said: 'He's a scoundrel!' When I came up to the wall where my sword was hanging I suddenly grasped it and said: 'You're a spy; defend yourself! *Du bist ein Spion, verteidige dich!' Ich gab ein Hieb* to the right, *ein Hieb* to the left, *und vun on the het. The spy fell!* I took my suitcase and money and jumped out of the window. *Ich nahm meinen Nantelsack und Beutel und sprang zum Fenster hinaus. Ich kam nach Ems.* There I got to know General Sazin. He took a liking to me, obtained a passport from the consul, and took me with him to Russia to teach his children. When General Sazin died your mama summoned me to her house. She said: 'Karl Ivanich! I'm entrusting my children to you; love them and I will never abandon you, I'll provide for your old age.' Now she's gone and everything's forgotten. Now, in return for twenty years of service, in my old age, I must go into the streets to seek my stale crust of bread. . . . *God sees and knows this and his sacred will be done, but I am sorry to part with you, childrens!"* concluded Karl Ivanich, drawing me to him by the hand and kissing me on the head.

XI

A Bad Mark

At the end of a year's mourning Grandmother recovered somewhat from the grief that had stricken her and began to receive guests from time to time, particularly children—our coevals.

On Lyubochka's birthday, December thirteenth, we were visited before dinner by Princess Kornakov and her daughters, Mme. Valakhin and Sonya, Ilinka Grap, and the two younger Ivin brothers.

We could already hear the sound of voices, laughter, and people running about down below, where the whole company had gathered, but were not allowed to join them until morning classes were over. The timetable that hung in the classroom bore the legend: *Lundi, de 2 à 3, Maître d'Histoire et de Géographie;* and so now we had to wait for this *Maître d'Histoire,* hear him out, and see him out before we could be free. It was already twenty past two and so far there was neither sight nor sound of the history teacher, not even on the street he had to come along, at which I was gazing with an urgent desire never to see him at all.

"It seems that Lebedev won't be coming today," said Volodya, tearing himself away for a moment from Smaragdov's book, in which he was preparing the lesson.

"Let's hope so, let's hope so. . . . I don't know a thing anyway . . . but . . . here he comes, I think," I added sorrowfully.

Volodya stood up and came to the window.

"No, that's not him, that's some *gentleman* or other," he said. "Let's wait till half past two," he added, stretching himself and at the same time scratching the top of his head, as he usually did when resting from his studies for a moment. "If he hasn't come by half past two, we can tell St.-Jérôme to take our notebooks away."

"What does he want to come at a-a-all for," I said, also stretching and brandishing Kaidanov's book overhead, holding it with both hands.

For lack of anything better to do I opened the book at the place from which our lesson had been set and started to read it. It was a long and difficult lesson. I knew nothing, and I saw that I could not possibly memorize any of it in the time left, especially since I was in that disturbed frame of mind in which one's thoughts absolutely refuse to remain on any subject whatsoever.

After the last history lesson, which always seemed to me to be the most boring and difficult subject, Lebedev had complained to St.-Jérôme about me and had given me a two in the mark-book, which was considered very bad. St.-Jérôme had told me then that if I got less than three for the next lesson I would be severely punished. And now the next lesson was upon us and I must admit that I was horribly afraid.

I was so engrossed in reading the unfamiliar lesson that the sound of galoshes being taken off in the anteroom suddenly startled me. I had hardly had time to look round when in the doorway there appeared the pockmarked and to me repulsive face and only too familiar and clumsy figure of the teacher, dressed in his blue buttoned-up frock coat with its scholarly buttons.

The teacher slowly placed his hat on the windowsill and his notebooks on his desk, spread the tails of his frock coat with both hands (as though this were very necessary) and sat down on his chair, puffing.

"Well, gentlemen," he said, rubbing his perspiring hands one against the other, "first let us go over what we did in the last lesson and then I shall attempt to acquaint you with further facts about the Middle Ages."

This meant: say your lessons.

While Volodya was answering him with the ease and confidence natural to those who know their subject well, I wandered aimlessly out onto the stairs, and, since I was forbidden to go down, it was entirely natural that, quite unwittingly, I found myself up on the landing. But I was just about to station myself at my usual observation post—behind the door—when suddenly Mimi, the perpetual source of all my troubles, bumped into me.

I felt myself completely in the wrong—both for not being in class and for being in such a forbidden spot; therefore I kept silent, lowered my head, and manifested in my person the most touching expression of repentance.

"No, this is absolutely unheard of!" said Mimi. "What are you doing here?" I remained silent. "No, this won't rest here," she repeated, tapping the bannister with the backs of her knuckles, "I'll tell the Countess everything."

It was already five to three when I returned to the classroom. The teacher, as though noticing neither my absence nor my presence, was explaining the next lesson to Volodya. When, having finished his explication, he began to gather up his notebooks and Volodya went into the next room to get his chit, I had the joyous idea that everything was over and that I would be forgotten.

But suddenly, with a devilish smile, the teacher turned to me.

"I trust you have learned the lesson," he said, rubbing his hands.

"I have," I said.

"Be so kind as to tell me something about the Crusade of Louis the Pious," he said, rocking on his chair and looking thoughtfully down at his feet. "First you will tell me of the reasons that led the French king to accept the cross," he said, raising his eyebrows and pointing his finger at the inkwell, "then you will explain to me the general characteristic features of this *Crusade*," he added, making a motion with his whole hand, as though wishing to catch something, "and, finally, the influence of this Crusade on the European states in general," he said, banging his notebooks on the left-hand side of his desk, "and on the French kingdom in particular," he concluded, banging the right-hand side of his desk and inclining his head to the right.

I swallowed several times, cleared my throat, bent my head to one side, and remained silent. Then, picking up the pen that lay on my desk, I began to pluck at it, but still was silent.

"Your pen, please," said the teacher, holding his hand out. "It will come in useful. Well?"

"Lou ... Lou ... Louis the Pious was ... was ... was ... a kind and clever tsar ..."

"What?"

"Tsar. He took it into his head to go to Jerusalem and *handed over the reins of government to his mother.*"

"What was her name?"

"B ... b ... lanka."

"What? Blanket?"

I grinned sort of crookedly and awkwardly.

"Well, is there anything else you know?" he said with a mocking smile.

I had nothing to lose, I cleared my throat and began to talk the first nonsense that came into my head. The teacher remained silent, brushing dust off the desk with the quill pen he had taken away from me, and looked past my ear, saying from time to time: "Good, very good." I felt that I knew nothing and that I was expressing myself not at all the way I should have been doing, and it was agony for me to see that the teacher neither stopped nor corrected me.

"Why did he take it into his head to go to Jerusalem?" he said, repeating my words.

"Since ... because ... for the reason that ..."

I dried up completely and said not a word more, and I felt that even if this devil-teacher remained silent and looked at me with that question in his eyes for a whole year, I would still not be capable of uttering another sound. The teacher looked at me for about three minutes; then, suddenly, an expression of profound sorrow appeared on his face and in a pained voice he said to Volodya, who was just coming into the room at that moment:

"Give me the book, please: to enter the marks in."

Volodya handed him the book and carefully placed the chit beside it.

The teacher opened the book and, carefully dipping his pen in the ink, wrote Volodya a handsome five in the columns for both achievement and behavior. Then, with his pen poised over the columns in which my marks were registered, he looked at me, shook some ink off, and grew thoughtful.

Suddenly his hand made an almost imperceptible motion and a handsomely drawn one and period appeared in the column; another motion—and another one and period appeared in the behavior column.

Shutting the mark-book carefully, the teacher stood up and walked to the door, as though unaware of my look compounded of despair, implorement, and reproach.

"Mikhail Larionich!" I said.

"No," he replied, understanding what it was I wanted to say to him, "that's no way to do your lessons. I don't want to take money for nothing."

The teacher donned his galoshes and camlet overcoat and wrapped himself up in his scarf with the greatest care. As though one could care about anything else after what had just happened to me! For him a mere motion of the pen, but for me the greatest misfortune!

"Is the class over?" asked St.-Jérôme, coming into the room.

"Yes."

"Is the teacher satisfied with you?"

"Yes," said Volodya.

"What mark did you get?"

"Five."

"And *Nicolas?*"

I kept silent.

"Four, I think," said Volodya.

He understood that I had to be rescued at least for today. Let them punish me, only not today, when there were guests.

"Voyons, messieurs (St.-Jérôme was in the habit of prefacing every word with *voyons)! Faites votre toilette et descendons."*

XII

THE KEY

We had hardly had time to go downstairs and greet all the guests when we were summoned to table. Papa was very gay (he was winning at this time), presented Lyubochka with an expensive silver service, and during dinner recalled that he had left in the wing a box of candies that was also intended for Lyubochka.

"Rather than send a servant, you go instead, Coco," he said to me. "The keys are in the shell on the big desk, do you know where I mean? . . . Well, get them and use the biggest key to open the second drawer on the right. There you'll find a box and some candies wrapped up in paper. Bring them all here."

"And shall I bring your cigars as well?" I asked, knowing that he always sent for them after dinner.

"Yes, but make sure you don't touch anything of mine!" he called after me.

Having found the keys in the appointed place I was about to open the drawer when my progress was arrested by a desire to find out what was opened by a tiny key that hung in the same bunch.

Among a thousand variegated objects lying on the desk there was, by the rail at the back, an embroidered wallet with a hanging lock, and I felt an urge to see if the little key fitted it. My experiment was crowned with complete success, the wallet opened and inside I found a whole wad of papers. A feeling of curiosity advised me with such persuasiveness to find out what these papers were that I failed to listen to the voice of conscience and began to examine the things in the wallet....

———

The childlike emotion of unconditional respect for all adults, and particularly for Papa, was so strong in me that my mind unconsciously refused to draw any kind of conclusions whatever from what I had just seen. I felt that Papa must live in a sphere altogether special and wonderful, which was unattainable and inaccessible to me, and that to try to penetrate the secrets of his life would be something in the nature of sacrilege on my part.

Therefore, the discoveries I had made almost inadvertently in Papa's wallet left me with no clear concept, except the dim awareness that I had behaved badly. I felt ashamed and awkward.

Under the influence of this feeling I wanted to close the wallet as quickly as possible, but I was fated, evidently, to undergo all possible misfortunes on that momentous day: having inserted the key in the keyhole, I turned it the wrong way; imagining that it was now locked, I removed the key and—oh horror!—my hand held only the head of the key. I tried carefully to reunite it with the half that had remained in the lock and by some sorcery or other to get it free; finally I was obliged to accustom myself to the horrifying thought that I had committed yet one more crime which, upon his return to the study, Papa was certain to discover that very day.

Mimi's complaint, the bad mark, the key! Nothing worse could happen to me. Grandmother, because of Mimi's complaint, St.-Jérôme, because of the bad mark, and Papa, because of the key . . . all this would be unleashed on me no later than that same evening.

"What will become of me? O-oh dear, what have I done!" I said aloud, walking over the soft carpet in the study. "Ha!" I said to myself as I got the candy and cigars, *"what must be, must be . . ."* And I ran to the house.

This fatalistic maxim, which as a child I had overheard Nikolai using, has always, at all difficult moments of my life, had a beneficial and temporarily soothing effect on me. When I entered the salon I was in a somewhat highly strung and unnatural, but also extraordinarily cheerful, state of mind.

XIII

The Deceiver

After dinner the *petits jeux* began and I took the liveliest part in them. While we were playing hide-and-seek, I was running somewhat clumsily after the Kornakovs' governess, who was playing with us, when I inadvertently stepped on her dress and tore it. Noticing that it gave all the girls, and particularly Sonyechka, great pleasure to see the governess go off, her face distraught, to the maids' room to sew up her dress, I resolved to afford them the same pleasure once more. As a consequence of this amiable intention, as soon as the governess returned to the room I took to galloping round her and continued to circle her until such time as I found a convenient moment to fasten my heel in her dress and tear it again. Sonyechka and the princesses could barely keep from laughing, which was very flattering to my vanity; but St.-Jérôme must have noticed my antics, for he came up to me, scowling (which I could not stand) and said that it appeared that no good could come of my high spirits and that if I were not more modest he would, despite the occasion, ensure that I was sorry for it.

But I was in that highly strung condition of a man who has lost more than he has in his pocket, who is afraid to tot up his losses, and who continues to lay desperate cards with no hope of recouping his position, but merely in order not to give himself the time to consider. I smiled insolently and walked away from him.

After hide-and-seek somebody started a game which we called, I believe, *Lange Nase*. The essence of this game consisted in placing two rows of chairs opposite one another and in the cavaliers and ladies splitting up into two parties and taking turns to choose one another.

The youngest princess chose the younger Ivin each time, Katyenka chose either Volodya or Ilinka, while Sonyechka chose Seryozha and was not in the least embarrassed when, to my extreme astonishment, Seryozha simply went and sat opposite her. She laughed her sweet musical laugh and nodded her head as a sign that he had guessed correctly. Nobody chose me. To the extreme discomfiture of my vanity, I realized that I was superfluous, *left over*, that they would have to say of me each time: 'Who's left over?' '*Why, Nikolyenka; go on, you take him.*' Therefore, when it was my turn to go, I either went straight up to my sister or else to one of the ugly princesses and, to my great misfortune, was never mistaken. Sonyechka, it seemed, was so occupied with Seryozha Ivin that I just did not exist for her at all. I do not know on what basis I mentally called her *deceiver*, for she had never promised to choose me and not Seryozha; but I was firmly convinced that she had treated me in the vilest possible way.

After the game I noticed that the *deceiver*, whom I despised, but from whom, however, I was unable to take my eyes, had gone into a corner with Seryozha and Katyenka and they were all talking secretly of something. Creeping up behind the piano in order to discover their secret, I saw the following: Katyenka was holding a batiste handkerchief at both ends in form of a screen in front of the heads of Seryozha and Sonyechka. "No, you lost, now you must pay!" said Seryozha. Sonyechka, her hands lowered, was standing in front of him as though guilty, and was saying blushingly: "No, I didn't lose, did I, *Mademoiselle Catherine?*" "I'm a lover of truth," replied Katyenka; "you lost the bet, *ma chère.*"

Katyenka had barely finished uttering these words when Seryozha bent over and kissed Sonyechka. Kissed her just like that on her rosy red lips. And Sonyechka laughed, as though it were nothing, as though it was great fun. Horrors!!! *Oh perfidious deceiver!*

XIV

ECLIPSE

Suddenly I felt contempt for the whole female sex in general and for Sonyechka in particular; I began to persuade myself that there was nothing jolly in these games at all, that they were suitable only for *little girls,* and I felt an extraordinary urge to run riot and commit such a heroic act as would astound everyone. The occasion was not long in presenting itself.

St.-Jérôme, after a few words with Mimi, left the room; the sound of his footsteps could be heard at first on the stairs and then overhead, in the direction of the classroom. It occurred to me that Mimi had told him where she had seen me during class time and that he had gone to look at the register. I did not suppose at that time that St.-Jérôme had any other aim in life than a desire to punish me. I have read somewhere that children between twelve and fourteen, i.e., those in the transitional stage to adolescence, are particularly prone to arson and even murder. Recalling my boyhood and particularly the mood I was in on this for me ill-fated day, I can understand quite clearly the possibility of the most horrible crime, without reason and without the desire to harm, but just *so*—out of curiosity, out of an unconscious need for action. There are moments when the future appears to man in such a gloomy light that he is afraid to let his mind's eye rest upon it; he puts a complete stop to the working of his mind and tries to convince himself that the past never was and that the future will never be. At such moments, when thought does not consider each formulation of the will in advance and bodily instincts remain the sole springs of action, I understand that a child who is particularly prone to such states can out of inexperience, without the least hesitation or fear and with a smile of curiosity, light and fan a fire under his own home, inside of which, fast asleep, are the brothers and mother and father whom he dearly loves. Under the influence of this temporary absence of thought—distraction almost—the peasant youth of seventeen, examining the blade of a newly sharpened ax beside a bench, on which his aged father lies asleep face down, suddenly brandishes the ax and watches with dull curiosity as blood from the severed neck trickles down beneath the bench; under the influence of this same absence of thought and instinctive curiosity a man finds a kind of pleasure in standing on the edge of a precipice and thinking: What if I throw myself down? Or in placing a loaded pistol to his head and thinking: What if I press the trigger? Or looking at some important personage, for whom all society cherishes servile respect, and thinking: What if I go up to him, take him by the nose and say: "All right, dear fellow, let's go?"

It was under the influence of just such an inward agitation and absence of reflection that, when St.-Jérôme came downstairs and told me I had no right to be there today because I had behaved and studied so badly, and should go upstairs at once, I stuck out my tongue at him and said I would not leave.

For the first moment St.-Jérôme was unable to utter a word from surprise and rage.

"*C'est bien,*" he said, catching up with me, "several times already I have promised you a punishment which your Grandmother wished to spare you; but now I see that nothing but a flogging will force you to obey and today you've fully earned it."

He said this so loudly that everyone heard his words. The blood surged to my heart with extraordinary force; I felt how strongly it was

beating, felt the blood leaving my face and felt my lips begin to tremble completely involuntarily. I must have been awful at that moment
because St.-Jérôme, avoiding my gaze, quickly came up to me and
grasped my hand; but the moment I felt his hand touch me I felt so
sickened that, beside myself with fury, I tore my hand away and struck
him with all my childish might.

"What's the matter with you?" said Volodya, coming up to me, having watched my action with horror and astonishment.

"Leave me alone!" I cried at him through my tears. "None of you
love me, you don't understand how unhappy I am! You're all horrible,
disgusting," I added in a kind of frenzy, addressing the whole company.

But at this moment, his face pale and resolute, St.-Jérôme came up
to me again and, before I had time to prepare myself, with a powerful
gesture seized both my hands in a viselike grip and dragged me away
somewhere. My head was spinning with excitement; I only know that
I thrashed about desperately with my head and knees as long as I had
any strength left; I remember that my nose bumped against someone's
thighs several times and that somebody's coat got into my mouth, and
that on all sides around me I felt the presence of someone's legs
and was assailed by the smell of dust and of the *violette* with which
St.-Jérôme always scented himself.

Five minutes later the door of the box room closed behind me.

"Vasile!" said *he* in a loathsome triumphant voice, "bring me the
birch rod...."

XV

DAYDREAMS

I hardly dared think at that time that I would remain alive after all the calamities that had overtaken me, and that there would come a time when I would recall them with composure....

Remembering what I had done, I could not conceive what would happen to me; but I had a dim foreboding that I was irrevocably lost.

Below and around me complete silence reigned at first, or at least it seemed so as a result of my great inner agitation, but little by little I began to distinguish various sounds. Vasily came downstairs and, having thrown some object, which sounded like a broom, onto the window ledge, yawned and settled himself on a chest. From downstairs came the loud voice of St.-Jérôme (he was probably speaking about me), then children's voices, then laughter and the sound of running, and in a few moments everything in the house resumed its former momentum, as though nobody knew or thought about the fact that I was languishing in the dark box room.

I did not cry, but my heart was weighed down as though by a stone. Thoughts and fancies passed through my disordered imagination with redoubled speed; but the recollection of the calamity that had overtaken me constantly interrupted their phantasmagoric procession and I re-entered the trackless labyrinth of uncertainty concerning my imminent fate, and of despair and terror.

Sometimes I thought that there must be some mysterious reason for the general dislike and even hatred of me. (At that time I was firmly convinced that everyone, beginning with Grandmother and ending with Filipp the coachman, hated me and took pleasure in my sufferings.) I must not be my mother and father's son, nor Volodya's brother, but an unfortunate orphan, a foundling accepted out of charity, I say to myself, and this absurd idea not only offers me a kind of melancholy consolation but even seems to me to be the absolute truth. It is very gratifying to think I am unhappy not because I am at fault but because such is my destiny from birth and because my fate is similar to that of the unfortunate Karl Ivanich.

But why hide this secret any longer, now that I myself have managed to discover it? I say to myself. Tomorrow I will go to Papa and say: "Papa, there's no point in concealing the secret of my birth; I know it." He will say: "It can't be helped, my friend, you were sure to find out sooner or later—you are not my son, but I have adopted you and if you are worthy of my love I will never abandon you." And I will say to him: "Papa, although I have no right to call you by this name, nevertheless I now utter it for the last time; I have always loved you and always will and I shall never forget that you are my benefactor, but I cannot remain in your house. Nobody loves me here and St.-Jérôme has sworn that I shall perish. Either he or I must leave your house, because I cannot answer for myself: I hate that man so much that I will do anything. I'll kill him"—just like that: "Papa, I'll kill him." Papa will start to plead with me, but I shall wave my hand and say: "No, my friend, my benefactor, we cannot live together; let me go." And I shall embrace him and say in French for some reason: *"Oh, mon père, oh mon bienfaiteur, donne moi pour la dernière fois ta bénédiction et que la volonté de dieu soit faite!"* And I, sitting on a trunk in that dark box room, begin to sob convulsively at the thought of it. But suddenly I remember the shameful punishment that awaits me, reality appears to me in its true light, and my dreams at once dissolve.

Sometimes I imagine myself at large again, outside the house. I join the hussars and go to war. The enemy swoops down on me from all sides, I brandish my saber and kill one of them, another flourish and I kill a second, a third. Finally, utterly exhausted by my wounds and fatigue, I fall to the ground and cry: "Victory!" A general comes up to me and asks: "Where is he, our deliverer?" They point to me; he flings his arms round me and cries: "Victory!" I recover and with my arm in a black sling I stroll along Tverskoy Boulevard. I am a general! But now I meet *His Majesty* and he asks who that wounded young man is. They tell him it is the well-known hero, Nikolai. His Majesty comes up to me and says: "I thank you. I will do whatever you ask of me." I bow deferentially and say, leaning on my saber: "I am happy, Your Majesty, that I was able to shed blood for my country, and I would like to die for her; but since you are so gracious as to allow me to petition you, I have just one request: allow me to destroy my enemy, the foreigner St.-Jérôme. I would like to destroy my enemy, St.-Jérôme." I stand menacingly in front of St.-Jérôme and say to him: "You are the author of my misfortunes, *à genoux!*" But suddenly it occurs to me that at any moment the real St.-Jérôme might come in with the birch rod and once more I see myself not as a general saving his country, but as a most pitiful, tearful creature.

Sometimes I begin to think of God and I ask Him impertinently why He is punishing me. "I don't believe I forgot my prayers either in the morning or at night, so why am I suffering?" I can definitely say that the first step in the direction of the religious doubts that disturbed me during my boyhood was taken now, not because unhappiness prompted me to resentment and disbelief, but because the idea of the injustice of providence, which came into my mind during this period of complete emotional dislocation and twenty-four-hour spell of isolation, lodged there, like a bad seed that falls on ploughed earth after rain, and speedily began to flourish and put out roots. At times I thought I would certainly die and I vividly imagined to myself St.-Jérôme's astonishment when he found in the box room not me but a lifeless corpse. Recalling Natalya Savishna's stories about the way the soul of a dead person remains in the house for forty days, I thought of my death and mentally floated invisibly through all the rooms in Grandmother's house and eavesdropped on Lyubochka's heartfelt tears, on Grandmother's regrets and on Papa's conversation with St.-Jérôme. "He was a wonderful boy," Papa will say with tears in his eyes. "Yes," St.-Jérôme will say, "but a terrible scapegrace." "You should have respect for the dead," Papa will say, "you were the cause of his death, you frightened him, he could not endure the humiliation you were preparing for him. . . . Get out of here, villain!"

And St.-Jérôme will fall to his knees and weep and beg forgiveness. After forty days my soul flies off to heaven; I see something there that is amazingly beautiful, white, transparent, and long and I sense that it is my mother. This white something surrounds and fondles me; but I feel disturbed and somehow do not recognize her. "If it really is you," I say, "then appear to me better so I can embrace you." And her voice answers me: "We are all like this here; I cannot embrace you any better. Do you not like it this way?" "Yes, I like it very much, but you are unable to tickle me and I am unable to kiss your hands . . ." "That's not necessary, it's wonderful the way it is here," she says, and I feel that it really is wonderful and together we fly higher and higher. At this point I seem to wake up and find myself once more on the trunk in the dark box room, my cheeks wet with tears, without a single thought in my head, repeating over and over again: *And we keep flying higher and higher.* For a long time I bend all my efforts to the task of clarifying my position in my own mind; but the only prospect my mind can see in the present is a terribly gloomy and impenetrable void. I try to return once more to those delicious happy dreams that interrupted my consciousness of reality, but to my surprise, as soon as I re-enter the realm of my former dreams I see that their continuation is impossible, and, what is even more surprising, they no longer afford me the slightest satisfaction.

XVI

It Will All Come Out in the Wash

I spent the night in the box room and nobody came to see me; only on the following day, Sunday, was I taken to a small room next to the classroom and locked in again. I began to hope that my punishment would be limited to confinement and under the influence of a sweet refreshing sleep, the bright sunlight playing on frost patterns on the window, and the normal sounds in the street, my thoughts began to calm down. But isolation was nonetheless a burden: I wanted to move about, to tell someone of all that had accumulated inside me, and yet there was not a living soul within reach. This situation was all the more unpleasant for me because, no matter how loathsome it was to me, I could not help but hear St.-Jérôme as he walked about his room, whistling some jolly tunes with complete *sang-froid*. I was fully convinced that he did not feel a bit like whistling but was doing it solely to spite me.

At two o'clock St.-Jérôme and Volodya went downstairs while Nikolai brought me my dinner, and when I got into conversation with him about what I had done and what awaited me, he said:

"Ah, master, don't brood about it, it will all come out in the wash."

Although this maxim, which helped me more than once to maintain my firmness of purpose in later years, consoled me somewhat, nevertheless it was precisely the fact that they had sent me not just bread and water but a whole dinner, including even the special pastry dessert, that forced me to reconsider the matter more intensively. If they had not sent me dessert it would have meant that I was being punished by confinement, but now it emerged that I was still not punished, that I had merely been isolated from the others as a pernicious person, and that my punishment still lay ahead. While I was engrossed in resolving this question, a key turned in my prison door and St.-Jérôme came into the room with a grim official expression on his face.

"We're going to see your Grandmother," he said, not looking at me.

Before leaving the room I was about to clean off the sleeves of my tunic, which were covered with chalk, but St.-Jérôme told me that this was completely useless, as though I were already in such a pitiful moral condition that it was not worth bothering about my external appearance.

As St.-Jérôme led me by the hand through the salon, Katyenka, Lyubochka, and Volodya looked at me in exactly the same way as we usually looked at the convicts who were led past our windows every Monday. And when I went up to Grandmother's armchair with the intention of kissing her hand, she turned away from me and hid her hand under her shawl.

"Yes, dear boy," she said after a fairly lengthy silence, during which she inspected me from head to foot with such a look that I did not know what to do with my eyes and hands, "I may say that you highly value my love and are a true consolation to me. Monsieur St.-Jérôme, who at my request," she added, lingering over every word, "was charged with your education, does not now wish to remain in my house. And why? Because of you, dear boy. I had hoped that you would be grateful," she went on after a brief pause, and in a tone which showed that her words had been prepared in advance, "for his care and labors, that you would know how to value his services, but you, you milksop, you brat, decided to raise your hand against him. Very nice! Excellent! I too am beginning to think that you are incapable of understanding noble behavior, that other, baser measures are needed for you. . . . Beg his pardon at once," she added in a sternly commanding voice, pointing to St.-Jérôme, "do you hear?"

I followed the direction of Grandmother's hand with my eyes and, catching sight of St.-Jérôme's coat, turned away and did not move from the spot; once more I began to feel a sinking sensation in my heart.

"What? Do you not hear what I say to you?"

I trembled all over, but did not move from the spot.

"Coco!" said Grandmother, probably noticing the inner agony I was going through. "Coco," she said no longer so much commandingly as tenderly, "is this you?"

"Grandmother! I will not beg his pardon, not for anything . . ." I said and stopped suddenly, sensing that I would be unable to hold back the tears that were choking me if I said any more.

"I order you, I beg you. What's the matter with you?"

"I . . . I . . . don't . . . want to. . . . I can't," I said, and the dammed tears that had accumulated in my breast suddenly burst the barrier that had restrained them and poured forth in a desperate torrent.

"C'est ainsi que vous obéissez à votre seconde mère, c'est ainsi que vous re-connaissez ses bontés," said St.-Jérôme in a tragic voice, *"à genoux!"*

"Good heavens, if she had lived to see this!" said Grandmother, turning away from me and wiping away some tears that had appeared. "If she had seen . . . but it's all for the best. Yes, she would not have withstood this blow, would not have withstood it."

And Grandmother wept more and more. I wept also, but did not even contemplate begging for pardon.

"Tranquillisez-vous au nom du ciel, Madame la comtesse," said St.-Jérôme.

But Grandmother was no longer listening to him, she covered her face with her hands, and her weeping soon changed to hiccoughing and hysterics. Mimi and Gasha ran into the room with frightened faces, there was a smell of spirits, and suddenly the whole house was filled with scurrying and whispering.

"Admire your handiwork," said St.-Jérôme, leading me upstairs.

My God, what have I done? What a terrible criminal I am! I thought.

Having told me to go to my room, St.-Jérôme had no sooner gone downstairs than I, unaware of what I was doing, ran down the main staircase that led onto the street.

Whether I wanted to run away completely or to drown myself I do not remember; I know only that, covering my face with my hands in order not to see anybody, I ran farther and farther down the stairs.

"Where are you off to?" asked a familiar voice all of a sudden. "You're just the person I'm looking for, my boy."

I was about to run past him, but Papa seized me by the hand and said sternly:

"Come with me, dear fellow! How dare you touch the wallet in my study," he said, leading me after him into the small sitting room. "Eh? Why are you silent, eh?" he added, taking hold of my ear.

"I'm sorry," I said. "I don't know what came over me."

"Oh, so you don't know what came over you, don't know, don't know, don't know, don't know," he repeated, tweaking my ear with every word. "Are you going to poke your nose into things that don't concern you in the future, are you, are you?"

Despite the fact that I felt a terrible pain in my ear, I did not cry but experienced a pleasantly moral feeling. No sooner had Papa released my ear than I seized his hand and commenced tearfully to cover it with kisses.

"Beat me some more," I said through my tears, "harder, so it hurts more, I'm worthless, I'm vile, I'm a wretched boy."

"What's the matter with you?" he said, pushing me away slightly.

"No, not for anything will I go away," I said, clinging to his coat. "They all hate me, I know that, but for God's sake you listen to me and defend me, or else drive me out of the house. I can't live with him, *he* does everything he can to humiliate me and orders me to kneel at his feet and wants to flog me. I can't stand it, I'm not a little boy, I shan't be able to bear it, I'll die, I'll kill myself. *He* told Grandmother that I'm worthless; now she's ill and she'll die because of me, I . . . he . . . for God's sake flog me . . . why . . . do they . . . torture me?"

My tears were suffocating me, I sat on the sofa and, unable to say another word, fell with my head in his lap, sobbing so much that I thought I was bound to die immediately.

"What is it, youngster?" said Papa sympathetically, bending over me.

"*He* tyrannizes over me ... torments me ... I'll die ... nobody loves me!" I was just able to say before I was overtaken by convulsions.

Papa took me in his arms and carried me up to the bedroom. I fell asleep.

When I awoke it was already very late, one candle was burning by my bed, and our family doctor, Mimi, and Lyubochka were sitting in the room. From their faces it was clear that they feared for my health. But I felt so well and easy after my twelve-hour sleep that I would have leaped out of bed immediately, had I not been reluctant to disturb their conviction that I was very ill.

XVII

Hatred

Yes, it was genuine hatred, not the hatred that is only written about in novels and in which I do not believe, the hatred that is supposed to delight in doing harm to a man, but a hatred that fills you with an unconquerable loathing for someone—someone who nevertheless deserves your respect—and makes his hair, his neck, his walk, the sound of his voice, all his limbs and all his movements disgusting to you, while at the same time some incomprehensible force draws you to him and forces you to keep a close and uneasy watch on his every little act. This was what I felt toward St.-Jérôme.

St.-Jérôme had been living with us for a year and a half at that time. Judging this man now dispassionately, I find that he was a good Frenchman, but a Frenchman in the highest degree. He was not stupid, was tolerably well educated, and carried out his duties conscientiously as far as we were concerned, but he had the distinctive qualities—common to all his countrymen but so contrary to the Russian character—of frivolous egotism, vanity, impudence, and ignorant self-assurance. All this I found very unpleasant. It goes without saying that Grandmother had explained to him her opinion on the subject of corporal punishment and he did not dare to strike us; but in spite of this he frequently threatened us, and especially me, with a flogging and pronounced the word *fouetter* (somehow as *fouatter*) so repulsively and with such intonation that it seemed to me that flogging me would have given him the greatest satisfaction.

I was not in the least afraid of the pain of being punished since I had never experienced it, but the mere thought that St.-Jérôme might strike me drove me into a painful state of suppressed fury and despair.

It had happened that Karl Ivanich, in a moment of irritation, had personally chastised us with a ruler or suspenders, but I can recall this without the slightest indignation. Even at the time I am speaking of (when I was fourteen), if Karl Ivanich had happened to thrash me I would have borne his blows quite calmly. I loved Karl Ivanich, I remembered him ever since I remembered myself and was accustomed to considering him a member of the family; but St.-Jérôme was a proud conceited man, for whom I felt nothing but that involuntary respect which all *grown-ups* inspired in me. Karl Ivanich was a ridiculous old man, a *valet*, whom I loved from the heart, but whom I nevertheless placed below me in my childish conception of the social order.

St.-Jérôme, on the contrary, was a young handsome and educated man-about-town, who tried always to be on an equal footing with everyone. Karl Ivanich always scolded and punished us dispassionately, and it was clear that he considered this an unavoidable but nevertheless unpleasant duty. St.-Jérôme, on the contrary, loved to display himself in the role of schoolmaster; it was clear when he punished us that he was doing it more for his own enjoyment than for our benefit. He used to get carried away by his own grandness. His magnificent French phrases, which he spoke with a strong emphasis on the last syllable, with an *accent circonflex*, were for me inexpressively repulsive. When Karl Ivanich was angry he said: "Don't make a scene, or naughty poys, or Shpanish fly." St.-Jérôme called us *mauvais sujet, vilain, garnement,* and similar names, which offended my self-esteem.

Karl Ivanich would make us kneel in the corner, face to the wall, and the punishment consisted in the physical discomfort produced by such a position; St.-Jérôme, puffing out his chest and making a grandiose gesture with his arm, would cry in a typical voice: *"À genoux, mauvais sujet!"* and would order us to kneel facing him and beg his pardon. The punishment consisted in the humiliation.

I was not punished and no one even referred to what had happened, but I was unable to forget everything that I had experienced—the despair, shame, terror, and hatred of those two days. Despite the fact that from that time onward St.-Jérôme apparently gave me up and hardly bothered with me at all, I was unable to accustom myself to looking upon him with indifference. Whenever our eyes met accidentally, it seemed to me that my look expressed a too-open hostility and I hastened to assume an air of indifference, but then it seemed to me that he understood my pretence and I blushed and turned away altogether.

In short, it was inexpressibly painful for me to have anything whatsoever to do with him.

XVIII

THE MAIDS' ROOM

I felt myself more and more lonely, and my chief pleasure now came from solitary meditations and observation. Of the subject of my meditations I shall speak in the following chapter; but the theater of my observations was primarily the maids' room, wherein a touching and for me extremely absorbing romance was taking place. It goes without saying that the heroine of this romance was Masha. She was in love with Vasily, who had known her before she became a maid and had promised to marry her then. Destiny, having separated them for five years, had brought them together again in Grandmother's house, but had placed a barrier before their mutual love in the person of Nikolai (Masha's uncle), who would not even hear of his niece's marriage to Vasily, whom he called *unbridled* and *incompatible*.

This barrier had caused Vasily, formerly somewhat cold and cavalier in his treatment of her, to fall suddenly in love with Masha, and to fall in love as only a house serf can, and moreover a tailor, with a pink shirt and oil on his hair.

Despite the fact that the manifestations of his love were extremely strange and incongruous (for instance, when meeting Masha he always tried to hurt her and would either pinch her or slap her with his hand, or else would hug her so fiercely that she could scarcely breathe), his actual love was sincere, which was proved by the fact that from the time Nikolai finally refused him his niece's hand, Vasily took to *drinking* from grief and began to hang around bars and get into scrapes—in short to behave so badly that he was more than once subjected to ignominious punishment in the cells. But these actions and their consequences, it seemed, were a merit in Masha's eyes and merely increased her love for him. When Vasily was being *kept in detention,* Masha wept for whole days without drying her eyes, complained of her bitter fate to Gasha (who took a lively interest in the affairs of the unfortunate lovers), and, scorning her uncle's abuse and blows, ran to the police station in secret in order to visit and console her friend.

Do not disdain, reader, the society into which I am bringing you. If the chords of love and sympathy have not withered away in your heart, there are notes in the maids' room which will evoke an answering response. Whether you do or do not see fit to follow me, I shall proceed to the landing from which I can see all that goes on in the maids' room. Here is the wide bench on which an iron stands, and a hand basin; over here is the windowsill with an untidy collection of objects on it: a piece of black wax, a skein of silk, a half-eaten green cucumber and a chocolate box; over there is the big red table with a calico-covered brick on it, holding down some half-finished sewing, and behind it *she* sits in my favorite pink linen dress and blue kerchief, which particularly attracts my attention. *She* is sewing, stopping from time to time to scratch her head with the needle or adjust the candle, while I gaze at her and think: Why was she not born a lady, with those bright blue eyes, that enormous braid of blonde hair and that firm bosom? How would she look sitting in a drawing room, wearing a bonnet with pink ribbons and a crimson silk robe, not like Mimi's but like the one I saw on Tverskoy Boulevard? She would be doing crochet work and I would look at her in the mirror, and whatever she wanted I'd do for her; I'd hand her her mantle, serve the food myself . . .

And what a drunken face and repulsive figure this Vasily makes in his tight coat over a dirty pink shirt, pulled out for display! In every movement and in every curve of his back I seem to see unmistakable signs of the repulsive punishment that has overtaken him. . . .

"What, again, Vasya?" said Masha, sticking her needle into the pincushion and not raising her head to greet the newly arrived Vasya.

"What of it? What good can you expect from him?" replied Vasily. "If only he'd settle the matter somehow, else I'll go to ruin for nothing, and all because of *him*."

"Will you have some tea?" said Nadezha, another maid.

"Thank you very much. And why does that thief of an uncle of yours hate me? Because I have real clothes of my own, because of my swank and walk. In short. Oh, well!" concluded Vasily with a wave of his hand.

"One should be obedient," said Masha, biting her thread off, "but you always..."

"I've had enough, that's why!"

At this moment there came the sound of Grandmother's door slamming and the grumbling voice of Gasha as she came upstairs.

"Just try and please her when she herself doesn't know what she wants... damned life this is, hard labor! There's just one thing I wish, but the Lord forgive me my sins for wishing it," she muttered, waving her arms about.

"My respects, Agafya Mikhailovna," said Vasily, rising to greet her.

"Oh, so you're here! What do I want with your respects!" she replied threateningly, looking at him. "And why do you come here? Is the maids' room a place for men to visit?"

"I wanted to ask how you were," said Vasily timidly.

"I'll kick the bucket soon, that's how I am," shouted Gasha at the top of her voice, still more angry than before.

Vasily laughed.

"There's nothing to laugh at in that, and when I say get out that means quick-march! Look at him, the scoundrel, and he wants to get married into the bargain, the villain! Well, scram, get going!"

And stamping her feet Gasha went through into her own room, slamming the door so hard behind her that the panes rattled in the windows.

For a long time afterwards she could be heard behind the partition, abusing everything and everyone, cursing her life, flinging her things about, and pulling her favorite cat by the ears; finally the door opened and out flew the pitifully mewing cat, flung by the tail.

"I think I'd better come another time for tea," whispered Vasily. "A very good day to you."

"It's nothing," said Nadezha with a wink. "I'll go take a look at the samovar."

"Yes, and I'll put an end to it once and for all," went on Vasily, sitting closer to Masha as soon as Nadezha had left the room. "Either I'll go straight to the Countess and say: 'So and so,' or else I'll . . . throw it all up and go off to the ends of the earth, I swear to God I will."

"And what will I do here?"

"It's you alone I feel sorry for, otherwise I'd have been out of here a-ages ago, I swear to God, I would, I swear to God."

"Why don't you bring me your shirts to wash, Vasya?" said Masha after a moment's silence. "Look how dirty it is," she added, taking hold of his shirt collar.

At this moment there came the sound of Grandmother's bell downstairs and Gasha came out of her room.

"Well, villain, what are you trying to get from her now?" she said, pushing Vasily, who had hastily risen at the sight of her, toward the door. "Look what the girl's been brought to and still you pester her; I suppose you enjoy seeing her tears, you bare-faced wretch. Clear out. Out of my sight. And what good can you find in him?" she went on, turning to Masha. "Didn't your uncle thrash you enough today on his account? But no, you must have your own way: I shan't marry anyone but Vasily Gruskov. Fool!"

"No, and I won't either, I don't love anybody else, even if they kill me stone-dead because of him," said Masha, dissolving into tears all of a sudden.

I was a long time gazing at Masha, who lay on the chest wiping her tears away with her kerchief, and I did everything I could to alter my view of Vasily and tried to discover the point of view from which he could seem attractive to her. But despite the fact that I sincerely sympathized with her grief, I was completely unable to comprehend how such a bewitching creature as Masha, or so she seemed to me, could love Vasily.

When I'm grown up, I reflected when I had gone upstairs to my room, the Petrovsky estate will come to me and Vasily and Masha will be my serfs. I shall sit in my study, smoking a pipe, and Masha will pass by on her way to the kitchen, holding an iron. I shall say: "Send Masha to me." She will come and there will be no one else in the room. . . . Suddenly Vasily will come in and when he sees Masha will say: "I am lost!" and Masha will also cry; and I shall say: "Vasily, I know that you love her and that she loves you, here are a thousand rubles for you; marry her, and may God make you happy!" And I shall go into the sitting room. . . . Among the innumerable thoughts and daydreams that pass through the mind and imagination without a trace, there are some that leave a deep sensitive furrow, so that frequently, while no longer remembering the essence of the thought, you remember that there was something pleasant in your mind, you are aware of the thought's traces and you try to resurrect it again. It was just such a deep trace that was left in my heart by the thought of sacrificing my feelings for the sake of Masha's happiness, a happiness which she could only find in being married to Vasily.

XIX

BOYHOOD

People will scarcely believe what were the favorite and most constant subjects of my meditations during boyhood—so incongruous were they with my age and situation. But, in my opinion, incongruity between a man's situation and his moral activity is the surest sign of truth.

In the course of the year during which I led a solitary moral life, turned in upon myself, I was already confronted by all the abstract questions concerning man's destiny, the future life, and the immortality of the soul; and my feeble childish mind endeavored with all the ardor of inexperience to comprehend those questions whose formulation constitutes the highest degree that man's mind can attain, but whose resolution is not granted to him.

It seems to me that the human mind in each individual follows the same path in its development as that of whole generations, that the ideas which serve as the basis of various philosophical theories constitute inalienable attributes of that mind, and that each man is more or less aware of them before he even knows of the existence of philosophical theories.

These thoughts occurred to my mind with such clarity and vividness that I even attempted to apply them in life, imagining that I was the *first* to discover such great and useful truths.

Once I had the idea that happiness does not depend on external causes but on our attitude to them, that a man accustomed to enduring suffering cannot be unhappy, and so, in order to accustom myself to hardship, I held, despite the terrible pain, Tatishchev's dictionaries outstretched at arm's length for five minutes at a time, or else went off to the box room and lashed my bare back with a rope so painfully that my eyes involuntarily filled with tears.

Another time, recollecting suddenly that death awaited me at any hour, at any minute, I decided, unable to understand how people had not realized it before, that man could not otherwise be happy than by taking full advantage of the present and not thinking of the past—and for three days, under the influence of this idea, I abandoned my lessons and occupied myself solely with lying on the bed, enjoying myself reading some novel or other, and eating gingerbread and honey, which I had bought with my last pocket money.

On one occasion I was standing before the blackboard and chalking various figures on it when I was suddenly struck by the thought: Why is symmetry pleasant to the eye? What is symmetry? It is an inborn feeling, I answered myself. But what is it based on? Not everything in life is symmetrical, is it? On the contrary, here is life—and I drew an oval figure on the board. After life the soul passes into infinity; here is infinity—and from one side of the oval I drew a line to the very edge of the board. Why is there no such line on the other side? And indeed, how can there be infinity on one side only? We must have existed before this life, although we've lost all recollection of it.

This argument—which seemed extraordinarily new and clear to me and whose thread I can only just manage to capture now—pleased me extraordinarily, and taking up a sheet of paper I thought to expound it in writing, but at this point such a welter of thoughts surged into my head that I was obliged to stand up and walk about the room. When I came to the window my attention was attracted by the water horse, which the coachman was harnessing at this moment, and all my thoughts concentrated on resolving the question: Into what animal or person will the soul of this water horse go when it expires? At that moment Volodya passed through the room and smiled when he noticed that I was meditating about something, and this smile was enough for me to realize that everything I was thinking was the most awful rubbish.

I have related this incident, which for some reason I find memorable, merely in order to give the reader an idea of the nature of my philosophizing.

But not one of the philosophical trends carried me away so completely as did skepticism, which at one time brought me to a condition bordering on madness. I imagined that, besides myself, nothing and no one existed in the whole world, that objects were not objects but images, which appeared only when I turned my attention to them, and that as soon as I ceased thinking of them these images disappeared. In short, I agreed with Schelling in the conviction that it was not objects that existed but only my attitude to them. There were moments when, under the influence of this *idée fixe*, I reached such a stage of lunacy that sometimes I would look quickly in the opposite direction, hoping to catch nothingness *(néant)* unawares while I was not there.

What a pitiful worthless spring of moral action is the mind of man!

My feeble mind was unable to penetrate the impenetrable and in this impossible labor it lost, one after the other, beliefs that, for my happiness in life, I ought never to have dared to touch.

From all this heavy moral labor I derived nothing except an agility of mind that diminished my will power and a habit of perpetual moral analysis that destroyed freshness of feeling and clearness of judgment.

Abstract ideas are formed as a result of man's ability to apprehend with his consciousness at any given moment the state of his mind and to transfer it to his memory. My fondness for abstract reasoning developed my consciousness to such an unnatural degree that frequently, when starting to think of the simplest thing, I entered a vicious circle of mental self-analysis, so that I no longer thought of the original question, but thought only of what I was thinking about. Asking myself: What am I thinking of? I would reply: I am thinking of what I am thinking. And what am I thinking of now? I am thinking that I am thinking of what I am thinking, and so on. My mind went round in circles. . . .

Nevertheless, the philosophical discoveries I made were extraordinarily flattering to my self-esteem: I frequently imagined myself to be a great man, discovering new truths for the good of all mankind, and I gazed at other mortals with proud consciousness of my merit; but, strange to say, when coming into contact with these mortals, I was shy in the presence of all of them and the higher I rated myself in my own opinion, not only was I the less capable with others of displaying my consciousness of this merit, but I could not even accustom myself to not feeling ashamed of every little word and gesture.

XX

VOLODYA

Yes, the further I go in describing this period of my life, the more difficult and painful it becomes for me. Rarely, rarely among my reminiscences of this time do I find moments of that genuine warmth of feeling that so vividly and continually illumined the beginning of my life. I involuntarily prefer to skip the desert of my boyhood and reach that happy time when a truly tender, noble feeling of friendship bathed the end of this period in brilliant light and established the beginning of a new period, one that was full of charm and poetry—youth.

I shall not trace my recollections hour by hour, but shall cast a swift glance at the most important ones from the moment that I have reached in my narrative until my association with a remarkable man who exerted a decisive and beneficial influence on my character and development.

Volodya is about to enter the university, teachers already come to him separately, and I listen enviously and with unwilling respect as, rapping the blackboard confidently with his chalk, he interprets functions, sines, coordinates, etc., which seem to me to be the expressions of inaccessible wisdom. And now, one Sunday after dinner, all the teachers and two professors assemble in Grandmother's room and in the presence of Papa and several visitors, conduct a rehearsal of the university entrance examination in which Volodya, to Grandmother's delight, displays remarkable learning. I am also asked questions on several subjects, but I turn out to be very poor and apparently the professors are endeavoring to conceal my ignorance from Grandmother, which confuses me even more. However, little attention is paid to me: I am only fifteen and therefore still have a year to wait before my examination. Volodya only comes down for dinner and spends whole days and even evenings upstairs at his studies, not from necessity but of his own volition. He is extraordinarily vain and wants not merely a pass but distinction.

But now the day of the first examination is here. Volodya dons a blue frock coat with bronze buttons, a gold watch, and patent leather boots; Papa's phaeton is brought to the front door, Nikolai throws the canopy back, and Volodya rides to the university with St.-Jérôme. The girls, Katyenka in particular, look out of the window with joyful, enraptured faces as the graceful figure of Volodya gets into the carriage and Papa says: "God grant, God grant," while Grandmother, who has also dragged herself to the window, with tears in her eyes, makes the sign of the cross over Volodya until the phaeton has disappeared around the corner into a side street, and whispers something.

Volodya returns. Everyone asks impatiently: "How was it? All right? How many?" but it is already clear from Volodya's beaming face that everything is all right. Volodya received full marks. The following day he is seen off with the same good wishes and anxiety, and greeted once more with the same impatience and delight. So it goes on for nine days. On the tenth day comes the last and most difficult examination—religious knowledge; we all stand at the window and await him with even greater impatience. Two o'clock already and no Volodya.

"Good heavens! Look!!! It's them!!! Them!!" shrieks Lyubochka, glued to the window.

And truly, there beside St.-Jérôme in the phaeton sits Volodya, but no longer in a blue frock coat and gray cap, but in student's uniform with an embroidered light-blue collar, wearing a three-cornered hat and with a gilded sword at his side.

"Oh, if only you were alive, my child!" exclaims Grandmother at the sight of Volodya and falls into a swoon.

Volodya runs into the front hall with a beaming face and kisses and embraces me, Lyubochka, Mimi, and Katyenka, who thereupon blushes to the ears. Volodya is beside himself with joy. And how handsome he is in his uniform! How well his light-blue collar suits his tentative young mustache! What a long slim waist he has and what a noble walk! On this red-letter day everyone dines in Grandmother's room, faces beam with delight, and after dinner, during dessert, the butler with a decently grave but at the same time cheerful countenance brings in a bottle of champagne wrapped in a napkin. Grandmother is drinking champagne for the first time since *maman* died; she drinks a whole glass in honor of Volodya and once more weeps for joy, looking at him. Volodya already goes out alone in his own carriage, receives *his guests in his room,* smokes, goes to balls, and once I even saw him drink two bottles of champagne in his room with his friends, and with each glass they drank the health of some mysterious persons and then quarreled over who would get *le fond de la bouteille.* He dines regularly at home, however, and after dinner sits in the sitting room the way he always used to and talks endlessly with Katyenka about something mysterious; but as far as I can make out—as a nonparticipant in their conversations—they talk only of the heroes and heroines they have read about in novels and of love and jealousy; and it is completely beyond me what they can find so interesting in such conversations and why they smile so delicately and argue so heatedly.

In general I notice that besides understandable friendship between childhood companions there exists between them some sort of peculiar relationship that separates them from us and binds the two of them closer together.

XXI

KATYENKA AND LYUBOCHKA

Katyenka is now sixteen; she is grown up; that angularity of figure, bashfulness, and awkwardness of movement natural to a girl in adolescence have given way to the harmonious freshness and gracefulness of a newly blossomed flower; but she has not changed. She has the same light-blue eyes and smiling regard, the same Roman nose, forming a straight line with her forehead, and with its firm nostrils, the same little mouth with its radiant smile, the same tiny dimples on her transparent pink cheeks, the same pale little hands . . . and for some reason the description of her as a *clean* little girl still suits her remarkably well. The only new things about her are the thick braid of blonde hair, which she wears like an adult, and her young breasts, whose appearance plainly delights yet shames her.

Although Lyubochka always grew up and was brought up with her, she is a completely different girl in every respect.

Lyubochka is short and as a result of having had rickets her legs are still bandy and her waist atrocious. The only good thing about her physically is her eyes, and these eyes are truly beautiful—large, black, and with such an indefinably pleasant expression of gravity and naïveté in them that they cannot fail to arrest the attention. Lyubochka is simple and natural in everything; Katyenka seems to wish to resemble someone else. Lyubochka always looks straight at people and sometimes, letting her enormous black eyes rest on someone, she keeps them there so long that she is scolded for this and told she is impolite; Katyenka, on the other hand, lowers her lashes, screws up her eyes, and says she is short-sighted, though I know for a fact that her vision is excellent. Lyubochka does not like to put on a pose in front of strangers and when some guest starts to kiss her she pouts and says she can't endure *sentiment;* Katyenka, on the other hand, always becomes particularly tender with Mimi when guests are present and loves to walk about the salon arm in arm with another girl. Lyubochka has a terribly loud laugh and sometimes, in an outburst of merriment, waves her arms about and runs about the room; Katyenka, on the other hand, covers her mouth with her handkerchief or her hand whenever she begins to laugh. Lyubochka always sits erect and walks with her hands at her sides; Katyenka holds her head slightly to one side and walks with her arms folded. Lyubochka is always terribly pleased when she has managed to talk to a grown-up man and says she definitely wants to marry a hussar; Katyenka says that all men disgust her and that she will never marry, and she changes completely, as if she is afraid of something, when a man talks to her. Lyubochka is always indignant with Mimi for lacing her corsets so that she "cannot breathe," and she likes eating; Katyenka, on the other hand, frequently hooks her finger under the point of her bodice to show us how much room she has, and she eats remarkably little. Lyubochka likes to draw heads; Katyenka draws only flowers and butterflies. Lyubochka plays Field's concertos extremely correctly and also some of Beethoven's sonatas; Katyenka plays variations and waltzes, slows down the tempo, uses the pedal constantly, and before beginning to play something dashes off three arpeggios with great enthusiasm....

But Katyenka, as I saw it then, was much more like a grown-up, and for that reason I liked her more.

XXII

PAPA

Papa has been particularly gay since Volodya entered the university and comes to dine with Grandmother more often than usual. The reason for his gaiety, however, as I have learned from Nikolai, is that lately he has been winning an extraordinary amount of money. It even happens that, before going to his club of an evening he comes in to us, sits down at the piano, gathers us around him, and sings gypsy songs, tapping out the time with his soft shoes (he cannot bear heels and never wears them). And one should see then the bliss of his favorite, Lyubochka, who for her part adores him as well. Sometimes he comes to the classroom and with a stern face listens to me saying my lessons, but from certain words that he uses in trying to correct me I notice that he himself has only a poor knowledge of what I am being taught. Sometimes he winks at us on the sly and makes signs when Grandmother starts to grumble and get angry at us for no reason. "Well, *we* got it in the neck that time, children," he says afterwards. On the whole he has come down somewhat in my eyes from that unattainable height on which my childish imagination had placed him. I still kiss his large white hand with the same sincere feelings of love and respect, but now

I allow myself to think about him, to judge his actions, and the thoughts of him that occur to me also frighten me. Never shall I forget the incident that inspired so many of these thoughts in me and caused me to undergo much moral suffering.

Once, late one evening, he came into the drawing room dressed in his black dress coat and white vest in order to take Volodya to a ball with him; Volodya was getting dressed in his room at the time. Grandmother was waiting in her room for Volodya to come and show himself to her (she had a habit of summoning him to her before each ball, blessing him, inspecting him, and giving him instructions). In the salon, which was lit by a single lamp, Mimi and Katyenka were walking back and forth, while Lyubochka was sitting at the piano practicing Field's second concerto, *maman*'s favorite piece.

Never in anyone have I met such a family likeness as between my mother and sister. This likeness lay neither in Lyubochka's face nor in her build, but in something intangible: in her hands, in her way of walking, and particularly in her voice and in certain of her expressions. When Lyubochka became angry and said: "It's ages since we were allowed out," the expression *it's ages,* which *maman* had also been in the habit of using, she pronounced in such a way that one thought one was hearing *maman.* She sort of drew it out: *it's a-a-ages;* but this likeness was most striking in her piano playing and in her mannerisms while at the piano: she adjusted her dress the same way, she turned the music pages with her left hand from the top the same way, and she would bring her fist down on the keys the same way when annoyed by her continuing inability to master a difficult passage, and say: "Oh, good heavens!" And she had that same elusive tenderness and precision in her playing, especially of that beautiful Fieldian music which is so well termed *jeu perlé,* and whose magic not all the hocus-pocus of our latest pianists can force one to forget.

Papa came into the room with quick little steps and went up to Lyubochka, who ceased playing at the sight of him.

"No, no, go on, Lyuba, go on," he said, pressing her back into her seat. "You know how I like to listen to you."

Lyubochka went on playing and Papa sat opposite her for a long, long time, chin in hand; then, with a quick twitch of his shoulder, he stood up and began to walk about the room. Each time he came close to the piano he stopped and looked at Lyubochka long and intently. From his movements and way of walking I could see that he was agitated. After having walked up and down the salon several times, he stopped behind Lyubochka's chair, kissed her black hair, then turned quickly and went on with his walking. When, having finished the piece, Lyubochka went up to him and asked: "Was it all right?", he took her head silently and began to kiss her forehead and eyes with such tenderness as I had never seen in him before.

"Oh, good heavens, you're crying!" said Lyubochka all of a sudden, letting his watchchain slip from her hands and fixing her big surprised eyes on his face. "Forgive me, darling Papa, I completely forgot that that was *Mama's piece.*"

"No, my friend, you must play it more often," he said, his voice quivering with emotion. "If only you knew how nice it is for me to weep with you . . ."

He kissed her once more and, still trying to overcome his inner disturbance, his shoulder twitching, went out of the door that led, via a corridor, to Volodya's room.

"*Waldemar!* Will you soon be ready?" he cried, stopping in the corridor. At that very moment the maid Masha passed by; at the sight of her master she lowered her eyes and wanted to walk round him. He stopped her.

"You're getting prettier and prettier," he said, leaning toward her.

Masha blushed and lowered her head still more.

"Excuse me," she whispered.

"*Waldemar,* come on, how much longer?" repeated Papa, shrugging and clearing his throat when Masha had passed and he caught sight of me.

I love my father, but man's mind leads a life independent of his heart and frequently harbors thoughts that offend his feelings and are cruel and incomprehensible to him. And these are the thoughts, despite my efforts to repel them, that sometimes come to me. . . .

XXIII

GRANDMOTHER

Grandmother is growing weaker from day to day; her bell, Gasha's grumbling voice, and the slamming of doors are heard more and more often in her room, and she no longer receives us in her study, sitting in her Voltaire armchair, but in her bedroom, lying on her high bed with its lace-bordered pillows. When I greet her I notice a sallow shiny swelling on her hand and in her room there is that oppressive smell that I noticed in Mama's room five years ago. The doctor comes to her three times a day and there have already been several consultations. But her character and her haughty ceremonious dealings with the whole household, and particularly with Papa, have not changed in the least; she draws out her words in exactly the same way as before and raises her eyebrows, saying "my dear man."

And now it is several days since we have been allowed in to see her and one morning, during classes, St.-Jérôme suggests I go for a sleighride with Lyubochka and Katyenka. Despite the fact that, as I enter the sleigh, I notice straw strewn on the street before Grand-mother's windows and some men in blue overcoats standing at our gate, I cannot conceive why we are being sent out for a ride at such an unsuitable hour. Today, for some reason, throughout our ride, Lyubochka and I happen to be in that particularly merry mood in which each simple incident, each word and each gesture send us into fits of laughter.

A peddler, clutching his tray, crosses the road at a trot and we burst out laughing. A tattered cabby overtakes us at a gallop, waving the ends of his reins about, and we roar with laughter. Filipp's whip gets caught under one of the runners; he turns round and says "Oh, bother," and we die of laughing. Mimi says, looking displeased, that only *idiots* laugh without reason and Lyubochka, all red from the pressure of suppressed laughter, gives me a sidelong look. Our eyes meet and we burst into such Homeric laughter that tears come to our eyes and we are completely incapable of containing the bursts of laughter that are suffocating us. And no sooner have we calmed down a little than I look at Lyubochka and say one of our code words, one that has been a favorite of ours for some time now and that always produces a laugh, and once more we split our sides.

As we approach the house on our return I have just opened my mouth to pull a superb face at Lyubochka when my eyes are struck by the black lid of a coffin, which is leaning against one of the double doors of our front entrance, and my mouth remains frozen in that distorted position.

"Votre grande-mère est morte!" says St.-Jérôme with a pale face, coming out to meet us.

The whole time Grandmother's body remains in the house I experience an oppressive feeling which is fear of death, that is the dead body reminds me vividly and unpleasantly of the fact that I too must die sometime; it is a feeling that for some reason people are accustomed to confuse with sorrow. I am not sorry for Grandmother, and indeed there is hardly a soul who feels sincerely sorry for her. Despite the fact that the house is full of mourners who have come to see Grandmother, nobody is sorry for her death, with the exception of one person whose violent grief astonishes me inexpressibly. And this person is—the maid, Gasha. She goes off to the attic, locks herself in and weeps incessantly, cursing herself, tearing her hair and refusing to listen to any advice, saying that death remains her only consolation after the loss of her beloved mistress.

I repeat that incongruity in the matter of feeling is the surest sign of truth.

Grandmother is no more, but reminiscences and various rumors about her live on in the house. These rumors are concerned primarily with the will, which she made shortly before her end and whose contents nobody knows, save for her executor, Prince Ivan Ivanich. I notice a certain excitement among Grandmother's servants and I often hear rumors about who is to get what, and I must confess that involuntarily and with pleasure I think of the fact that the inheritance will come to us.

After six weeks Nikolai, the perpetual newspaper in our house, tells me that Grandmother has left her whole estate to Lyubochka, entrusting the guardianship of it until her marriage not to Papa but to Prince Ivan Ivanich.

XXIV

Me

Only a few months remain now until I enter the university. I am studying well. Not only do I await my teachers without fear, but I even experience a certain pleasure in class.

I enjoy repeating the lesson I have learned clearly and precisely. I am preparing to enter the faculty of mathematics and I have made this choice, to tell the truth, solely because I have an extraordinary liking for such words as sines, tangents, differentials, integrals, and so on.

I am much shorter than Volodya, broad-shouldered, beefy, and still as ugly and still tormented by it. I try to seem original. One thing consoles me: this is that Papa once said of me that I have a *clever puss*, and I fully believe it.

St.-Jérôme is pleased with me, he praises me, and not only do I not hate him, but, when he sometimes says of me that *with my abilities, with my intelligence*, I ought to be ashamed of not doing so-and-so and so-and-so, it even seems to me that I like him.

My watch on the maids' room has long since come to an end; I am ashamed to hide behind the door, and moreover the conviction that Masha really is in love with Vasily has somewhat cooled my ardor.

And I am finally cured of this unfortunate passion by Vasily's marriage, which I myself, at his request, have petitioned my father for.

When the *newlyweds* come to thank Papa with a tray of candies and Masha, wearing a bonnet with blue ribbons on it, also thanks us for something or other and kisses each one of us on the shoulder, I am aware only of the smell of pink hair oil coming from her and am not in the least excited.

In general I am beginning to be cured of my boyhood shortcomings, except, that is, for the main one, which is still destined to cause me a great deal more harm in life—and that is my bent for philosophizing.

XXV

VOLODYA'S FRIENDS

Although in the company of Volodya's friends I played a role that offended my self-esteem, I loved to sit in his room when he had visitors and silently observe what went on. Those who came to see Volodya most were an adjutant by the name of Dubkov and a student named Prince Nekhlyudov. Dubkov was a small sinewy fellow with a dark complexion; he was no longer so very young and was somewhat short in the legs, yet he was quite good-looking and always gay. He was one of those narrow-minded people who are especially attractive precisely because of their narrow-mindedness, who are incapable of seeing things from different sides and who are always being carried away. Such people's judgments are one-sided and mistaken, but they are always candid and engaging. Even their narrow egotism seems for some reason pardonable and appealing. Apart from this Dubkov had for Volodya and me a dual fascination: his military appearance and, more important, his age—which for some reason young men are in the habit of confusing with the concept of gentlemanliness *(comme il faut)*, which is highly prized by them at this time of life. However, Dubkov really was what one calls *un homme comme il faut*. The only thing I disliked was that Volodya sometimes seemed to be ashamed in his presence of even my most innocent actions, and most of all of my youth.

Nekhlyudov was unattractive: his little gray eyes, low steep forehead, and disproportionately long arms and legs could hardly be called handsome. The only attractive things about him were his remarkable height, the delicate coloring of his face, and his beautiful teeth. But this face was endowed with such an original and energetic character by his close-set gleaming eyes and mobile expression—now stern, now vaguely childlike and smiling—that it was impossible not to be struck by it.

Evidently he was very shy, because every trifle made him blush to the ears; but his bashfulness was not like mine. The more he blushed the more resolute his face looked. As though he were angry at himself for his weakness.

Despite the fact that he seemed very friendly with Dubkov and Volodya, it was clear that only chance had brought them together. Their attitudes were totally different: Volodya and Dubkov seemed to be afraid of anything that resembled a serious discussion or emotion; Nekhlyudov, on the contrary, was enthusiastic in the highest degree and frequently, despite the others' mockery, launched into discussions of philosophical questions and the emotions. Volodya and Dubkov liked to talk of the objects of their love (and were suddenly in love with several people and both with the same ones); Nekhlyudov, on the other hand, always became really angry when they hinted at his love and referred to some *redhead*.

Volodya and Dubkov often allowed themselves, jokingly, to make fun of their relatives; Nekhlyudov, on the other hand, could be driven to fury by an unfavorable reference to his aunt, whom he worshipped almost ecstatically. Volodya and Dubkov used to go somewhere after supper and called him a *pretty girl.* . . .

Prince Nekhlyudov impressed me from the very first both by his conversation and his appearance. But despite the fact that I found much in his attitude that coincided with mine—or perhaps precisely for that reason—the feelings he aroused in me the first time I saw him were far from friendly.

I did not like his swift glance, his firm voice, and his proud demeanor, but most of all I disliked the complete indifference which he showed to me. Often during a conversation I felt a terrible desire to contradict him, to outargue him as a punishment for his haughtiness, and to prove to him that I too was intelligent, despite the fact that he did not wish to pay attention to me. But my shyness prevented me.

XXVI

DISCUSSIONS

Volodya was lying with his feet up on the sofa and leaning on one elbow, reading a French novel, when I went in to see him—as I usually did—after my evening classes. He raised his head for a second to look at me and resumed his reading again—a perfectly simple and natural gesture, but one that made me blush. It seemed to me that his glance held a question: why had I come there, and the swift bending of his head a desire to conceal from me the meaning of this glance. This tendency to endow the simplest gesture with meaning was a characteristic trait of mine at that age. I went to the table and also picked up a book; but before I began to read, it occurred to me that it was somehow funny for the two of us, not having seen one another all day, to say nothing to one another.

"What, are you staying home this evening?"

"I don't know, why?"

"I just asked," I said, seeing that the conversation was not getting anywhere, then took the book and started to read.

It is odd that when Volodya and I were alone together we passed whole hours in silence, but it was sufficient for even the most taciturn third person to be present and we struck up the most varied and interesting conversations. We felt that we knew one another too well. And knowing too much of one another inhibits intimacy as much as knowing too little.

"Is Volodya home?" came Dubkov's voice from the vestibule.

"Yes," said Volodya, taking his feet off the sofa and putting his book on the table.

Dubkov and Nekhlyudov came into the room in their hats and coats.

"Well, are you coming to the theater, Volodya?"

"No, I've no time," replied Volodya, turning red.

"A likely story! Come on, let's go."

"I don't have a ticket."

"You can get as many as you like at the door."

"Just a minute, I'll be right back," replied Volodya evasively, and with a twitch of his shoulder left the room.

I knew that Volodya was very keen to go to the theater with Dubkov, that he had refused only because he had no money and that he had gone out in order to get a loan of five rubles from the butler until his next allowance.

"How are you, *diplomat!*" said Dubkov, giving me his hand.

Volodya's friends called me the *diplomat* because once, after they had dined at Grandmother's, she had somehow, in their presence, expanded on the subject of our futures and had said that Volodya would be a soldier and that she hoped to see me a *diplomat* in a black frock coat and with my hair *à la coq*, which in her opinion constituted an indispensable condition of diplomatic service.

"Where did Volodya go?" Nekhlyudov asked me.

"I don't know," I replied, blushing at the thought that they were sure to guess what he had gone out for.

"I don't suppose he has any money! Right? Oh, *diplomat!*" he added affirmatively, interpreting my smile. "I don't have any either, what about you, Dubkov?"

"Let's have a look," said Dubkov, getting his purse out and with extreme care fingering some small change with his stubby fingers. "Here's five copecks, here's a little twenty-copeck piece—and that's about it," he said, making a comical gesture with his hand.

At this moment Volodya entered the room.

"All right, shall we go?"

"No."

"How comical you are!" said Nekhlyudov. "Why don't you say you have no money. Take my ticket if you want."

"And what about you?"

"He'll join his cousins in their box."

"No, I won't go at all."

"Why?"

"Because, as you know, I don't like to sit in a box."

"Why?"

"I don't like to, I feel awkward."

"The same old story again! I don't understand how you can feel awkward when everyone's glad to have you there. It's absurd, *mon cher.*"

"What's to be done, *si je suis timide?* I'm sure you've never blushed in your life, while I do it every minute and over the smallest trifles!" he said, blushing this time as well.

"Savez vous d'où vient votre timidité? . . . D'un excès d'amour propre, mon cher," said Dubkov in a patronizing tone.

"Where does *excès d'amour propre* come into it?" replied Nekhlyudov, stung. "On the contrary, I'm shy because I have too little *amour propre;* I always think the opposite, that I'm unpleasant and boring . . . because of that . . ."

"Get dressed, Volodya!" said Dubkov, seizing him by the shoulders and taking his coat off. "Ignat, get your master dressed!"

"Because of that it often happens that I . . ." went on Nekhlyudov.

But Dubkov was no longer listening. "Tra-la-la ta-ra-ra-la-la." He was humming a tune.

"You haven't gotten away with it," said Nekhlyudov. "I'll prove to you that shyness has nothing to do with pride."

"You'll prove it if you come with us."

"I said I wouldn't go."

"Well then, stay here and prove it to the *diplomat;* and when we come back he can tell us."

"I shall, too," retorted Nekhlyudov with childish petulance. "Only hurry back."

"What do you think: am I proud?" he said, sitting down closer to me.

Despite the fact that my mind was already made up on that score, I was so taken aback by this unexpected question that I was unable to answer for a while.

"I think you are," I said, aware that my voice was trembling and that my face had colored at the thought that the time had come to prove to him that *I was clever*. "I think that every man is proud and that everything a man does he does out of pride."

"So what is pride, in your opinion?" said Nekhlyudov, smiling somewhat contemptuously, it seemed to me.

"Pride," I said, "is the conviction that I am better and cleverer than all other people."

"Then how can everyone be convinced of the same thing?"

"Well, I don't know whether it's true or not, but nobody except me admits it; I am convinced that I am cleverer than anyone in the world and I'm sure that you too believe the same thing."

"No. I'd be the first to admit that I'd met people who were cleverer than myself," said Nekhlyudov.

"Impossible," I replied confidently.

"Do you really think so?" said Nekhlyudov, gazing at me intently.

"Seriously," I replied.

And then another thought occurred to me which I immediately voiced.

"I'll prove it to you. Why do we love ourselves more than others? . . . Because we consider ourselves better than others, more deserving of love. If we found others better than ourselves we would love them more than ourselves, and this never happens. If it does, well, I'm still right," I added with an involuntary smile of self-satisfaction.

Nekhlyudov was silent for a moment.

"You know I had no idea you were so clever!" he said to me with such a pleasant good-natured smile that it suddenly seemed to me I was remarkably happy.

Praise has such a powerful effect not only on man's feelings but also on his mind that under its agreeable influence I seemed to myself to become much much cleverer, and ideas rushed into my head with extraordinary speed. From pride we passed imperceptibly to love and this topic seemed inexhaustible. Despite the fact that to a chance listener our discussions might have seemed complete nonsense—so vague and partial were they—to us they were highly significant. Our hearts were so well attuned that the least touch of a chord by one would immediately evoke an answering echo in the other. We found delight precisely in this mutual response to the various chords we touched upon in our conversation. It seemed to us there were neither words nor time enough to express to one another all those thoughts of ours that begged to be released.

XXVII

The Beginning of a Friendship

From that time on somewhat strange but extraordinarily pleasant relations were established between me and Dmitri Nekhlyudov. In the presence of others he paid hardly any attention to me; but as soon as ever we were alone we settled in some cozy corner and commenced our discussions, forgetting everything and not noticing how the time flew.

We discussed the future life, the arts, government service, marriage and the bringing up of children, and not once did it occur to us that everything we said was the most awful rubbish. It did not occur to us because the rubbish we talked was intelligent and agreeable rubbish; and in youth one still cherishes intelligence and believes in it. In youth all one's inner forces are directed toward the future, and this future takes on such various, vivid, and enchanting shapes under the influence of hope—founded not on experience of the past but on the imagined possibility of happiness in the future—that mere dreams alone of a future happiness, when once understood and shared, do in themselves constitute true happiness at this age. In the metaphysical discussions that formed one of the chief subjects of our conversations

I used to love that moment when ideas began to follow one another faster and faster, becoming more and more abstract, until finally they attained such a degree of fogginess that one saw absolutely no possibility of expressing them, and while supposing that one said one thing one was saying something completely different. I used to love that moment when, soaring higher and higher in the realm of thought, one suddenly comprehends the whole of its immensity and realizes the impossibility of going any further.

At one time, during Shrovetide, Nekhlyudov was so absorbed in various pleasures that although he came several times to spend the day with us, not once did he talk to me, and I was so offended that I again thought of him as a haughty, unpleasant person. I was waiting only for the chance to show him that I did not in the least value his company and had no particular attachment to him. The first time he wanted to talk to me again after Shrovetide I said I had to prepare my lessons and went upstairs; but a quarter of an hour later someone opened the door of the classroom and Nekhlyudov came up to me.

"Am I disturbing you?" he said.

"No," I replied, despite the fact that I wanted to say that I really did have work to do.

"Then why did you leave Volodya's room? It's ages since we discussed anything. And now I've got so used to it that I seem to be missing something."

My annoyance passed in a moment and Dmitri again became in my eyes the same kind person.

"You probably know why I went away, don't you?" I said.

"Perhaps," he replied, sitting down beside me, "but even if I make a guess I won't be able to say why, whereas you can," he said.

"I'll tell you then: I went away because I was angry with you . . . not angry but annoyed. In short: I'm always afraid that you look down on me for still being so young."

"Do you know why we've become such good friends?" he said, responding to my confession with a good-humored sensible smile, "and why I like you more than the people whom I know better and with whom I have more in common? I've just decided. You have one astonishing and rare quality—frankness."

"Yes, I always say the very things I'm ashamed to admit," I agreed, "but only to those I can be sure of."

"But in order to be sure of a man you have to be close friends with him, and we're still not close friends, *Nicolas*. Do you remember what we said about friendship? To be true friends you have to be sure of one another."

"To be sure that you will not tell the things I tell you to anyone else," I said. "But then the most important and interesting thoughts are precisely those we wouldn't tell one another for anything."

"And what vile thoughts they are! Such abominable thoughts that, if we knew we were bound to confess them, we would not dare admit them to our minds. Do you know what just occurred to me, *Nicolas?*" he added, standing up and rubbing his hands with a smile. "*Let's do it*, and you'll see how it will help us both: we'll give our word to confess everything to one another. We shall know one another and we will not be ashamed; and so as not to have to worry about outsiders, we'll promise *never to say anything to anybody* about one another. Let's do it."

"Let's," I said.

And we really *did* do it. I shall describe what came of it later.

Carr has said that every close relationship has two sides: one loves and the other permits itself to be loved, one kisses and the other offers the cheek. This is quite correct; and in our friendship I kissed while Dmitri offered his cheek; but he too was prepared to kiss me. We loved equally, because our knowledge of and esteem for one another was reciprocal; but this did not prevent him from exercising an influence over me, nor me from subordinating myself to him.

It goes without saying that under Nekhlyudov's influence I involuntarily assimilated his attitude too, the essence of which was an ecstatic adoration of the ideal of virtue and a firm belief that it was man's destiny to be constantly perfecting himself. Then the reform of all mankind and the elimination of all human vices and miseries seemed a feasible prospect—it seemed extremely easy and simple to reform oneself, to acquire all the virtues and to be happy. . . .

God alone knows, however, whether these noble dreams of youth really were absurd or who was to blame for the fact that they did not come true. . . .

III: YOUTH

I

WHAT I CONSIDER THE BEGINNING OF MY YOUTH

I have said that my friendship with Dmitri revealed to me a new view of life and its aims and relationships. The essence of this view consisted in the firm belief that man's destiny is to strive for moral perfection and that such perfection is easy and possible and would be eternal. But until now I had merely reveled in discovering the new ideas that stemmed from this belief and constructing dazzling plans for a morally active future; but my life followed the same old trivial confused and idle routine.

Those virtuous ideas which I discussed in conversation with my adored friend, Dmitri—*wonderful Mitya,* as I sometimes called him when talking to myself—still appealed only to my reason, not to my heart. But there came a time when these ideas struck my mind with all the fresh force of a moral discovery, so that I became frightened at the thought of how much time I had wasted and desired at once, that very instant, to apply these ideas to life, firmly intending never to be untrue to them again.

And this moment I consider to be the beginning of my *youth.*

At that time I was almost sixteen. I continued to receive private lessons from various teachers, St.-Jérôme was supervising my studies and willy-nilly, against my inclination, I was preparing to enter the university. Apart from studying, my occupations were as follows: dreaming solitary and incoherent daydreams and thinking; doing gymnastics in order to make myself the strongest man in the world; wandering through all the rooms and especially the corridor leading to the maids' room without any particular aim or thoughts in mind; and examining myself in the mirror, from which, however, I always retreated with an oppressive feeling of dejection and even revulsion. I became convinced not only that my appearance was unprepossessing, but that I could not even console myself with the normal consolations in such cases. I could not say that my face looked expressive intelligent or noble. Of expressiveness there was not a jot—I had the most ordinary coarse and ugly features; my tiny eyes, which were gray, especially when I looked in the mirror, looked more stupid than intelligent. Of manliness there was still less: despite the fact that I was quite tall and very strong for my age, all the features of my face were soft flabby and ill-defined. There was no nobility in it even: on the contrary, my face was like a simple peasant's and my hands and feet were too large; and this seemed very shameful to me at that time.

II

SPRING

The year I entered the university Easter came late in April, so that the examinations were set for the week following Low Sunday, while during Holy Week I was supposed both to fast and to make my final preparations.

After some wet snow, which Karl Ivanich had been wont to characterize as "the son following the father," the weather had been calm clear and warm for about three days. There was not a single patch of snow left in the streets and dirty dough had given way to wet gleaming pavement and swift-rushing streams. On the rooftops the last of the thawing snow was already melting in the sun, buds swelled on the trees in the garden, and in the yard there was a dry path leading to the stables past a frozen heap of manure, while blades of mossy grass showed green between the stones around the porch. It was that particular time of spring that most powerfully affects a man's soul: brilliant sunshine gleaming on everything, but not hot, rushing streams and thawing snow, a fragrant freshness in the air and a delicately blue sky streaked with long transparent clouds. I do not know why, but it seems to me that the influence of this first period of spring's birth is more palpable and affects the soul more powerfully in a large town—you see less but sense more. I was standing by a window, through whose double panes the morning sun was casting dusty rays onto the floor of my intolerably constricting classroom, and working out some long algebraic equation on the blackboard. In one hand I held a soft tattered copy of Franker's *Algebra* and in the other a small piece of chalk, with which I had already succeeded in dirtying both hands, my face, and the elbows of my jacket. Nikolai, wearing an apron and with his sleeves rolled up, was knocking putty out with a pair of pincers and bending back nails on the window that looked out onto the front garden. This job and the noise he was making were distracting my attention. Moreover I was in an extremely bad and discontented mood. Somehow nothing would go right for me: I made a mistake at the beginning of my calculations, so that I had to begin everything over again; I dropped the chalk twice, I felt that my face and hands were all smeared with chalk, I had lost the eraser, and the noise that Nikolai was making played painfully on my nerves. I felt like flying into a tantrum and cursing him; I threw down the chalk and algebra book and started to walk about the room. But I recollected that today was the Wednesday before Easter, that we had to go to confession today and that I ought to refrain from all wrong; and suddenly I found myself in a particularly meek mood and went up to Nikolai.

"Let me help you, Nikolai," I said, trying to make my voice as meek as possible, and the thought that I was acting virtuously, suppressing my irritation and helping him, strengthened this meekness of mood still more.

The putty had been knocked away and the nails bent back, but in spite of the fact that Nikolai was tugging at the crosspieces with all his might, the frame would not come out.

If the frame comes out straight away now as soon as I pull with him, I thought, that means it would be a sin to study any more today and I won't. . . . The frame gave way on one side and came out.

"Where shall I put it?" I said.

"It's all right, I'll take care of it," replied Nikolai, visibly surprised and apparently none too pleased by my zeal. "They mustn't be mixed up, I have them numbered in the attic."

"I'll mark it," I said, picking the frame up.

It seemed to me that if the attic had been a mile away and the frame had weighed twice as much I would have been quite content. I wanted to completely tire myself out performing this service for Nikolai. When I returned to the room the tiles and little bags of salt were already arranged on the windowsill and Nikolai was brushing sand and sleepy flies out of the open window with a bird's wing. Fresh, fragrant air had already inundated the room and filled it. From outside the window came the hum of the city and the twittering of sparrows in the front garden.

Everything was brightly illuminated, the room cheered up, and a light spring breeze fluttered the leaves of my algebra book and Nikolai's hair. I went to the window, sat on the sill, leaned out over the garden, and grew thoughtful.

A new, for me, extraordinarily strong and pleasant feeling suddenly invaded my heart. The damp earth, pierced here and there by vivid-green needles of grass with yellow stalks, the streams of water gleaming in the sunshine, with lumps of earth and chips of wood twisting along them, the russet twigs of lilac with swollen buds swaying just beneath my window, the fussy twittering of the birds swarming in the shrubbery, the blackish fence, wet with melting snow, and most of all the damp fragrant air and joyous sunshine—all spoke to me distinctly and clearly of something new and beautiful, something that, although I cannot render it the way it revealed itself to me, I shall endeavor to render the way I perceived it—everything spoke to me of beauty, happiness, and virtue and said that just as one, so was the other easy and possible for me, that one could not exist without the other and even that beauty, happiness, and virtue were one and the same thing. . . . How is it I did not understand this before, how bad I've been, and yet how good and happy I could have been and can be in the future! I said to myself. At once, at once, this very minute, I must become a different man and begin to live differently. . . . In spite of this, however, I continued to sit in the window for a long time, daydreaming and doing nothing. Has it ever happened to you that you have gone to sleep on a gloomy wet summer's day and, waking at sunset and opening your eyes, have caught sight through the expanding rectangle of the window, beneath the canvas blind which has ballooned out and is beating its rod on the windowsill, of the shadowy violet side of the lime avenue, all wet with rain, and the damp garden path, lit up with bright slanting rays, and heard suddenly the joyful bird life in the garden, seen insects hovering in the aperture of the window, translucent in the sunlight, and smelled the scent of the rain-washed air and thought: How shameful of me to sleep away such an evening, and jumped up hastily in order to go into the garden and rejoice in life? If it has, then that is an example of the strong emotion that overcame me at that moment.

III

DAYDREAMS

Today I shall go to confession and cleanse myself of all my sins, I thought, and never again will I . . . (at this point I remembered all the sins that troubled me most). I shall definitely go to church every Sunday and read the Bible for a whole hour afterwards, and then out of the twenty-five rubles I get every month when I enter university I shall definitely give two and a half (one-tenth) to the poor, and in such a way that nobody knows: and not to beggars either; I shall seek out the poor, an orphan or an old woman, that no one knows about.

I shall have a room of my own (probably St.-Jérôme's) and I shall clean it myself and keep it in perfect condition and I shan't ask my manservant to do anything for me. He's a man just like myself, isn't he? Then I shall go to the university every day on foot (and if I'm given a droshky I shall sell it and put that money away for the poor as well) and do everything properly (what this "everything" was I could not possibly have said at the time, but I had a vivid understanding and sense of it being "everything" in a sensible, moral and irreproachable life). I shall prepare my lectures and even go over the subjects beforehand, so that I shall be first in the first course and shall write a dissertation; for the second course I shall learn everything in advance and they will be able to transfer me straight to the third course, so that at eighteen I shall graduate top of the class with two gold medals, then I'll take a master's degree, then a doctor's, and I'll become the leading scholar in Russia . . . I can even be the leading scholar in the whole of Europe. . . . And then? I asked myself, but at that point I remembered I was day-dreaming—pride was a sin that I would have to confess to the priest that very evening. I returned to the beginning of my speculations. . . . In order to prepare for lectures I shall go on foot to the Vorobyov Hills; there I shall pick out a spot under a tree and read the lectures; some-times I shall take a bite to eat along with me: some cheese or a cake from Pedotti's, or something. I'll rest a while and then read some good book, or I shall sketch the landscape or play some instrument (I must definitely learn to play the flute). And then *she* will also go walking in the Vorobyov Hills and one day she'll come up and ask me who I am. I shall give her a sorrowful look and say that I'm the son of a certain priest and that I am happy only when here, when I am alone, com-pletely on my own. She will give me her hand, say something, and sit down beside me. Thus we shall go there every day, we shall be friends, and I shall kiss her. . . . No, that's no good. On the contrary, from this day forth I shall not look at a woman. Never, never shall I go to the maids' room, nor even try to walk past; and in three years I shall have come of age and shall marry, definitely. I shall purposely take as much exercise as possible and do gymnastics every day, so that when I am twenty-five I shall be stronger than Rappeau. On the first day I shall hold sixteen pounds in each hand at arm's length for five minutes, on the second day twenty-one pounds, on the third twenty-two, and so on until finally I shall hold over sixty pounds in each hand, so that I shall be stronger than any of the peasants; and if somebody suddenly takes it into his head to insult me or speaks disrespectfully of *her,* I shall sim-ply take him by the chest, lift him a yard or two off the ground with one hand and just hold him there, for him to feel my strength, and let him go; but that is bad too, actually; no, I won't do him any harm, but just show him that I. . . .

Let no one reproach me because the daydreams of my youth were as childish as those of my childhood and boyhood. I am convinced that if I should ever live to a ripe old age and my story keeps pace with my age, I shall daydream just as boyishly and impractically as an old man of seventy as I do now. I shall dream of some enchanting Maria, who will love me, a toothless old man, as she did Mazeppa, or of how my feeble-minded son suddenly becomes a minister as a result of some extraordinary occurrence, or of how I shall suddenly receive countless millions of rubles. I am convinced that there is not a single human being or age group that is bereft of this beneficent and comforting capacity to daydream. But, their general impossibility excepted, the magic of these dreams and each man's and each age group's dreams have their own distinctive character. During the period of time that I consider to be the end of my boyhood and beginning of my youth, my dreams were based on four sentiments: love for *her*, for the imaginary woman of whom I dreamed always in the same way and whom I was constantly expecting to meet somewhere at any moment. This *she* had a little of Sonyechka in her, a little of Masha, Vasily's wife, when she was doing the laundry in the tub, and a little of a woman with pearls round her white neck whom I had seen once at the opera a long time ago in the box next to ours. The second sentiment was love of love. I wanted everyone to know and love me. I wanted to say my name, Nikolai Irtenyev, and have everyone astonished by this news and crowd around me and thank me for something. The third sentiment was the hope of some extraordinary vainglorious happiness—a hope that was so strong and firm that it verged on madness. I was so confident that soon, as the result of some extraordinary occurrence, I would suddenly become the richest and grandest man in the world that I lived in constant and excited expectation of some sort of magical happiness. I was always expecting that it was *about to begin* and that I would attain everything a man can desire, and I always hurried everywhere in the supposition that it was *already beginning* somewhere where I wasn't. The fourth and most important sentiment was disgust with myself and remorse, but remorse that was to such a degree mingled with the hope of happiness that it had nothing sad about it. It seemed to me so easy and natural to break away from my whole past, to change and forget everything that had been and to begin my life completely anew, together with all its relationships, that the past neither oppressed nor fettered me. I even reveled in detesting the past and tried to see it as gloomier than it was. The blacker the circle of memories from the past, the purer and brighter against such a background seemed the pure bright spot of the present and the unfolding rainbow hues of the future. It was this voice of remorse and passionate desire for perfection that constituted my chief new emotional sensation during this period of my development, and it was this that provided new premises for my view of myself, other people, and the whole of this world. Oh, blessed comforting voice, how many times since then, at grievous moments when the soul yields in silence to the power of life's falsehood and vice, have you boldly protested against every untruth, ferociously denouncing the past, indicating and forcing me to love that bright spot of the present and promising me happiness and good fortune in the future—blessed comforting voice! Is it possible you will one day cease to speak?

IV

Our Family Circle

Papa was seldom at home that spring. But on the other hand, whenever he was he was extremely gay, strummed his favorite pieces on the piano, made soppy eyes at us and thought up jokes about us all, including Mimi—to the effect that a Georgian prince had seen Mimi out riding and had fallen so in love with her that he had petitioned the synod for a divorce; or that I was to be appointed assistant to our ambassador in Vienna—and all this was announced with a serious face; he frightened Katyenka with spiders, which she could not bear; he was very affable with our friends, Dubkov and Nekhlyudov, and never ceased telling them and us about his plans for the coming year. Despite the fact that these plans changed practically every day and contradicted one another, they were so attractive that we listened with delight and Lyubochka gazed unwinkingly at Papa's mouth in order not to miss a single word. At one time the plan consisted in leaving us at the university in Moscow while he and Lyubochka went to Italy for two years, at another in buying an estate in the Crimea, on the southern shore, in order to go there every summer, then in moving the whole family to St. Petersburg, and so on. But apart from this special gaiety, another change had taken place in Papa just lately that surprised me greatly. He had had some fashionable clothes made—an olive-green coat, fashionable trousers with footstraps, and a long overcoat that suited him very well, and he often smelled of some wonderful scent when he went visiting, especially if it were to one particular lady, of whom Mimi never spoke but with a deep sigh and with such a face that you could practically read on it: "Poor orphans! What an unfortunate passion! A good job *she's* no longer here," and so on. I learned from Nikolai—since Papa never told us anything about his gambling affairs—that he had been particularly lucky this winter; he had won an awful lot and placed it in the bank and did not want to play any more this spring. It was probably because of this and for fear of not holding out that he was so eager to get away quickly to the country. He had even decided to leave for Petrovsky with the girls immediately after Easter, without waiting for me to enter the university, while Volodya and I were to follow later.

All this winter and right up to the spring Volodya was inseparable from Dubkov (though the two of them had become coldly estranged from Dmitri). Their main pleasures, so far as I could judge from the conversations that I heard, consisted entirely in endlessly drinking champagne, driving in a sleigh beneath the windows of a young lady with whom, it seemed, both of them were in love at the same time and dancing *vis-à-vis,* not at children's dances any more but at real grown-up balls. This last circumstance, despite the fact that Volodya and I were both fond of one another, separated us a lot. We sensed too great a difference—between the little boy who still has tutors and the man who already dances at grown-up balls—to feel able to confide our thoughts in one another. Katyenka was now completely grown up and read lots of novels, and the thought that she might get married soon no longer seemed like a joke to me; but despite the fact that Volodya was grown up too, they did not get on together and it seemed that they even despised one another. In general Katyenka did nothing at all when she was home alone, except read novels, and most of the time she was just bored; but whenever there were any men from outside she became very animated and charming and did such things with her eyes that it was completely beyond me what she could have meant by them.

Only later, when I heard from her in conversation that the sole form of coquetry permissible to young ladies is coquetry of the eyes, was I able to explain to myself these weird unnatural grimaces, which no one else, it seemed, was at all surprised by. Lyubochka was also beginning to wear almost full-length dresses so that her bandy legs were almost invisible, but she was just as much a crybaby as before. Now she no longer dreamed of marrying a hussar but preferred a singer or a musician, and to this end was diligently studying music. St.-Jérôme, who knew that he was to remain in the house only until my examinations were over, had found himself a place with some count or other and since then had regarded everyone at home with a sort of disdain. He was rarely there, had begun to smoke cigarettes, which was then the height of dandyism, and was constantly whistling various cheerful little tunes through a piece of cardboard. Mimi was becoming more and more embittered with every day and it seemed that ever since the day we all began to grow up she had ceased to expect anything good of anything or anyone.

When I came down to dinner I found only Mimi, Katyenka, Lyubochka, and St.-Jérôme in the dining room; Papa was not at home and Volodya was preparing for an examination with some friends in his room and had asked for dinner to be sent up. In general lately it was Mimi who for the most part sat at the head of the table, and since none of us had any respect for her, dinner had lost a lot of its charm. Dinner was no longer, as it had been with *maman* or Grandmother, a sort of ritual, bringing the whole family together at a certain hour and dividing the day into two. We allowed ourselves to be late, to arrive during the second course, to drink wine from tumblers (St.-Jérôme himself set this example), to lounge about on our chairs, to get up before dinner was finished, and similar liberties. From that time forth dinner ceased to be, as formerly, a joyful family daily ceremony. What a difference at Petrovsky, where at two o'clock everyone would be sitting washed and dressed in the drawing room, ready for dinner, talking gaily and waiting for the appointed hour. At precisely the moment when a clock in the footmen's room whined preparatory to striking two, Foka would step quietly into the room with a napkin over his arm and a dignified and somewhat severe expression on his face. "Dinner is served!" he would proclaim in a loud deliberate voice and everyone, their faces gay and content, the elders in front, the young ones behind, with a rustle of starched skirts and a squeaking of boots and shoes, would move into the dining room, conversing quietly as they took their places. Or what a difference there had been in Moscow when everyone stood about the ready-set table in the salon, talking and waiting for Grandmother, whom Gavrilo had already gone to inform that dinner was ready: suddenly the door would open, one heard the rustle of a dress and the scrape of feet and out from her room would sail Grandmother, wearing a bonnet with some extraordinary lilac bow on it, turning sideways and either smiling or scowling gloomily, according to the state of her health. Gavrilo would rush to her chair, there would be a scrape of chairs and, feeling a cold shiver run down your spine— portent of a good appetite—you would pick up your dampish starched napkin, consume a crust of bread, rub your hands under the table with an impatient and cheerful craving, and fix your eyes on the steaming bowls of soup as they were distributed by the butler, according to rank, age, and Grandmother's estimation of those present.

Now I no longer experienced either joy or trepidation when I came down to dinner.

The gossip of Mimi, St.-Jérôme, and the girls about the awful boots worn by our Russian teacher and the dresses with flounces that the princesses Kornakov had, and so forth—this gossip, which had formerly filled me with genuine contempt that I had not even tried to hide, particularly with regard to Lyubochka and Katyenka, did not now destroy my new virtuous disposition. I was extraordinarily humble; smiling, I listened to them extra courteously; deferentially, I requested them to pass the kvas and I concurred with St.-Jérôme when he corrected a phrase I used after dinner, saying that *je puis* was more elegant than *je peux*. I must confess, however, that I was somewhat ruffled by the fact that nobody paid any special attention to my humility and virtuousness. After dinner Lyubochka showed me a piece of paper on which she had written all her sins; I thought this all very well, but that it was still better to write one's sins on one's heart because "that wasn't it at all."

"Why not?" asked Lyubochka.

"Oh well, that's all right too; you wouldn't understand." And I went upstairs to my room, having told St.-Jérôme that I was going to study, although actually I was intending before confession, which was still an hour and a half away, to write down for myself a schedule of all my duties and studies for the rest of my life, and to set out on paper both my life's objectives and the rules by which I should act henceforth, without ever deviating from them.

V

RULES

I took a sheet of paper and first of all intended to set about scheduling my duties and occupations for the coming year. For this I had to rule the paper. But since I could not seem to find a ruler I used a Latin dictionary instead. Apart from the fact that after having drawn my pen along the edge of the dictionary and then lifted it off, it transpired that instead of a line I had merely made a long puddle of ink on the paper, the dictionary was in any case not long enough for the paper and the line bent around by its soft corner. I took another sheet of paper and by moving the dictionary managed to draw some sort of line. Having divided my duties into three kinds: duties to myself, to my neighbor, and to God, I started to write the first ones down, but there turned out to be so many and with so many kinds and subdivisions that first I had to write down *Rules for Life,* and only then could I start my schedule. I took six sheets of paper, threaded them together into a notebook, and wrote at the top: *Rules for Life.* These words were written so crookedly and irregularly that I was a long time wondering whether to rewrite them or not, and for a long time afterwards I worried about the look of my tattered schedule and this deformed heading. Why was everything so beautiful and clear in my mind, and yet came out so grotesquely on paper and in life generally, whenever I tried to apply some of my thoughts in practice? . . .

"The confessor has arrived, please come downstairs to hear his instructions," announced Nikolai.

I hid the notebook in my desk, looked in the mirror, brushed my hair up because this, in my opinion, gave me a thoughtful air, and descended to the sitting room, where the table had already been covered and bore an icon and lighted wax candles. Papa entered by the other door simultaneously with me. Our confessor, a gray monk with a severe old man's face, gave Papa his blessing. Papa kissed his short broad and withered hand and I did the same.

"Call *Waldemar*," said Papa. "Where is he? Oh yes, he's taking communion at the university."

"He's studying with the prince," said Katyenka and looked at Lyubochka. Lyubochka suddenly blushed for some reason, winced, pretending she had a pain somewhere, and left the room. I went out after her. She halted in the drawing room and noted something fresh down on her paper with a little pencil.

"What, have you committed a new sin?" I asked.

"Oh no, it's nothing," she replied, blushing.

At this moment Dmitri's voice sounded in the front hall as he bade farewell to Volodya.

"Look, always new temptations for you," said Katyenka, coming into the room and speaking to Lyubochka.

I could not understand what was wrong with my sister: she was so confused that tears came to her eyes and her embarrassment, becoming extreme, turned to vexation with both herself and Katyenka, who evidently was teasing her.

"It's obvious that you're a *foreigner* (nothing could have been more insulting to Katyenka than the word *foreigner*, which was why Lyubochka used it), since you are upsetting me on purpose before such a solemn ceremony," she went on in an important tone of voice, "you ought to realize . . . it's no joke . . ."

"Do you know what it was she wrote, Nikolyenka?" said Katyenka, cut to the quick by the word *foreigner,* "she wrote . . ."

"I didn't expect you to be so spiteful," said Lyubochka, completely blubbering now and walking away from us, "at such a time and on purpose; for ages now you've been leading me into sin. I don't get onto you about your feelings and sufferings."

VI

CONFESSION

It was with these and similarly distracted thoughts that I returned to the sitting room when everyone gathered there and our confessor, standing up, prepared to lead the prayer before confession. But the moment the monk's stern expressive voice rang out amid the general silence, saying the prayer, and especially when he addressed us with the words *Reveal all your sins without shame, concealment or excuses and your soul will be cleansed before God, but if ye conceal anything your sin shall be great* I was revisited by that feeling of reverent trepidation that I had experienced in the morning when I thought of the coming sacrament. I even experienced a sensation of pleasure in this state and tried to prolong it, stopping all the thoughts that entered my mind and striving to be afraid of something.

Papa was the first to go into confession. He stayed a very long time in Grandmother's room and during the whole of this time all of us in the sitting room remained quiet or else talked in whispers about who was to go first. At last we again heard the sound of the monk saying a prayer and of Papa's footsteps. The door gave a squeak and he emerged coughing, as was his custom, and shrugging one shoulder and without looking at anyone.

"Well, now you go in, Lyubochka, and make sure you say everything. You're one of our biggest sinners," said Papa cheerfully, pinching her on the cheek.

Lyubochka turned pale and then red, took out her list from her apron and put it back again, lowered her head so that her neck became somehow foreshortened, as though awaiting a blow from above, and went through the door. She was not in there long, but when she came out her shoulders were heaving with sobs.

Finally, after pretty Katyenka, who came out smiling, my turn came. With that same blank fear and with a desire purposely to inflate that fear more and more, I went into the half-lit room. The confessor was standing before a lectern and turned his face slowly toward me.

I remained in Grandmother's room no longer than five minutes, but emerged from there a happy and, I then believed, completely pure and morally reborn new man. Despite the fact that I was disagreeably affected by being in the same old situation, having the same old rooms around me, the same old furniture and even the same old body (I would have liked to have my whole exterior altered in the way that I thought my interior self had altered)—despite this fact I remained in this blissful state of mind until bedtime.

I was already dropping off to sleep and going over in my imagination all the sins of which I had cleansed myself when suddenly I recalled one shameful sin that I had concealed at confession. The words of the prayer before confession came back to me and rang in my ears incessantly. All my peace of mind vanished in an instant. "But if ye conceal anything your sin shall be great . . ." came back incessantly and I saw myself as such a terrible sinner that no punishment was sufficient for me. For a long time I tossed from side to side, thinking my position over and from moment to moment expecting God's punishment or even sudden death—a thought that threw me into indescribable horror. But suddenly I had a happy thought: at first light I would ride or walk to our confessor at the monastery and make a new confession— and then I calmed down.

VII

A Trip to the Monastery

I woke up several times during the night in my fear of oversleeping and at six o'clock I was already up. There was hardly a glimmer of light at the window. I put on my clothes and boots, which lay in a dirty heap by my bed, since Nikolai had not yet had time to clear them away, and without praying or washing, went out into the street alone for the first time in my life.

A chill misty dawn glowed red behind the green roof of the large house across the street. A fairly hard spring-morning frost froze the mud and streams, crackled underfoot and nipped my face and hands. I had counted on taking a cab in order to get there quicker and get back, but there was still none to be seen in our street. There were just some carts trailing slowly along Arbat and two stonemasons who walked along the sidewalk talking to one another. After going about a quarter of a mile I began to meet men and women with baskets on their way to market, and water carts going for water; a confectioner came out of his shop at the crossroads; a bakery was opening; and by Arbat Gate I came across a cabby, a little old man asleep and rocking back and forth on his shabby patched and sort of blueish droshky, with a tired horse harnessed to it. It must have been in his sleep that he demanded only twenty copecks of me to go to the monastery and back, because suddenly he remembered himself and just as I was about to get in lashed his nag with the ends of his reins and almost left me behind. "Have to feed the horses! Sorry, master," he muttered.

It was with difficulty that I persuaded him to stop by offering him double the money. He stopped his horse, inspected me carefully and said: "Get in, master." I must confess that I was somewhat afraid lest he take me to some secluded side street and rob me. Catching hold of the collar of his tattered old coat, at which his wrinkled neck was somehow pitifully bared over his acutely bent back, I climbed up and sat astride the blue, curved and rocking seat and we jolted our way down Vozdvizhenka. On the way I managed to note that the back of the droshky was lined with a piece of the same greenish material as the driver's coat had been made of; this circumstance for some reason reassured me and I no longer feared that the cabby would take me to a secluded side street and rob me.

The sun had already risen fairly high and was brightly gilding the church cupolas when we arrived at the monastery. Frost still persisted in the shade, but swift muddy streams covered the whole road and the horse splashed its way through the thawing mud. When we had entered the monastery enclosure, I asked the first person I saw where I might find our confessor.

"His cell is over there," said a passing monk, pausing for a moment and pointing to a little hut with a tiny porch.

"Thank you most kindly," I said.

But what could the monks have thought of me as they all looked at me, coming out of the church one by one? I was neither a grown-up nor a child; my face was unwashed, my hair uncombed, my clothes covered in fluff and my boots uncleaned and still covered with mud. To what class of people did the monks mentally assign me as they looked at me? And they looked closely enough. However, I still walked in the direction the young monk had indicated.

On the narrow path leading to the cells I was met by an old man in black with a gray bushy beard who asked me what I wanted.

There was a moment when I wanted to say "nothing" and run back to the cabby and return home, but despite his knitted brows the old man's face inspired confidence. I said that I needed to see my confessor and mentioned his name.

"Come, young sir, I'll show you the way," he said, turning round and seeming to have guessed my situation at once. "The father is at matins, he'll soon be back."

He opened a door and led me through a spotlessly clean vestibule and hallway, over a clean linen mat, into the cell.

"You can wait here," he said with a kindly reassuring expression and went out.

The room in which I found myself was extremely small and remarkably clean and tidy. Its whole furniture consisted of a small table, covered with oilcloth and standing between two tiny shuttered windows on whose sills stood two pots of geraniums and a stand with some icons on it, and a lamp hanging in front of them, and an armchair and two ordinary chairs. A wall clock hung in the corner with flowers painted on its dial and pulled-up brass weights on chains; on a partition that was joined to the ceiling by whitewashed wooden planks (and which probably concealed a bed) two surplices hung on nails.

The windows faced a white wall which showed about five feet away. Between them and the wall there was a small shrub of lilac. Not a sound from outside came into this room, so that in such a silence the regular pleasant tick of the pendulum seemed a loud noise. As soon as I remained alone in this quiet retreat, all my former thoughts and recollections suddenly vanished from my head as though they had never been and I became wholly absorbed in an inexpressibly pleasant reverie. This yellowing nankeen surplice with its fraying lining, these books with their worn black-leather bindings and brass clasps, these dull-green plants with their carefully watered soil and washed leaves, and particularly the monotonously intermittent sound of the pendulum—all spoke to me clearly of a new life that till now had remained unknown to me, a life of solitude, prayer, and quiet peaceful happiness. . . .

Months, years pass, I thought, and he is always alone, always calm, and always feels that his conscience is clear before God and that his prayers have been heard. I sat on the chair for about half an hour, trying not to move or breathe loudly in order not to disturb the harmony of the sounds which were so eloquent for me. And the pendulum ticked on and on—louder on the right, quieter on the left.

VIII

A Second Confession

The steps of my confessor aroused me from this reverie.

"Good morning," he said, smoothing his gray hair with his hand. "What can I do for you?"

I asked him to bless me and kissed his small yellowy hand with particular pleasure.

When I explained the nature of my request to him, he said nothing, went up to the icons and commenced the confession.

When the confession was over and I, overcoming my shame, had told him everything that was on my mind, he placed his hands on my head and in his quiet resonant voice enounced: "May our Heavenly Father's blessing be upon you, my son, and may He always preserve you in faith, meekness, and humility. Amen."

I was completely happy; tears of happiness welled up in my throat; I kissed the lining of his woolen cassock and raised my head. The monk's face was completely calm.

I felt that I was overcome with tender emotion and, afraid of dispersing it in some way, hurriedly took my leave of my confessor and without looking to either side, in order not to be distracted, left the enclosure and once more mounted the striped, rocky droshky. But the jolting of the carriage and the vividness of the objects that flashed by my eyes soon dispersed this feeling; and soon I was already thinking of how the confessor must be thinking that never in his life had he met a young man with such a beautiful soul as I, and never would, and that no others even existed. I was convinced of this; and this conviction evoked in me the sort of feeling of bonhomie that absolutely insisted on being communicated to someone.

I had a terrible desire to talk to someone, but since there was nobody else to hand besides the cabby, I turned to him.

"Well, was I long?" I asked.

"No, not very, but it was time to feed my horse ages ago; you see I'm a night driver," replied the little old cabby, who now, evidently because of the sunshine, was more cheerful than before.

"It seemed to me I was no more than a minute," I said. "And do you know why I went to the monastery?" I added, moving into a hollow on the droshky that was closer to the little old man.

"What business is it of ours? We only take a customer wherever he wants to go," he replied.

"No, but still, what do you think?" I continued to pester him.

"Well, you've probably got to bury someone and went to buy a plot," he said.

"No, my friend. Do you know why I went?"

"I can't, master, can I?" he replied once more.

The cabby's voice sounded so nice to me that I decided, for his edification, to tell him the reasons for my trip and even about the feeling I had experienced.

"I'll tell you if you like. You see."

And I told him everything and described all my beautiful feelings. And even now I blush at the recollection of it.

"Yes, sir," said the cabby dubiously.

And for a long time after this he was silent and sat motionless, merely adjusting from time to time the tail of his coat, which kept getting out from under his striped leg as it bounced up and down, with a big boot on the end of it, on the droshky's running board. I was already thinking that he thought the same about me as my confessor—that is that there did not exist in the whole world another such fine young man as myself; but suddenly he spoke to me:

"Well, master, that's a matter for gentlemen."

"What?" I asked.

"Yep, a matter for gentlemen," he repeated, moving his toothless lips in a mumble.

No, he has not understood me, I thought, but did not say any more to him until we reached home.

Although it was not the same feeling of tenderness and reverence, still a sense of self-satisfaction at having experienced it remained with me the whole way, despite the people who formed a motley throng on the streets in the bright sunlight; but as soon as I reached home this feeling vanished completely. I did not have forty copecks to pay the driver with. Gavrilo the butler, to whom I was already in debt, would not lend me any more. Seeing me run across the yard twice in my search for money, the cabby must have guessed the reason for my running and got down from his droshky; and despite the fact that he had seemed so nice to me, began to speak loudly—with the obvious intention of stinging me—about swindlers who did not pay their fares.

Everyone was still asleep at home so that, apart from the servants, there was no one from whom I could borrow the forty copecks. Finally Vasily, not in exchange for my most sacred word of honor, which (I could see by his face) he did not trust in the least, but simply because he loved me and remembered the service I had done him, paid the cabby for me. Thus this feeling of mine vanished like smoke. When I began to dress for church in order to go to communion with all the others and it turned out that my best clothes had not yet been altered and could not be worn, I committed an avalanche of sins. Having put on some other clothes, I went to communion in a sort of strange state of mental tumult and with utter distrust of my finer impulses.

IX

HOW I PREPARED FOR THE EXAMINATIONS

On Easter Thursday Papa, Lyubochka, Mimi, and Katyenka left for
the country, so that in the whole of Grandmother's big house there remained only Volodya, myself, and St.-Jérôme. The mood I was in on
the day of my confession and my trip to the monastery had completely
vanished and left behind only a vague though pleasant recollection,
which became more and more overlaid with new impressions of my
life of freedom.

The notebook headed *Rules for Life* was also put away, along with my
school notebooks. Despite the fact that the idea of the possibility of
composing for myself rules to cover every contingency in life and always being guided by them appealed to me and seemed extraordinarily simple and at the same time grand, and I still intended to apply it
in real life, I again seemed to forget that it was necessary to do this at
once and I always put it off to another time. I was consoled, however,
by the fact that every thought that occurred to me nowadays fitted
neatly into some one or other of the subdivisions of my rules and duties: either it fitted the rules affecting my neighbor, or else myself, or
else God. When the time comes I'll put that down, plus all the other

thoughts that will come to me then on this subject, I said to myself. Often I ask myself now: when was I better and closer to the truth: then when I believed in the omnipotence of the human mind, or now, when I have lost the power to develop, and doubt the power and significance of the human mind? And I cannot give myself a positive answer.

The sense of freedom and that spring feeling of expectation, which I have already spoken of, disturbed me to such a degree that I was completely incapable of controlling myself and prepared for the examinations very badly. Sometimes, for instance, you'd be studying in the classroom in the morning and you'd know that it was essential to work, because tomorrow you were going to be examined in the subject for which you still had two whole questions to read, but suddenly there'd be a smell of some sort of spring fragrance coming in at the window, it would seem as though there was something extremely urgent you had to remember, your hands would lower the book of their own accord, your legs would begin to move of their own accord and walk back and forth, and in your head it was as though someone had released a spring and set a machine in motion, it would feel so light and natural in your head and various gay and vivid daydreams would begin to race through it at such speed that you only had time to notice their flashing by. And one hour, two, would pass unnoticed. Or else you'd be sitting over a book and somehow or other concentrating all your attention on what you were reading when suddenly you would hear the sound of a woman's steps and the rustle of a dress in the corridor—and everything would fly out of your head and there was not the slightest chance of remaining in your seat, although you knew very well that besides Gasha, Grandmother's old maid, no one else could possibly be using the corridor. "Well, but what if it's *her* all of a sudden?" would come into your head, "Well, what if it's just beginning and I'm missing it?"—and you leapt out into the corridor and saw that it really was Gasha; but for a long time afterwards your mind would be out of control. The spring would have been released and all chaos let loose once more. Or in the evening you'd be sitting alone in your room with a tallow candle; suddenly, in order to trim the candle or adjust your seat, you would tear yourself away for a moment from your book and see that everywhere—in the doorway and in the corners—it was dark, and you would become aware that the whole house was quiet: again it would be impossible not to pause and listen to the silence and gaze into the darkness through the open door and around the dark room, and not to remain for a long long time quite still or else go downstairs and walk through all the empty rooms. Often, in the evenings, I would also sit for a long time in the salon unnoticed, listening to the sounds of "The Nightingale" as Gasha picked it out on the piano with two fingers, sitting alone in the salon with a tallow candle. And then, when it was moonlight, I positively had to get up out of bed and settle myself on the windowsill that looked out over the garden, and there, gazing at the illuminated roof of the Shaposhnikovs' house, at the graceful belfry of our local church and at the nocturnal shadows of the fence and shrubbery, I just had to sit for so long that afterwards, in the morning, I would have difficulty in awakening even at ten o'clock.

Thus if it had not been for the tutors, who still came to see me, for St.-Jérôme, who reluctantly pricked my ambition from time to time, and most of all for my desire to seem a clever fellow in the eyes of my friend Nekhlyudov, that is to pass the examination with distinction, which, according to his views, was an extremely important matter—if it had not been for this, then spring and freedom would have made me forget even that which I already knew and I would never have passed the examinations at all.

X

THE HISTORY EXAMINATION

On the sixteenth of April, under the protection of St.-Jérôme, I entered the great university hall for the first time. We arrived together in our somewhat flashy phaeton. I was wearing a dress coat for the first time in my life and all the clothes I was wearing, even my stockings and underwear, were absolutely new and of the best quality. When the porter helped me out of my overcoat downstairs and I appeared before him in all my glory, I even felt somewhat ashamed of being so dazzling. However, I had no sooner entered the brightly lit parqueted hall, which was filled with people, and caught sight of the hundreds of young men in high school uniforms and dress coats, some of whom glanced at me with indifference, and important professors walking casually about among the tables at the far end and sitting in large armchairs, than I was at once disillusioned in any hopes I might have had of attracting general attention with my clothes, and the expression on my face, which at home and even in the vestibule downstairs had signified a sort of regret for looking, against my will, so noble and distinguished, gave way to an expression of the greatest timidity and even a certain dejection. I even went to the other extreme and was terribly pleased when on the nearest bench I caught sight of an extraordinarily badly and untidily dressed man, still not old but almost completely gray already, who was sitting at a distance from all the others on the last bench. I immediately sat down next to him and started to inspect the examinees and draw my own conclusions about them. There were all sorts of figures and faces there, but they could all, according to me at that time, be easily divided into three categories.

First of all there were those like myself who had come to the examination with their tutors or parents, including the younger Ivin, with Frost, whom I also knew, and Ilinka Grap, who was there with his old father. All these had downy chins, showed off their linen, and sat quietly, without opening the books and notebooks they had brought with them, and they looked at the professors and examination tables with obvious timidity. The second kind of examinees wore high school uniforms and many of them were already shaving. These for the most part knew one another, talked loudly, called the professors by name, prepared for questions on the spot, passed notebooks to one another, stepped over the benches and brought cakes and sandwiches in from the vestibule, which they at once ate, merely bending their heads slightly in order to be on a level with the backs of the benches. And then, finally, the third kind of examinees, of whom, however, there were very few, were quite old and some wore dress coats and displayed no visible linen. These bore themselves extremely seriously, sat apart, and looked very gloomy. The man who had consoled me by being decidedly worse dressed than I belonged to this last category. Resting his head in both hands, with his disheveled gray hair sticking out between his fingers, he was reading a book, and having glanced up at me none too amiably for a split second with his glittering eyes, he scowled darkly and in addition stuck out a shiny elbow in my direction to stop me from moving any closer. The high school boys, on the other hand, were a bit too sociable and I was a little afraid of them. One of them, thrusting a book into my hand, said: "Give this to him over there"; another said as he passed by me: "Let me through, old boy"; and a third, as he clambered over one of the benches, leaned on my shoulder as though it were the back of a bench. All this I found outrageous and disagreeable; I regarded myself as much superior to these high school boys and considered that they had no right to allow themselves to be so familiar with me. Finally they started to call out our names; the high school boys went up boldly and for the most part answered well, returning cheerfully to their seats; our group was much shyer and, as it seemed, answered worse. Of the older ones, some of them were outstanding and some very bad. When the name Semyonov was called, my neighbor with the gray hair and glittering eyes elbowed me roughly as he clambered over my legs and went to the table. It was obvious from the look of the professors that he answered boldly and excellently. Returning to his seat, he calmly picked up his books and left, without inquiring what his mark was. Several times already I had started at the sound of the voice calling out the names, but in the alphabetical list my name had not yet been reached, although names beginning with *K* had already been called. "Ikonin and Tenyev" cried someone suddenly from the professors' corner. A shiver ran down my back and through my hair.

"Who was that? Who's Bartenyev?" said voices around me.

"Ikonin, get going, you're being called; but who's this Bartenyev, Mordenyev? I don't know, I must say," said a tall ruddy high school boy standing behind me.

"It's you," said St.-Jérôme.

"My name's Irtenyev," I said to the ruddy high school boy. "Did they say Irtenyev?"

"Yes, yes; why don't you get going? . . . My, what a dandy!" he added in a lower tone, but so that I could hear his words as I emerged from between the benches. Ikonin was just in front of me, a tall young man of about twenty-five who belonged to the third group, the older ones. He was wearing a tight olive-colored dress coat and a blue satin cravat on which his long fair hair rested behind, carefully cut à la muzhik. I had noticed his appearance while we were still sitting down. He was quite attractive and talkative; and I was particularly struck by the strange red hair that he had grown on his throat and the even stranger habit he had of constantly unbuttoning his vest and scratching his chest under his shirt.

Three professors were sitting behind the table that Ikonin and I approached: not one of them replied to our greeting. A young professor was shuffling the question slips like a pack of cards, another professor with a medal on his coat was watching a high school boy as he spoke very fast about the Emperor Charlemagne, adding the words *at last* to every phrase, and the third professor, a little old man wearing glasses, lowered his head, looked at us through his glasses, and pointed to the slips. I felt that his glance was directed jointly at Ikonin and myself and that there was something about us that he did not like (perhaps it was Ikonin's red beard), because he made an impatient gesture with his head, again looking at the pair of us, indicating that we should hurry up and take our slips. I was vexed and offended, first because no one had replied to our greeting and second because I was evidently classed with Ikonin in the same category of examinee, and they were already prejudiced against me because of Ikonin's red beard. I took a slip without shyness and prepared to answer; but the professor was aiming his glance at Ikonin. I read my slip through: the topic was familiar to me and as I calmly awaited my turn, I watched what was going on in front of me. Ikonin did not seem in the least shy and was even too bold as he moved, twisting the whole of one side of his body to take his slip, then tossing his hair back and briskly reading what was written on it. He was about, as it seemed to me, to open his mouth in order to begin his answer when the professor with the medal, having praised and dismissed the high school boy, suddenly looked at him. Ikonin appeared to remember something and stopped. General silence ensued for about two minutes.

"Well?" said the professor with the glasses.

Ikonin opened his mouth but was silent again.

"You're not the only one, you know. Are you going to answer or not?" said the young professor, but Ikonin did not even glance at him. He stared at the slip and said not a single word. The professor with the glasses looked at him through his glasses, over his glasses, and without his glasses, since during this period he had had time to take them off, clean the lenses carefully and put them on again. Ikonin said not a single word. Suddenly his face lit up with a smile, he gave a toss of his head, again twisted sideways to the table, replaced his slip, looked at all the professors in turn, then at me, turned on his heel and, swinging his arms, walked briskly back to his place. The professors looked at one another.

"A fine specimen!" said the young professor. "Paying his own way."

I moved closer to the table, but the professors continued to talk among themselves almost in a whisper, as though none of them even suspected my presence. I was firmly convinced at the time that all three professors were extraordinarily interested in whether I would pass the examination or not and whether I would pass well, but that it was merely in order to seem important that they pretended to be completely indifferent to this and pretended not to notice me.

When the professor with the glasses turned to me indifferently and invited me to answer the question, I looked him straight in the eye and felt somewhat ashamed on his behalf that he should so play the hypocrite with me, and I somewhat faltered with the beginning of my answer; but then things became easier and easier, and since the question concerned Russian history, which I knew very well, I ended brilliantly and was so carried away that, in a desire to show the professors I was no Ikonin and should not be confused with him, I proposed to take another slip; but with a nod of his head the professor said: "That's enough," and noted something in his register. Returning to the benches I immediately learned from the high school boys, who, God knows how, seemed to know everything, that I had been given a five.

XI

The Mathematics Examination

At the following examination, apart from Grap, whom I did not deem worthy of my acquaintance, and Ivin, who for some reason fought shy of me, I already had many new friends. Some of them were already greeting me. Ikonin was even overjoyed to see me and informed me that he was going to take the history examination again, and that the history professor had had a grudge against him ever since last year's examination, at which, evidently, he had also *tripped him up*. Semyonov, who was going to enter the same faculty as I, the mathematics faculty, continued to fight shy of everyone right up to the end of the examinations and sat silent and alone, resting his head in his hands and thrusting his fingers into his gray hair. He did excellently in the examinations and finished second; first was a high school student from high school number one. This was a tall thin fellow with dark hair, extremely pale, with his cheek tied up in a black scarf and a pimple-covered forehead. His hands were thin and red, with extraordinarily long fingers, and his fingernails had been so bitten down that the ends of his fingers seemed to have threads running round them. All this seemed wonderful to me and just the way things ought to be with the *top high school boy*. He spoke to everybody just like anyone else and even

I got to know him, but nevertheless, it seemed to me that there was something about his walk and the motions of his lips and black eyes that was clearly extraordinary and *magnetic.*

I arrived for the mathematics examination earlier than usual. I knew the subject pretty well, but there were two algebra questions that I had somehow concealed from my teacher and that I had not the slightest idea about. They were, as I remember, combinations theorem and Newton's binomial theorem. I sat on the rear bench and looked through the two unfamiliar questions; but being unused to studying in a noisy room and being also aware that there was insufficient time, I was prevented from concentrating on what I was reading.

"There he is; this way, Nekhlyudov," came the familiar sound of Volodya's voice behind me.

I turned around and saw my brother and Dmitri who, with coats unbuttoned and arms swinging, were making their way toward me between the benches. It was at once clear that they were second-year students who felt quite at home in the university. The mere appearance of their unbuttoned coats expressed disdain for us who were entering, and we who were entering were filled with envy and respect. It was extremely flattering for me to think that everyone around me would see that I was acquainted with two second-year students, and I hurriedly stood up to greet them.

Volodya was bursting to express his sense of his own superiority.

"Ha, you poor wretch!" he said. "What? Not been examined yet?"

"No."

"What are you reading? Aren't you prepared?"

"Yes, but there are two questions I'm not sure of. Here, I don't understand this bit."

"What? This here?" said Volodya, and started to explain Newton's binomial to me, but went so fast and unclearly that, having read disbelief of his knowledge in my eyes, he glanced at Dmitri, whereupon, having read the same in his eyes, he blushed, but still went on saying something that I did not understand.

"No, wait a minute, Volodya! Let me go over it with him if there's time," said Dmitri, with a glance at the professors' corner, and sat down beside me.

I noticed immediately that my friend was in that complacently humble mood that always came upon him when he was satisfied with himself and that I particularly liked in him. Since he had a good knowledge of mathematics and spoke clearly, he explained the question to me so splendidly that I remember it to this very day. But hardly had he finished than St.-Jérôme said in a loud whisper: "*À vous, Nicolas!*" and I followed Ikonin out from the benches without having had time to look at the second question. I went up to a table at which two professors were sitting and where a high school boy was standing in front of a blackboard. He was briskly working some formula out, banging his chalk on the board and breaking it, and continued to write even though the professor had already told him: "Enough," and had ordered us to take our slips. What if I get the combinations theorem? I thought, taking a slip with trembling fingers from the soft pile of cut-up pieces of paper. Ikonin, with the same bold gesture as at the last examination, with a sideways lunge took the topmost slip, looked at it, and scowled irately.

"Always the same old stinkers!" he muttered.

I looked at mine.

Oh, horrors! It was the combinations theorem! . . .

"What do you have?" asked Ikonin.

I showed him.

"I know that," he said.

"Do you want to change?"

"No, it makes no difference, I don't feel up to it," Ikonin barely had time to whisper before the professor called us to the blackboard.

Well, all's lost! I thought. Instead of the brilliant performance I thought I would give I shall cover myself in shame forevermore, worse than Ikonin. But suddenly, right under the professor's eyes, Ikonin turned to me, snatched the slip from my hands and gave me his. I looked at it. It was Newton's binomial.

The professor was not an old man and had a pleasant intelligent expression that was particularly reinforced by the extraordinary prominence of the lower part of his forehead.

"What's this, are you exchanging slips, gentlemen?" he said.

"No, he just gave me his to look at, Professor," improvised Ikonin, and again the word *professor* was the last word he uttered at the examination; and again, as he walked past me on his way back, he glanced at the professors and at me, smiled, and shrugged his shoulders, as if to say: "It doesn't matter, friends!" (Later I learned that this was the third year Ikonin had taken the entrance examinations.)

I gave an excellent answer to the question I had only just reviewed. The professor even told me that I had done better than required and gave me five.

XII

THE LATIN EXAMINATION

Everything went beautifully until the Latin examination. The high school boy with the scarf was first, Semyonov was second, and I was third. I even began to feel proud and to think seriously that in spite of my youth I was not to be taken lightly.

Ever since the first examination people had been talking with trepidation about the Latin professor, who was alleged to be some kind of monster who delighted in bringing about the downfall of young men, especially paying students, and spoke allegedly only in Greek or Latin. St.-Jérôme, who was my Latin teacher, gave me encouragement, and it seemed to me that in any case—being able to translate Cicero and several of Horace's odes without a dictionary and having an excellent knowledge of Zumpt—I was prepared just as well as the others; but it transpired otherwise. All one heard the whole morning was of the downfall of those preceding me: this one got nought, that one got one, another one was harangued and threatened with being sent out, and so on and so forth. Only Semyonov and the top high school boy, as usual, went up calmly and came back with five a piece. I already had a premonition of disaster when Ikonin and I were called out together to the little table at which the professor sat completely alone. The terrible professor was a thin yellow little man with long greasy hair and with an extremely preoccupied expression on his face.

He gave Ikonin a volume of Cicero's speeches and made him translate from it.

To my great astonishment Ikonin not only read but even translated several lines with the aid of the professor, who prompted him. Aware of my superiority to such a weak rival, I could not suppress a smile that even grew somewhat disdainful when it came to the problem of parsing and Ikonin, as before, lapsed into what was obviously an irrevocable silence. I intended by this intelligent and slightly mocking smile to please the professor, but it came out to the contrary.

"You evidently know it better, since you are smiling," said the professor in bad Russian. "We'll see. Here, tell me the answer."

I learned subsequently that the Latin professor was a patron of Ikonin and that Ikonin even lived with him. I answered the question on syntax that had been put to Ikonin immediately, but the professor put on a sorrowful face and turned away from me.

"Good. Well, your turn will come and we shall see what you know," he said without looking at me, and began explaining the question to Ikonin.

"You may go," he added, and I saw him write four in his notebook for Ikonin. Well, I thought, he's not at all as severe as they said. After Ikonin's departure he spent a good five minutes—which seemed like more than five hours to me—arranging books and question slips, blowing his nose, straightening his armchair, sprawling out in it, and gazing down the hall and around him and everywhere but in my direction. All this play-acting, however, still seemed insufficient for him, since he opened a book and pretended to be reading it, as though I were not there at all. I moved closer and coughed.

"Oh, yes! Are you next? Well, try translating something," he said, handing me some book or other. "No, better take this one." He leafed through a volume of Horace and gave it to me open at a place that, it seemed to me, nobody in the world could have translated.

"I haven't prepared this," I said.

"Oh, you wish to have something that you've learned by heart—wonderful! No, you translate this."

Somehow I began to make sense of it, but in response to each inquiring glance of mine he shook his head, sighed, and merely said No. At last he closed the book with such nervous haste that he slammed it shut on his finger; having jerked it out angrily from there, he handed me a slip on grammar, leaned back in his chair, and maintained a most ominous silence. I was about to begin my reply, but the expression on his face paralyzed my tongue and everything I might have said seemed wrong to me.

"That's wrong, wrong, quite wrong," he said suddenly with his disgusting pronunciation, quickly changing his position, leaning his elbow on the table, and playing with a gold ring that hung loosely on one of the thin fingers of his left hand. "That's no way, gentlemen, to prepare for entry to an establishment of higher learning; all you want is a uniform to wear with a blue collar; you skim the surface a bit and you think you can be students; no, gentlemen, you have to have a thorough knowledge of your subject," and so on and so forth.

During the whole of this speech, uttered in mangled Russian, I watched his lowered eyes with blank attention. At first I was tormented by the disillusionment of not coming third, then by fear of failing the examinations altogether, and finally by an additional awareness of a sense of injustice, of outraged pride and undeserved humiliation. Above all, my contempt for the professor for not being, in my view, a man who was *comme il faut*—a fact that I discovered by looking at his short, strong, rounded fingernails—inflamed all these feelings in me still further and made them poisonous. Glancing up at me and noticing my trembling lips and tear-filled eyes, he must have translated my agitation as a plea for him to increase my mark, and as though taking pity on me he said (this in the presence of another professor who came up at this time):

"All right, although you don't deserve it, I'll give you a pass (this meant a two), but it's only out of consideration for your youth and in the hope that you will not be so frivolous once you are at the university."

This last phrase of his, spoken in the presence of another professor—who looked at me as if to say: "There, you see, young man!"—completed my confusion. There was one moment when a mist veiled my eyes: the terrible professor and his table seemed to me to be in the far distance and with terrible one-sided vividness the wild thought entered my head: "What if? . . . What would happen?" But for some reason I did not do it; on the contrary, unconsciously I bowed with extra courtesy to both professors and with a slight smile, the same, I believe, as that smiled by Ikonin, walked away from the table.

The injustice of this had such a powerful effect on me at the time that if I had had freedom of action I would not have gone to any more examinations. I had lost all ambition (since it was now unthinkable that I could come third) and I let all the other examinations go by without any particular effort or even trepidation. My average mark at the end, however, was four something, but this no longer interested me in the least; I made up my mind and even proved to myself with great clarity that it was extraordinarily stupid and even *mauvais genre* to try to come first and that one had to try to do not too badly and not too well, like Volodya. I was also determined to stick to this henceforward in the university as well, despite the fact that in this I departed for the first time from the opinions of my friend.

Now I thought only of my uniform, my three-cornered hat, my own droshky, my own room and—most important of all—my freedom.

XIII

I Am Grown-up

Even these thoughts had their charm, however.

Returning from my last examination, religious knowledge, on May eighth, I found at home an apprentice whom I knew from Rozanov's, who had called once before with my hastily run-up uniform and frock coat of shimmering glossy black cloth and had chalked out the lapels; and now he had brought the completely finished outfit with its glittering gold buttons wrapped in paper.

Having donned the outfit and finding it excellent, although St.-Jérôme assured me that it was wrinkled at the back, I went downstairs with a self-satisfied smile that spread completely involuntarily over my whole face, and went to Volodya's room, sensing but pretending not to notice the looks the servants fixed greedily upon me from the front hall and corridor. Gavrilo, the butler, overtook me in the salon, congratulated me on my success, handed me, on Papa's instructions, four twenty-five-ruble bills and told me that henceforth, also on Papa's instructions, the driver Kuzma, a droshky, and the bay Krasavchik would be at my complete disposal. I was so overjoyed by this almost unexpected good fortune that I was completely incapable of pretending indifference before Gavrilo and, somewhat overcome, gasped and said the first thing that came into my head—something, I believe, to the effect that "Krasavchik's an excellent trotter." Glancing at the heads thrust out from the doors of the front hall and corridor, I could no longer restrain myself and galloped through the salon in my new coat with its glittering gold buttons. Just as I entered Volodya's room I heard behind me the voices of Dubkov and Nekhlyudov, who had come to congratulate me and propose that we go out to dine somewhere and drink champagne in honor of my success. Dmitri told me that, although he did not like drinking champagne, he would go with us today in order to drink a toast with me; Dubkov said that for some reason I resembled a colonel; Volodya did not congratulate me and merely said extremely curtly that now we could leave for the country the following day. Although he was glad of my success, it was as though he were a little displeased that I was now a grown-up like him. St.-Jérôme, who also came in, said very pompously that his duties were now at an end, that he did not know whether they had been well or ill discharged but that he had done everything he could and that the following day he would move to his count's. In reply to everything that was said to me I felt a syrupily happy and somewhat foolishly self-satisfied smile blossom on my face against my will and I noticed that this smile even communicated itself to everyone who talked to me.

So here I was without a tutor, with my own droshky, my name printed in the directory of students, a sword at my waist, and sentries might salute me from time to time. . . . I was grown-up; I was, it seems, happy.

We had decided to dine at Yar's after four; but since Volodya had gone to Dubkov's and Dmitri, in his usual fashion, had also disappeared somewhere, saying he had something to do before dinner, I had two hours in which to do as I liked. For quite a long time I walked through all the rooms looking at myself in all the mirrors, now with my coat buttoned up, now with it completely unbuttoned, and finally with it buttoned on the top button only, and all ways seemed excellent to me. Then, no matter how ashamed I felt of showing too much joy, I could not resist going to the stables and coachhouse and inspecting Krasavchik, Kuzma, and the droshky before returning to the house once more, strolling through all the rooms, looking in the mirrors and counting the money in my pocket, all with the same ecstatic smile on my face. However, not an hour of the time had passed before I experienced a certain boredom or rather regret that no one was seeing me in this dazzling state, and I felt a desire for movement and action. Consequently I ordered the droshky to be harnessed and decided that it would be best of all to go to Kuznetsky Bridge to make some purchases.

I recalled that when Volodya entered the university he had bought himself some lithographs of horses done by Victor Adam, some tobacco, and some pipes, and it seemed essential to me that I do the same.

With eyes turned upon me from all sides and with the sun sparkling brightly on my buttons, cockade, and sword, I arrived at Kuznetsky Bridge and halted beside Daziaro's picture shop. Looking around me in all directions, I went in. I did not want to buy horses by Adam in order not to be reproached with aping Volodya, but out of shame for the trouble I was causing the obliging shopman, I hastened to make a choice as quickly as possible and took a gouache of a woman's head that was standing in the window, for which I paid twenty rubles. Having spent twenty rubles in the shop, however, I still felt ashamed of having bothered the two handsomely dressed shopmen with such a trifle; moreover it seemed that they still regarded me much too casually. Wishing to impress upon them what sort of a man I was, I directed my attention to a silver object that lay under glass, and upon learning that it was a *porte-crayon* costing eighteen rubles, asked to have it wrapped up, paid the money, discovered further that it was possible to find good tobacco and briars in the tobacco store next door, and with a polite bow to the two shopmen went out into the street with the picture under my arm. In the neighboring store, which had a sign with a Negro on it smoking a cigar, I bought, also out of a desire to imitate no one, not ordinary Zhukov but Turkish tobacco, together with a Stamboul pipe and two briars of lime and rosewood. As I left the shop to return to my droshky I caught sight of Semyonov, who with his head lowered and wearing civilian clothes was stepping swiftly along the sidewalk. I was irritated that he did not recognize me. Saying "Drive on!" in a fairly loud voice, I boarded the droshky and overtook Semyonov.

"Hello," I said.

"Good day to you," he replied, walking on.

"Why aren't you wearing a uniform?" I asked.

Semyonov halted, screwed up his eyes, bared his teeth, as if it were hurting him to look at the sun, but actually in order to show his indifference to my droshky and uniform, looked at me silently and then continued on his way.

After Kuznetsky Bridge I called in at a pastry shop on Tverskoy Boulevard, and although I wanted to pretend that it was principally the newspapers that interested me, I could not hold back and began to eat one sweet cake after another. Despite the fact that I felt ashamed in the presence of a gentleman who gazed at me with curiosity from behind a newspaper, I ate eight cakes with extraordinary rapidity—all the kinds they had in the pastry shop.

When I arrived home I felt a touch of heartburn; but disregarding it, I busied myself with examining my purchases, of which the picture so displeased me that I not only did not frame it or hang it up in my room, as Volodya had done, but carefully hid it behind the chest of drawers where nobody could see it. I did not like the *porte-crayon* either now that I was at home; I put it in my desk, consoling myself, however, with the thought that it was silver and an asset, which for a student was very useful. As for my smoking apparatus, I at once decided to put it into action and test it.

Having unsealed the package and carefully filled my Stamboul pipe with fine-cut Turkish tobacco, I put a glowing tinder to it and, holding the pipe between my middle and fourth fingers (a position that specially appealed to me), began to inhale.

The smell of the tobacco was very pleasant, but there was a bitter taste in my mouth and it was difficult to breathe. Bracing myself, however, I breathed in the smoke for quite a long time and tried to blow smoke rings and inhale. Soon the room was completely filled with clouds of bluish smoke, the pipe began to wheeze, the hot tobacco to jump, my mouth felt bitter, and there was a slight dizziness in my head. As soon as I tried to rise just to take a look at myself with a pipe in the mirror, to my amazement I began to stagger; the room went in circles and when I looked in the mirror, which I approached with difficulty, I saw that my face was as white as a sheet. I barely had time to flop down on the sofa before I experienced such nausea and such feebleness that, imagining the pipe to have been fatal to me, I thought I was dying. I grew seriously alarmed and was even about to call for help and send for a doctor.

But this terror did not last long. I soon realized what the matter was and for a long time lay there on the sofa, enfeebled, with a terrible headache and gazing dully at the crest of Bostonzhoglo depicted on the tobacco paper, at the pipe, tobacco embers, and remains of the patisserie cakes lying on the floor; and in sad disillusionment I thought: I mustn't be completely grown-up yet if I can't smoke like the others; evidently I'm not fated, like the others, to hold a pipe between my middle and fourth fingers and inhale and expel the smoke through my blond whiskers.

It was in this disagreeable state that Dmitri found me when he called for me after four. After drinking a glass of water, however, I was nearly well again and was ready to go with him.

———

"What on earth did you want to smoke for?" he said, looking at the traces of my smoking. "It's all nonsense and a senseless waste of money. I promised myself I'd never smoke. . . . However, let's go quickly; we still have to pick up Dubkov."

XIV

What Volodya and Dubkov Were Doing

As soon as Dmitri entered my room I realized from his walk and from a gesture that was characteristic of him in a bad mood—that of blinking his eyes and jerking his head to one side in a grimace, as though straightening his tie—that he was in that coldly stubborn mood that usually came over him when he was dissatisfied with himself, and that always had a cooling effect on my feelings for him. Lately I had already begun to observe and judge my friend's character, but our friendship was not in the least affected by this: it was still so young and strong that no matter from which side I looked at Dmitri I could not fail to see his perfection. He contained two different men, both of whom were wonderful to me. One, whom I loved passionately, was kind affectionate humble gay and conscious of these lovable qualities. When he was in this mood his whole appearance, his tone of voice and all his gestures seemed to say: "I am humble and virtuous and I revel in being humble and virtuous and you can all see it." The other, whom I was only now beginning to recognize and whose majesty I worshiped, was a cold man, stern toward himself and others, proud, religious to the point of fanaticism, and pedantically moral. At the moment he was the second of these men.

With the frankness that constituted an indispensable condition of our relations with one another, I told him when we had got into the droshky that it pained and saddened me to see him in such a dismal and to me disagreeable mood on what was such a happy day for me.

"Something must have upset you: why don't you tell me about it?" I said.

"Nikolyenka!" he replied with deliberation, nervously putting his head to one side and blinking. "If I gave you my word never to conceal anything from you, you have no reason to suspect me of secrecy. It is impossible to be always in the same mood, and if something has upset me I myself cannot say what it is."

What a wonderfully open and honest character he has, I thought and said no more.

We drove to Dubkov's in silence. Dubkov's apartment was remarkably fine, or so it seemed to me. Everywhere there were rugs, pictures, curtains, vivid wallpaper, portraits, bent-wood chairs and Voltaire chairs, while on the walls hung guns, pistols, tobacco pouches, and some sort of cardboard heads of wild animals. At the sight of his study I realized whom Volodya was imitating in the furnishings of his own room. We found Dubkov and Volodya playing cards. A gentleman who was unknown to me (and who must have been unimportant, judging by his humble attitude) was sitting beside the table and following the game with rapt attention. Dubkov himself was wearing a silk dressing gown and soft slippers. Volodya was sitting opposite him on the sofa, coatless, and—judging by his flushed face and the discontented hasty glance that he flung at us, tearing himself away from the cards for a moment—was very much absorbed in the game. Catching sight of me he flushed still further.

"Come, it's your turn to deal," he said to Dubkov. I realized that it disturbed him for me to know he played cards. But there was no embarrassment discernible in his expression; it seemed to say to me: "Yes, I play cards, and you are surprised about it only because you are still young. It's not only not bad but necessary at our age."

I immediately sensed and understood this.

Dubkov, however, did not commence to deal but got up, shook us by the hand, found us seats, and offered us pipes, which we refused.

"So here he is, our diplomat, the guest of honor," said Dubkov. "I swear he looks terribly like a colonel."

"Hm!" I mumbled, feeling that foolishly self-satisfied smile break out once more over my face.

I admired Dubkov as only a sixteen-year-old boy can admire a twenty-seven-year-old aide-de-camp whom all the grown-ups declare to be a remarkably decent young man, who is an excellent dancer, speaks French and, although despising me in his heart of hearts for my youth, makes an evident effort to conceal it.

And yet God knows why, despite my admiration for him, I found it difficult and awkward throughout the whole of our acquaintance to look him straight in the eye. And I have since observed that there are three sorts of people whom it is difficult for me to look in the eye— those who are much worse than I, those who are much better than I, and those with whom I get into a situation where neither of us can bring himself to say something to the other that we both know to be true. Perhaps Dubkov was better than I, perhaps he was worse, but what was certain was that he had frequently lied without admitting it and that I had detected this weakness in him, but of course had not been able to bring myself to speak to him of it.

"Let's play one more game," said Volodya, shrugging one shoulder like Papa, and shuffling the cards.

"He's so persistent!" said Dubkov. "We'll play on later. Oh well, one more hand then—go on."

While they played I watched their hands. Volodya had large handsome hands; the angle of his thumb and the way he bent his other fingers when holding the cards reminded me so much of Papa's hand that for one moment it even seemed to me that Volodya held his hand that way on purpose in order to look like a grown-up; but one glance at his face immediately told me that he was thinking of nothing but the game. Dubkov's hands, on the contrary, were small, plump, and bent inward and were extremely nimble and had soft fingers; they were precisely the kind of hands that normally have rings on them and belong to people who enjoy handicrafts and like to possess beautiful things.

Volodya must have been losing because the gentleman who was watching his cards said that Vladimir Petrovich was having atrocious luck while Dubkov, taking out his notebook, wrote something in it, showed what he had written to Volodya, and said: "Right?"

"Right!" said Volodya, pretending to look absently at the notebook. "Now let's go."

Volodya took Dubkov and Dmitri took me in his phaeton.

"What were they playing?" I asked Dmitri.

"Piquet. A stupid game. Gambling in general is stupid, anyway."

"Are they playing for large stakes?"

"No, not very, but it's still not right."

"Don't you gamble?"

"No, I promised I wouldn't. But Dubkov can't help beating the others."

"Well, that's a bit off on his part, isn't it?" I said. "I suppose Volodya's not as good as he is?"

"Of course it's a bit off, but there's nothing particularly bad about it. Dubkov likes to play and plays well, but nonetheless he's an excellent fellow."

"Well, I had no idea . . . ," I said.

"Well, you mustn't think ill of him because really he's a wonderful man. And I like him very much and always will like him, despite his weaknesses."

For some reason it seemed to me that precisely because Dmitri stood up for Dubkov so overenthusiastically he no longer liked or respected him, but would not admit it out of stubbornness and so that no one could accuse him of inconstancy. He was one of those people who love their friends for a whole lifetime, not so much because these friends remain constantly dear to them as because, once, even mistakenly, having loved a man, they consider it dishonorable to change toward him.

XV

My Success Is Celebrated

Dubkov and Volodya knew all the people at Yar's by name and, from the doorman to the proprietor, everybody showed them the greatest respect. We were immediately assigned a private room and served a superb dinner, chosen by Dubkov from the French menu. A bottle of chilled champagne, which I tried to look upon with as much indifference as possible, had already been prepared for us. Dinner passed very agreeably and merrily, despite the fact that Dubkov, in his usual manner, related the oddest stories which he claimed to be true—among others how his grandmother, with a blunderbuss, had killed three brigands who attacked her (at this I blushed, lowered my eyes, and turned away from him)—and also despite the fact that Volodya winced visibly every time I started to say something (which was completely superfluous because, so far as I remember, I said nothing that was particularly disgraceful).

When the champagne was served everyone congratulated me and I drank *Bruderschaft*, with linked arms, with Dubkov and Dmitri, and embraced them. Since I did not know to whom the bottle of champagne they served belonged (it was a joint bottle, I learned afterward) and wanted to treat my friends with my own money—which I was fingering ceaselessly in my pocket—I surreptitiously extracted a ten-ruble bill, called the waiter over to me, gave him the money and whispered to him—although everyone heard me because they watched me in silence—to bring *if you please another half bottle of champagne.* Volodya turned so red and began to twitch and look at me and the others in such consternation that I felt I had made a mistake, but the half bottle was brought and we drank it up with great satisfaction. Things continued to seem very jolly. Dubkov told story after story without stopping and Volodya also related such funny things and so well that I never would have expected it of him, and we laughed a great deal. The nature of their wit, that is Dubkov's and Volodya's, consisted in imitating and extending that well-known joke that goes: "Oh, so you've been abroad, have you?" says one man supposedly. "No, I haven't," says the other, "but my brother can play the violin." They attained such perfection in this species of nonsense humor that the anecdote itself even came out as: "My brother never played the violin either." Every question from one another they answered in the same way and sometimes they even tried to link two totally different things together without a question, and said this nonsense with such serious faces that it all seemed very funny. I began to understand what was going on and also wanted to say something funny, but they all looked at me fearfully or tried not to look at me at all while I was talking and my story did not come off. Dubkov said: "You're talking nonsense, my dear diplomat," but I felt so good from the champagne I had drunk and from being in the company of grown-ups that this remark only inflicted on me a very slight scratch. Only Dmitri, despite the fact that he had kept pace with our drinking, remained in that severe serious mood of his, which somewhat restrained the general merriment.

"Now listen, gentlemen," said Dubkov. "After dinner we shall have to take the diplomat in hand. What say we go to Auntie; we'll soon settle his hash there."

"Nekhlyudov won't go," said Volodya.

"An impossible lamb you are, an impossible lamb!" said Dubkov, turning to him. "Come with us and you'll see what a wonderful lady Auntie is."

"Not only will I not come, but I won't let him go, either," replied Dmitri, blushing.

"Who? The diplomat? You want to go, don't you, Diplomat? Look at him, his whole face lit up as soon as we mentioned Auntie."

"It's not that I won't let him," went on Dmitri, getting up from his chair and starting to walk about the room without looking at me, "but I don't advise him to go and I hope he won't. He's not a child now, and if he wants to he can go alone, without you. But you ought to be ashamed of yourself, Dubkov. Just because you behave badly yourself, you want others to do the same."

"What's wrong with it?" said Dubkov, winking at Volodya. "Just because I invited you all to Auntie's for a cup of tea? Well, if you don't like the fact that we're going, it's up to you: Volodya and I are going. Coming Volodya?"

"Mm, mm!" said Volodya affirmatively. "We'll drop in there and then go back to my place and go on with our piquet."

"Well, do you want to go with them or not?" said Dmitri, coming up to me.

"No," I replied, moving along the sofa to give him room to sit down, which he did. "I don't want to go anyway, and if you advise me not to then I wouldn't go for anything in the world."

"No," I added afterward. "I'm not telling the truth when I say I don't want to go with them; but I'm glad I'm not going."

"And quite right too," he said. "Live your own life and don't dance to anybody's tune, that's best of all."

This little argument not only did not spoil our enjoyment but even increased it. Dmitri suddenly fell into that humble mood of his that I liked best. As I had occasion to notice more than once later, this was the influence that consciousness of a good action had upon him. Now he was pleased with himself for having stood up for me. He cheered up considerably, ordered another bottle of champagne (which was against his principles), called some unknown man into the room and started giving him drinks, sang *"Gaudeamus igitur,"* asked us all to sing the chorus, and suggested that we go to Sokolniki for a ride, at which Dubkov remarked that this was too, too sentimental.

"Come on, let's be merry today," said Dmitri smilingly. "In honor of his success I'm making myself drunk for the first time. Well, so be it." This jollity seemed somewhat odd in Dmitri. He resembled a tutor or a kind father who is pleased with his children, has let himself go, and wishes to entertain them and at the same time show that it is possible to make merry honorably and decently; but in spite of this it seemed that his unexpected jollity was infectious, the more so in that each of us by now had drunk almost a half bottle of champagne.

It was in this agreeable mood that I went out into the main restaurant to light a cigarette that Dubkov had given me.

When I got up from my seat I noticed that my head felt a little dizzy and that my legs would move and my hands stay in their natural position only when I concentrated my attention on them. Otherwise my legs took themselves off to either side and my arms described certain gestures. I fixed my whole attention on these members, commanded my hands to rise, button my coat, and smooth down my hair (at which they threw my elbows up horribly high in the air), and commanded my legs to walk to the door, which they did, but stepping somehow either very firmly or else overgently, especially my left foot, which kept getting up on tiptoe. A voice called out to me: "Where are you going? They're bringing a candle." I guessed that this voice belonged to Volodya and I was pleased to think that I had been able to guess it, but in reply to him I merely smiled slightly and continued on my way.

XVI

A Quarrel

In the main restaurant a short thick-set gentleman in civilian clothes and with a ginger mustache was sitting at a little table eating something. Next to him sat a tall dark man who was without a mustache. They were talking in French. Their glance disturbed me but nonetheless I made up my mind to light my cigarette from the burning candle standing before them. Looking away in order to avoid their eyes, I approached their table and proceeded to put my cigarette into the flame. When the cigarette was alight I could not resist it any longer and glanced at the gentleman who was eating. His gray eyes were fixed upon me intently and were filled with animosity. Just as I was about to turn away, his ginger mustache quivered and he said in French:

"I don't like people to smoke when I am eating, sir."

I muttered something unintelligible.

"No, I don't like it," went on the mustachioed gentleman severely, stealing a quick glance at the mustacheless gentleman, as though inviting him to admire the way in which he was going to give me a dressing down. "I don't like it, sir, nor people who are so discourteous as to come and smoke under your nose; I don't like them either." I realized immediately that this gentleman was taking it out on me, but it seemed to me at first that I was very much in the wrong.

"I did not think it would disturb you," I said.

"Ah, you didn't think you were a lout, either, but I did," shouted the gentleman.

"What right do you have to shout at me like that?" I said, feeling that he was insulting me and beginning to grow angry myself.

"This much, that I shall never permit anyone to show disrespect to me and shall always teach young pups like you a lesson. What's your name, sir? And where do you live?"

I was enraged, my lips trembled violently, and my breath came with difficulty. But I still felt myself in the wrong, probably because I had drunk so much champagne, and I did not offer this gentleman any insults; on the contrary, my lips informed him of my name and our address in the humblest possible fashion.

"My name is Kolpikov, sir, and you should have more respect in future. You will be hearing from me (*vous aurez de mes nouvelles*)," he concluded, since the whole conversation had been conducted in French.

All I said was: "Delighted," trying to imbue my voice with as much firmness as possible, then turned, and with my cigarette, which by now had gone out, returned to our room.

I did not tell either my brother or our friends about what had happened to me, the more so in that they were engaged in some heated argument, but sat down alone in one corner and debated upon this strange incident to myself. The words: "You're a lout, sir [*un mal élevé, Monsieur*]" resounded in my ears, making me more and more indignant. My intoxication had completely passed. When I pondered on the way I had behaved in the affair, the terrible thought occurred to me that I had acted like a coward.... What right did he have to attack me? Why did he not simply say that I was disturbing him? He was in the wrong, wasn't he? Why, when he told me I was a lout, didn't I say to him: he, sir, is a lout who permits himself rudeness? Or why didn't I simply yell *Shut up!* at him? That would have been excellent; why didn't I challenge him to a duel? No, I didn't do any of those things, but swallowed the insult like a despicable little coward. "You're a lout, sir!" rang in my ears incessantly, irritating me.... No, I can't leave it like that, I thought and stood up with the firm intention of going once more to that gentleman and saying something awful to him, and perhaps even hitting him over the head with the candlestick if necessary. I mused over this last idea with the greatest of pleasure, but it was not without certain misgivings that I re-entered the main restaurant. Fortunately Mr. Kolpikov was no longer there; there was only one waiter in the restaurant, clearing the table. For a moment I wanted to inform the waiter about what had happened and explain to him that I was not at all in the wrong, but for some reason I changed my mind and went back to our room in the blackest possible mood.

"What's happened to our diplomat?" said Dubkov. "He's probably deciding the fate of Europe now."

"Oh, leave me alone," I said sullenly, turning away. After this, as I walked up and down the room, I began to dwell for some reason on the idea that Dubkov was not at all a good man. And why all these endless jokes and calling me "diplomat"—there's nothing friendly about it. All he wants to do is win off Volodya and then go to see some auntie or other. . . . And there's nothing nice about him. Everything he says is a lie or something vulgar, and he always wants to make fun of someone. It seems to me he's just stupid and a bad man into the bargain. With such thoughts as these I passed about five minutes, feeling my hostility to Dubkov grow and grow. Dubkov, though, paid no attention to me and this increased my spite still more. I even grew angry with Volodya and Dmitri for continuing to speak to him.

"Do you know what, gentlemen? We have to pour water over the diplomat," said Dubkov all of a sudden, glancing at me with a smile; this smile seemed mocking and even treacherous to me. "Otherwise he'll be in a bad way. I swear to God he's in a bad way!"

"And you need some water too, you're in a bad way yourself," I replied, smiling venomously and forgetting even to use the familiar *thou*.

This reply must have surprised Dubkov, but he turned away from me indifferently and continued to talk to Volodya and Dmitri.

I tried for a moment to join in their conversation, but was completely incapable of pretending and again retired to my corner, where I remained until our departure.

When we had paid the bill and were getting into our overcoats, Dubkov said to Dmitri:

"Well, and where are Orestes and Pylades going? Home, I suppose, to talk of *love*; we'll do better, we'll pay a call on dear Auntie—it's better than your sour friendship."

"How dare you say such things and laugh at us," I said, going up very close to him and waving my arms about. "How dare you laugh at feelings you don't understand? I won't allow it. Shut up!" I cried and then fell silent myself, not knowing what else to say and gasping with excitement. Dubkov was taken aback at first; then he was about to smile and take it as a joke, but finally, to my immense surprise, he looked alarmed and lowered his eyes.

"I'm not laughing at you and your feelings at all," he said evasively. "I was just talking."

"Aha!" I shouted, but at that very moment I felt ashamed of myself and sorry for Dubkov, whose red disturbed face expressed genuine sorrow.

"What's the matter with you?" said Volodya and Dmitri in unison. "Nobody was trying to insult you."

"No, he was trying to insult me."

"He's a desperate case, your brother," said Dubkov as he got outside the door, so that he could not hear anything I might say in reply.

Perhaps I would have dashed after him and said all sorts of more rude things to him, but at this moment that same waiter who had been present during my contretemps with Kolpikov offered me my overcoat and I immediately calmed down, merely pretending in front of Dmitri to be as angry as seemed indispensable to prevent my sudden calmness from seeming queer. The following day Dubkov and I met at Volodya's and did not refer to this affair, but we remained on formal terms and it became even harder for us to look one another in the eye.

The recollection of my quarrel with Kolpikov, who, by the way, never gave me *de ses nouvelles*, either on the following day or afterwards, remained horribly vivid and painful to me for many years. Five years after this I would still give a start and exclaim every time I remembered that unavenged insult and I consoled myself complacently with the thought that on the other hand I had behaved like a hero in the affair with Dubkov. Only much later did I begin to regard this affair in a different light and recall my quarrel with Kolpikov with humorous satisfaction, and repent of the undeserved insult I had inflicted on that *good fellow* Dubkov.

When I told Dmitri that same evening about my adventure with Kolpikov, whose appearance I described to him in detail, he was extremely surprised.

"Oh, so that's the one!" he said. "Just imagine, that Kolpikov's a notorious rogue and card-sharp, but the main thing is he's a coward and was drummed out of his regiment by his comrades because his face was slapped and he wouldn't fight. Where did he get the spunk, I wonder?" he added with a good-natured smile, looking at me. "Did he not say anything more than just *lout*?"

"No," I replied, blushing.

Only much later, when I could think about the incident calmly, did I come to the fairly plausible conclusion that Kolpikov, feeling after many years that he could safely attack me, revenged himself upon me in the presence of his mustacheless companion for the slap he had received before, just as I immediately revenged myself for his "lout" on the innocent Dubkov.

XVII

I Prepare to Make Some Calls

When I awoke the following day my first thought was of my adventure with Kolpikov; again I let out a strangled cry and ran about the room, but there was nothing to be done; moreover, today was my last day in Moscow and I had, on Papa's instructions, to make certain visits which he had written out for me on a piece of paper. Father's care of us had less to do with morality and education than it had with social relations. Written on the paper in his hasty angular handwriting was the following: (1) Prince Ivan Ivanich *without fail,* (2) the Ivins *without fail,* (3) Prince Mikhailo, (4) Princess Nekhlyudov and Mme. Valakhin if you have time. And of course go to the university president, the rector, and the professors.

Dmitri dissuaded me from paying these last calls, saying that not only was it unnecessary but would even be improper, but the rest should all be made that day. Of these the first two visits, beside which *without fail* was written, frightened me in particular. Prince Ivan Ivanich was a full general, an old man, a wealthy man, and alone; that meant that I, a sixteen-year-old student, had to come into direct contact with him, a situation which could not, I felt, prove at all flattering to me. The Ivins were also wealthy and their father was an important top-ranking civil servant who had only been to us once—when Grandmother was alive. After Grandmother's death I noticed that the younger Ivin fought shy of us and seemed to put on airs. The elder, I knew by report, had already completed his law studies and was now working for the government in St. Petersburg; the second one, Sergei, whom I had once worshiped, was also in St. Petersburg as a big fat cadet in the Corps of Pages.

In my youth I not only did not like to associate with people who considered themselves above me, but such associations were intolerably painful to me, owing to my constant fear of being insulted and the straining of all my mental faculties in order to prove my independence to them. Since, however, I was not going to carry out Papa's last order, it was necessary to ease my guilt by complying with the first ones. I was walking about my room, eyeing my clothes, sword, and hat laid out on some chairs and just preparing to go, when old man Grap arrived to congratulate me together with Ilinka. Grap senior was a Russianized German who was unbearably obsequious and sycophantic and extremely frequently under the influence; for the most part he only came to us to ask for something and Papa sometimes entertained him in his study, but he was never invited to dine with us. His abjectness and persistent begging were so mingled with surface good nature and familiarity with our household that everyone placed high value on his attachment to us all, but I for some reason did not like him and whenever he spoke I always felt ashamed for him.

I was extremely displeased by the arrival of these guests and did not attempt to conceal my displeasure. I was so accustomed to looking down on Ilinka and he was so accustomed to thinking we had a right to do this that I felt somewhat piqued that he should be a student just like me. It seemed to me that he too felt somewhat ashamed in my presence of this equality. I greeted them coldly and without inviting them to take a seat, because I was ashamed to and thought that they might do it without an invitation from me, ordered my carriage to be got ready. Ilinka was a kind, very honorable, and not in the least stupid young man, but he was what was called a bit touched; he was always in some extreme mood and always without reason it seemed—one moment it was tearfulness, then a giggling fit, then a disposition to take offense at the least little trifle; and now, it seemed, he was in this last mood. He did not say anything but looked balefully at me and his father, and only when spoken to did he smile the submissive constrained smile beneath which he was accustomed to conceal his feelings, especially a feeling of shame for his father, which was unavoidable in our presence.

"So, Nikolai Petrovich," said the old man, following me about the room as I dressed, and slowly and respectfully revolving in his pudgy fingers a silver snuffbox, given to him by Grandmother, "as soon as I learned from my son that you'd passed the examinations so brilliantly—you're well known for your brains, anyway—I immediately came to congratulate you, dear boy; I used to carry you on my shoulders, you know, and God sees that I love you all as my own; and Ilinka kept begging to come and see you. He's got used to you too."

During this time Ilinka sat silently by the window, apparently examining my three-cornered hat and barely audibly muttering something in an angry undertone.

"Well, and I wanted to ask you, Nikolai Petrovich," went on the old man, "how was my Ilinka, did he pass the examinations well? He said he's going to be in the same faculty as you, so please don't abandon him; keep an eye on him and give him advice."

"Why, he did extremely well," I replied, glancing at Ilinka; the latter, feeling my glance on him, blushed and ceased moving his lips.

"And can he spend the day with you?" said the old man with such a timid smile that it seemed as though he were very frightened of me, and continued to follow so close behind me, wherever I moved, that the alcohol and tobacco fumes of which he reeked did not cease to assail me even for a second. I was irritated with him for placing me in such an invidious position vis-à-vis his son and for distracting my attention from what was for me an extremely important task—dressing; but the main thing was that being pursued by this alcoholic stench so infuriated me that I told him extremely coldly that I could not be with Ilinka because I would be away from home all day.

"But you wanted to go and see your sister, Father, didn't you?" said Ilinka, smiling and not looking at me. "And anyway I have some work to attend to." I felt even more annoyed and ashamed and in order to soften my refusal somehow I hastened to inform them that I had to visit *Prince* Ivan Ivanich, *Princess* Kornakov, and Ivin, the one who held such an important post, and that I would probably be dining at *Princess* Nekhlyudov's. I thought that once they knew what important people I was visiting they could no longer make any claims on me. When they were preparing to leave I invited Ilinka to visit me another time; but Ilinka merely mumbled something and smiled with a strained expression. It was clear that he would never set foot over my threshold again.

I followed them out in order to make my calls. Volodya, whom I had invited that morning to accompany me so that I would feel less awkward than if alone, refused on the grounds that it would have been too soppy—*two little brothers* riding together in *one little carriage.*

XVIII

THE VALAKHINS

And so I set off alone. My first call was on Mme. Valakhin, who lived nearest in Sivtsev Vrazhek. I had not seen Sonyechka for three years and my love for her, of course, had long since passed, but lively and touching recollections of that old childish love still lingered deep inside me. During these past three years I had sometimes remembered her with such force and clarity that I had shed tears and felt myself to be in love once more, but it had only lasted a few minutes and had not repeated itself all that soon.

I knew that Sonyechka and her mother had been abroad and had remained there for about two years and that their carriage was said to have been overturned and Sonyechka's face badly cut by flying glass, so that her looks were supposed to have badly deteriorated. On the way there I recalled the former Sonyechka vividly and wondered how I would find her now. As a result of her two-year stay abroad I imagined her for some reason as being extremely tall, with a superb waist, serious and dignified, but extraordinarily attractive. My imagination refused to picture her with her face disfigured by scars; on the con-

trary, having heard somewhere of a passionate lover who had remained faithful to his love in spite of her disfigurement by smallpox, I
tried to think that I was in love with Sonyechka in order to have the
merit of remaining true to her in spite of her scars. In general I was not
in love as I approached the Valakhins' house, but having stirred up old
memories of love inside me I was well prepared to fall in love and
strongly desired it; besides, I had long felt grieved, contemplating all
my friends who were in love, at being left so far behind them.

The Valakhins lived in a neat little wooden house which was entered from the yard. After I had rung the bell, which was then still a
great rarity in Moscow, the door was opened for me by a tiny but
neatly dressed boy. He was not able or did not wish to tell me whether
the family was at home and left me alone in a dark anteroom while he
ran off down a still darker corridor.

I remained alone in this dark room for quite a long time; besides the
entrance to the corridor it contained one other door that was locked
and I half-wondered at the gloomy character of the house and half-
supposed that this was the way it always was with people who had been
abroad. After about five minutes the door to the salon was unlocked
from inside by the agency of the same little boy and he conducted me
into a tidy but not luxurious drawing room into which I was followed
by Sonyechka.

She was seventeen. She was extremely short and extremely thin and
her face was a sallow, unhealthy color. No scars were visible on her
face and her wonderful prominent eyes and bright good-naturedly
merry smile were the same I had known and loved in childhood. I had
not expected to find her like this at all and therefore was completely
incapable at first of lavishing on her the feelings I had prepared en
route. She gave me her hand in the English fashion, which at that time
was as great a rarity as a bell, shook my hand sincerely, and made me
sit beside her on the sofa.

"Oh, how glad I am to see you, dear *Nicolas*," she said, looking into
my face with such a genuine expression of pleasure that I detected in
the words *dear Nicolas* a friendly and not a patronizing tone. After her
visit abroad she was, to my surprise, still simpler and sweeter and
friendlier in her behavior than before. I noticed two tiny scars by her

nose and on her brow, but her wonderful eyes and smile corresponded exactly with my recollections and shone in the old manner.

"How you've changed!" she said. "You've become quite grown-up. Well, and what about me—how do you find me?"

"Oh, I'd never have known you," I replied, despite the fact that at that very moment I was thinking I would have known her anywhere. Once again I felt in that carefree merry mood in which I had danced the *grossvater* with her five years before at Grandmother's ball.

"Well, do I look much worse?" she asked with a toss of her head.

"No, not at all; you've grown a bit, got a bit older," I replied hastily, "but on the contrary . . . you're even . . ."

"Oh well, it makes no difference. Do you remember our dances and games, and St.-Jérôme, and Madame Dorat? (I did not remember any Madame Dorat; she was evidently carried away by her enthusiasm for childhood memories and was getting mixed up.) Oh, what a wonderful time that was," she went on, and that same smile, even better than the one I carried in my memory, and those same eyes, shone in front of me. While she was speaking I found time to think over the position I was in at that moment and decided to myself that at that moment I was in love. As soon as I decided this my happy carefree mood disappeared at once, some sort of fog obscured everything before me—even her eyes and smile. I became ashamed of something and blushed and lost my ability to talk.

"Times have changed now," she went on, sighing and raising her brows slightly. "Everything's got much worse, and we are worse, isn't that so, *Nicolas?*"

I could not reply and looked at her in silence.

"Where are all those Ivins and Kornakovs now? Do you remember?" she went on, looking into my blushing frightened face with a certain amount of curiosity. "What a wonderful time it was!"

I was still unable to answer.

I was rescued from this difficult position by the arrival in the room of Mme. Valakhin. I got up, bowed, and once more acquired my powers of speech; but on the other hand, the arrival of her mother produced a strange change in Sonyechka. All her gaiety and friendliness suddenly disappeared, even her smile changed, and suddenly, except for her height, she became that young lady just returned from abroad that I had imagined I would find in her. It would seem that there was no need for such a change, for her mother smiled just as agreeably and was just as gentle in all her movements as in the old days. Mme. Valakhin sat in a large armchair and motioned me to a seat beside her. To her daughter she said something in English and Sonyechka immediately left the room, which afforded me even greater relief. Mme. Valakhin questioned me about my relatives, my brother and my father, then told me of her own troubles—the loss of her husband—and, sensing at last that there was nothing more to talk about, looked at me in silence, as much as to say: "If you stand up now, bow, and depart you will be doing just the right thing, dear boy," but a strange thing happened to me. Sonyechka returned to the room with some needlework and sat in the other corner of the drawing room, so that I could feel her glances upon me. While Mme. Valakhin was telling me about the loss of her husband, I remembered once more that I was in love and also thought that the mother had probably guessed this, and I was again visited by a fit of bashfulness so violent that I felt myself incapable of moving a single limb naturally. I knew that in order to stand up and go away I would have to think of where to place my feet and what to do with my head and hands; in short, I felt almost exactly the same as the day before when I had drunk half a bottle of champagne. I had a foreboding that I would not be in control of myself in all this and therefore would be unable to stand up, and indeed I was unable to stand up. Mme. Valakhin must have been astonished to see my face, red as a beet, and my complete immobility; but I decided that it was better to sit in this stupid position than to risk rising and making a ridiculous departure. Thus I sat there for quite a long time, waiting for some unforeseen incident to rescue me from this position. This incident occurred in the person of an insignificant-looking young man who, with the air of someone at home, entered the room and treated me to a courteous bow. Mme. Valakhin stood up, excused herself by saying that she had to speak with her *homme d'affaires*, and looked at me with a puzzled expression that said: "If you want to go on sitting there forever, I won't drive you out." Somehow, making a tremendous effort with myself, I stood up, but found myself incapable of bowing, and as

I left the room, to the accompaniment of pitying looks from both mother and daughter, I tripped over a chair that was not at all in my way—but which I did because all my attention was concentrated on not tripping over the carpet beneath my feet. Outside, however—after fidgeting and mumbling so loudly that even Kuzma asked me several times: "What was that, sir?"—this feeling vanished and I began to meditate fairly calmly on my love for Sonya and her relations with her mother, which seemed odd to me. When I told Father later about my noticing that Mme. Valakhin and her daughter did not seem to get on well together, he said:

"Yes, she leads the poor girl a dog's life with her meanness. And it's strange, you know," he added with greater emotion than he could ever have felt simply over a relative, "but she was such a sweet delightful wonderful woman! I can't understand why she's so changed. Did you not happen to see some man there, her secretary? And what's a Russian lady doing with a secretary?" he said, walking away angrily.

"Yes, I saw him," I replied.

"What's he like, good-looking at least?"

"No, not at all good-looking."

"Incomprehensible," said Papa and shrugged his shoulder angrily and coughed.

And so I'm in love, I thought, driving on in my droshky.

XIX

THE KORNAKOVS

The second call on my route was to the Kornakovs. They lived on the first floor of a large house on Arbat. The staircase was extremely smart and spruce but not sumptuous. There were strips of matting everywhere held down by highly polished brass rods, but no flowers or mirrors. The salon, across whose brightly polished floor I walked to get to the drawing room, was arranged equally severely, coldly and tidily, and everything gleamed and seemed solid although not quite new, but no pictures or drapes or any ornaments were in evidence anywhere. Several princesses were in the drawing room. They were sitting so precisely and were so unoccupied that it was immediately clear that they did not sit that way when there were no guests.

"*Maman* will be here in a minute," said the eldest of them and came and sat nearer to me. For a quarter of an hour this princess engaged me in conversation so fluently and skillfully that the conversation did not flag even for a single second. But it was all too obvious that she was entertaining me and therefore I was not pleased. She told me among other things that their brother Stepan, whom they called Etienne and who had been sent to cadet school two years previously, had already been promoted to an officer. When she spoke of her brother and particularly of the fact that he had joined the hussars against his mother's wishes, she made a frightened face, and all the younger princesses, sitting there silently, also made frightened faces; when she spoke of Grandmother's death she made a sorrowful face and all the younger princesses did the same; when she recalled how I had struck St.-Jérôme and been led out of the room she laughed and showed her bad teeth and all the princesses laughed and showed their bad teeth.

The Princess came in: the same lean little woman with restless eyes and with a habit of looking round at other people while she was talking to you. She took my hand and raised her own hand to my lips for me to kiss it, which I would certainly not have done otherwise, since I did not see any need for it.

"How pleased I am to see you," she said in her usual voluble manner, looking round at her daughters. "Ah, how like his mama he is. Isn't that so, Lise?"

Lise said it was, although I know for sure that I did not bear the slightest resemblance to my mother.

"So here you are, and so big too! And my Etienne, you remember him, don't you, he's your second . . . no, not second; which is it, Lise? My mother was Varvara Dmitryevna, the daughter of Dmitri Nikolayich, and your grandmother was Dmitri's sister."

"Then it's third cousin, *maman*," said the eldest princess.

"Oh dear, you always mix things up," cried her mother at her angrily. "It's not second cousin at all but *issus de germains*—like you and my Etiennekin, you see. He's already an officer, did you know? It's bad that he has too much freedom, though. You young people need a firm hand, and I mean *firm*! . . . Don't be angry with me, your old aunt, for telling you the truth; I was always strict with Etienne and I find that it's necessary."

"Yes, this is how we're related," she went on. "Prince Ivan Ivanich was my uncle and was uncle to your mother. Therefore your mother and I were cousins—no, second cousins, yes, that's it. Well, tell me now: have you been to see Prince Ivan yet?"

I said that I had not but would go that day.

"Oh dear, how is that possible!" she exclaimed. "You should have made that your first visit. You know, don't you, that Prince Ivan's virtually a father to you? He doesn't have any children, therefore his only heirs are you and my children. You should revere him both for his age and for his position in the world and for everything. I know that you people of today have no respect for kinship and don't like your elders; but you listen to me, your old aunt, because I love you and I loved your *maman* and I also loved and respected your grandmother very much. No, you must go without fail. Without fail you must go."

I said that I would go without fail and since, in my opinion, the visit had lasted quite long enough, stood up with the intention of leaving, but she detained me.

"No, wait a moment. Where's your father, Lise? Call him in here; he'll be so pleased to see you," she went on, turning to me.

A minute or two later Prince Mikhailo did indeed enter. He was a short thick-set man, extremely sloppily dressed and unshaven and with such a kind of apathetic expression on his face that it even looked stupid. He was not in the least pleased to see me, or at any rate did not show it. But the Princess, of whom, evidently, he was very afraid, said to him:

"Doesn't *Waldemar* [she must have forgotten my name] look like his *maman?*" and made such a sign with her eyes that the Prince, probably guessing what she meant, came up to me with the most unenthusiastic and even discontented expression on his face and offered me his unshaven cheek, which I was supposed to kiss.

"I see you're not dressed yet and you have to go out," began the Princess immediately afterward, speaking to him in an angry tone that was evidently natural to her with members of the family. "You want to make people angry again, you want to turn them against you again."

"At once, at once, madam," said Prince Mikhailo and went out. I bowed and went out also.

This was the first time I had heard we were Prince Ivan Ivanich's heirs and this news had an unpleasant effect on me.

XX

THE IVINS

It became even more painful for me to contemplate the unavoidable visit that was in prospect. But on the way to the Prince's I had to call in at the Ivins. They lived on Tverskoy Boulevard in an enormous handsome house. It was not without trepidation that I went in through the main entrance, where a doorman stood with a mace.

I asked him if they were at home.

"Whom do you want? The general's son is at home," said the doorman.

"And the general?" I said bravely.

"You will have to be announced. Whom shall I say?" said the doorman and rang the bell. A footman's gaitered feet appeared on the stairs. I became so nervous, I do not know why, that I told the footman not to announce me to the general, since I would go first to the general's son. While I was mounting that large staircase I felt I had grown terribly small (not in the metaphorical but in the genuine meaning of that word). It was the same feeling as the one I had experienced when my droshky came up to the main entrance: it had seemed to me then that both the droshky and the horse and the driver had all become small.

The general's son was lying on a sofa with an open book before him and sleeping when I entered his room. His tutor, Herr Frost, who still remained in their house, followed me into the room with his dashing walk and roused his charge. Ivin did not evince any special joy at seeing me and I noticed that in his conversation with me he looked at my eyebrows. Although he was very polite, it seemed to me that he was entertaining me, just as the Princess had done, and that he neither felt any particular attraction toward me nor indeed had any need of my acquaintance, since he probably had his own different circle of acquaintances. All this I deduced primarily because he looked me in the brows. In short, no matter how disagreeable it was for me to admit it, his attitude to me was practically the same as mine to Ilinka. I began to get irritated and to intercept Ivin's every glance, and when his and Frost's eyes met I translated this as the question: "And why did he have to come to us?"

Having talked to me for a while, Ivin said that his father and mother were at home, so why did we not go downstairs together.

"I'll get dressed right away," he added, going into another room, despite the fact that even in his own room he was well dressed—in a new coat and white vest. A few moments later he came out wearing his uniform, which was buttoned up all the way, and together we went downstairs. The reception rooms, which we passed through, were extremely large, lofty and, it seemed, sumptuously appointed: there was marble and gold, and something swathed in muslin, and mirrors. Mme. Ivin entered a small room behind the drawing room at the same time we did, coming in by another door. She received me in an extremely friendly and cordial manner, sat me beside her, and questioned me sympathetically about my whole family.

I had only caught glimpses of Mme. Ivin once or twice before, but now I examined her carefully and liked her very much. She was tall, thin, and very pale and seemed to be permanently melancholy and exhausted. Her smile was sorrowful, but extremely kind; her eyes were big, tired, and somewhat squinting, which made her expression even more sorrowful and attractive. As she sat she not so much hunched her back as slumped with her whole body, and all her movements were floppy. She spoke languidly, but the sound of her voice and her pronunciation, with its indistinct *r*s and *l*s, were very pleasant. She was not entertaining me. She evidently took a melancholy interest in my answers about my family, as though, while listening to me, she was sadly recalling better days. Her son went away somewhere and she looked at me for a moment or two in silence and then suddenly started to weep. I sat before her and was completely unable to think of anything to say or do. She continued to weep without looking at me. At first I felt sorry for her, then I thought: Shouldn't I perhaps comfort her? But how does one do it? and finally I felt annoyed with her for placing me in such an awkward position. Do I really have such a pitiful appearance, I thought, or is she perhaps doing it on purpose to see what I will do in such a situation?

It would be a bit awkward to leave now, I thought, as though I were running away from her tears. . . . I twisted on my chair in order to at least remind her of my presence.

"Oh, how silly I am!" she said, looking at me and attempting to smile. "There are some days when one cries without reason."

She began to search for her handkerchief on the couch beside her and suddenly started weeping still more violently.

"Oh, goodness gracious! How ridiculous it is of me to keep crying like this. I was so fond of your mother, we were such . . . good friends . . . and . . ."

She found her handkerchief, covered her face with it, and continued to weep. My awkward position was repeated and continued for quite a while. Her tears seemed genuine, but I kept thinking that she was weeping not so much because of my mother as because she herself was now unhappy and because once, in the old days, things had been much better. I do not know how it would have ended if young Ivin had not come in and said that Ivin senior was asking for her. She stood up and was about to leave when Ivin himself came into the room. He was a short, sturdy, gray-haired gentleman with thick black brows, completely gray close-cropped hair, and an extremely severe and hard expression about the mouth.

I got up and bowed to him, but Ivin, who wore three medals on his coat, not only did not reply to my bow but hardly glanced at me at all, so that suddenly I felt not like a person but like some sort of thing not worthy of notice—an armchair or a window, or, if a person, then one who differs not in the slightest from an armchair or a window.

"You still haven't written to the Countess, my dear," said he to his wife in French, with an impassive but severe expression on his face.

"Good day, *Monsieur Irteneff*," said Mme. Ivin, with a sudden proud nod of her head, looking, as her son had done, in the direction of my eyebrows. I bowed once more both to her and to her husband, and again my bow had the same effect on the elderly Ivin as if someone had opened or closed the window. The student Ivin, however, accompanied me to the door, informing me en route that he was transferring to the University of St. Petersburg, because his father had been given a post there (he named some extremely important post).

Well, as Papa wishes, I muttered to myself as I boarded my droshky, but I shall never set foot here again; that ninny weeps and looks at me like some poor unfortunate creature and Ivin, the pig, doesn't even bow; I'll pay him back. . . . How I was going to pay him back I do not know, but those were the words that came out.

Afterwards I frequently had to endure the exhortations of my father, who said that it was essential to *cultiver* this acquaintance and that I could not demand of a man in Ivin's position that he bother himself about a mere boy like myself; but I maintained my stand for quite a long time.

XXI

Prince Ivan Ivanich

"Now to Nikitskaya for our last call," I said to Kuzma and we drove off to Prince Ivan Ivanich's house.

After undergoing several ordeals by visit I usually acquired more self-confidence, and now I was on my way to the Prince in a fairly calm frame of mind; but suddenly I remembered Princess Kornakov's words that I was an heir, and in addition to that I caught sight of two carriages at the door and my former shyness returned.

It seemed to me that both the old doorman who opened the door, and the footman who took my coat, and the three ladies and two gentlemen I found in the drawing room, and, in particular, Prince Ivan Ivanich himself, who was sitting on a couch there, dressed in civilian clothes—it seemed to me that they all looked upon me as an heir and, as a consequence of this, were hostile. The Prince was very affectionate with me: he kissed me; that is, he placed his soft cold dry lips to my cheek for a second, questioned me about my studies and plans, joked with me, asked me whether I still wrote verses like the ones I had written for Grandmother's name day, and asked me to stay to dinner with him. But the more affectionate he was, the more it seemed to me that he wanted to show me so much kindness merely in order that I would not notice how disagreeable it was to him to think that I was his heir. He had a habit—stemming from the fact that his mouth was full of false teeth—of raising his upper lip toward his nose whenever he said anything and of seeming to draw this lip into his nostrils, thus producing a slight hissing sound; and when he did this now I kept thinking that he was saying to himself: "Youngster, youngster, you needn't remind me: my heir, my heir," and so on.

When we were children we called Prince Ivan Ivanich Granddad, but now, as an heir, I could not get my tongue round the word *Granddad* and to say Your Highness, as one of the gentlemen present did, seemed degrading to me, so that during our whole conversation I tried to avoid giving him a title at all costs. But I was embarrassed most of all by the old Princess, who was also an heir and who lived in the Prince's home. During the whole of dinner, during which I sat next to the Princess, I assumed that the Princess was not speaking to me because she hated me for being one of the Prince's heirs, like herself, and that the Prince was not paying any attention to our side of the table because we—the Princess and I, his heirs—were equally obnoxious to him.

"You wouldn't believe how unpleasant it was for me," I said that same evening to Dmitri, wishing to brag to him about the revulsion I felt at the thought that I was an heir (it seemed to me that this was an excellent sentiment), "how unpleasant it was to stay for two whole hours at the Prince's. He's a wonderful man and was very affectionate with me," I said, wishing among other things to impress upon my friend that I was not saying all this because I felt I had been humiliated by the Prince, "but," I went on, "the thought that they might look upon me as they do the Princess, who lives there in his house and sucks up to him, is a horrible thought. He's a marvelous old man and is extremely kind and tactful with everyone, but it's painful to see the way *il maltrait* that Princess. This disgusting money ruins all relationships!

"You know, I think it would be much better to have an open explanation with the Prince," I said, "to say to him that I respect him as a man but that I am not thinking of an inheritance and to beg him not to leave me anything, and that only in this case will I visit him." Dmitri did not burst into laughter when I said this; on the contrary, he became thoughtful, was silent for several minutes, and then said to me:

"Do you know what? You're wrong. Either you shouldn't suppose that they could think of you as they think of that Princess of yours, or, if you're going to suppose that, you should suppose further, that is that you know they can think of you in that light, but that such thoughts are so far from you that you despise them and will do nothing on that basis. You must suppose that they are supposing that you suppose . . . but, in short," he added, sensing that he was mixing up his argument, "it's much better not to suppose anything of the sort."

My friend was quite right; only much much later did I come to the conclusion, from my experience of life, that it is bad to think, and even worse to say, much that seems very noble at the time but that should be kept in each man's heart and forever concealed from others—and also that noble words rarely go together with noble deeds. I am convinced that once a good intention has been announced it is difficult, and indeed in the majority of cases impossible, to carry out that good intention. But how to desist from speaking out about the complacently noble impulses of one's youth? Only much later does one recall and regret them, like a flower which one cannot resist tearing up before it has blossomed and sees later on the ground, faded and trampled.

I, who had only just spoken to my friend Dmitri about the way money spoils relationships, asked him the following day, immediately prior to our departure for the country (when it transpired that I had squandered all my money on various pictures and pipes), for a loan of twenty-five rubles in bills for the journey, which he freely offered me and which I continued to owe him for a long time afterward.

XXII

A Heart-to-Heart Talk with My Friend

This talk of ours took place in the phaeton on the way to Kuntsevo. Dmitri had dissuaded me from paying his mother a visit in the morning and had called for me after dinner to take me to the country house where they all lived to spend the whole evening and even the night there. Only when we had left the town behind and the dirty motley streets and intolerable deafening noise of the cobbles had given way to a broad vista of fields and the soft crunch of wheels on the dusty road, and fragrant spring air and a sense of spaciousness enfolded me, only then did I recover somewhat from the various new impressions and the sensation of freedom that had completely confused me for the past two days. Dmitri was convivial and gentle; he did not adjust his tie by moving his head, nor blink nervously, nor scowl; I was satisfied with the noble sentiments I had expressed to him and supposed that because of them he had completely forgiven me that shameful episode with Kolpikov and did not despise me for it; and so we talked in a friendly way about many things so intimate that it is not always one is able to talk about them. Dmitri told me about his family, whom I had not yet met—his mother, his aunt, his sister, and the girl whom

Volodya and Dubkov held to be the passion of his life and whom they called The Redhead. He spoke of his mother in terms of cold solemn praise, as though intending to forestall any objections on that score; about his aunt he was enthusiastic, although somewhat condescending; he spoke very little of his sister and seemed reluctant to mention her; but on the subject of The Redhead, whose name was in fact Lyubov Sergeyevna and who was a spinster and lived in the Nekhlyudov home because of certain family connections, he waxed eloquent.

"Yes, she's a wonderful girl," he said, blushing shyly, but because of this looking me even more boldly in the eye; "she's no longer young, she's even old, rather, and not at all attractive to look at, but then how stupid and nonsensical to love beauty! That I cannot understand, it's so stupid (he said this as though having just discovered a brand new and extraordinary truth), and what a soul, what a heart, what principles.... I'm sure you won't find another girl like her nowadays." (I do not know where Dmitri acquired the habit of saying that all good things were rare nowadays, but he was fond of using this expression and somehow it suited him).

"Only I'm afraid," he continued calmly, having completely annihilated with his dictum all those who were stupid enough to love beauty, "I'm afraid it will take you some time to understand and get to know her: she is modest and even secretive, she does not like to show her wonderful, extraordinary qualities. Take Mama, for instance, who, as you will see, is a fine intelligent woman—she has known Lyubov Sergeyevna for several years now and cannot and will not understand her. Even yesterday I ... let me tell you why I was in a bad mood when you questioned me. The day before yesterday Lyubov Sergeyevna wanted me to go with her to see Ivan Yakovlyevich—you've probably heard about Ivan Yakovlyevich: he's supposed to be mad but actually he's a remarkable man. Lyubov Sergeyevna, I must tell you, is extremely religious and completely understands Ivan Yakovlyevich. She often visits him, chats with him, and gives him money, which she herself earns, to give to the poor. She's an extraordinary woman; you'll see. Well, and so I went with her to visit Ivan Yakovlyevich and I'm very grateful to her for enabling me to see that remarkable man. But Mama absolutely refuses to understand this and calls it superstition.

And yesterday for the first time in my life I quarreled with Mama, and fairly violently," he concluded, with a convulsive motion of his neck, as though recalling the feelings he had experienced during that quarrel.

"Well, what do you think? I mean, how, when do you think something will come of it ... or do you talk to her about what's going to happen and how your love or friendship will end?" I asked, wishing to distract him from these unpleasant memories.

"You're asking me if I'm thinking of marrying her?" he asked, blushing once more, but boldly turning his head in order to look me in the face.

Well, what of it? I thought, reassuring myself, it's nothing, we're two *grown-up* friends, riding in a phaeton and discussing our future life. Anyone would even enjoy listening to us now and watching us secretly.

"Why not?" he went on after I had answered in the affirmative. "My aim, like that of any other sensible man, is to be happy and good as far as is possible; and with her, provided she wishes it—and when I am completely independent—I can be happier and better than with the greatest beauty in the world."

Conversing thus we did not even notice that we were nearing Kuntsevo—nor that the sky had grown overcast and that a squall was gathering. The sun was now low, away to the right, over the ancient trees in the Kuntsevo garden, and half its brilliant red disk was obscured by a gray, barely translucent raincloud; showers of splintering fiery rays burst from the other half and lit up with astonishing brilliance the old trees in the garden, whose dense green crowns gleamed motionless against a clear bright patch of azure sky. This gleam and the brightness of this edge of sky were in sharp contrast to the heavy indigo cloud that had settled before us over a young birch wood that we could see on the horizon.

A little to the right we could already see, behind the trees and shrubbery, the multicolored roofs of some summer cottages, of which some reflected the sun's brilliant rays while others assumed the doleful character of the other part of the sky. Lower down on the left showed a still, blue pond, surrounded by pale green osiers that were reflected darkly on its lusterless, seemingly convex surface. Beyond the pond, halfway up the hill, a field of fallow land was spread out black before us and the straight line of vivid greenery dividing it in the middle receded into the distance until it joined the leaden, thundery horizon. On both sides of the soft road, along which the phaeton swayed regularly, lush shaggy rye showed sharply green and in one or two places had already begun to sprout stalks. The air was perfectly still and exhaled freshness; the verdure of the trees, leaves, and rye was motionless and extraordinarily pure and vivid. Every leaf, every shoot seemed to be living its own separate full and happy life. By the side of the road I noticed a blackish footpath that twisted its way through the dark-green rye, which was more than a quarter grown by now, and for some reason this footpath reminded me extremely vividly of our village, and as a result of this village recollection, by some strange chain of ideas, reminded me extremely vividly in turn of Sonyechka and the fact that I was in love with her.

Despite my friendship for Dmitri and the pleasure I derived from his frankness, I did not feel like hearing any more about his feelings and intentions with regard to Lyubov Sergeyevna, but was eager instead to tell him of my love for Sonyechka, which seemed to me to be love of a much higher caliber. But for some reason I could not make up my mind to tell him straight out about my suppositions of how nice it would be, after marrying Sonyechka, to live in the country, and how I would have little children who would crawl about the floor and call me Papa, and how overjoyed I would be when he and his wife, Lyubov Sergeyevna, arrived in their traveling clothes . . . and instead of all this I said, pointing to the setting sun: "Look, Dmitri, how lovely!"

Dmitri said nothing, visibly displeased that to his confession, which must have cost him an effort, I had responded by directing his attention toward nature, to which he was in general indifferent. Nature had a wholly different effect on him from what it had on me: it affected him not so much by its beauty as by its interest; he loved it more with his mind than with his heart.

"I am extremely happy," I said to him immediately after this, paying no attention to the fact that he was obviously busy with his own thoughts and was completely indifferent to anything that I might say to him. "I believe I told you, remember, about a certain young lady with whom I was in love as a child; well, I saw her today," I continued animatedly, "and now I'm definitely in love with her."

And despite the expression of indifference his face continued to exhibit, I told him of my love and of all my plans for future married happiness. And strange to say, as soon as I spoke in detail of the strength of my feeling, at that same moment I sensed my feeling begin to wane.

The rain overtook us just after we had entered the birch avenue leading to the house, but we did not get wet. I knew that it was raining only because several drops fell on my nose and hand and because something splashed onto the young sticky leaves of the birch trees which, their curly branches drooping motionlessly, seemed to delight in accepting these pure transparent drops upon themselves and expressed their delight in the powerful fragrance with which they filled the avenue. We dismounted from our carriage in order to get to the house more quickly by running through the garden. But at the very entrance to the house we collided with four ladies, two with needlework, one with a book, and one with a little dog, who were approaching with rapid steps from the other direction. Dmitri at once introduced me to his mother, sister, and aunt and to Lyubov Sergeyevna. For a moment they halted, but the raindrops started coming faster and faster.

"Let's go to the veranda; there you can introduce him again," said the one I took to be Dmitri's mother, and together with the ladies we went upstairs.

XXIII

THE NEKHLYUDOVS

At first sight the one out of all this company who struck me most was Lyubov Sergeyevna, who, holding a spaniel in her arms and wearing thick woolen shoes, mounted the staircase behind the others, halted once or twice, looked round at me attentively and then kissed her little dog. She was extraordinarily unattractive: red-haired, thin, short, and somewhat lopsided. And what made her ugly face still uglier was her queer hair style, with the parting on one side (one of those hair styles that bald-headed women dream up for themselves). No matter how I tried in deference to my friend, I could not find a single good feature in her. Even her brown eyes, their kind expression notwithstanding, were too small and dull and were definitely unappealing; even her hands, that telltale feature, although small and not badly formed, were rough and red.

When I had followed them onto the terrace each of the ladies, with the exception of Varyenka, Dmitri's sister, who merely looked at me attentively with her big dark-gray eyes, said a few words to me before taking up her work again, while Varyenka began to read aloud from a book she held on her knees, using her finger as a bookmark.

Princess Marya Ivanovna Nekhlyudov was a tall graceful woman of about forty. She might have been taken for older, judging by the graying curls that showed frankly from under her bonnet, but her fresh and extraordinarily delicate face, almost without a wrinkle, and particularly the merry lively gleam of her big eyes, made her seem a great deal younger. Her eyes were brown and very frank; her lips too thin and a trifle severe; her nose fairly regular and slightly to the left; and her hand was ringless, large and almost masculine, with beautiful long slender fingers. She was wearing a dark-blue high-necked dress that tightly hugged her slim, still-youthful waist, of which she was obviously very proud. She was sitting remarkably erect and sewing a dress. When I reached the verandah she took me by the hand, drew me to her, as though wishing to make a closer examination of me, and said, looking at me with that same somewhat cold, frank look her son had, that she had long known me from Dmitri's stories and that, in order for me to get to know them all properly, would I not stay for a whole day.

"Do whatever you feel like doing and don't mind us in the least, just as we shan't mind about you—go for a walk, read, listen, or even sleep if that's what you prefer," she added.

Sofya Ivanovna was an old maid and the Princess's younger sister, but in appearance she seemed older. She had that special overstuffed kind of build that is only met with in short and very fat old maids wearing corsets. It was as though all her health had risen up with such force that it threatened at any moment to choke her. Her short fat little arms could not meet below the protruding point of her bodice and the very tip of this point, which was tight to bursting, she could not see at all.

In spite of the fact that Princess Marya Ivanovna had black hair and black eyes, while Sofya Ivanovna was fair and had big, lively, and at the same time (which is very rare) calm blue eyes, the sisters bore a great family likeness to one another; the same expression, the same nose, the same lips; but with Sofya Ivanovna her nose and lips were somewhat thicker and went slightly to the right when she smiled, while with the Princess they went to the left. Judging by her clothing and hair style, Sofya Ivanovna was evidently still trying to look young and would not have displayed *her* gray curls if she had had any. For the first moment her glance and attitude toward me struck me as haughty and embarrassed me; whereas with the Princess, on the contrary, I felt completely at ease. Perhaps it was her stoutness and a certain likeness to a portrait of Catherine the Great that struck me in her that made her seem haughty in my eyes; but I was thoroughly abashed when with an intent stare at me she said: "The friends of our friends are always our friends." Only when, having said these words, she paused, opened her mouth, and sighed heavily did I regain my composure and suddenly change my opinion of her. Probably on account of her stoutness she must have had this habit, after saying a few words, of opening her mouth, rolling her big blue eyes a little, and sighing deeply. This habit was for some reason so expressive of amiable good nature that immediately after her sigh I lost all fear of her and found that she even appealed to me. Her eyes were lovely, her voice musical and agreeable, and even those well-rounded lines of her figure seemed to me at that period of my youth to be not wholly lacking in beauty.

Lyubov Sergeyevna, as a friend of my friend (I supposed), ought now to say something very friendly and confidential to me, and she even looked at me in silence for quite a long time, as though undecided whether what she wanted to say to me was perhaps a bit too friendly or not; but she interrupted this silence only to ask which faculty I was in. Then, once more, she gazed at me intently for quite a long time and was obviously hesitating whether to say that friendly confidential something or not; and I, noticing her doubt, begged her with the expression on my face to say all, but she said: "They say that nowadays the sciences are unpopular at the university," and called her dog Suzette to her.

The whole evening Lyubov Sergeyevna talked for the most part in similar phrases that had nothing to do either with anything important or with each other; but I had so much faith in Dmitri and he spent the whole evening looking so anxiously first at me and then at her, with an expression that seemed to be saying: "Well, what do you think?"—that, as often happens, although in my heart of hearts I was already convinced that Lyubov Sergeyevna was nothing special, I was still far far away from expressing this thought even to myself.

Finally, the last member of the family was Varyenka, a very plump young girl of about sixteen.

Only her big, dark-gray eyes, whose expression combined merriment with calm attentiveness, which bore a remarkable resemblance to her aunt's eyes, and her very thick fair hair and delicate handsome hands—only these were attractive about her.

"It must be boring for you, I think, *Monsieur Nicolas,* to listen from the middle," said Sofya Ivanovna to me with her good-natured sigh, as she turned over some pieces of material she was stitching.

The reading had ended at this moment because Dmitri had gone out of the room for some reason.

"Or perhaps you've read *Rob Roy* before?"

At that time, if only because I wore a student's uniform, I considered it my invariable duty when with people I did not know well to give an extremely *clever and original* answer to even the simplest question, and I regarded as things to be unutterably ashamed of such brief and clear answers as: yes, no, I'm bored, I like it, and so forth. With a glance at my new fashionable trousers and the glittering buttons on my coat I replied that I had not read *Rob Roy* but that I was very interested in listening because I preferred to read books from the middle rather than from the beginning.

"It's twice as interesting: you can guess about what's gone before and what's to come," I added, smiling complacently.

The Princess laughed what sounded like an unnatural laugh (I observed subsequently that she had no other laugh).

"However, that must be true," she said. "Well, and will you be staying here long, *Nicolas?* You won't take offense if I drop the *monsieur?* When will you be leaving?"

"I don't know, perhaps tomorrow, and perhaps we shall stay for quite a long time," I replied for some reason, despite the fact that we definitely had to leave the following day.

"I hope you can stay, both for your sake and for my Dmitri's," remarked the Princess, looking away into the distance. "At your age friendship's a wonderful thing."

I felt that everyone was looking at me and waiting for what I was going to say, although Varyenka pretended to be examining her aunt's work; I felt that they were setting me some kind of examination and that I had to show myself in the best possible light.

"Yes, for me," I said, "Dmitri's friendship is very useful, but I cannot be of any use to him: he's a thousand times better than I." (Dmitri was unable to hear what I was saying, otherwise I would have been afraid lest he sense the insincerity of my words.)

The Princess again laughed her unnatural—to her natural—laugh.

"There, but to hear him talk," she said, *"c'est vous qui êtes un petit monstre de perfection."*

Monstre de perfection—that's excellent; I must remember that, I thought.

"However, even apart from you he's a master at that," she went on, lowering her voice (which was specially pleasant for me) and indicating Lyubov Sergeyevna with her eyes. "He's discovered in *poor auntie* (as they called Lyubov Sergeyevna), whom with her Suzette I have known for twenty years now, such perfections as I never even suspected. . . . Varyenka, ask them to bring me a glass of water," she added, looking once more into the distance, considering probably that it was still too early or perhaps entirely unnecessary to initiate me into the family secrets. "Or no, better let *him* go. He's doing nothing, so you go on reading. Go straight through that door there, my friend, and after fifteen paces halt and say in a loud voice: 'Pyotr, bring Marya Ivanovna a glass of water with some ice in it,'" she said and again laughed lightly with her unnatural laugh.

She probably wants to talk about me, I thought as I left the room; she probably wants to say what an extremely clever young man I am. I had barely managed to take the fifteen paces, however, when stout panting Sofya Ivanovna overtook me with her quick light steps.

"Merci, mon cher," she said. "I am going there myself so I'll tell them."

XXIV

LOVE

Sofya Ivanovna, as I learned later, was one of those rare middle-aged women, born for family life, whom fate has denied this happiness and who, as a result of this denial, decide suddenly to pour out that reserve of love, which has grown, strengthened, and been stored up in their hearts so long for their husband and children, upon certain chosen ones. And the reserve in old maids of this sort is so inexhaustible that, although there are many chosen ones, much love is still left that is poured out on all surrounding them, on whomever they happen to come into contact with, whether good or bad.

There are three sorts of love:

1. Beautiful love
2. Self-sacrificing love, and
3. Active love.

I am not speaking about the love of a young man for a young woman, or vice versa; I fear these niceties and have been unfortunate enough in life never to see the least spark of truth in this sort of love, but only falsehood, in which sensuality, marriage relationships, money, and a desire either to bind or to free one's hands have so distorted the emotion itself that it was impossible to make head or tail of it. I am speaking about love for one's neighbor, which, according to the greater or lesser capacity of the soul, concentrates itself on one or on a few, or else pours itself out on the many; about love for one's mother, father, brother, children, comrade, friend, fellow countryman, about love for one's neighbor.

Beautiful love consists in loving the beauty of the feeling itself, or its expression. For people who love thus, the beloved object is loved only insofar as it evokes that agreeable feeling in the consciousness and expression of which they take delight. People who experience beautiful love are very little concerned about reciprocity, regarding it as a circumstance that has little influence on the beauty and agreeableness of the feeling. They frequently change the object of their love, since their main aim consists only in ensuring that the agreeable feeling of love is constantly evoked. In order to maintain this agreeable feeling in themselves they constantly talk of their love in the most refined possible terms, both to the object itself and even to those who have no interest in this love. In our homeland people of a certain class who love *beautifully* not only tell everyone about their love but invariably tell them in French. It sounds an absurd and strange thing to say, but I am convinced that there have been and still are many people of a certain class, particularly women, whose love for their friends, husbands, and children would immediately be destroyed if they were forbidden to speak of it in French.

The second sort of love, *self-sacrificing love,* consists in loving the process of sacrificing oneself for the sake of the beloved object while paying no attention whatever to whether the beloved object is any the worse or better for these sacrifices. "There is no unpleasantness that I could not bring myself to inflict upon myself in order to prove my devotion to *him* or *her* and to the whole world." This is the formula for this sort of love. People who love this way never believe in reciprocity (because it is even worthier to sacrifice oneself for somebody who does not understand one) and are always sickly, which also heightens the value of the sacrifice; they are, for the most part, constant, for it would be painful for them to lose the value of the sacrifices they have already made for the beloved object; they are always ready to die in order to prove their devotion to *him* or *her,* but they neglect the small daily proofs of love since they do not require any particular effort of self-sacrifice. It is all the same to them whether you have eaten well or slept well, or whether you are cheerful or healthy, and they do nothing to secure these comforts for you whether it is in their power to do so or not; but to face bullets, to throw themselves into the water or flames, or to pine away for love—for these they are always prepared, if only the opportunity presents itself. Apart from this, people inclined to self-sacrificing love are always proud of their love, exacting, jealous, and mistrustful—and, strange to say, they desire danger for their beloved objects, in order to be able to rescue them; unhappiness, in order to comfort them; and even vices, in order to be able to reform them.

You live alone in the country with your wife, who loves you self-sacrificingly. You are well and at peace and you have your work, which you love; your wife is so weak that she can cope with neither the housework, which is passed to domestics, nor the children, who are handed over to nurses, nor indeed with any work that she would love, because she loves nothing but you. She is *visibly* ailing, but does not want to tell you this for fear of grieving you; she is *visibly* bored, but for your sake she is prepared to be bored for the rest of her life; she is *visibly* crushed because you are so engrossed in your work (whatever it might be: hunting, books, farming, government service); she sees that this work will ruin you—but she continues to suffer in silence. Then suddenly you fall ill—your loving wife forgets her own sickness and never leaves your bedside, despite your entreaties to her not to tire herself out unnecessarily; and every moment you feel her condoling glance upon you that says: "Well, I told you so, but nevertheless I won't leave you." In the morning you feel a little better, you go into the other room. The room is unheated and has not been cleaned; the soup that is all you are allowed to eat has not been ordered from the kitchen, your medicine has not been sent for; but, exhausted by her nocturnal vigil, your loving wife looks at you with that same expression of condolence, walks about on tiptoe, and whispers vague uncustomary orders to the servants. You want to read—your loving wife says with a sigh that she knows you will not listen to her, she has grown accustomed to that by now, but it is better for you not to read; you want to walk up and down your room—it is better for you not to do that either; you want to talk with a visiting friend—it is better not to talk. At night you have a fever again, you want to lose yourself in sleep, but your loving wife, thin, pale and sighing from time to time, sits opposite you in an armchair in the gloom of the night light and with each little movement, each little sound arouses feelings of impatience and irritation in you. You have a servant who has been with you for twenty years, to whom you are accustomed and who serves you gladly and efficiently, because he has been able to sleep during the day and is paid for his work, but she will not allow him near you. She does everything with her own feeble and unaccustomed fingers, and you cannot help watching with suppressed fury as those white fingers struggle in vain to unstopper a phial, snuff a candle, pour out medicine, or touch you squeamishly. If you are an impatient hot-tempered man and you ask her to leave, your inflamed sick man's hearing will detect her sighing submissively behind the door and weeping and whispering some nonsense or other to your servant. Finally, if you do not die, your loving wife, who has not slept during the twenty nights of your illness (as she tells you repeatedly), herself becomes ill, wastes away, suffers and becomes still less capable of any work, and at the very time when you are back to normal expresses her self-sacrificing love merely in humble boredom, which is involuntarily communicated to you and all about you.

The third sort of love, *active love*, consists in striving to satisfy all the needs, desires, whims and even vices of the beloved person. People who love in this way love always for a whole lifetime, because the more they love the more they learn about the object of their love, and the easier it becomes to love them, i.e., to satisfy their desires. Their love is rarely put into words, and if it is, it is not only not expressed complacently and elegantly but comes out bashful and awkward, because they are always afraid that their love is insufficient. These people love even the vices of the beloved person, because these vices give them the opportunity to satisfy ever new desires. They desire reciprocity, willingly deceiving themselves, and believe in it and are happy if they get it; but their love is just the same even in the opposite case, and not only do they desire happiness for the object of their love, but they endeavor constantly with all the moral and material, big and little means at their disposal to secure it for him.

And so it was this active kind of love for her nephew and niece, for her sister, for Lyubov Sergeyevna and even for me, because Dmitri loved me, that shone in the eyes and in every word and gesture of Sofya Ivanovna.

Only much later did I fully appreciate Sofya Ivanovna, but even then it occurred to me to ask myself: why was it that Dmitri, who strove to understand love quite differently from the usual way of young people and who had the sweet loving Sofya Ivanovna constantly before his eyes, why had he fallen passionately in love with the incomprehensible Lyubov Sergeyevna and yet merely conceded that his aunt also had some good qualities? Clearly there is truth in the saying that a prophet is not without honor, save in his own country. There are two possibilities: either there is truly more bad than good in man, or else man is more receptive to the bad than the good. Lyubov Sergeyevna he had only known a short while, whereas he had been bathed in his aunt's love ever since birth.

XXV

I Become Better Acquainted

When I returned to the verandah they were not talking at all about me, as I had supposed; Varyenka was no longer reading, but, having set her book aside, was having a heated argument with Dmitri, who, pacing up and down, was straightening his tie with his neck and frowning. The subject of the argument was ostensibly Ivan Yakovlyevich and superstition; but the argument was too heated for the underlying subject not to be something else, something that was closer to home. The Princess and Lyubov Sergeyevna sat in silence, listening carefully to every word and visibly wishing at times to take part in the argument themselves, but restraining themselves and allowing themselves to be represented, one by Varyenka, the other by Dmitri. When I entered, Varyenka glanced at me with a look of such indifference on her face that it was clear she was deeply absorbed in the argument and was quite unconcerned that I should be there and hear what she was saying. The Princess's face bore the same expression and she was evidently on Varyenka's side. But Dmitri began to argue even more heatedly in my presence, while Lyubov Sergeyevna appeared to be very apprehensive of me and said, not speaking to anyone in particular: "The old are quite right when they say *si jeunesse savait, si vieillesse pouvait.*"

But this saying did not put an end to the argument, but merely led me to the thought that Lyubov Sergeyevna's and my friend's side was in the wrong. Although I felt somewhat embarrassed to be present at a minor family squabble, it was nonetheless agreeable to me to see the real family relationships as they revealed themselves because of this argument and to feel that my presence did not hinder this revelation. How often does it happen that for years and years you see a family beneath the same false veil of propriety, while the true relations between its members remain a secret (and I have even noticed that the more impenetrable and therefore becoming the veil, the coarser are the true relationships concealed from you)! But then one day, completely unexpectedly, there happens to arise within the family circle some seemingly insignificant question about some blonde or other or a trip made with the husband's horses—and for no apparent reason the argument grows fiercer and fiercer; it becomes too restricted under the veil for a proper resolution of the matter and suddenly, to the horror of the protagonists themselves and the astonishment of onlookers, the true coarse relationships emerge into view, the veil, no longer concealing anything, flutters uselessly between the warring sides and merely reminds you of how long you have been deceived. Frequently it is not so painful to bang one's hand on a lintel at full speed as it is just barely to touch a spot that is painful and already sore. And such a sore painful spot exists in every family. In the Nekhlyudov family this sore spot was Dmitri's strange love for Lyubov Sergeyevna, which aroused in his sister and mother if not a feeling of jealousy then an offended family feeling. It was because of this that the argument about Ivan Yakovlyevich and superstition had such deep significance for them.

"You're always trying to see things in what other people laugh at and despise," said Varyenka in her musical voice, enunciating every syllable distinctly. "It's precisely in all this that you try to find some extraordinary virtue."

"In the first place, only the most *frivolous person* could speak of despising such a remarkable man as Ivan Yakovlyevich," replied Dmitri, convulsively jerking his head in the opposite direction from his sister, "and in the second place, on the contrary, it is *you* who are purposely trying not to see the good that stares you in the face."

When she returned to where we were, Sofya Ivanovna looked fearfully several times first at her nephew, then at her niece, and then at me, and a couple of times, as though having mentally said something, opened her mouth and sighed.

"Varya, please, go on with your reading," she said, handing her the book and patting her hand affectionately. "I must know whether he found her again or not." (I don't believe there was any mention in the novel of anyone finding anyone else.) "And you, Dmitri dear, would do better to wrap up your cheek; it's cool in here and you'll get the toothache again," she said to her nephew, in spite of the displeased glance he threw at her, probably because she had interrupted the logical thread of his argument. The reading continued.

This little quarrel did not in the least disturb that domestic calm and sensible accord with which this feminine circle was imbued.

This circle, which obviously received its direction and character from Princess Marya Ivanovna, had for me an entirely new and attractive flavor that was somehow logical and yet at the same time simple and refined. This flavor was expressed for me both in the beauty, purity, and stability of the things there—the bell, the book binding, the armchair, the table—and in the upright corseted posture of the Princess, and in the gray curls out on display, and in her way of calling me simply *Nicolas* and *he* at our first meeting, and in the things they were doing, the reading and sewing, and in the extraordinary whiteness of the women's hands. (All of them had one family feature in common in their hands, which was that the soft part of their palms on the outside was a deep rose color and was divided by a sharp straight line from the extraordinary whiteness of the upper part of their hands.) But most of all this flavor expressed itself in the manner all three of them had of speaking excellent Russian and French and pronouncing every syllable distinctly, completing every word and phrase with pedantic exactitude. All this, and especially the fact that in this company they treated me simply and seriously, like a grown-up, offering me their opinions and listening to mine—something to which I was so little accustomed that, despite my shining buttons and blue piping, I was in constant fear they would suddenly say to me: "Surely you don't think we are taking you seriously? Go back to your studies"—all this resulted in my feeling not in the least embarrassed in their company. I stood up and sat down several times in various places and boldly talked to everyone, excepting Varyenka, with whom it seemed improper and forbidden to talk on this first occasion.

Listening to her pleasant musical voice as she read, and glancing from her to the sandy path of the flower garden, on which round darkening spots of rain made their marks, and at the lime trees, upon whose leaves occasional drops of rain continued to patter from the pale edge, shot through with blue, of the thundercloud that had enveloped us, and back to her again, and then at the last purple rays of the setting sun that lit up the branchy old birch trees, dripping with rain, and at Varyenka again—I decided that she was not at all as plain as I had thought in the beginning.

What a pity that I'm already in love, I thought, and that Varyenka's not Sonyechka; how nice it would be to become suddenly a member of this family: suddenly I should gain both a mother and an aunt and a wife. . . . At the same time as I was thinking this I gazed fixedly at Varyenka as she read and thought that I would magnetize her and make her look at me. Varyenka lifted her head from the book, glanced at me, and, meeting my eyes, looked away.

"It hasn't stopped raining, though," she said.

And suddenly I experienced a strange sensation: it came back to me that everything happening to me now was an exact repetition of something that had already occurred: that then too there had been exactly the same sort of light rain and the sun had been setting behind some birch trees and I had looked at *her* and she had been reading and I had magnetized her and she had looked around, and I had even recollected that this had happened before that.

Can she be . . . *she*? I thought. Can it really be *beginning*? But I quickly decided that it was not *she* and that it was not yet beginning. . . . In the first place she's plain, I thought, and then she's just a girl and I met her in the most ordinary way, whereas *she* will be extraordinary and I shall meet her in some extraordinary place somewhere; and then, I reasoned, I like this family so much only because I haven't seen anything else yet, but there must be others and I shall meet many more during my lifetime.

XXVI

I Am Seen to My Best Advantage

During tea the reading ceased and the ladies engaged in conversation among themselves about people and circumstances I was unacquainted with, solely, it seemed to me, in spite of my cordial welcome, in order to give me to understand the full difference that existed between us both in years and in our positions in the world. In the general conversations in which I was able to participate, in an effort to atone for my former silence I tried to show off my remarkable intelligence and originality, which I felt in honor bound to do for the sake of my uniform. When the conversation turned to country houses I related suddenly that Prince Ivan Ivanich had such a house near Moscow, that people came from London and Paris to see it, and that he had some railings there worth three hundred and eighty thousand rubles, and that Prince Ivan Ivanich was a very close relative of mine and I had dined with him today and he had invited me to go and live with him at his country house for the whole summer, but I had declined because I knew that house very well, having been there several times, and all those railings and bridges held no interest for me because I could not bear luxury, especially in the country, but preferred the country to be completely like the country. . . . Having uttered this terribly complicated lie, I became confused and blushed, so that everyone must have noticed I was lying. Varyenka, who was handing me a cup of tea at the time, and Sofya Ivanovna, who was looking at me as I spoke, both turned away from me and began to speak of something else, with an expression on their faces that I frequently met later in kindhearted people when a very young man began to lie to their faces, an expression that meant: "We know he's lying, but why does he do it, poor boy!"

The reason I said that Prince Ivan Ivanich had a country house was that I could not find a better excuse for telling them of my being related to Prince Ivan Ivanich and of having dined with him that day; but for what reason I talked about railings worth three hundred thousand and about having visited him frequently, when in fact I had not once and could not have been there, since Prince Ivan Ivanich lived only in Moscow or Naples, a fact which the Nekhlyudovs were quite well aware of—for what reason I said this I am completely at a loss to understand. Neither in childhood nor boyhood, nor later at a more mature age have I detected in myself the vice of lying; on the contrary, I was if anything too truthful and frank; but during this first period of my youth I frequently experienced a strange desire, without any apparent reason, to lie in the most desperate manner. I say "desperate manner" precisely because I always lied in cases where it was extremely easy to find me out. It seems to me that the main reason for this strange inclination was a vainglorious desire to represent myself as being completely other than I was, joined to the hope, unrealizable in life, of lying without being discovered.

After tea, the rain having passed and the evening weather being calm and clear, the Princess proposed to go for a walk in the lower garden and admire her favorite spot. Sticking to my rule of always being original and believing that such intelligent people as the Princess and I should be above mundane politeness, I replied that I detested aimless walking and that when I walked I preferred to walk alone. I was completely unaware that I was simply being rude; it seemed to me then that since there was nothing more despicable than vulgar compliments, so there was nothing more endearing and original than a certain ill-mannered frankness. Extremely satisfied with my reply, however, I nonetheless went for a stroll with the whole company.

The Princess's favorite spot was a long way down, right at the very bottom of the garden, on a little bridge spanning a small narrow swamp. The view was extremely limited, but very affecting and graceful. We are so used to mixing up art and nature that very often those manifestations of nature that we have never met in painting seem artificial to us, as though nature were unnatural, and vice versa: those manifestations that are too often repeated in art seem hackneyed, while certain views that we meet in reality are too much imbued with a single thought or feeling and seem bizarre. The view from the Princess's favorite spot was of this kind. It was made up of a small pool overgrown round the edges, a steep slope rising immediately behind the pool covered with enormous old trees and bushes that frequently had their various leaves and branches entangled in one another, and an old birch tree which, arching over the pool at the bottom of the slope and partly holding on by its thick roots sunk in the marshy edge of the pool, rested its crown against a tall slender ash and hung its curly branches over the smooth surface of the pool, which in turn reflected both the branches and the surrounding foliage.

"How charming!" said the Princess, shaking her head and not speaking to anyone in particular.

"Yes, wonderful, but it looks terribly like a stage set to me," I said, wishing to show that I had my own opinion about everything.

As though not having heard my remark, the Princess continued to admire the view and, turning to her sister and Lyubov Sergeyevna, pointed out some details: a crooked overhanging bough and its reflection in the water, which particularly pleased her. Sofya Ivanovna said that it was all wonderful and that her sister used to spend several hours here at a time, but it was clear that she said all this just to please the Princess. I have noticed that people endowed with the capacity to love actively are rarely receptive to the beauties of nature. Lyubov Sergeyevna also expressed her admiration and among other things asked: "How does that birch tree stay up? Will it stay there for long?" and constantly glanced at her Suzette, who ran back and forth over the bridge on her crooked little legs, wagging her fluffy tail, and with such a preoccupied expression as though this were the first time in her life she had been let out of a room. Dmitri started up an extremely logical discussion with his mother to the effect that it was impossible for a view with a restricted horizon to be beautiful. Varyenka said nothing. When I looked around at her, she was leaning on the bridge rail with her profile turned toward me and looking in front of her. Something must have interested her deeply and even moved her, for she was obviously far away and was oblivious of herself and of the fact that she was being watched. There was so much concentrated attention and calm clear intelligence in the expression of her big eyes, and so much relaxation and, despite her small stature, even grandeur in her posture that once more I was struck as though by a recollection of her and once more I asked myself: Is it beginning? And once more I told myself that I was already in love with Sonyechka and that Varyenka was just a girl—my friend's sister. But she attracted me at that moment and I experienced a vague desire to do something or say something slightly unpleasant to her.

"Do you know what, Dmitri," I said to my friend, moving closer to Varyenka so that she could hear what I was going to say, "I find that even if it weren't for the mosquitoes there would be nothing good about this place. And now," I added, slapping my forehead and really crushing a mosquito, "it's perfectly dreadful."

"You don't like nature, I gather?" said Varyenka to me without turning her head.

"I find that it's an idle useless occupation," I replied, highly satisfied that I had nonetheless got my little unpleasantness in, and an original one at that. Varyenka barely raised her eyebrows for an instant with an expression of pity and continued to look straight in front of her just as calmly as before.

I felt annoyed with her, but in spite of this the grayish parapet of the little bridge with its faded paint, on which she was leaning, the dark pool's reflection of the leaning birch tree's drooping bough, which seemed to wish to be united with the hanging branches, the smell of the swamp, the feel of the crushed mosquito on my forehead, and her intent gaze and majestic posture—all this would suddenly rise up later completely unexpectedly in my imagination.

XXVII

Dmitri

When we returned home after our walk, Varyenka did not sing as she usually did in the evenings and I was presumptuous enough to put this down to my account, imagining that what I had said to her on the bridge was the reason for it. The Nekhlyudovs did not eat supper and retired early and since Dmitri, as Sofya Ivanovna had predicted, actually began to suffer with toothache, we went to his room even earlier than usual. Supposing that I had done all that might have been required of me by my blue collar and buttons and that everyone was very pleased with me, I was in an extremely agreeable and self-satisfied frame of mind; but Dmitri, on the other hand, as a result of the argument and his toothache, was taciturn and morose. He sat at his desk, took out his notebooks—a diary and a book in which he had the habit each evening of noting down his past and future tasks—and wrote in them for quite a long time, constantly wincing and putting his hand to his cheek.

"Oh, leave me alone," he shouted at the maid whom Sofya Ivanovna had sent to ask how his teeth were, and did he not want a poultice for them. After that, having said that my bed would soon be prepared and that he would soon return, he went to see Lyubov Sergeyevna.

What a pity that Varyenka isn't pretty and in general isn't Sonyechka, I mused, remaining alone in the room. How nice it would be when I left the university to come to them and offer her my hand. I would say: "Princess, I am no longer young—I cannot love passionately, but I shall always love you as a dear sister." And I would say to her mother: "You I already respect, and for you, Sofya Ivanovna, believe me, I have the very highest regard. So tell me plainly and simply: will you be my wife?" "Yes." And she will give me her hand and I shall squeeze it and say: "My love is not in words but in deeds." And what, I thought, if Dmitri were suddenly to fall in love with Lyubochka—after all, Lyubochka's in love with him—and to want to marry her? Then one of us would be unable to marry. And that would be excellent. Here's what I would do then. I would realize it immediately and would say nothing, but I'd go to Dmitri and say: "It would be useless, my friend, for us to try and conceal things from one another: you know that my love for your sister will end only with my death; but I know all; you have deprived me of my highest hopes, you have made me unhappy; but do you know how Nikolai Irtenyev repays you for making the rest of his life unhappy? Here is my sister," and I would give him Lyubochka's hand. He would say: "No, not for anything!" but I would say: "Prince Nekhlyudov! In vain you wish to be more generous than Nikolai Irtenyev. Nowhere in the whole world is there a man more generous than he." I would bow and depart. Dmitri and Lyubochka, in tears, would come running after me and implore me to accept their sacrifice. And I could agree and would be very very happy if only I were in love with Varyenka. . . . These dreams were so pleasant that I was eager to tell my friend about them, but in spite of our vow to be frank with one another, I felt for some reason that this was a physical impossibility.

Dmitri returned from Lyubov Sergeyevna with some drops that she had given him for his tooth; the pain was even greater and as a consequence of this he was even gloomier. My bed had still not been prepared and the boy who was Dmitri's servant came to ask him where I was to sleep.

"Go to hell!" yelled Dmitri, stamping his foot. "Vaska! Vaska! Vaska!" he cried as soon as the boy had gone, raising his voice each time. "Vaska, make up my bed on the floor."

"No, let me sleep on the floor," I said.

"Well, it's all the same, put the bed somewhere," went on Dmitri in the same irate voice. "Vaska! Why don't you get a move on?"

But Vaska obviously did not understand what was wanted of him and stood there without moving.

"Well, what's wrong with you? Get moving, get moving! Vaska! Vaska!" cried Dmitri, flying into a kind of rage all of a sudden.

But Vaska, who still did not understand, looked timid and did not stir.

"So you're determined to rui—to provoke me?"

And Dmitri, jumping up from his chair and flying at the boy, struck Vaska on the head with his fist several times with full force, while the latter fled headlong from the room. Stopping by the door, Dmitri looked round at me and the look of rage and cruelty that had appeared on his face for a second gave way to such a meek contrite and loving childlike expression that I began to feel sorry for him, and much as I wished to turn away, I resolved not to do so. He did not say a word to me, but for a long time walked about the room in silence, glancing at me from time to time with that same look of begging forgiveness; then he took a notebook from his desk, wrote something in it, took off his coat, folded it carefully, went to the corner where the ikon was hanging, folded his big white hands on his chest and commenced to pray. He prayed for so long that Vaska had time to bring a mattress and make it up on on the floor, while I gave him directions in a whisper. I undressed and lay on the bed on the floor, while Dmitri continued to pray. Gazing at Dmitri's slightly stooped back and at the soles of his feet, which were somehow humbly presented to me as he bowed to the ground, I loved him even more strongly than before and kept thinking: Shall I tell him or not what I dreamed about our sisters? Finishing his prayers, Dmitri came and lay on my bed and, leaning on one elbow, looked at me for a long time in silence, with an affectionate and contrite look on his face. It was evidently painful for him to do this, but he was punishing himself. I smiled as I looked at him. He smiled too.

"Well, why don't you tell me that I acted despicably?" he said. "That's what you were thinking, isn't it?"

"Yes," I replied, although I had been thinking something else; but it seemed to me that I really had been thinking that too. "Yes, that was very bad, I would never have expected it of you," I said, experiencing a special pleasure at that moment in using the *thou* form. "Well, and how are your teeth?" I added.

"Better. Oh, Nikolyenka, my friend!" said Dmitri, so affectionately that it seemed there were tears in his shining eyes. "I know, I feel how bad I am, and God sees that I want and implore him to make me better; but what can I do when I have such an unfortunate abominable character? What can I do? I try to restrain myself, reform myself, but then it's impossible to do it at once and on one's own. I need someone to support me and help me. Lyubov Sergeyevna, for instance—she understands me and has helped me a lot in this. I know from my notes that during the year I've improved a great deal. Oh, Nikolyenka, my dear!" he went on with particular and unusual tenderness, and his tone was calmer after this confession. "How much it means to be influenced by such a woman as she! My God, how fine it could be, when I am independent, to have a friend like her beside me! I am a completely different man when I am with her."

And after this Dmitri began to unfold to me his plans for marriage, living in the country, and working constantly at self-improvement.

"I shall live in the country, you'll come to see me, and perhaps you'll be married to Sonyechka," he said. "Our children will play together. All this sounds ridiculous and foolish, doesn't it, but it might come to pass, you know."

"Absolutely! It's very possible," I said, smiling and thinking at that moment that it might be even better if I married his sister.

"Do you know what?" he said after a brief silence. "You only imagine that you're in love with Sonyechka, but as far as I can see it's not serious—you still don't know what the genuine feeling is like."

I did not object because I almost agreed with him. We were silent for a while.

"You must have noticed that I was in a foul mood again today and quarreled nastily with Varyenka. Then it was terribly disagreeable for me, particularly because you were there. Although she has wrong ideas about a lot of things, she's a wonderful girl, a fine girl, you'll see for yourself when you get to know her better."

His transition in his conversation from the fact that I was not in love to praises of his sister pleased me terribly and made me blush, but I still did not say anything to him about his sister and we went on to talk of something else.

In this way we talked until second cock-crow and pale dawn was already peeping in the window when Dmitri went over to his own bed and extinguished the candle.

"Well, let's go to sleep now," he said.

"Yes," I replied. "But just one last word."

"Well?"

"It's a grand life, isn't it?" I said.

"It's a grand life," he replied in such a voice that it seemed to me in the dark that I could see the expression of his merry caressing eyes and childlike smile.

XXVIII

IN THE COUNTRY

The following day Volodya and I set off for the country by post-chaise. Sorting in my mind through my various memories of Moscow en route, I also remembered Sonyechka Valakhin, though even then only in the evening when we had gone five stages. . . . But it's queer, I thought, that I'm in love and yet forgot about it completely; I must think of her, and I began to think of her the way one does when traveling—disconnectedly but vividly, and I thought myself into such a state that, once in the country, for two days I considered it essential for some reason to seem sad and preoccupied in front of everyone at home, particularly Katyenka, whom I considered a great connoisseur in matters of this nature and to whom I dropped one or two little hints about the state of my heart. But in spite of all my efforts at pretending to others and myself, in spite of deliberately acquiring all the signs that I had noticed in others who were in love, only during the course of two days, and even then not continually, but predominantly in the evenings, did I remember that I was in love, and finally, as soon as I entered the new round of country life and occupations, I completely forgot about my love for Sonyechka.

We arrived in Petrovsky at night and I was sleeping so soundly that I saw neither the house nor the birch avenue nor any of the household, who were all in their rooms and long since sleeping. Old Foka, bent double, barefoot, wearing a sort of woman's quilted bed jacket and with a candle in his hand, unlocked the door for us. At the sight of us he shook with joy, kissed us on the shoulder, hastily put his mattress away and started to get dressed. I passed through the front hall and up the stairs without being thoroughly awake, but in the anteroom the lock of the door, the bolt, the crooked floorboard, the chest, the old candlestick splashed with wax, just as in the old days, the shadow thrown by the cold crooked just-lit wick of the tallow candle and the always dusty double window that was never removed, behind which, I remember, there was a rowan tree—all this was so familiar, so full of memories, and so harmoniously arranged, as though united by a single idea, that I suddenly felt the caress of this dear old house upon me. Involuntarily I asked myself the question: How had we, the house and I, managed to remain so long apart?—and hastening somewhere, I ran to see whether all the other rooms were just the same. Everything was the same, only it had all grown smaller, lower, while I seemed to have grown taller, heavier, and rougher; but the house took me joyfully into its arms even as I was and every floorboard, every window, every step on the stairs and every sound awoke in me a host of images, feelings, and incidents from the happy irrecoverable past. We went into our childhood bedroom: all those childhood horrors lurked just the same in the dark corners and doorways; we walked through the drawing room—every object in the room was still imbued with that same quiet tender motherly love; we passed through the salon—boisterous carefree childish merriment seemed still to linger in this room and waited merely to be brought to life again. In the sitting room, to which we were led by Foka and where he prepared our beds, it seemed that everything—the mirror, the screens, the old wooden ikon, and every irregularity on the wall, now covered with white paper—everything spoke of suffering, death, and that which would never come again.

We got into bed and Foka, wishing us good night, left us.

"It was in this room that *maman* died, wasn't it?" said Volodya.

I did not answer him and pretended to be asleep. If I had said anything I would have wept. When I awoke the next morning Papa, who was still not dressed, wearing his dressing gown and soft bootees, with a cigar in his mouth, was sitting on Volodya's bed and talking and laughing with him. With a merry twitch he jumped up from Volodya's bed, came over to me, slapped me on the back with his big hand, put out his cheek to me, and pressed it against my lips.

"Well, excellent, thank you, Diplomat," he said with that particular joking affection of his, gazing at me with his tiny shining eyes. "Volodya says that you passed your exams well, put up a good show—that's wonderful. When you make up your mind not to fool around, you too can be a wonderful fellow. Thank you, my friend. Now we can have a wonderful time together and in the winter, perhaps, we'll go to St. Petersburg; only it's a pity the hunting season is over, else I could have kept you entertained; well, can you hunt with a gun, *Waldemar*? There's no end of game, I'll go with you myself one day, perhaps. Well, and next winter, God willing, we'll move to St. Petersburg, you can meet some people, make connections; you're big lads now; I was just saying to *Waldemar* that you can stand on your own feet now, my business is done, you can find your own way, and as for me, if you want my advice, ask for it, I'm not your nurse any more but a friend, at least that's what I want to be—a friend, comrade, and adviser if I can, and nothing more. How does that fit in with your philosophy, Coco? Eh? Good or bad, eh?"

I said, naturally, that it was excellent, and truly I found it so. Today Papa had some sort of particularly attractive gay and happy look about him and this new attitude to me as an equal and a comrade made me love him all the more.

"Well, tell me everything; did you go to see all our relatives? The Ivins? Did you see the old man? What did he say to you?" he continued to interrogate me. "Did you go to see Prince Ivan Ivanich?"

And we talked for so long without getting dressed that the sun was already beginning to disappear from the sitting-room windows and Yakov (who was just as old and who still twirled his fingers in the same way behind his back and said *but there again*) came into our room and informed Papa that the carriage was ready.

"Where are you going?" I asked Papa.

"Oh yes, I almost forgot," said Papa, with a vexed shrug and a cough. "I promised to go to the Epifanovs today. Do you remember the Epifanov girl, *la belle Flamande*? She used to visit your *maman*. They're wonderful people." And Papa, shyly, it seemed to me, shrugging his shoulder, went out of the room.

During our chat Lyubochka had come to the door several times and kept asking: "Can I come in?" but Papa shouted to her each time through the door "It's out of the question because we're not dressed yet."

"What a tragedy! I've seen you in your dressing gown, haven't I?"

"You are not allowed to see your brothers without their unmentionables," he shouted to her. "Listen, each of them will come and knock on your door, will that satisfy you? Go and knock, boys. But it's improper for them even to speak to you in such a state of undress."

"Oh, how hateful you all are! Well, at least hurry up and come to the drawing room; Mimi's so eager to see you," shouted Lyubochka from behind the door.

As soon as Papa went away, I quickly dressed in my student uniform and went to the drawing room; Volodya, on the other hand, took his time and remained a long time upstairs talking to Yakov about where there were most woodcock and snipe. As I have said before, there was nothing in the world he feared more than tenderness with his "brotherkin, pappy, or sissy," as he put it, and in avoiding any expression of sentiment he went to the other extreme—that of coldness, which frequently mortally offended people who did not understand the reasons for it. In the anteroom I bumped into Papa, who with quick little steps was on his way to his carriage. He was wearing his new fashionable Moscow coat and smelled of scent. Catching sight of me he nodded his head cheerfully, as much as to say: "Pretty good, eh" and I was again struck by the happy expression of his eyes which I had noticed that morning.

The drawing room was the same bright high room with its yellowy English piano and big open windows, into which the green trees and reddish-yellow garden paths glanced cheerfully. Having kissed Mimi and Lyubochka and gone up to Katyenka, it suddenly occurred to me that it would be improper now to kiss her and I halted, blushing and silent. Katyenka, not in the least embarrassed, offered me her whitish little hand and congratulated me on entering the university. When Volodya came into the drawing room, the same thing happened between him and Katyenka. It really was difficult after having grown up together and seen one another every day throughout all this time to decide how we ought now to greet one another after our first separation. Katyenka blushed far more than the rest of us; Volodya was not in the least put out and, after having bowed to her slightly, went over to Lyubochka, with whom he also talked a little, although not seriously, and then went off somewhere to walk alone.

XXIX

OUR RELATIONS WITH THE GIRLS

Volodya had such odd views about the girls that he could be interested in whether they had eaten enough or slept enough or whether they were properly dressed or made mistakes in French, which he would be ashamed of in front of strangers, but he would not admit the idea that they might have any human thoughts or feelings and still less would he admit the possibility of ever discussing anything with them. Whenever they happened to go to him with any serious question (which, however, they already tried to avoid) or if they asked his opinion about some novel or other or about his studies at the university, he would pull a face at them and walk away in silence, or else reply with some mangled French phrase such as *kom si tri joli,* and so on; or else, pulling a serious and deliberately foolish face, he would utter some word that was completely meaningless and had nothing whatever to do with the question, saying, his eyes suddenly turning blank: *bread roll* or *let's go* or *cabbage,* or something of that sort. Whenever I happened to repeat to him something that Lyubochka or Katyenka had told me, he always said:

"Hm! So you still have discussions with them? No, you're still in a bad way, I see."

And one had to hear and see him as he said it to appreciate the profound immutable contempt conveyed by this sentence. Volodya had been grown-up for two years now and was constantly falling in love with all the pretty women he met; but despite the fact that he saw Katyenka every day, and she too had been wearing a long dress for two years now and was growing prettier from day to day, it did not even occur to him that it was possible to fall in love with her. Whether this proceeded from the fact that prosaic memories of childhood— droshkys, sheets, naughtiness—were still too fresh in his mind, or from the horror that very young men feel of everything domestic, or from the general human weakness, when meeting something good and beautiful early on in life, of going round it and saying to oneself: "Ah! There will be lots more of this in my life"—at all events until now Volodya had not looked upon Katyenka as a woman.

Volodya was visibly bored the whole of this summer; his boredom proceeded from contempt for us and, as I have said, he made no attempt to conceal it. The constant expression on his face said: "Phoo! How boring, and there's no one to talk to!" All morning he would either be out hunting with a gun or else remain in his room undressed until dinner time, reading a book. If Papa were not at home he would even bring his book to the dinner table and continue reading there without talking to anyone, as a result of which we all felt somehow guilty before him. In the evenings, too, he would lie with his feet up on the couch in the drawing room and sleep, with his head propped on his elbow, or else with a perfectly straight face spout the most terrible rubbish, some of which at times was not absolutely proper, so that Mimi would grow angry and come out in red spots and we would all die of laughter; but never did he deign to speak seriously with anyone in the whole family, except for Papa and occasionally me. Quite involuntarily I aped my brother in his view of the girls, despite the fact that I was not afraid of tendernesses, as he was, and my contempt for them was far from being as firm or deep. This summer I even tried several times, out of boredom, to get closer to Lyubochka and Katyenka and to talk to them, but I invariably encountered such inability to think logically and such ignorance of the simplest and most ordinary things, such as, for instance, what money was, what one studied at the university, what war was, and so on, and such indifference to having these things explained to them that these efforts merely reinforced my unfavorable opinion of them.

I remember one evening when Lyubochka was repeating some intolerably boring passage on the piano for the hundredth time and Volodya, lying in the drawing room and dozing on the couch, was muttering from time to time, without speaking to anyone in particular, such ironies as: "Look at her go . . . what a musician . . . *Bithoven!* (he pronounced this name with particular irony) great . . . and now once more . . . that's right," and so forth. Katyenka and I had remained at the tea table and I don't remember how, but Katyenka had turned the conversation to her favorite topic—love. I was in the mood for philosophizing and began loftily to define love as a desire to acquire in another that which one has not oneself, and so on. But Katyenka replied that on the contrary, it was not love if a girl wished to marry a rich man and that in her opinion money was the most worthless of things, but that true love was only that which could endure parting (by this I realized that she was hinting at her love for Dubkov). Volodya, who must have overheard our conversation, raised himself suddenly on one elbow and cried questioningly: "*Katyenka!* Any Russians?"

"You and your nonsense!" said Katyenka.

"*In a pepper-pot?*" went on Volodya, emphasizing each vowel. And I could not help thinking that Volodya was absolutely right.

Apart from the general faculties, developed to a greater or lesser degree in individuals, of intelligence, sensibility, and artistic feeling, there is a particular faculty, developed to a greater or lesser degree in various circles of society and especially in families, that I choose to call *understanding.* The essence of this faculty consists in an agreed sense of measure and in an agreed bias in one's view of things. Two members of a single circle or a single family, possessing this faculty, will always permit the expression of feeling to a given identical point, beyond which they both see only words; at one and the same instant they will perceive where praise ends and irony begins, where enthusiasm ends and pretense begins—which might seem quite different to people with another kind of understanding. For people with a single understanding, each object strikes them identically—and predominantly in its ridiculous, beautiful, or repellent aspect. In order to facilitate this identical understanding among people in the same circle or family, a special language is established with its own turns of phrase and even words which define those nuances of meaning that do not exist for others. In our family, between Papa and us brothers, this kind of understanding was developed in the highest degree. Dubkov also fitted in well with our circle and *understood,* whereas Dmitri, despite the fact that he was much more intelligent, was blind in this respect. But with no one was this faculty developed to such a pitch of subtlety as with Volodya and myself, who had grown up together in identical circumstances. Even Papa was far behind us in this respect and much that was as clear as twice two makes four to us was incomprehensible to him. For instance, Volodya and I had established, God knows how, the following words with their corresponding meanings: *raisin* meant a vain desire to show that one had some money, *bigwig* (at which the fingers had to be placed together and special emphasis laid on the two *gs*) meant something fresh healthy and elegant, but not ostentatious; nouns used in the plural meant an unjustifiable liking for that object, and so on and so forth. However, the meaning depended more upon the facial expression and upon the general sense of the conversation, so that no matter what new expression one of us might think up to gain a fresh nuance of meaning, the other would understand exactly what he meant from a mere hint alone. The girls did not have our understanding and this was the main reason for our moral separation and the contempt we felt for them.

Perhaps they had their own understanding, but it was so different from ours that where we saw fine words they saw feeling, and our irony was for them serious, and so on. But at that time I did not understand that they were not at fault in this respect and that this absence of understanding did not prevent them from being clever attractive girls, and so I despised them. Furthermore, having once hit upon the idea of frankness and having taken the application of this idea to an extreme in myself, I convicted Lyubochka's serene trusting nature of secrecy and insincerity, merely because she saw no need to dig out and examine all her ideas and spiritual tendencies. For instance, the fact that Lyubochka made the sign of the cross over Papa every evening before bed, the fact that she and Katyenka used to cry at the chapel whenever we went to hold a memorial service for Mama, and the fact that Katyenka used to sigh and roll her eyes when playing the piano—all this seemed terribly insincere to me and I asked myself where they had learned to pretend like grown-ups and why they were not ashamed of themselves.

XXX

My Occupations

In spite of this, I came closer to our girls this summer than in other years as the result of a sudden passion of mine for music. That spring a neighbor came to us in the country to introduce himself, a young man, and as soon as he entered the drawing room he kept looking at the piano and imperceptibly moving his chair closer to it, talking all the while with Mimi and Katyenka. Having talked for a time of the weather and the delights of country living, he skillfully led the conversation round to piano tuners, music, and the piano and finally announced that he played, and played three waltzes in very short order, at which Lyubochka, Mimi, and Katyenka stood round the piano and watched him. This young man never once came to see us again, but I was very attracted by his playing, his posture at the piano, the tossing of his hair, and particularly his way of playing octaves with his left hand, swiftly shooting his little finger and thumb out to the width of an octave, slowly lowering them and then swiftly shooting them out again. This graceful gesture, his casual posture, the tossing of his hair and the regard which our ladies displayed for his talent gave me the idea of taking up the piano. Having convinced myself as a result of this idea that I had both talent and a passion for music, I commenced to learn. In this respect I acted in exactly the same way as millions of people of the male and particularly the female sex who learn without a good teacher, without a real vocation, and without the slightest idea of what art can give and how to approach it in order that it may make this gift. For me music, or rather piano playing, was a means of enticing girls by way of their feelings. With the aid of Katyenka and having learned the notes and broken in my thick fingers a little, at which, by the way, I spent two months of such zealous effort that I even worked on my recalcitrant fourth finger on my knee at dinner and on my pillow in bed, I immediately started to play *pièces* and played them, of course, with feeling—*avec âme,* on which Katyenka agreed—but completely out of time.

The choice of pieces was familiar—waltzes, galops, romances (*arrangés*), and so on—all by those nice composers of whose work any man in a music shop with healthy taste will pick you out a sheaf from a pile of good things and say: "You don't need to play these because nothing more useless tasteless and senseless was ever set to music," and which, probably for that reason, you are sure to find on every Russian girl's piano. It is true we had those unfortunates—crippled forever by our young ladies—the *Sonate Pathétique* and C minor sonata by Beethoven, which Lyubochka used to play in memory of *maman,* and some other good things given to her by her Moscow teacher, but we also had some of this teacher's compositions, ridiculous marches and galops, which Lyubochka also used to play. Katyenka and I did not like serious things and preferred above all "*Le Fou*" and "The Nightingale," which Katyenka played so fast that her fingers were invisible and which I also had begun to play fairly loudly and consecutively. I mastered the young man's gesture and frequently regretted that there were no outsiders to see my playing. But soon Liszt and Kalkbrenner proved beyond my powers and I realized the impossibility of catching up with Katyenka. As a result of this, imagining that classical was easier, and partly in order to be original, I decided suddenly that I liked academic German music, began to go into ecstasies whenever Lyubochka played the *Sonate Pathétique,* although, to tell the truth, I had long since become sick to death of it, and myself started playing

Beethoven and pronounced it *Bate-hoven*. Through all this muddle and pretense, however, so far as I can remember now, there really was something resembling talent in me, because often music affected me to the point of tears even and somehow the things that I liked I managed to pick out on the piano without notes; so that if someone had taught me then to regard music as an end in itself, as an independent delight, and not as a means of fascinating girls with the speed and sensitivity of my playing, I might well have become a reasonable musician.

My other occupation that summer was reading French novels, of which Volodya had brought a lot with him. At that time the *Monte-Cristo* series and various "mysteries" had only just begun to appear and I buried myself in the novels of Sue, Dumas, and Paul de Kock. All the most unnatural personages and events were as vivid to me as reality; I not only did not dare to suspect the author of falsehood but the author himself did not even exist for me and real people and events rose up before me from the printed page entirely of their own volition. If I had never met such personages as the ones I read about, still I did not doubt for a single second that they *would one day exist.*

I discovered in myself all the passions described there and a resemblance to all the characters, both the heroes and villains, in every novel, just as an impressionable man finds in himself the symptoms of all possible illnesses when he reads a medical book. What pleased me in these novels were the cunning thoughts and fiery emotions and fantastic events and whole characters: the good man was completely good, the bad man completely bad—just as I imagined people to be during my early youth; what I liked very very much also was the fact that all this was in French and that I could memorize the noble words uttered by the noble heroes and refer to them on some noble occasion. How many different French phrases I could have thought up with the help of these novels for Kolpikov, should I ever meet him again, and for *her,* when at last I met her and declared my love! I prepared such things to say to them as would make them die on the spot. On the basis of these novels I even evolved new ideals of the moral excellences I wished to attain. Most of all I desired to be *noble* in all my deeds and actions (I use the French word, *noble,* and not the Russian one, *blagorodny,* because the French word has a different meaning, a fact which the Germans understood when they adopted the word *nobel* without mixing it up with the concept of *ehrlich*), then to be *passionate*, and finally, something to which I had been inclined even before, to be as much *comme il faut* as possible. Even in my appearance and habits I tried to be like the heroes who had some of these qualities. I remember that in one of the hundred or so novels I read that summer there was one extraordinarily passionate hero with bushy eyebrows, and I so desired to be like him in appearance (morally I felt myself to be exactly like him) that, examining my eyebrows in the mirror one day, I conceived the idea of trimming them a little so that they would grow thicker, but when I began to trim them, it came out that I had cut too much off in one spot and it was necessary to even them up—it ending finally, to my horror, with me seeing myself in the mirror browless and consequently very ugly. I consoled myself, however, with the hope that I would soon grow bushy eyebrows, like the passionate hero, and merely worried about what to say to the family when they saw me eyebrowless. I obtained some powder from Volodya, rubbed it on my eyebrows and lit it. Although the powder did not flare up, I looked sufficiently burned for no one to guess my subterfuge, and truly, when I had already forgotten about the passionate hero my eyebrows did grow out much thicker.

XXXI

COMME IL FAUT

In the course of this story I have already hinted several times at the concept corresponding to this French heading and now I feel the need to devote a whole chapter to this concept, which was one of the most false pernicious concepts in my life, implanted in me both by upbringing and society.

The human race can be divided into numerous categories—rich and poor, good and evil, military and civilian, clever and stupid, and so on and so forth, but each man has his own favorite subdivision into which he unconsciously places each new person he meets. My own favorite and most important subdivision of people at the time I am writing of was into people who were *comme il faut* and those who were *comme il ne faut pas*. The second class was subdivided further into people who actually were not *comme il faut* and the common people. People who were *comme il faut* I respected and considered worthy of being on an equal footing with me; the second sort I pretended to despise, but in reality I hated them and they evoked in me a sort of sense of personal affront; the third did not exist for me—I despised them utterly. My sense of *comme il faut* consisted, first and foremost, in an excellent knowledge of French, particularly pronunciation. A man who pronounced French badly immediately evoked a feeling of hatred in me. "Why do you try to speak like us when you can't?" I would ask him mentally with venomous scorn. The second condition of being *comme il faut* was fingernails—long, manicured and clean; the third was an ability to bow, dance, and make conversation; the fourth, and a very important one, was aloofness toward everything and a constant expression of a kind of refined superior boredom. Besides these there were general signs on the basis of which, without speaking to a man, I decided to which class he belonged. The most important of these signs, apart from the state of his room, his seal, his handwriting, and his carriage, were his legs. The relationship between a man's boots and his trousers immediately decided his position in my eyes. Boots without heels and with a squarish toe, and narrow trousers without footstraps—this was *plain;* a boot with a pointed rounded-off toe and heel and narrow trousers with footstraps closely hugging the feet, or wide trousers with footstraps which arched over the toes like canopies—this was a man of *mauvais genre,* and so on.

It is strange that this concept should have taken such a hold on one like me, who was decidedly incapable of *comme il faut.* But perhaps it took such deep root in me precisely because it cost me such enormous effort to acquire *comme il faut.* It is dreadful to recall how much priceless time of that best sixteen-year-old period of my life I wasted in acquiring this quality. Everyone that I imitated—Volodya, Dubkov, and the larger part of my friends—seemed to achieve it quite easily. I watched them enviously and labored in secret over my French, over the art of bowing, regardless of whom I bowed to, over my conversation, dancing, and the cultivation in myself of boredom and indifference to everything, over my fingernails, whereupon I cut my flesh with the scissors—and still I felt that much work lay ahead of me before I could achieve my aim. And my room, desk, carriage—all this I was completely unable to arrange so that it was *comme il faut,* even though I forced myself, despite my aversion to practical affairs, to occupy myself with them. With others, however, things seemed to go excellently without the slightest effort, as though nothing could be otherwise. I remember once, after working diligently but fruitlessly at my fingernails,

I asked Dubkov, whose nails were astonishingly good, how long they had been like that and what he had done to them. Dubkov replied: "I haven't done anything for them to be like that ever since I can remember and I don't understand how a gentleman's nails could possibly be otherwise." This reply incensed me. I still did not know that one of the main conditions of *comme il faut* was secrecy with regard to the labors by which *comme il faut* was acquired. *Comme il faut* was for me not merely an important merit, an excellent quality, and an accomplishment that I desired to attain, it was an indispensable condition of life, without which there could be neither happiness, nor glory, nor anything good in the world. I would have respected neither a renowned artist, nor a scholar, nor a benefactor of the human race if he had not been *comme il faut*. A man who was *comme il faut* stood higher than and beyond comparison with them; he left it to them to paint pictures, write books and music, or do good—he even praised them for it; why not praise what is good in no matter whom—but he could not be on the same level with them, because he was *comme il faut* and they were not—and that was all. It seems to me, even, that if we had had a brother, mother, or father who was not *comme il faut*, we would have said that it was unfortunate but that between us and them there could be nothing in common. But neither the loss of valuable time, used up in constant worrying about the observance of all those conditions of *comme il faut* that were so difficult for me and excluded any kind of serious study, nor my hatred and contempt for nine tenths of the human race, nor my absence of interest in anything good that lay outside the circle of *comme il faut*—none of these constituted the main evil caused me by this concept. The main evil consisted in a conviction that *comme il faut* was a self-sufficient position in society, that a man did not need to try to be a civil servant or a coachmaker or a soldier or a scholar if he was *comme il faut*; that having reached this position he was thereby fulfilling his vocation and even became higher than the majority of people.

At a certain point in his youth, after many mistakes and diversions, every man normally feels the necessity of taking an active part in the life of society, chooses some branch of activity and devotes himself to it; but this rarely happens with a man who is *comme il faut*. I have known and know very very many older, proud and self-confident people, sharp in their judgments, who in answer to the question, should it be posed them in the next world: "Who are you? And what did you do down there?" will be able to say nothing but: *"Je fus un homme très comme il faut."*

This fate awaited me.

XXXII

Youth

Despite the confusion of ideas taking place in my head that summer, I was young, innocent, free, and therefore almost happy.

Sometimes, and fairly often at that, I would get up early. (I used to sleep in the open air on the terrace and the brilliant slanting rays of the morning sun used to wake me.) I would dress quickly, tuck a towel and a volume of a French novel under my arm and walk to the river to swim in the shade of a birch grove about a quarter of a mile from the house. There I would lay down on the grass in the shade and read, tearing my eyes away from time to time in order to glance at the surface of the river, violet in the shade and just beginning to stir in the morning breeze, at the field of ripening rye on the other side, at the light-red rays of morning light as they tinctured the white boles of the birch trees ever lower and lower, which, hiding behind one another, receded before me into depths of sheer forest, and I reveled in the consciousness inside me of the same fresh young forces of life as those which nature breathed all around me. When gray wisps of morning cloud had appeared in the sky and I was chilled after my swim, often I would set off to walk at random through the woods and fields, joyously feeling the fresh dew soak through my boots and wet my feet. At this time I would dream vividly of the heroes of the last novel I had read and would imagine myself now a general, now a minister, now an extraordinary strong man and now a passionate man, and with a certain amount of trepidation I would look about me constantly in the hope of suddenly meeting *her* somewhere in a glade or behind a tree. Whenever I met peasant men or women at work on these walks of mine, despite the fact that the *common people* did not exist for me, I always experienced a powerful subconscious embarrassment and tried to avoid being seen by them. When it was already getting hot and the ladies had still not come out for tea, I often went to the garden or orchard to eat all the vegetables and fruits which were ripe by then. And this occupation afforded me one of my greatest pleasures. Sometimes you'd make your way into the apple orchard, into the very center of a tall dense thicket of raspberry canes. Overhead was the hot bright sky, around you pale-green prickly raspberry leaves intermingled with growths of weeds. A dark-green nettle with a delicate flowering crown reaches up gracefully; a bushy burdock with unnatural, violet, hooked flowers rudely overtops the raspberries and even your head, and in one or two places, together with the nettles, reaches even to the pale-green drooping branches of the ancient apple trees, on whose tops apples that are still sour, round and shiny like ivory, are ripening full in the sunlight. Down below, a young raspberry bush, almost dry, leafless and twisted, reaches for the sun; green spears of grass and a young thistle, pushing up through last year's leaves and moist with dew, show richly green in the eternal shade, as though unaware that bright sunshine is playing on the leaves of the apple tree.

In this thicket it is always damp, it smells of deep constant shadow, spiders' webs, fallen apples that already lie blackening on the fusty ground, of raspberries and at times even of forest bugs, which you would sometimes swallow accidentally with a raspberry and then hastily eat another. Moving forward, you startle the sparrows that always dwell in this inaccessible spot, you hear their hurried twittering and the sounds of their swift little wings striking against the twigs, you hear the stationary buzzing of a bumblebee and somewhere along the path the steps of the gardener, the simpleton Akim, and his perpetual mumbling. You think to yourself: No, nobody in the world can find me here, not even him ... and with hands to right and left you pick off the juicy raspberries from their white conical stalks and swallow them blissfully one after the other. Your legs are soaking wet, even above the knees, some terrible rubbish is running through your head (you keep on repeating to yourself a thousand times a-a-and twe-e-e-nty here and se-e-even there), your arms and your legs through your soaked trousers are being stung by nettles, the sun's perpendicular rays are already beginning to penetrate the thicket and scorch your head, your desire to eat has long since vanished and yet you continue to sit there in the thicket, looking, listening, thinking, and mechanically plucking and swallowing the best berries.

At about eleven o'clock, mostly when tea is over and the ladies have already sat down to work, I normally go to the drawing room. By the first window, with its unbleached canvas shade lowered against the sun and bright sunlight pouring through the chinks, casting such brilliant dazzling circles on everything it finds that it hurts the eyes to look at them, there stands an embroidery frame with flies quietly strolling on its white linen. Mimi sits at the frame, ceaselessly tossing her head in vexation and moving about to escape the sun, which, making a sudden breakthrough somewhere, extends a brilliant stripe now here now there over her face or across her arm. Through the other three windows the sun forms vivid complete rectangles with the frame shadows in them. In one of them, on the unpainted drawing-room floor, Milka lies out of old habit, pricking up her ears and staring at the flies walking about in the bright rectangle. Katyenka knits or reads, sitting on the sofa, and impatiently waves her whitish little hands, seeming transparent in the brilliant light, or, frowning, gives a shake of her little head in order to drive off a fly that has got tangled in her thick golden hair and is buzzing there. Lyubochka either walks up and down the room with her hands clasped behind her back, waiting for everyone to go into the garden, or else plays the piano, playing some piece whose every note I have known for ages. I sit down somewhere, listen to the music or the reading and wait till I can go to the piano myself. After dinner I sometimes deign to go riding with the girls (I considered walking incompatible with my age and position in the world). And our outings, during which I take them to unusual places and ravines, are very pleasant. Sometimes we have adventures in which I show myself to be quite a hero and the ladies praise my bravery and horsemanship and consider me their protector. In the evening, if there are no guests, after drinking tea on the shady verandah and walking round the estate with Papa, I settle down in my old spot in the Voltaire armchair and, listening to Lyubochka or Katyenka playing, read and at the same time dream as of old. Sometimes, remaining alone in the drawing room while Lyubochka plays one of our old pieces of music, I involuntarily abandon my book and gaze through the open balcony door at the curly hanging branches of the tall birch trees, already touched by the evening shadows, and at the clear sky, where, if you look closely, a kind of dusty yellowish spot appears suddenly and then disappears again; and listening to the sounds of music coming from the salon, to the creaking of the gate, the sound of peasant women's voices and cattle returning to the village, I have a sudden vivid image of Natalya Savishna, and *maman*, and Karl Ivanich, and I become sad for a moment. But my heart at this time is so full of life and hope that the recollection merely brushes me with its wings and flies on.

After supper and occasionally an evening stroll with someone in the garden—I was afraid to walk through those dark avenues alone—I would go off alone to sleep on the floor of the verandah, which, despite the fact that I would get bitten by millions of mosquitoes, afforded me great satisfaction. At the full moon I would often spend whole nights successively sitting up on my mattress, gazing at the light and shadow, listening to the noises and silence, dreaming of various things, but primarily of a voluptuous poetic bliss that seemed to me then to be the highest happiness in life, and mourning the fact that till now I had been able only to dream about it. At times, no sooner had everyone dispersed for the night and the lights from the drawing room been transferred upstairs, whence would then come the sound of women's voices and the noise of windows being opened and closed, than I would go to the verandah and start to walk up and down, greedily listening to all the sounds of the retiring house. As long as there was the tiniest irrational hope of even partial happiness of the kind I dreamed of, I was unable to construct calmly my imaginary happiness.

At every sound of bare feet, every cough, every sigh, bump of a window or rustle of a dress I would leap up out of bed, listen and peer about furtively and become all excited for no apparent reason. But then the lights would go out in the upstairs windows, the sound of footsteps and talking would give way to snores, the night watchman would begin tapping on his board, the garden would get darker and then lighter as soon as the bright stripes of red light coming from the windows disappeared from it, the last light from the pantry would move to the front hall, throwing a strip of light across the dewy garden, and through the window I would see the bent figure of Foka, wearing a smock and with a candle in his hand, on his way to bed. Often I would get enormous palpitating pleasure out of creeping over the wet grass in the black shadow of the house, going up to the window of the front hall and listening with baited breath to the boy's snores, the groaning of Foka, who supposed that no one could hear him, and the sound of his old man's voice going on and on with his prayers. Finally this last candle of his would go out too, the window would slam shut and I would remain completely alone, looking about me timidly to either side to see whether there was perhaps a white lady somewhere beside the flowers or beside my bed—and then scamper back to the verandah. And only then would I lie down in bed facing the garden, cover myself up as best I could to escape the mosquitoes and bats, gaze into the garden, listen to the sounds of the night, and dream of love and happiness.

Then everything would acquire a different character for me: the sight of the old birch trees, their curly branches gleaming on one side in the moonlit air, while on the other they darkly obscured the shrubbery and road with their black shadows, and the calm sumptuous sheen of the pond, swelling steadily like a sound, and the moonlit gleam of dewdrops on the flowers by the verandah, which also laid their graceful shadows across the gray flowerbed, and the sound of quail beyond the pond, and a man's voice coming from the main road, and the quiet barely audible creak of two birch trees rubbing together, and the buzzing of a mosquito by my ear under the blanket, and the falling onto dry leaves of an apple that had been caught on a twig, and the leaping of frogs who sometimes came up as far as the terrace steps, their greenish backs gleaming somehow mysteriously in the moonlight—all this acquired a strange character for me—of excessive beauty and sort of uncompleted happiness. And then *she* would appear, with long black hair and a high bosom, always sad and always beautiful, with naked arms and voluptuous embraces. She loved me and I sacrificed my whole life for one moment of her love. But the moon climbed higher and higher up the sky and shone brighter and brighter, the pond's sumptuous sheen, intensifying like a sound, grew clearer and clearer, the shadows became blacker and blacker and the light more and more transparent, and, gazing at all this, listening to all this, something told me that even *she*, with her naked arms and ardent embraces, was still far, far from being the whole of happiness, and that loving her was far, far from being the whole of bliss; and the more I looked at the high full moon, the more true beauty and bliss seemed higher and higher to me, purer and purer, and nearer and nearer to Him, the source of all beauty and bliss, and tears of a kind of dissatisfied but disturbing joy welled up in my eyes.

And still I was alone and still it seemed to me that mysteriously grandiose nature, together with the bright hypnotic disk of the moon, which had stopped for some reason at one elevated but indistinct spot in the pale-blue sky, though at the same time being everywhere and seeming to fill the whole of infinite space with itself, and I, an insignificant worm, already corrupted by all the poor petty passions of humanity, but with an infinite mighty fund of imagination and love—still it seemed to me at these moments as though nature, the moon, and I were all one and the same.

XXXIII

THE NEIGHBORS

I had been extremely surprised the first day after our arrival to hear Papa call our neighbors, the Epifanovs, wonderful people, and still more surprised by the fact that he was visiting them. From time immemorial there had been a lawsuit going on between us and the Epifanovs over some land or other. As a child I had several times heard Papa fly into a rage over this lawsuit, abuse the Epifanovs and summon various people, as I thought then, to his defense, and I had heard Yakov calling them our enemies and *dark people*, and I remembered *maman* begging us not even to mention their name in her presence.

On the basis of this evidence I had in childhood composed for myself such a firm and clear concept of the fact that the Epifanovs were our enemies, prepared to strangle or cut the throat not only of Papa but even of his son if they caught him, and that they literally were dark people, that when I saw Avdotya Vasilyevna Epifanov, *la belle Flamande,* waiting upon Mama the year she died, I had difficulty in believing that she was from this family of dark people, and still retained the lowest possible opinion of the family. Despite the fact that we saw a great deal of them this summer, I continued to be strangely prejudiced against the whole family. In reality, this is who the Epifanovs were. The family consisted of a mother, a fifty-year-old widow, still a youthful and merry old lady, her beautiful daughter, Avdotya Vasilyevna, and a son who stuttered, Pyotr Vasilyevich, a retired bachelor cornet with a very serious disposition.

Anna Dmitriyevna Epifanov had lived apart from her husband for twenty years before he died, part of the time in St. Petersburg, where she had relatives, but most of the time in her village of Mitishchi, which was a mile and a half from us. Such horrors were related in the surrounding district about her way of life that in comparison with her, Messalina was an innocent child. It was because of this that Mama begged us not even to mention the name of Epifanov in her house; but without the least irony, it was impossible to believe even a tenth of this most malicious of all gossip—country-neighbor gossip. But at the time when I came to know Anna Dmitriyevna, although she had a peasant steward in the house named Mityusha, who, with his hair always oiled and curled and wearing a coat in the Circassian manner, used to stand behind Anna Dmitriyevna's chair during dinner, and in whose presence she would often invite the guests, in French, to admire his handsome eyes and mouth, there was nothing even remotely resembling the things that rumor continued to assert. Indeed, it seemed that for ten years now, ever since Anna Dmitriyevna had recalled her dutiful son Pyotr to her from the Army, she had completely changed her way of life. Anna Dmitriyevna's estate was not large, merely a hundred serfs or so, while expenses during her gay life *had* been large, so that ten years ago, the mortgages and double mortgages that had of course been taken out on the estate then fell due and its sale by auction seemed inevitable. It was in these extreme circumstances that Anna Dmitriyevna, supposing the activities of the trustees, the inventorying of the estate, the arrival of the judge, and similar unpleasantnesses to be due not so much to her failure to pay the interest as to the fact that she was a woman, wrote to her son's regiment for him to come and rescue his mother from her predicament. Despite the fact that Pyotr Vasilyevich's career was going so well that he could hope soon to have his own little nest egg, he abandoned everything, went into retirement, and as a dutiful son who considers it his first duty to comfort his mother in her old age (as he wrote with complete sincerity in his letters), came to the village.

In spite of his plain face, clumsiness, and stutter, Pyotr Vasilyevich Epifanov was a man of firm principle and remarkable practical sense. Somehow or other, by means of small loans, deals, petitioning, and promises he kept possession of the estate. Having become an estate owner, Pyotr Vasilyevich donned his father's lumber jacket that had been kept in storage, abolished the horse and carriages, dissuaded guests from coming to Mitishchi, and on the other hand dug drains, increased the tillage, reduced the peasants' land, himself had some trees cut down and sold them economically—and put his affairs in order. Pyotr Vasilyevich made and kept one promise—not to wear any clothes other than his father's lumber jacket and a canvas coat that he had made himself, and not to ride in anything other than a simple cart with peasant horses until such time as all his debts had been paid. As far as he was permitted by his servile respect for his mother, which he considered his duty, he tried to extend this stoical way of life to the whole family. In the drawing room he would fawn stammeringly on his mother, fulfill her every desire, and scold the servants for not doing what Anna Dmitriyevna told them to, but in his study and in the office he would take them sternly to task for serving a duck at table without his orders, or sending a peasant to a neighbor on Anna Dmitriyevna's instructions to inquire about her health, or sending peasant girls to the woods for raspberries when they should have been weeding the kitchen garden.

After three years the debts had all been paid and Pyotr Vasilyevich made a trip to Moscow and returned wearing new clothes and in a new tarantas. But in spite of the flourishing state of his affairs, he retained the same stoical propensities and seemed gloomily proud of them, saying before his own family and before strangers, stammering frequently, that "anyone who really wants to see me will be equally glad to see me in my sheepskin coat, and to eat cabbage soup and gruel," adding "I myself eat it." Each word and gesture of his expressed pride based on the knowledge that he had sacrificed himself for his mother and retrieved the estate, and contempt for others for not having done something similar.

The mother and daughter had characters completely different from his and were in many ways quite different from one another. The mother was one of the pleasantest possible women and always equally good-tempered and jolly in company. Anything that was nice or cheerful truly delighted her. She even had a characteristic that is met with in only the best-tempered of older people, the ability to enjoy the sight of young people making merry, and this she had in the highest degree. Her daughter, Avdotya Vasilyevna, had on the contrary a more serious disposition, or rather that particular apathetically dreamy and quite unwarrantedly haughty demeanor that is usually met with in young unmarried beauties. Whenever she tried to be gay, her gaiety came out rather oddly, so that you did not know whether she was laughing at herself, the person she was talking to, or the whole world, something, evidently, that she did not intend. Often I was amazed and asked myself what exactly she meant when she uttered such phrases as: *yes, I'm astonishingly pretty; of course, everybody's in love with me,* and so on. Anna Dmitriyevna was always active; she had a passion for fixing up her "little home" or "little garden," for flowers, canaries, and pretty knickknacks. Her little rooms and little garden were quite small and modest, but everything was arranged so tidily and neatly and everything bore such a general character of that dainty gaiety that is expressed in a waltz or a polka that the word *toy,* often used by visitors as a form of praise, was particularly suited to Anna Dmitriyevna's little garden and rooms. And Anna Dmitriyevna herself was a toy—tiny, delicate, with pretty little hands, always cheerful and always attractively dressed. Only the slightly too prominent purplish veins on her tiny hands disturbed this general impression. Avdotya Vasilyevna, on the contrary, hardly did anything at all and not only did not like bothering with knickknacks or flowers, but even paid too little attention to herself and always ran off to get dressed whenever guests came. But once dressed, she would look extraordinarily pretty when she returned to the room, except for that cold insipid expression of the eyes and smile that is common to all very beautiful faces. Her strictly regular, beautiful face and slender figure seemed constantly to be saying: "Go ahead, you may look at me."

But in spite of the mother's lively nature and the daughter's apathetically absent-minded appearance, something told you that the former had never—neither in the past nor now—loved anything, other than prettiness and gaiety, while Avdotya Vasilyevna was one of those people who, having once loved, devote their whole lives to the beloved.

XXXIV

Father's Marriage

Father was forty-eight years old when he took Avdotya Vasilyevna Epifanov for his second wife.

I imagine that when he arrived in the country alone that spring with the girls he was in that extra-nervously happy and affable frame of mind that gamblers usually find themselves in when having retired from the tables after a large win. He felt that he still had a large reserve of unexploited luck which, if he did not wish to expend on cards, he could expend on general success in life. Moreover it was spring, he had an unexpected quantity of money, he was completely alone, and he was bored. Upon discussing his affairs with Yakov and recalling the endless lawsuit with Epifanov, and the beautiful Avdotya Vasilyevna, whom he had not seen for a long time, I can imagine him saying to Yakov: "You know, Yakov Kharlamich, why should we drag on with this lawsuit; I think we should simply let them have that accursed piece of ground, eh? What do you think?"

I can imagine how Yakov's fingers twirled negatively behind his back at such a question and how he proved that "*there again* we are in the right, Pyotr Aleksandrovich."

But Papa ordered the carriage to be prepared, donned his fashionable olive-green tunic, combed his remaining hair, sprinkled his handkerchief with scent, and in the most cheerful mood, inspired by the belief that he was behaving aristocratically and, more important, by the hope of seeing a pretty woman, set off to see his neighbors.

All I know is that on his first visit Papa did not find Epifanov at home, the latter being in the fields, and so spent an hour or two with the ladies. I can imagine how Papa was profuse with his compliments, how he charmed them, tapping his soft boots, lisping and making eyes at them. I can imagine also how the merry old lady suddenly conceived a tender affection for him and how animated her cold beautiful daughter became.

When one of the servant girls, puffing and panting, ran up to Epifanov to tell him that old Irtenyev was there in person, I can imagine him answering angrily: "Well, what if he is?" and because of this returning home as slowly as possible, calling in, perhaps, at his study in order to put on his dirtiest overcoat and sending to inform the cook that under no circumstances, not even if the ladies ordered it, should he make any additions for dinner.

I often saw Papa with Epifanov subsequently, therefore I can vividly imagine their first meeting. I can imagine how Epifanov, in spite of Papa's proposal to end the lawsuit peacefully, was gloomy and angry at having sacrificed his career for his mother, Papa, of course, having done nothing of the sort; how nothing surprised him and how Papa, appearing not to notice this gloominess, was playful, gay, and treated him as a wonderful jester, by which Epifanov was offended now and then but to which he could not help but surrender sometimes in spite of himself. Papa, with his tendency to make a joke out of everything, for some reason called Epifanov colonel, and despite the fact that Epifanov, stuttering worse than usual and blushing with annoyance, remarked once in my presence that he was not a c-c-c-colonel but a c-c-c-cornet, within five minutes Papa was calling him colonel again.

Lyubochka told me that before we arrived in the country they had seen the Epifanovs every day and that it had been extraordinarily jolly. Papa, with his flair for arranging everything somehow originally, humorously, and at the same time simply and elegantly, had got up hunts, fishing trips, and even a sort of fireworks display, to which the Epifanovs always came. And things would have been even jollier had it not been for that unbearable Pyotr Vasilyevich, who sulked, stuttered, and spoiled everything, said Lyubochka.

Since we arrived the Epifanovs had only been to us twice and once we had all gone together to their place. But after St. Peter's day on June 29, Papa's name day, when they and scores of other guests came, our relations with the Epifanovs for some reason came to a complete halt and only Papa continued to visit them on his own.

During the brief time that I was able to see Papa with Dunyechka, as her mother called Avdotya Vasilyevna, here is what I was able to note. Papa was constantly in that happy mood that had astonished me in him on the day of our arrival. He was so young, gay, happy, and full of life that the rays of his happiness spread out to all around him and involuntarily put them in the same mood. He did not leave Avdotya Vasilyevna's side for a moment when she was in the room, and constantly showered her with such sugary compliments that I felt embarrassed for him, or else, looking at her in silence, would twitch his shoulder somehow passionately and complacently and cough, and sometimes, with a smile, would even whisper to her; but he did all this looking as if it were just a joke, as was characteristic of him in really serious matters.

Avdotya Vasilyevna seemed to have acquired from Papa the expression of happiness that shone almost constantly in her big blue eyes at this time, except for those moments when she was suddenly attacked by such a fit of bashfulness that I, knowing this feeling, found it pitiful and painful to look at her. At such moments she was visibly afraid of every glance and movement; it seemed to her that everyone was looking at her, thinking only of her and finding everything about her unacceptable. She would look round at everybody apprehensively, the color constantly rushing to her face and leaving it again, and then she would begin to speak loudly and boldly, talking foolishness for the most part, feeling it and feeling that everyone, including Papa, could hear it, and then she would blush still more. But in such cases Papa would not even notice her foolishness and would go on coughing and looking at her just as passionately and with the same cheerful delight as before. I noticed that although Avdotya Vasilyevna's fits of bashfulness could occur for no reason at all, they sometimes followed immediately upon the mention in Papa's presence of some other beautiful young woman. Her frequent transitions from thoughtfulness to that kind of strange awkward gaiety I have already mentioned, the repetition of some of Papa's favorite words and turns of phrase, the continuation with others of conversations begun with Papa—all this, if my own father had not been involved and I had been older, would have made clear to me the relations existing between Papa and Avdotya Vasilyevna, but I suspected nothing at that time, not even when Papa, in my presence, received some sort of letter from Epifanov, became extremely agitated, and ceased going to the Epifanovs until the end of August.

At the end of August Papa again started visiting our neighbors and the day before Volodya's and my departure for Moscow, announced his intention to marry Avdotya Vasilyevna Epifanov.

XXXV

How We Took the News

On the eve of this official announcement everyone in the house already knew about it and had different opinions about it. Mimi did not leave her room the whole day and wept. Katyenka sat with her and emerged only for dinner, with a sort of offended expression on her face that was obviously borrowed from her mother; Lyubochka, on the contrary, was extremely gay and said over dinner that she knew a wonderful secret, which she would not, however, tell to anyone.

"There's nothing wonderful about your secret," said Volodya, not sharing her satisfaction. "If you were able to think of anything serious you'd realize that on the contrary it's very bad."

Lyubochka stared hard at him in astonishment and kept quiet.

After dinner Volodya was about to take me by the hand, but taking fright, probably because it would have looked like tenderness, merely touched me on the elbow and nodded in the direction of the salon.

"Do you know what secret Lyubochka was talking about?" he asked me after reassuring himself that we were alone.

Volodya and I rarely talked face to face or about anything serious, so that whenever this happened we felt a kind of mutual awkwardness and our eyes began to jump about like grasshoppers, as Volodya put it; but now, in answer to the embarrassment in my eyes, he continued to look me directly and seriously in the face with an expression that said: "There's nothing to get embarrassed about, after all we're brothers and we have to consult one another about an important family matter." I understood him and he went on:

"Papa's marrying the Epifanov girl, did you know?"

I nodded because I had already heard about it.

"Well, it's very bad," went on Volodya.

"Why?"

"Why?" he replied with annoyance. "How very pleasant to have that stuttering colonel for an uncle and that whole family. And she seems nice and all right for now, but who knows what's to come? We can suppose it makes no difference to us, but Lyubochka will have to come out very soon. It's not very nice with a *belle mère* like that; she even speaks bad French, and what manners she might give her! *Une poissarde,* a fishwife and nothing more; a nice one, perhaps, but nonetheless *une poissarde,*" concluded Volodya, obviously very pleased with the designation *poissarde.*

Strange as it was for me to hear Volodya thus calmly passing judgment on Papa's choice, it seemed to me he was right.

"Why is Papa marrying?" I asked.

"It's a mysterious business, God only knows, all I know is that Epifanov persuaded him to marry her, demanded it and Papa didn't want to, but then he got some nonsense in his head about chivalry—a mysterious business. I've only just begun to understand Father," went on Volodya (his calling him *Father* and not *Papa* gave me a painful stab), "he's a fine man, clever and kind, but so frivolous and irresponsible that ... it's amazing! He can't look at a woman and keep a cool head. Do you know he falls in love with every woman he gets to know! There was Mimi too, you know."

"What?"

"I'm telling you. Not long ago I found out that he had been in love with Mimi when she was young and wrote poems to her, and there was something between them. Mimi's still suffering from it." And Volodya laughed.

"Impossible!" I said in amazement.

"But the main thing is," went on Volodya, serious once more and suddenly beginning to speak in French, "how nice this wedding will be for the rest of our family! And she's sure to have children."

I was so stunned by Volodya's foresight and good sense that I did not know what to reply.

At this moment Lyubochka came up to us.

"So you know then?" she said with a beaming face.

"Yes," said Volodya, "only I'm amazed at you, Lyubochka: you're no longer a baby in swaddling clothes, you know; how can you be so over-joyed at Papa marrying some piece of trash?"

Lyubochka's face suddenly became serious and thoughtful.

"Volodya! Why trash? How dare you talk that way about Avdotya Vasilyevna? If Papa's marrying her she can't be trash."

"No, not trash, I didn't mean that, but nevertheless . . ."

"No, no *nevertheless*," interrupted Lyubochka heatedly. "I never said the girl you were in love with was trash, did I? So how can you say that about Papa and about an excellent woman? You may be my elder brother, but don't say that to me, you ought not to say it."

"But why shouldn't I discuss . . ."

"You mustn't," interrupted Lyubochka again, "you mustn't discuss such a father as ours. Mimi can, but not you, an older brother."

"No, you don't understand yet," said Volodya contemptuously, "you listen to me. Do you think it a good thing for some *Dunyechka* Epifanov to take the place of your dead mother?"

Lyubochka was silent for a moment and suddenly tears appeared in her eyes.

"I knew you were conceited, but I didn't think you were malicious," she said and left us.

"*Bread roll,*" said Volodya, making a seriocomic face and lackluster eyes. "What's the use of talking to them," he went on, as though re-proaching himself for having forgotten himself to the point of conde-scending to talk to Lyubochka.

The following day the weather was bad and neither Papa nor the ladies had yet come out for tea when I entered the drawing room. A cold autumnal rain had fallen during the night and now the remains of clouds that had emptied themselves overnight still scudded across the sky, with the sun's bright disk, already quite high, wanly showing through them. It was windy, damp and raw. The door to the garden was open and pools of last night's rain were drying out on the rain-blackened floor of the terrace. The open door, held back by an iron catch, shuddered in the wind and the footpaths were wet and muddy. The old birch trees with their stripped white branches, the shrubbery, grass, stinging nettles, currant bushes, and elders with their leaves turned up to show their pale underside, all thrashed about where they stood and seemed to want to break away from their roots; round yellow leaves came flying down the avenue of lime trees, twisting and turning and overtaking one another, then grew wet and flattened themselves on the wet path and on the wet newgrown grass in the meadow. My mind was busy with Papa's forthcoming marriage from the point of view outlined by Volodya. The future seemed to promise nothing good for either our sister or for us, or even for Father himself. I was appalled by the thought that an outsider, a strange and, most important, *young* woman, with no right whatsoever to it, was suddenly in many respects to take the place of—of whom—a simple *young* girl was actually to take the place of poor dead Mama! My heart was heavy and Father seemed more and more to blame. At that moment I heard his and Volodya's voices in the footmen's room. I did not want to see Father just then and moved away from the door, but Lyubochka came up behind me and said that Papa was asking for me.

He was standing in the drawing room with one hand resting on the piano and was looking impatiently and at the same time solemnly in my direction. His face no longer bore that youthful and happy expression I had always noticed on it lately. He was sorrowful. Volodya, holding a pipe in his hand, was walking up and down the room. I went up to Father and greeted him.

"Well, my friends," he said decisively, raising his head and using that special hurried tone of voice reserved for things that are obviously unpleasant but that have gone too far for second thoughts, "you know, I believe, that I am marrying Avdotya Vasilyevna." He was silent a moment. "I never intended marrying again after your *maman*, but . . ." he paused for a second, "but . . . but, it's fate, I suppose. Dunyechka's a good sweet girl and is no longer so very young; I hope you will love her, children; she already loves you sincerely, she's a good girl. And now," he said, speaking to me and Volodya and seeming to hurry his words so that we should not have time to interrupt him, "it is time for you to travel. I shall remain here until the New Year and then come to Moscow," he faltered again, "together with my wife and Lyubochka this time." It pained me to see Father seeming so timid and guilty before us and I moved closer to him, but Volodya, still smoking and with head lowered, continued to walk about the room.

"Yes-yes, my friends, that's what your old man's been up to," concluded Papa, blushing, clearing his throat and offering his hand to Volodya and me. There were tears in his eyes as he said this and I noticed that the hand he held out to Volodya, who at this moment was at the other end of the room, was trembling slightly. The sight of this trembling hand had a painful effect on me and there occurred to me a strange thought that moved me even more—the thought that Papa had been in the Army during the war against Napoleon and was known as a brave officer. I kept hold of his big sinewy hand and kissed it. He pressed mine hard and suddenly, with a tearful sob, took Lyubochka's dark head in both his hands and began to kiss her on the eyes. Volodya pretended to have dropped his pipe, bent down surreptitiously, wiped his eyes with his fist and, trying not to be noticed, left the room.

XXXVI

University

The wedding was to be in two weeks, but our lectures had already begun and at the beginning of September, Volodya and I went to Moscow. The Nekhlyudovs had also returned from the country. Dmitri (who had sworn with me on parting that we would write to one another, though naturally neither of us had written a word) immediately came to see me and we decided that the following day he would take me to the university for the first time to hear the lectures.

It was a bright sunny day.

As soon as I entered the auditorium I felt my individuality melting away in this crowd of gay young people that surged noisily in the bright sunlight pouring in through the big windows. This feeling of being conscious of myself as a member of this enormous company was very pleasant. But out of all these people only a few were known to me and even then our acquaintanceship was limited to a nod of the head and the words: "How are you, Irtenyev?" All around me people were shaking hands and chatting, and words of friendship, smiles, greetings, and jokes flourished on all sides. Everywhere I sensed the bond that held the whole of this young company together and I felt sadly that somehow this bond had missed me. But this was only a momentary impression. Because of it and the chagrin it provoked in me I even found, on the contrary, that it was a very good thing that I did not belong to this whole company, that I ought to have my own circle of the right sort of people, and I sat down in the third row with Count B, Baron Z, Prince R, Ivin, and other men of the same kind, out of whom I was acquainted with Ivin and Count B. But these men looked at me in such a way that I did not feel as though I quite belonged to their society either. I started to watch everything going on around me. Semyonov, with his tousled graying hair and white teeth and wearing his coat unbuttoned, was sitting not far from me, leaning on the bench and chewing his pen. The high school boy who had come out first in the examinations was sitting on the front bench, still with his cheek wrapped up in a black neckcloth, and playing with a silver watch key that hung on his velvet vest. Ikonin, who had nonetheless entered the university, was sitting on the topmost bench, wearing piped blue trousers that completely covered his boots, roaring with laughter and shouting that he was on Parnassus. Ilinka, who to my astonishment bowed to me not only coldly but even contemptuously, as though wishing to remind me that we were all equal here, was sitting in front of me with his thin legs up extra carelessly (for my benefit, as it seemed to me) on the bench in front of him and talking to another student, casting occasional glances in my direction. Beside me Ivin's group was talking in French. These gentlemen seemed terribly stupid to me. Every word I heard of their conversation seemed to me not only senseless but incorrect, it simply was not French (*ce n'est pas Français,* I said to myself in my thoughts), while the posture, words, and actions of Semyonov, Ilinka, and the others seemed to me ignoble, improper, and not *comme il faut.*

I did not belong to any group and feeling myself isolated and incapable of friendship, became resentful. One student on the bench in front of me was biting his nails, which were all in red hangnails, and I found this so repulsive that I even moved farther away from him. That day, I remember, I felt very sad inside.

When the professor entered there was a general stir and then silence and I remember that I extended my satirical view to him as well, and was amazed when the professor began his lecture with an introductory phrase that, in my opinion, contained no sense at all. I wanted the lecture to be so clever from beginning to end that it would be impossible either to take away or add a single word. Disappointed in this, I immediately took out the handsomely bound notebook I had brought with me and under the heading "First Lecture," written inside it, drew eighteen profiles which formed a circle in the shape of a flower, and only occasionally did I draw my hand over the paper in order to make the professor (who I was sure was taking a great interest in me) think that I was taking notes. Having decided at this lecture that it was unnecessary and would even be stupid to note down anything that any professor said, I kept to this rule for the rest of the semester.

At following lectures I no longer felt my isolation so keenly; I got to know many people, shook hands with them and conversed, but for some reason no real rapprochement took place between me and my comrades and I still had frequent occasion to sorrow inwardly and pretend. I could not get closer to Ivin's group and the aristocrats, as everyone called them, because, as far as I remember, I was rough and rude with them and bowed to them only when they bowed to me, and they evidently had very little need of my friendship. But with the majority this happened for quite a different reason. As soon as I felt a comrade beginning to feel friendly toward me, I immediately gave him to understand that I was used to dining with Prince Ivan Ivanich and that I had my own carriage. I said all this only to show myself in the most favorable possible light and so that my comrade would like me still more because of it; but on the contrary, almost every time, as a result of my information about being related to Prince Ivan Ivanich and having a carriage, my comrade, to my surprise, would turn cold and haughty with me.

Among us there was a student from a government-supported boarding school, Operov, a modest but very capable and hardworking young man who always kept his hand as stiff as a board when offering it, without bending the fingers or making any movement with it, so that sometimes the humorists among his companions would offer him their hands in the same way and called this the "boardshake." I almost always sat next to him and we often talked. I particularly liked Operov for the free opinions he expressed concerning our professors. He defined the merits and defects of each professor's teaching extremely clearly and succinctly and even mocked them at times, which had a particularly strange and striking effect on me, coming as it did from his tiny little mouth and uttered in his quiet little voice. In spite of this, however, he carefully wrote down all the lectures without exception in his small handwriting. He and I were now beginning to grow closer and had decided to study together, and his little gray short-sighted eyes were beginning to regard me with pleasure as I came to take my place next to him. But once in conversation I found it necessary to explain to him that my mama, when she died, had begged Father not to send us to a government boarding school and that I was coming to believe that all boarding-school students, although perhaps well-educated, were for me ... well, not the right sort of people, *ce ne sont pas des gens comme il faut,* I said, faltering and sensing that for some reason I was blushing. Operov said nothing, but at following lectures did not greet me first, did not offer me his board, and did not talk to me, and when I sat down in my seat, bent his head away from me, lowered it to within an inch of his notebooks and pretended to be peering at them. I was amazed at Operov's baseless cooling toward me. But *pour un jeune homme de bonne maison* I considered it improper to make up to the boarding-school student, Operov, and left him alone, although, I must confess, his coolness grieved me. One day I arrived before him and since it was a lecture by one of the favorite professors, attended by students who were not in the habit of always coming to lectures, and the seats were all full, I sat down in Operov's seat, placed my books on the bench in front of me and went out for a moment. Returning to the auditorium I saw that my books had been moved to the rear bench and that Operov was sitting in his seat. I remarked to him that my books had been there.

"I don't know," he replied, flaring up suddenly and not looking at me.

"I'm telling you that I put my books here," I said, purposely beginning to lose my temper with the intention of frightening him with my bravery. "Everybody saw me," I added, looking round at the other students; but although many of them looked at me with curiosity, nobody answered.

"You can't book seats here; it's first come first served," said Operov, angrily settling himself in his seat and casting an indignant glance at me for an instant.

"That means you're a cad," I said.

I believe that Operov also muttered something, muttered even, I believe: "And you're a stupid little brat," but I definitely did not hear him. And anyway, what use would it have been if I had heard him? Just to insult one another like a couple of *manants* and nothing more? (I was very fond of this word *manant* and it provided me with an answer and solution to many complicated situations.) Perhaps I would have said something more, but at that moment the door banged and the professor, wearing a blue coat and scraping his feet, hurried across to his desk.

Before the examination, however, when I needed the notes, Operov remembered his promise, offered me his notebooks, and invited me to study with him.

XXXVII

AFFAIRS OF THE HEART

Affairs of the heart kept me fairly busy that winter. I was in love three times. Once I fell passionately in love with a very stout lady who used to ride in my presence at Freytag's riding school, as a consequence of which, every Tuesday and Friday—the days she rode—I would go to the riding school to watch her, but each time was so afraid that she would see me and therefore always stood so far away from her and ran away so quickly from any spot that she was due to pass, and turned away so indifferently whenever she looked in my direction, that I did not even see her face properly and do not know to this day whether she was really attractive or not.

Dubkov, who knew this lady and who found me one day at the riding school, where I stood hiding behind the footmen and the fur coats they were holding, knowing of my passion from Dmitri, so alarmed me with a proposal to introduce me to this Amazon that I fled posthaste from the riding school and the mere thought that he had mentioned me to her kept me from ever daring to go there again, even as far as the footmen, for fear of meeting her. Whenever I was in love with strangers and particularly with married women, I was subject to a bashfulness that was a thousand times stronger than that I had experienced with Sonyechka. More than anything else in the world I feared lest my beloved should ever learn of my love or even of my very existence. It seemed to me that if she learned of the feelings I had for her she would be so insulted that she would never be able to forgive me. And indeed, had this Amazon known in detail how I dreamed, gazing at her from behind the footmen, of abducting her and carrying her off to the country and of how I would live and what I would do with her, perhaps she would have been justified in feeling insulted. But I was unable to grasp the fact that by knowing me she still could not learn thereby all my thoughts about her, and that therefore there was nothing shameful in simply making her acquaintance.

Another time I fell in love with Sonyechka when I saw her visiting my sister. My second love for her had long since passed, but I fell in love with her a third time as a result of being given by Lyubochka a book of verse that Sonyechka had copied out, in which many gloomy love passages in Lermontov's "The Demon" had been underlined in red ink and flowers had been pressed between the pages. Remembering how last year Volodya had kissed his lady's purse, I tried to do the same and truly, when I began to muse one evening in my room, gazing at one of the flowers, and to place it to my lips, I fell into a pleasantly lachrymose mood and was in love once more, or so I supposed for several days.

Finally I fell in love a third time that winter with a girl Volodya was in love with who used to visit us. As far as I can remember there was absolutely nothing good about this girl and especially none of the goodness that usually appealed to me. She was the daughter of a Moscow woman, well known for her intelligence and learning, a tiny, thin little girl with long blonde English ringlets and with a transparent profile. Everyone said that this girl was even more intelligent than her mother; but I was never able to judge because, experiencing a kind of craven fear at the thought of her intelligence and learning, I only spoke to her once, and then with inexpressible trepidation. But the raptures of Volodya, who was never embarrassed by the presence of others when expressing his rapture, were communicated to me so powerfully that I also fell passionately in love with this young lady.

Sensing that Volodya would dislike hearing that *two little brothers were in love with one pretty maid,* I did not tell him of my love. For I, on the contrary, got most pleasure of all out of my feeling from the thought that our love was so pure that, in spite of its object being one and the same delightful creature, we would remain friends and be prepared, if the necessity arose, to sacrifice ourselves for one another. However, it seems that Volodya did not quite share my opinion on the score of preparedness for self-sacrifice, because he was so passionately in love that he wanted to slap the face of the man—a real diplomat—who they said was supposed to marry her, and challenge him to a duel. But I thought it would be very pleasant to sacrifice my feeling, perhaps because it would have cost me so little effort, seeing that I had only made one pretentious remark to the young lady concerning classical music, and my love, try as I might to sustain it, disappeared the following week.

XXXVIII

Society

The pleasures of society to which, upon entering the university, I had dreamed of abandoning myself in imitation of my elder brother, completely disillusioned me this winter. Volodya danced a great deal and Papa also went to balls with his young wife; but I must have been considered either too young or else unfitted for these pleasures, since nobody introduced me into those houses where balls were given. In spite of my promise of frankness to Dmitri, I did not tell anyone, not even him, how much I wanted to go dancing and how hurt and vexed I was that they forgot about me and thought of me, evidently, as some kind of philosopher, a role I consequently played up to.

But that winter there was a *soirée* at Princess Kornakov's. She herself invited all of us, including me, and for the first time I was to go to a ball. Before leaving, Volodya came to my room and wanted to see how I would dress. I was extremely surprised and puzzled by this action of his. It seemed to me that a desire to be well dressed was something to be ashamed of and should be concealed; but he, on the contrary, considered this desire so natural and indispensible that he said quite openly that he was afraid I might disgrace myself. He ordered me to be sure to put on patent leather boots, was horrified when I wanted to put on suede gloves, arranged my watch in some special way and carried me off to the hairdresser's at Kuznetsky Bridge. My hair was waved. Volodya stepped back and viewed me from a distance.

"Yes, that's fine now, only can't you smooth those tufts down?" he said, speaking to the hairdresser.

But try as Monsieur Charles might to gum my tufts down with some sort of sticky stuff, they still stuck up when I put my hat on and in general my waved appearance struck me as much worse than before. My sole salvation was to affect indifference. Only with such an aspect would my appearance amount to anything.

Volodya apparently held the same opinion because he asked me to destroy the waves, and when I had done so and it was still no good, he did not look at me any more and was sad and silent the whole way to the Kornakovs.

In company with Volodya I entered the Kornakovs' house boldly; but when the Princess invited me to dance I said for some reason, in spite of the fact that I had come with the sole idea of dancing a great deal, that I could not dance, then grew timid, remaining alone among unfamiliar people, and lapsed into my usual insurmountable and constantly increasing bashfulness. I stood silently in the same spot for the whole evening.

During a waltz one of the young princesses came up to me and with the official politeness characteristic of the whole family asked me why I was not dancing. I remember how I grew shy at this question and also how, completely unintentionally on my part, a complacent smile spread over my face and I began in French and in the most pompous language, with lots of parentheses, to spout such utter rubbish that even now, after dozens of years, I am ashamed to recall it. It must have been the effect of the music on me, stimulating my nerves and drowning, as I supposed, the less intelligible things I said. I said something about high society, about the vacuity of men and women, and in the end got so involved that I stopped halfway through a word and in the middle of a sentence that there was not the remotest possibility of finishing.

Even the princess, sophisticated by nature, was embarrassed and looked at me reproachfully. I smiled. At this critical moment Volodya, who had noticed me speaking animatedly and probably wanted to know how I was compensating in conversation for the fact that I was not dancing, came up to us, along with Dubkov. Catching sight of my smiling face and the princess's frightened expression, and hearing the frightful rubbish with which I ended, he blushed and turned away. The princess stood up and moved off. I still smiled, but I was suffering so much at that moment from the consciousness of my own stupidity that I was ready to sink through the ground and felt the need, come what may, to move about and say something in order somehow to change my situation. I went up to Dubkov and asked him if he had danced many waltzes with *her*. This was supposed to show me as playful and gay, but in reality I was begging help from that same Dubkov whom I had told to shut up at the dinner at Yar's. Dubkov pretended not to hear me and turned away. I moved closer to Volodya and said with an effort, also trying to give my voice a joking tone: "Well, Volodya, are you *played out* yet?" But Volodya looked at me as though wishing to say: "You don't talk to me like that when we are alone," and walked away from me in silence, evidently afraid lest I somehow accost him once more.

My God, even my brother's abandoning me! I thought.

However, for some reason I did not have the strength to leave. I stood gloomily in one spot until the end of the evening and only when everyone was leaving and had crowded into the front hall and a footman caught the back of my hat with the overcoat he was helping me on with, so that the hat tipped back, did I laugh painfully through my tears and say, addressing no one in particular: *"Comme c'est gracieux."*

XXXIX

A DRINKING PARTY

Despite the fact that under Dmitri's influence I had not yet abandoned myself to the usual student entertainments known as "drinking parties," I did happen once that winter to take part in such a celebration and the impression it left me with was not very agreeable. This is how it happened. One day at a lecture at the beginning of the year Baron Z, a tall blond young man whose regular features always bore an extremely serious expression, invited us all to his place for a social evening. By all I mean all those in our course who were more or less *comme il faut*, which did not include, of course, either Grap or Semyonov or Operov, or all those other nasty little men. Volodya smiled contemptuously when he heard I was going to a drinking party for first-year students; but I expected to derive great and remarkable pleasure from this to me entirely unfamiliar pastime and punctually at the appointed hour, eight o'clock, I arrived at Baron Z's.

Baron Z, in a white vest and with his coat unbuttoned, welcomed the guests in the brilliantly lit salon and drawing room of the small house where his parents lived, the latter having ceded the reception rooms to him for the evening's celebration. The dresses and heads of curious servant girls could be seen in the corridor, and in the buffet I glimpsed the dress of a lady whom I took to be the Baroness herself. There were twenty guests present, with the exception of Herr Frost, who had come together with Ivin, and a tall ruddy gentleman in civilian clothes who was in charge of the revelries and who was introduced to everyone as the Baron's relative and a former student of Dorpat University. At first the excessively brilliant lighting and usual formal arrangement of the reception rooms had such a cooling effect on the whole of this youthful company that everyone involuntarily hugged the walls, except for a few bold spirits and the Dorpat student, who, his vest already unbuttoned, seemed to be in every room and in every corner of every room at the same time and to fill the whole room with his pleasant, resonant and unflagging tenor voice. But his fellows were quiet for the most part or else talked modestly about the professors, science, examinations, and subjects that were on the whole more serious and uninteresting. All without exception glanced repeatedly in the direction of the buffet and although they tried to conceal it, all had an expression that said: "Well, it's time to begin." I also felt that it was time to begin and awaited the *beginning* with impatient delight.

After the guests had been served tea by the footmen, the Dorpat student asked Frost in Russian:

"Can you make punch, Frost?"

"*Oh, ja!*" replied Frost, flexing his calves, but the Dorpat student said again in Russian:

"Then you look after that" (they were on familiar terms as comrades of Dorpat University); and Frost, taking big strides with his bandy muscular legs, commenced to go from drawing room to buffet and back from buffet to drawing room again, and soon there appeared on the table a large soup bowl with a ten-pound loaf of sugar suspended over it, supported by three crossed student swords. During this time Baron Z kept going up to each of his guests, who had all gathered in the drawing room to look at the soup bowl, and with an invariably serious expression on his face would say almost exactly the same thing to every one of them: "Come, gentlemen, let's all drink a cup in proper student fashion, *Bruderschaft*, otherwise there's absolutely no comradeship in our year. Go on, unbutton your coats, or even take them right off like him." And indeed the Dorpat student, having taken his coat off and rolled the sleeves of his white shirt up to above his white elbows, with his feet planted firmly apart, was already setting fire to the rum in the soup bowl.

"Gentlemen, put out the candles!" shouted the Dorpat student all of a sudden and so heartily and loudly as would only have been appropriate if we had all shouted at the same time. We for our part all looked in silence at the soup bowl and at the Dorpat student's white shirt, and all felt that the triumphal moment had come.

"Löschen Sie die Lichter aus, Frost!" shouted the Dorpat student again, this time in German and probably from over-excitement. Frost and the rest of us set about extinguishing the candles. It became dark in the room, only the white shirts and the hands supporting the sugar loaf on the swords were illuminated by the bluish flames. The Dorpat student's loud tenor was no longer alone because talking and laughter broke out in all four corners of the room. Many people took their coats off (especially those who had fine quality and freshly laundered shirts), and I did the same and realized that *it had begun.* Although there was nothing gay about it yet, I was firmly convinced that nevertheless it would be excellent once we had all drunk a glass of the prepared drink.

The drink was ready. The Dorpat student, spilling it liberally on the table, poured the punch into glasses and shouted: "Now then, gentlemen, let's go!" As each of us took a full sticky glass into his hand the Dorpat student and Frost struck up a German song in which the exclamation *Juchhe!* was frequently repeated. We all joined in raggedly with them, began to clink our glasses, to shout something, to praise the punch, and to drink the sweet and powerful liquid either simply or with our arms linked together. Now there was nothing more to wait for, the drinking party was in full swing. I had already drunk one whole glass of punch and was poured another; there was a hammering in my temples, the flames seemed crimson, there was shouting and laughter all around me, but not only did it still not seem gay to me, but I was even convinced that both I and everybody else there were bored and that I and everybody else were only pretending that we found it gay because we felt we had to for some reason. Only the Dorpat student, perhaps, was not pretending; he was getting even ruddier and more ubiquitous, filling everybody's empty glasses and spilling more and more on the table, which had become all sweet and sticky. I do not remember what followed what or in what order that evening, but I do remember that I became awfully fond of the Dorpat student and Frost, learned a German song by heart, and kissed the two of them on their sweet lips; I remember also that I came to hate the Dorpat student that evening and wanted to hurl a chair at him, but was held back. I remember that apart from that sensation of the insubordination of all my limbs, which I had experienced on the day of that dinner at Yar's, my head ached and swam so much that evening that I was terribly afraid of dying on the spot; I remember also that we all sat on the floor for some reason, waved our arms about to imitate the movements of oars, and sang "Down Old Mother Volga," and that I thought at the time that this was completely unnecessary; I remember furthermore that, lying on the floor with legs interlocked, we wrestled gypsy fashion, and that I dislocated someone's neck and thought that this would not have happened had he not been drunk; I remember furthermore that we had supper and drank something else, that I went outside to cool off and my head felt cold, and that upon leaving I noticed how frightfully dark it was and that the carriage running board had become steep and slippery, and it was impossible to hold on to Kuzma because he had become weak and swayed about like a rag; but the main thing I remember is that throughout the entire evening I never stopped feeling that I was acting very stupidly, pretending that I felt very gay, that I liked drinking very much and that I had no intention of becoming drunk, and I never stopped feeling that the others were acting very stupidly too, pretending to feel the same things. It seemed to me that each one individually found it unpleasant, just as I did, but, supposing that he was alone in experiencing such unpleasant sensations, pretended gaiety in order not to destroy the general merriment; furthermore—strangely enough—I felt obliged to pretend if only because three bottles of champagne at ten rubles a bottle and ten bottles of rum at four rubles a bottle had gone into the soup bowl, totaling seventy rubles in all, with supper still to come. I was so convinced of this that at lectures the following day I was extremely surprised to hear that my comrades at Baron Z's entertainment not only were not ashamed to recall what they had done there but talked about it so that the other students could hear them. They said it had been an outstanding party, that the Dorpat fellows were first-rate at these things, and that twenty men there had drunk forty bottles of rum, and many had lain dead drunk under the tables. I could not understand why they not only talked about it but also told lies about themselves.

XL

FRIENDSHIP WITH THE NEKHLYUDOVS

That winter I saw a good deal not only of Dmitri, who frequently came to see us, but of his whole family, to whom I was getting closer.

The Nekhlyudovs—mother, aunt, and daughter—spent all their evenings at home and the Princess liked having young people visit her, men of the sort who, as she put it, were able to spend a whole evening without cards or dancing. But evidently such men were few, since I, who visited them almost every evening, rarely met any other guests there. I had got used to the members of this family, to their various moods, I already had a clear concept of their relations with one another, was used to the rooms and furniture and, when there were no guests, felt perfectly at ease there, except on those occasions when I remained alone in a room with Varyenka. It always seemed to me as if, not being very pretty, she was anxious for me to fall in love with her. But even this embarrassment began to pass. She had such a natural way of showing that it did not matter to her whether she talked to me, her brother, or Lyubov Sergeyevna that I too acquired the habit of regarding her as simply a person to whom it was not in the least shameful or dangerous to reveal the pleasure one derived from her company. During the whole period of my acquaintance with her she seemed to me—for days at a time—now extremely ugly, now not too bad-looking a girl, but I did not even once ask myself whether I was in love with her or not. Sometimes I talked to her directly, but more often I would talk to her by addressing my remarks to Lyubov Sergeyevna or Dmitri, and this last method particularly appealed to me. I took great pleasure in speaking in her presence, in listening to her sing and in general in being aware of her presence in the same room where I was; but thoughts of what my future relations with Varyenka would be like and dreams of sacrificing myself for the sake of my friend, should he fall in love with my sister, now came rarely to me. And if such thoughts and dreams did come to me, I, feeling myself quite satisfied with the present, would unconsciously try to drive away all thoughts of the future.

In spite, however, of this growing closeness, I continued to consider it my bounden duty to conceal from all the Nekhlyudovs and particularly from Varyenka my true feelings and inclinations and I tried to display myself as a completely different young man from the one I was in reality, and even the sort of man I could not possibly have been in reality. I tried to seem passionate, went into ecstasies, groaned, made passionate gestures when something allegedly pleased me, and at the same time tried to seem indifferent to all ordinary occurrences that I saw or was told about; I tried to seem a cruel iconoclast who held nothing sacred, and at the same time a subtle observer; I tried to seem logical in all my actions, precise and tidy in my life, and at the same time scornful of all material things. It is quite safe to say that I was much better in reality than the strange creature I strove to make of myself; but nevertheless the Nekhlyudovs took to me even with all my pretensions and fortunately did not, it seems, believe in my playacting. Only Lyubov Sergeyevna, who, I believe, considered me a terrible egoist, atheist, and iconoclast, did not like me and argued frequently with me, growing angry and flooring me with her spasmodic, incoherent phrases. But Dmitri still maintained his strange, more than friendly relations with her and said that no one understood her and she had done him a remarkable amount of good. His friendship with her continued to aggravate his family as before.

Once when talking to me about this incomprehensible alliance, Varyenka explained it as follows:

"Dmitri is vain. He's overproud, and his great intelligence notwithstanding, he likes to be praised and to surprise people, he likes always to be first; and *aunty* in all her innocence admires him for it and hasn't sufficient tact to conceal her admiration from him, so that in fact she flatters him—not out of hypocrisy but sincerely."

This judgment stuck in my mind and later, turning it over by myself, I could not help thinking that Varyenka was very intelligent, as a consequence of which I took pleasure in raising my estimate of her. This sort of raising of my estimate of her as a result of her newly discovered intelligence and other moral qualities, however, although done with pleasure, was also kept within the bounds of a certain severe moderation and never reached the extreme where I was enraptured by her. Thus when Sofya Ivanovna, who never tired of speaking about her niece, told me once how Varyenka, four years ago in the country, had given all her dresses and shoes away to the peasant children without permission, so that they had had to be taken back afterward, I did not at once accept this fact as entitling her to be raised in my estimation and even sneered at her mentally for having such an impractical view of things.

When the Nekhlyudovs had guests, including, sometimes, Volodya and Dubkov, I would, complacently and with the certain calm consciousness of strength of the man who is at home, retire into the background, say nothing, and listen to what the others were saying. And everything that the others said seemed so incredibly stupid that I was inwardly surprised how such an intelligent logical woman as the Princess and all her logical family could listen to such rubbish and reply to it. If it had ever occurred to me then to compare what the others were saying with what I myself said when alone there, I would probably have been not in the least surprised. And I would have been still less surprised had I been able to believe that our womenfolk—Avdotya Vasilyevna, Lyubochka, and Katyenka—were just the same as all other women, not in the least inferior to others, and had I remembered that Dubkov, Katyenka, and Avdotya Vasilyevna used to spend whole evenings talking and smiling gaily; and that almost every time Dubkov found a pretext he would declaim the verses: *"Au banquet de la vie, infortuné convive . . ."* or snatches of "The Demon"; and in general how they enjoyed talking such utter rubbish for several hours on end.

Naturally Varyenka paid less attention to me when there were guests than when we were alone—and then there was no reading or music, which I used to enjoy listening to. When talking to guests she lost what was for me her chief charm—her calm reasonableness and simplicity. I remember how staggered I was by her conversations about the weather and the theater with my brother Volodya. I knew that Volodya avoided and detested small talk more than anything else in the world and that Varyenka also laughed always at affectedly absorbing conversations about the weather, and so on—yet why, when together, did they both constantly talk the most intolerable rot and yet pretend to be ashamed for one another? Always after such conversations I would grow angry with Varyenka and make fun of the guests the following day, but I took still greater pleasure in being alone in the Nekhlyudovs' family circle.

In any event, I began to take greater pleasure in being with Dmitri in his mother's drawing room than alone with him face to face.

XLI

Friendship with Nekhlyudov

Just at this time my friendship with Dmitri was hanging by a thread. I had begun to judge him too long ago for me not to have found any faults in him; and in first youth we love only passionately and therefore only perfect people. But once the fog of passion starts to disperse or the clear light of reason begins involuntarily to pierce it, and we see the object of our passion in its true light, with all its virtues and failings—only the failings, being so unexpected, stand out for us vividly and in magnified form, and the attractions of the new and hopes that perfection is not impossible in another person encourage not only coolness in us but also disgust with the former object of our passion, and we abandon it pitilessly and rush on, seeking a new perfection. If this did not happen to me in connection with Dmitri, it was only because of his stubborn pedantic and intellectual rather than emotional attachment to me, which made me ashamed to betray it. Moreover we were bound together by our odd rule of frankness. Parting, we were too afraid of leaving all those shameful moral secrets we had confided in one another in one another's power. However, our frankness rule, as was clear to us, had long since ceased to be observed and frequently embarrassed us and produced strange relations between us.

That winter, practically every time I visited Dmitri I found one of his university comrades with him, the student Bezobyedov, in whom he was taking an interest. Bezobyedov was a thin pockmarked little man with tiny freckled hands and a great shock of unkempt ginger hair; he was always ragged and filthy and was even badly educated and a poor student. Dmitri's relations with this man, as with Lyubov Sergeyevna, were incomprehensible to me. The sole reason he could have had for choosing him from among all his companions and becoming friendly with him could only have been that no one in the whole university was worse than Bezobyedov. And it must have been precisely for this reason that Dmitri delighted in going against everyone and offering him his friendship. Through all his relations with this student there ran the following implication: "I don't care who you are, everyone's the same for me; I like him too, therefore he's all right."

I was surprised that he did not find it unpleasant to be continually forcing himself, and that the unfortunate Bezobyedov was able to put up with his awkward position. I did not like their friendship at all.

Once I went to see Dmitri one evening in order to spend the evening in his mother's drawing room, talking and listening to Varyenka's singing and reading; but Bezobyedov was sitting upstairs. Dmitri told me sharply that he could not come downstairs because, as I could see, he had a visitor.

"And what's the fun of sitting down there?" he added. "Much better to sit up here and talk." Although I was not at all attracted by the idea of sitting for an hour or two with Bezobyedov, I could not bring myself to go down to the drawing room alone and so, feeling resentment at my friend's eccentricity, I sat down in a rocking chair and began to rock back and forth in silence. I was extremely annoyed with Dmitri and Bezobyedov for depriving me of the pleasure of being downstairs; I waited for Bezobyedov to leave quickly and fumed at him and Dmitri as I listened to their conversation in silence. A pleasant sort of guest! Go on, sit there with him! I thought when a footman brought tea and Dmitri had to ask Bezobyedov about five times to pick up his glass, because for the first two glasses his timid guest considered it his duty to refuse and say: "You have some yourself." Dmitri, clearly forcing himself, kept his guest in conversation and several times made vain efforts to draw me in. I remained gloomily silent.

There's no point in pulling a face to say: don't dare think I'm bored, I said mentally to Dmitri, rocking regularly back and forth in my chair in silence. Gradually and with a certain pleasure, I fanned my feeling of quiet hatred for my friend more and more. What a fool, I thought. He could be spending a pleasant evening with his own dear family, but no—he has to sit up here with this swine; and time's running out now and soon it will be too late to go to the drawing room, and I glanced several times at my friend round the wing of my chair. Both his arm and his posture and his neck and particularly the back of his head and his knees seemed so repulsive and offensive to me that it would have given me great pleasure at that moment to inflict on him some sort of—major, even—insult.

Finally Bezobyedov stood up, but Dmitri could not let such a pleasant visitor leave at once; he invited him to stay the night, which Bezobyedov, fortunately, refused and then went out.

Having seen him out, Dmitri returned and with a slight self-satisfied smile on his face and rubbing his hands—probably over the fact that nevertheless he had kept his end up and that he was delivered, at last, from boredom—started to walk up and down the room, glancing at me from time to time. I found him even more disgusting. How dare he walk up and down and smile? I thought.

"What are you mad about?" he said all of a sudden, stopping opposite me.

"I'm not mad at all," I replied, as people always reply in these circumstances. "I'm just annoyed that you're pretending to me and to Bezobyedov and to yourself."

"What rubbish! I never pretend to anyone."

"I haven't forgotten our frankness rule and I'm telling you straight," I said. "I'm convinced you can't stand Bezobyedov any more than I can, because he's stupid and God knows what else, but you like to put on airs in front of him."

"No! In the first place, Bezobyedov's a wonderful fellow . . ."

"And I'm telling you *yes;* I'm telling you even that your friendship with Lyubov Sergeyevna is also based on the fact that she looks on you as a god."

"And I'm telling you it's not."

"And I'm telling you it is, because I know so," I replied with the warmth of suppressed irritation and trying to disarm him with my frankness. "I've told you before and I repeat that I've always thought I like the people who say pleasant things to me, but when I look at it closer I see there's no real attachment there at all."

"No," continued Dmitri, straightening his tie with an angry movement of his neck, "when I love someone, neither praise nor blame can change my feelings."

"That's not true; didn't I admit to you that when Papa called me worthless I hated him for a while and desired his death? It's the same when you . . ."

"Speak for yourself. It's a pity if that's the way you are . . ."

"On the contrary," I cried, leaping out of my chair and looking him in the eye with desperate boldness, "that wasn't a nice thing to say; didn't you once say about my brother—I won't remind you of it because that would be unfair—but didn't you say . . . and I'm telling you how well I understand you now . . ."

And trying to wound him more deeply than he me, I began to demonstrate to him that he loved no one and to say to his face everything that I thought I had a right to reproach him with. I was extremely satisfied that I was able to tell him everything, completely forgetting that the sole permissible aim of this outspokenness, which would have consisted in him admitting the faults that I was castigating him with, could not be achieved at the present time, when he was in a terrible temper. I never said any of this to him when he was calm and capable of admitting it.

Our argument was already turning into a quarrel when Dmitri suddenly fell silent and left me to go into the next room. I was about to follow him, still talking, but he did not answer me. I knew that hot-temperedness was on his list of vices and that he was now trying to master himself. I cursed all his lists.

So this was where we had been led by our rule *to tell one another everything we felt and never to say a word to anyone else about one another.* Carried away by our frankness we had made the most shameless confessions to one another, passing off, to our own shame, suppositions and dreams as though they were desires and emotions, like, for instance, what I had just said to him; and these confessions not only had not tightened the bond between us but had dried up emotion itself and come between us; and now, suddenly, vanity prevented him from making the most trivial of admissions and we, in the heat of our quarrel, made use of the very weapons that we had formerly placed in one another's hands and which now inflicted terrible wounds upon us.

XLII

OUR STEPMOTHER

Despite the fact that Papa wanted to come to Moscow with his wife only in the new year, he came in the autumn, in October, while there was still excellent hunting to be had with the hounds. Papa said that he had changed his plans because his case was due to be heard in the Supreme Court; but Mimi told us that Avdotya Vasilyevna had been so bored in the country, had spoken about Moscow so often, and had so feigned illness that Papa had decided to meet her wishes.

"Because she's never loved him and only made everybody's ears buzz with her love because she wanted to marry a rich man," added Mimi, sighing thoughtfully, as much as to say: That's not what *certain people* would have done for him, had he known how to value them.

Certain people were unjust to Avdotya Vasilyevna; her love for Papa, passionate devoted self-sacrificing love, was evident in every look and gesture. But such a love did not in the least preclude, together with the desire not to be separated from her adored husband, a desire to have that extraordinary bonnet from Madame Annette, that hat with the extraordinary blue ostrich feather in it and red Venetian velvet, or that dress which would artistically reveal those shapely white breasts and arms, till now shown to no one except her husband and maids. Katyenka, of course, was on her mother's side, while between us and our stepmother some sort of strange joking relationship was at once established from the very day of her arrival. As soon as she emerged from the carriage Volodya, putting on a serious face and glazed eyes, scraping his feet and swaying back and forth, approached her hand and said, as though introducing someone:

"I have the honor to congratulate dear Mamma on her arrival, and kiss her little hand."

"Ah, my dear son!" said Avdotya Vasilyevna, smiling her beautiful fixed smile.

"And don't forget your second son," I said, also going up to her hand and unconsciously trying to adopt Volodya's manner and tone of voice.

If we and our stepmother had been sure of our mutual affection, this expression could have signified disdain for any expression of the marks of love; if we had already been ill-disposed toward one another it might have signified irony or contempt or hypocrisy or a desire to conceal from our father, who was present, the real state of our relationship and of many other thoughts and feelings; but in the present case this expression, which suited Avdotya Vasilyevna's taste very well, signified absolutely nothing at all and merely concealed the absence of any relationship whatsoever. Subsequently I have often noticed that in other families, when their members sensed that the real relationships were not going to be very good, a similar sort of joking substitute relationship took their place; and this was the kind of relationship unconsciously established between Avdotya Vasilyevna and us. We hardly ever departed from it, we were always hypocritically polite with her, spoke in French, scraped and bowed and called her *chère maman,* which she always responded to with jokes of the same nature and her beautiful fixed smile. Only crybaby Lyubochka, with her bandy legs and ingenuous conversations, really took to our stepmother and tried terribly naïvely and sometimes awkwardly to bring her closer to the whole family; on the other hand the sole person in the world, not counting her passionate love for Papa, for whom Avdotya Vasilyevna had the least hint of affection was Lyubochka. Avdotya Vasilyevna had even a kind of enthusiastic admiration and timid respect for her that greatly surprised me.

At first Avdotya Vasilyevna, calling herself Stepmother, often liked to hint at how children and servants always have a bad and unjust opinion of stepmothers and how difficult her position was in consequence. But, although foreseeing all the unpleasantness of this situation, she never did anything to avoid it by being nice to this person, giving a gift to that one, and not being grumpy, which was very easy for her because by nature she was easygoing and kind. And not only did she not do this but, on the contrary, foreseeing all the unpleasantness of her situation, prepared to defend herself without having been attacked, and, assuming that all the servants wanted to insult and be unpleasant to her by all the means at their disposal, saw bad intentions everywhere and considered her most dignified course to be to endure in silence, thus, naturally, earning by her passivity not love but dislike. Moreover, she was so lacking in that capacity of instinctive understanding which was developed to such a high degree in our home and about which I have already spoken, and her habits were so contrary to those already deeply rooted in our house that this alone worked to her disadvantage. In our neat orderly house she always lived as though she had only just arrived: she got up and went to bed now early and now late; sometimes she came down to dinner, sometimes she did not; one day she ate supper, another not. When there were no visitors she almost always went around half-dressed and was not ashamed to appear before us and even the servants dressed only in a white petticoat, with a shawl thrown over her shoulders and her arms bare. At first this simplicity appealed to me but then very soon, precisely because of this simplicity, I lost the last respect I had for her. Even more odd for us was the fact that, in the presence or absence of guests, she was two completely different women: one, in the presence of guests, was a cool healthy young beauty, sumptuously dressed, not clever, not stupid, but gay; the other, in the absence of guests, was a no longer young, exhausted, and apathetic woman, sloppy and bored, though very affectionate. Often, looking at her as she returned from paying some calls, smiling, red-cheeked from the winter cold and happy in the knowledge of her beauty, and as she took off her hat and went to look at herself in the mirror, or, rustling her sumptuous low-cut ball dress, blushing and at the same time proud in front of the servants, as she walked to her carriage, or at home when we had little evening gatherings, as, in a high-necked silk dress with some delicate lace about her soft neck, she beamed her fixed but beautiful smile in all directions—I have thought, looking at her: what would those who rave about her now say if they could see her as I have seen her when she stays at home in the evenings, waiting up after midnight for her husband to come home from the club, dressed in some sort of robe, her hair uncombed, and walking through the dimly lit rooms like a shadow. One moment she would go to the piano and play—frowning with concentration—the one waltz she knew, then pick up a novel, read a few lines in the middle and throw it down again, then, in order not to wake the servants, go to the pantry herself, take out a cucumber and some cold veal and eat it there, standing by the pantry window, and then start wandering from room to room again, aimless weary and apathetic. But most of all we were alienated from her by her lack of understanding, expressed above all in her characteristic way of listening deferentially when people spoke to her of things she did not understand. She was not to blame that she had made an unconscious habit of smiling slightly with her lips alone and inclining her head when people spoke to her of things that held little interest for her (and apart from herself and her husband nothing interested her); but this smile and inclination of the head, frequently repeated, were unbearably distasteful. Her merriment, which seemed to be directed at herself, you, and the whole world, was also awkward and infected no one; her sentimentality was too sugary. But the main thing was that she was not ashamed to talk to everyone constantly about her love for Papa. Although she was telling no lie in saying that her whole life consisted in her love for her husband, and although she proved it with her whole life, to our way of thinking such brazen incessant assertion of her love was repellent and we blushed for her when she talked of it to outsiders even more than when she made mistakes in French.

She loved her husband more than anything else in the world and her husband loved her, especially in the early period and when he saw that he was not the only one she appealed to. The sole aim of her life was to obtain her husband's love; but she seemed on purpose to do everything that could possibly be disagreeable to him, and all with the aim of proving to him the full power of her love and her readiness for self-sacrifice.

She liked fine dresses and Father liked seeing her as a society beauty, exciting praise and admiration; she sacrificed her passion for fine dresses for Father's sake and got more and more used to sitting at home in a gray blouse. Papa, who always considered freedom and equality to be an indispensable condition of family relationships, hoped that his favorite, Lyubochka, and his good young wife would come together sincerely and be friends; but Avdotya Vasilyevna sacrificed herself and considered it essential to show the *real mistress of the house*, as she called Lyubochka, an unseemly respect that mortally wounded Papa. He gambled a great deal that winter, lost a lot toward the end of it and, as usual, not wanting to involve his gambling with his family life, concealed his gambling losses from everyone at home. Avdotya Vasilyevna sacrificed herself and considered it her duty, whether ill at times or even pregnant toward the end of winter, to go down in her gray blouse, swaying about, her hair uncombed, even at four or five in the morning, to meet Papa when he returned, sometimes tired, shamefaced after having lost, after eight fines, from the club. She would ask him absent-mindedly if he had been lucky and would listen with deferential attention, smiling and shaking her head, to what he told her of what he had done at the club and how he begged her for the hundredth time never to wait up for him. But although his losses and winnings, upon which, because of his way of playing, Papa's whole fortune depended, did not interest her in the least, she was again the first to meet him every night whenever he returned from the club. She was impelled to these meetings, moreover, apart from her craving for self-sacrifice, by a secret jealousy, from which she suffered to a terrible extent. Nobody in the whole world could have convinced her that Papa was returning late from the club and not from a mistress. She tried to read Papa's love secrets on his face; and reading nothing there, she would sigh, luxuriating in her grief, and give herself up to a contemplation of her woes.

As a result of these and many other continual sacrifices, there was already becoming noticeable in Papa's attitude toward his wife during the last months of that winter, when he was losing a lot and therefore out of sorts most of the time, an intermittent feeling of quiet hatred, of that suppressed repugnance for the object of one's affections that is expressed in a subconscious desire to cause that object all manner of petty mental irritations.

XLIII

New Companions

Winter passed imperceptibly and the thaw had already set in again and the examination timetable pinned up at the university when I suddenly remembered that I had to take examinations in the eighteen subjects I had been attending and not one of which I had listened to, noted down, or prepared. It is strange how such a simple question as: How do I pass the examinations? had never once occurred to me. But I had been in such a fog all winter as a result of my delight in being grown-up and *comme il faut*, that, even when it occurred to me to ask: How do I pass the examinations?, I compared myself with my companions and thought: They will pass and the majority of them aren't even *comme il faut*, therefore I have an extra advantage over them so I'm bound to pass. I went to lectures only out of habit and because Papa sent me out of the house. Furthermore I had lots of friends and I often enjoyed myself at the university. I liked the noise and buzz of talking and laughter in the lecture room; I liked during the lectures, sitting on the back bench, to dream of something or other and watch my comrades to the regular sound of the professor's voice; I liked to slip down to Matern's sometimes with a companion to drink some vodka and have a snack, knowing that I might be reprimanded afterwards by the professors, and to make the door creak cautiously as I entered the auditorium; I liked to take part in scuffles when course launched itself laughingly on course in the corridors. All this was great fun.

By the time everyone had started attending all the lectures properly, the physics professor had already finished his course and taken his leave until the examinations, while the students had started to collect their notebooks together and revise in groups. I also thought of revising. Operov, to whom I still bowed but with whom my relations were extremely cold, as I mentioned earlier, not only offered me his notebooks but invited me to go over them with himself and some other students. I thanked him and agreed, hoping by this honor completely to smooth over my former rift with him, but requested only that everyone should meet at my place each time since I had a nicer apartment.

I was told that they would take turns, going first to one person and then another, wherever was nearest. We gathered at Zukhin's the first time. This was a tiny little room behind a partition in a large house on Trubnoy Boulevard. I was late the first day and arrived after they had begun reading. The tiny room was full of smoke, and not even from good tobacco but from some cheap shag that Zukhin was smoking. On the table there was a jug of vodka, a wineglass, bread, salt, and a mutton bone.

Zukhin, without getting up, invited me to drink some vodka and take off my coat.

"I guess you're not used to this sort of stuff," he added.

They were all wearing dirty calico shirts with false shirtfronts. Trying not to show my contempt for them, I took off my coat and stretched out on the sofa like *one of the boys*. Checking the various notebooks from time to time, Zukhin spoke while the others stopped him and asked questions, which he would answer clearly, concisely, and intelligently. I began to listen too and not understanding much of it, because I had not heard what went before, asked a question.

"Hey, there's no point in you listening if you don't know that, old boy," said Zukhin. "I'll lend you the notebooks and you can go over it for tomorrow, otherwise there's no point in explaining."

I felt ashamed of my ignorance and at the same time, aware of the justice of Zukhin's remark, stopped listening and took to watching my new companions. According to the division of people into *comme il faut* and not *comme il faut* they belonged, obviously, to the second class and therefore awakened in me not only feelings of contempt but also a certain sense of personal hatred, which I felt for them because, although not *comme il faut*, they seemed not only to look upon me as being equal to them but even patronized me good-naturedly. This feeling was also awakened in me by their feet and their dirty fingers with bitten-down fingernails, and one long fingernail that Operov had allowed to grow on his little finger, and their pink shirts and shirtfronts, and the swear words that they used affectionately with one another, and the dirty room, and Zukhin's habit of blowing his nose constantly by pressing his finger over one nostril, and in particular their way of saying, using, and pronouncing certain words. For instance they used words like *nincompoop* instead of fool, *whither* instead of where, *splendid* instead of nice, and certain old-fashioned turns of phrase, and so on, that struck me as stilted and extremely bad form. But this *comme il faut*–type hatred of mine was fanned still more by the way they pronounced certain words and especially foreign words: e.g., they would say things like áutomobile instead of automobíle, contróversy instead of cóntroversy, rendezvóus instead of réndezvous and Quijote instead of Quixote, and so on and so forth.

In spite of what was for me at that time their repulsive appearance, I sensed something good in these people and, envying the cheerful comradeship that bound them together, felt attracted to them and wished to come closer to them, no matter how difficult it might be for me. I already knew the gentle honest Operov; now the jaunty and extraordinarily clever Zukhin, who clearly dominated this circle, appealed to me tremendously. He was a short sturdy dark-haired man with a somewhat swollen and always shiny, but remarkably intelligent, animated and independent-looking face. This expression was especially due to the low forehead that bulged out over his deep black eyes and to his short bristly hair and heavy black growth of beard, that always made him look unshaved. He seemed not to think of himself (which always appealed to me in people), but it was clear that his mind never stopped working. He had one of those expressive faces that suddenly appear different to you several hours after you have seen them for the first time. This happened to me with Zukhin's face toward the end of the evening. Suddenly new lines appeared on his face, his eyes became deeper, his smile changed and his whole face was so transformed that I would have had difficulty in recognizing him.

When they had finished reading Zukhin, some other students and myself, in order to prove our desire to be good comrades, each drank a glass of vodka so that there was hardly anything left in the jug. Zukhin asked if anyone had a quarter-ruble in order to send the old woman that cleaned for him for more vodka. I started to offer him some of my money, but as though not hearing me Zukhin turned to Operov, who took out a beaded purse and gave him the required coin.

"Watch out you don't drink too much," said Operov, who did not drink himself.

"Don't worry," replied Zukhin, sucking the marrow from a mutton bone (I remember thinking at the time that this was what made him so clever).

"Don't worry," went on Zukhin, smiling slightly, and his smile was the sort that you noticed involuntarily and felt grateful to him for, "even if I do it won't matter; now we'll see, brother, who's going to outsmart whom, he me or me him. It's all in there, brother," he added, tapping his forehead boastfully. "But Semyonov has to watch out, he's been hitting the bottle pretty heavily."

Indeed, that same Semyonov with the graying hair who had so delighted me at the first examination by being worse to look at than I, and who had come out second in the entrance examinations, after attending lectures punctually the first month had taken to hard drinking and toward the end of the year had ceased appearing at the university at all.

"Where is he?" asked someone.

"I've even lost sight of him myself," went on Zukhin. "The last time we were together was when we broke up the Lisbon. We had a splendid time. Then, they say, there was some sort of scandal. . . . A great character! What fire there is in the man, what brains! It'll be a pity if he goes to rack and ruin. But he will for sure: he's not the sort of boy to sit quiet at the university, not with those outbursts of his."

After some more talk we all started to leave, agreeing to meet at Zukhin's on the other days as well because his apartment was the most central for everyone else. When we all went outside I felt somewhat ashamed that everybody else was on foot while I alone had a carriage, so, embarrassed, I offered Operov a lift. Zukhin left at the same time as we did and after borrowing a ruble from Operov went to spend the whole night somewhere with some friends. On the way home Operov told me a great deal about Zukhin's character and way of life and once at home I lay awake for a long time thinking of these new acquaintances of mine. Unable to drop off to sleep for a long time, I hovered between on the one hand respecting them, to which I was inclined by their knowledge, simplicity and honesty, and the poetry of their youth and audacity, and on the other being repelled by their slovenly appearance. In spite of my wholehearted desire to do so, it was literally impossible for me at that time to become friends with them. Our ideas were quite different. There was a host of nuances that constituted the whole charm and point of life for me and that were incomprehensible to them, and vice versa. But the main reasons why it was impossible for us to be friends were the twenty-ruble cloth of my coat, my carriage, and my Holland shirts. This reason was particularly important for me: it seemed to me that I involuntarily offended them with the marks of my good fortune. I felt guilty before them, and now humbling myself and now rebelling against my undeserved humiliation and going to the other extreme of arrogance, I was in no way able to enter into sincere equal relations with them. But the coarse depraved side of Zukhin's character was so outweighed for me at the time by the powerful poetry of that audacity I sensed in him that it did not have any unpleasant effect on me at all.

For about two weeks I went almost every evening to study at Zukhin's. I worked very little because, as I said before, I was behind my comrades and, not having the strength of mind to study alone and catch up, merely pretended to listen and to understand what was being said. I believe my comrades must have divined my pretense, because I often noticed that they skipped parts they all knew themselves without even asking me.

With every day I became more and more lenient toward the indecorum of this circle, feeling more and more drawn into its way of life and finding much that was poetic about it. Only the promise I had given to Dmitri never to go on the spree with them held me back from wishing to share their pleasures.

Once I wanted to boast to them of my knowledge of literature, particularly French, and led the conversation round to this topic. To my surprise it turned out that although they pronounced the foreign titles with a Russian accent, they had read much more than I and knew and appreciated not only English but even Spanish writers and Lesage, whom I had not even heard of at that time. Pushkin and Zhukovsky were for them literature (and not, as for me, little books in yellow bindings that I had read and learned from as a child). They had an equal contempt for Dumas, Sue, and Féval and were, particularly Zukhin, far clearer and better judges of literature than I, which I could not help but acknowledge. Nor had I any advantage over them in knowledge of music. To my even greater surprise, Operov played the violin, another of the students studying with us played the cello and piano, and both of them played in the university orchestra and knew and appreciated music. In short, they knew everything that I wished to boast about, except for my pronunciation of French and German, better than I and were not in the least proud of the fact. I might have boasted, in my position, of my society manners, but I did not have them the way Volodya did. So what was the height from which I looked down on them? My acquaintanceship with Prince Ivan Ivanich? French pronunciation? My carriage? Holland shirts? Fingernails? But this was all rubbish, wasn't it? Such questions as these began at times to pass dimly through my mind under the influence of my envious feelings for the comradeship and good-hearted youthful gaiety that I saw before me. They were all on intimate terms with one another. The simplicity of their manners approached rudeness, but beneath this rude surface one could constantly see their fear of offending one another even only very slightly. The words *rogue* and *swine* that they used affectionately jarred only on me and provided me with an excuse for inwardly jeering at them, but they were not in the least offended and it did not prevent them from being on the sincerest and friendliest terms among themselves. In their relations with one another they were as careful and tactful as only the very poor and the very young can be. But the main thing was that I scented something wholehearted and hellish about Zukhin's character and his exploits at the Lisbon. I sensed that these outings had to be something quite different from the shamming with rum punch and champagne that I had taken part in at Baron Z's.

XLIV

ZUKHIN AND SEMYONOV

I do not know which class of society Zukhin belonged to, but I know that he had been at S high school, had no money, and was not, apparently, a nobleman. He was eighteen then, although he looked much older. He was extremely clever and especially quickwitted: it was easier for him to grasp instantly a whole complex subject and foresee all its particulars and consequences than to consider with his conscious mind the laws that produced these consequences. He knew that he was clever, was proud of the fact, and because of this pride was equally simple and good-natured in his relations with everyone. He must have experienced a great deal in his life. His fiery sensitive nature had already had time to receive the imprint of both love and friendship, business and money. Although on a small scale and among the lower orders of society, there was not a thing that he had not experienced and for which he did not feel not exactly contempt but a sort of indifference and disinterest, both of which stemmed from the excessive easiness with which he achieved everything. He seemed to take up each new thing so enthusiastically only in order, on having attained his object, to disdain the thing he had attained, and his capable nature always attained its object and the right to disdain it. The same thing operated with regard to science: without studying very much or taking notes he had an excellent knowledge of mathematics and was not boasting when he said he would outwit the professor. He thought there was a lot of rubbish in the lectures he heard, but with the unconscious practical trickery that came naturally to him, immediately adapted himself to what the professors required and was popular with all of them. He was direct in his dealings with the administration and the administration respected him. He not only did not like or respect science, but even despised those who seriously studied something that came so easily to him. Science, as he understood it, did not occupy a tenth of his capacities; life in his position as a student offered nothing at all of the sort that he could wholly give himself up to, but his fiery active nature craved life, and so he resorted to loose living as far as his means permitted, and abandoned himself to it with passionate intensity and a desire to extend himself *to the limit of his strength*. Now, just before the examinations, Operov's prediction had come true. He disappeared for about two weeks, so that for the last part of the time we studied at another student's. But at the first examination he appeared in the hall—pale, exhausted, with trembling hands—and passed brilliantly into the second year.

At the beginning of the year there had been eight people in the gang of revelers headed by Zukhin. They included Ikonin and Semyonov at first, but the former had left the company because he could not stand up to the ferocious dissipation to which they had abandoned themselves at the beginning of the year, while the latter left it because even this was not enough for him. In the beginning everyone in our course had regarded them with a kind of horror and had related their exploits to one another.

The main heroes of these exploits were Zukhin and—at the end of the year—Semyonov. For the whole time recently Semyonov had come to be regarded with a sort of awe even and whenever he came to a lecture, which happened fairly rarely, there was excitement in the auditorium.

Just before the examinations Semyonov concluded his dissipated career in the most spectacular and original manner, to which I myself was a witness thanks to my friendship with Zukhin. This is how it was. One evening after we had just arrived at Zukhin's and Operov, his head bent over his notebooks and with a tallow candle in a candlestick and a tallow candle in a bottle standing beside him, had just begun to read in his high-pitched little voice from his finely handwritten physics notes, Zukhin's landlady came into the room and informed him that someone had come with a message for him.

Zukhin went out and soon came back with his head lowered and a thoughtful look on his face, holding an open note in his hand, written on gray wrapping paper, and two ten-ruble bills.

"Gentlemen! An extraordinary occurrence," he said, raising his head and looking at us with a sort of solemn gravity.

"What, been paid for your tutoring?" said Operov, leafing through his notebook.

"Well, get on with the reading," said someone.

"No, gentlemen! No more reading for me," went on Zukhin in the same tone of voice. "I'm telling you there's been an incomprehensible occurrence! Semyonov's just sent a soldier to me with these twenty rubles he borrowed from me some time ago, and he writes that if I wish to see him I should go to the barracks. You know what that means?" he added, looking round at all of us. We all remained silent. "I'm going to see him right away," went on Zukhin. "Anyone who wants to can come too."

Everyone at once donned their coats and prepared to go and see Semyonov.

"Won't it be a bit awkward," said Operov in his high-pitched voice, "if we all troop in to look at him like some rarity?"

I was completely in agreement with Operov's remark, particularly as far as I was concerned, since I hardly knew Semyonov, but it was so pleasant to think of myself taking part in a general comradely act and I so wanted to see Semyonov himself that I said nothing on the subject.

"Rubbish!" said Zukhin. "What's awkward about us all going to say good-bye to a friend, no matter where he is. It's nonsense. Whoever wants to, come."

We called some cabs, took the soldier along with us, and set off. The duty noncom did not want to let us into the barracks, but Zukhin somehow persuaded him and the soldier who had brought the message led us into a large room, almost dark and feebly lit by several night lights, where recruits wearing gray topcoats and with shaven foreheads lay or sat about on the bunks that lined both sides. Inside the barracks I was struck by the particular powerful smell and the sound of several hundred men snoring, and as I walked behind our guide and Zukhin, who was walking firmly between the bunks ahead of us all, I peered with trepidation at each recumbent form and endowed each one with my mental recollection of Semyonov's thickset sinewy figure, with his long, tousled and almost gray hair, white teeth, and gloomy shining eyes. In the far corner of the barrack room, by the last clay pot filled with black oil, in which a bent guttering wick smoked sootily, Zukhin quickened his pace and suddenly stopped.

"Hello, Semyonov," he said to a recruit whose head was shaved just like the others and who, wearing thick Army underwear and with a gray topcoat slung over his shoulders, was sitting with his feet up on his bunk, talking with another recruit and eating something. It was *he*, with his graying hair close-cropped, a blue shaved forehead, and his habitual gloomy and energetic expression on his face. I was afraid lest my glance offend him and therefore looked away. Operov, who seemed to share my opinion, was standing behind all the others; but the sound of Semyonov's voice as he greeted Zukhin and the others in his usual jerky manner completely reassured us and we hastened to go forward and offer—I my hand and Operov his board, but Semyonov stretched his big black hand out even before us, thus rescuing us from the unpleasant feeling of seeming to do him an honor. He spoke reluctantly and calmly, as always:

"How are you, Zukhin. Thanks for coming. Well, gentlemen, sit yourselves down. You clear off, Kudryashka," he spoke to the recruit with whom he had been having supper and talking, "we'll finish our talk later. Sit down. What? Surprised, eh, Zukhin? Eh?"

"Nothing surprises me about you," replied Zukhin, seating himself beside him on the bunk, somewhat with the expression of a doctor seating himself on a patient's bed. "I'd have been surprised if you'd come to the examinations, that I would. But tell us where you got to and how it all happened."

"Where did I get to?" he replied in his deep strong voice. "Oh, bars, dives, and various other establishments. But sit down, gentlemen, there's plenty of room. Hey, pull your legs up," he shouted imperiously, showing his white teeth for an instant at a recruit lying on the bunk to his left, who was resting his head on his arm and regarding us with idle curiosity. "I lived it up. It was disgusting. And good fun," he went on, the expression of his energetic face changing with each jerky sentence. "You know about that business with the merchant, don't you: the bastard died. They were going to kick me out. What money I had I threw away. That was nothing, though. I had stacks of debts left—nasty ones, too. And nothing to pay them with. And that's all."

"How on earth did such an idea occur to you?" said Zukhin.

"Easy: I was living it up at Yaroslavl—you know, at Stozhenka—drinking with some merchant gentleman. He provides recruits for the Army. 'Give me a thousand rubles,' I said, 'and I'll go.' And I went."

"But how can you; you're a nobleman," said Zukhin.

"Rubbish! Kirill Ivanov fixed all that."

"Who's Kirill Ivanov?"

"The one who bought me (at this his eyes flashed particularly oddly, quizzically, and mockingly and he seemed to smile). They got permission from the Supreme Court. I had some more fun, paid off my debts, and then went. That's all there is to it. Why not? They can't flog me . . . I'm five rubles to the good. . . . And perhaps there'll be a war . . ."

Then he started to tell Zukhin about his strange incredible adventures, constantly changing the expression of his energetic face while his eyes flashed gloomily.

When it was no longer possible to remain in the barracks we began to take our leave. He offered everyone his hand, shook ours firmly, and without getting up to see us out said:

"Drop in again, gentlemen; they say they won't be pushing us on till next month," and again he seemed to smile.

Zukhin, however, after taking a few steps, turned back. I wanted to see their farewell, so I also slowed my steps and saw Zukhin take some money from his pocket and offer it to him, but Semyonov pushed his hand away. Then I saw them embrace and heard Zukhin shout fairly loudly as he returned to us once more:

"Good-bye, egghead! I bet that before I finish my course you'll be an officer."

In answer to this Semyonov, who never laughed, roared with loud uncustomary laughter that astonished and pained me terribly. We left.

The whole way back, while we talked, Zukhin was silent and kept constantly sniffing, putting his finger first to one nostril and then the other. When we arrived home he immediately left us and from that day on drank heavily right up to the examinations.

XLV

I Fail

At last the first examination came—differential and integral calculus—and I was still in a kind of queer fog and had no clear conception of what awaited me. In the evenings, after meeting with Zukhin and my other companions, it would occur to me that I ought to alter my ideas somehow, that there was something wrong and bad about them, but in the morning, with the sun shining, I would again become *comme il faut,* was very satisfied with this and did not wish for any changes in myself.

It was in such a mood that I arrived for the first examination. I sat on a bench in that part of the hall where the princes, counts and barons sat and started to talk to them in French, and (strange as it may seem) it did not even occur to me that in a moment I would have to answer questions on a subject that I had no knowledge of whatsoever. I coolly watched those who were going up to be examined and even allowed myself to make fun of some of them.

"Well, Grap," I said to Ilinka when he returned from the front, "did you get the wind up?"

"We'll see how you get on," said Ilinka, who ever since he entered the university had completely rebelled against my influence, no longer smiled when I spoke to him, and was ill-disposed toward me.

I smiled scornfully at Ilinka's answer, in spite of the fact that the doubts he expressed frightened me for a moment. But the fog once more obliterated this feeling and I continued absentminded and indifferent, so that I even promised to go to Matern's for a snack with Baron Z immediately after having been examined (as though this were the most trivial matter possible for me). When my name was called together with Ikonin's, I adjusted the pleats in my uniform and approached the examination table with complete nonchalance.

A slight shiver of fright ran down my back only when the young professor, the same one who had examined me at the entrance examination, looked me straight in the face and I stretched out my hand to the notepaper on which the questions were written. Ikonin, although he took his slip with that same lunging movement of his whole body as he had done at the former examination, managed to give some sort of answer, although a very bad one; while I did what he had done at the first examination, but even worse, because I took a second slip and could give no answer at all to it. The professor looked me in the face regretfully and said in a quiet but firm voice:

"You will not pass to the second course, Mr. Irtenyev. Don't bother to attend the other examinations. We have to weed out the faculty. You too, Mr. Ikonin," he added.

Ikonin begged permission to take the examination again as though begging for alms, but the professor replied that he would not succeed in doing in two days what he had failed to do in a whole year and that he would never pass. Ikonin implored him again, pitifully and abjectly, but the professor again refused.

"You may go, gentlemen," he said in the same subdued but firm voice.

Only then did I bring myself to leave the table and I felt ashamed that by my silent presence I had seemed to participate in Ikonin's abject pleading. I do not remember how I traversed the hall past the other students, what I replied to their questions, how I emerged into the vestibule, and how I reached home. I was insulted and humiliated, I was truly unhappy.

For three days I did not leave my room, saw no one and, as in child-

hood, found relief in tears and wept a great deal. I looked for pistols
with which to shoot myself should I feel like it. I thought that Ilinka
Grap would spit in my face when he saw me and would be justified in
doing so; that Operov rejoiced in my misfortune and was telling everyone he met about it; that Kolpikov was quite right to insult me at Yar's;
that my stupid conversations with Princess Kornakov could not have
had any other consequences, and so on and so forth. All the painful
moments of my life, when my self-esteem had been wounded, passed
through my mind one after the other; I tried to blame someone for my
misfortune: I thought that someone had done it all on purpose,
thought up a whole plot against myself, railed at the professors and my
comrades, at Volodya and Dmitri, and at Papa for sending me to the
university; I railed at Providence for allowing me to live through such
a disgrace. Finally, conscious of my utter ruin in the eyes of all who
knew me, I begged Papa to allow me to join the hussars or go to the
Caucasus. Papa was displeased with me, but seeing how terribly
wounded I was, comforted me by saying that no matter how bad it was,
it could all be put right by my joining another faculty. Volodya, who
also saw nothing catastrophic in my misfortune, said that in another
faculty I would not at least feel ashamed in front of my new comrades.

Our ladies understood not at all and did not want to or were not
able to understand what an examination was and what it meant not to
pass, and merely pitied me because they saw my grief.

Dmitri came to see me every day and was extraordinarily tender
and humble the whole time; but precisely because of this it seemed to
me that he had cooled toward me. I always felt pained and insulted
when he came upstairs and sat close to me in silence, looking somewhat like a doctor who seats himself by a man who is seriously ill.
Sofya Ivanovna and Varyenka sent me books by him that I had formerly wished to have and hoped that I would visit them; but it was
precisely in this solicitousness that I saw the haughty and to me offensive condescension that is offered to a man who has fallen too low.
After about three days I calmed down a bit, but did not leave the house
until our departure for the country; thinking constantly of my grief, I
wandered aimlessly from room to room, trying to avoid everyone at
home.

I thought and thought and late one night, sitting alone downstairs and listening to Avdotya Vasilyevna's waltz, I suddenly jumped up, ran upstairs, took out my notebook headed *Rules for Life* and opened it—and experienced a moment of repentance and moral fervor. I wept, but they were no longer the tears of despair. Straightening up, I resolved once more to write rules for my life and was firmly convinced that I would never do anything bad again, that I would not spend a single minute idle and that I would never be false to my rules.

Whether this moral fervor continued for long, what it consisted of, and what new impetus it gave to my moral development I shall relate in the second and happier half of my youth.

A NOTE ON THE TYPE

The principal text of this Modern Library edition
was set in a digitized version of Janson, a typeface that
dates from about 1690 and was cut by Nicholas Kis,
a Hungarian working in Amsterdam. The original matrices have
survived and are held by the Stempel foundry in Germany.
Hermann Zapf redesigned some of the weights and sizes for
Stempel, basing his revisions on the original design.

MODERN LIBRARY IS ONLINE AT
WWW.MODERNLIBRARY.COM

MODERN LIBRARY ONLINE IS YOUR GUIDE
TO CLASSIC LITERATURE ON THE WEB

THE MODERN LIBRARY E-NEWSLETTER

Our free e-mail newsletter is sent to subscribers, and features sample chapters, interviews with and essays by our authors, upcoming books, special promotions, announcements, and news.

To subscribe to the Modern Library e-newsletter, send a blank e-mail to: **join-modernlibrary@list.randomhouse.com** or visit **www.modernlibrary.com**

THE MODERN LIBRARY WEBSITE

Check out the Modern Library website at
www.modernlibrary.com for:

- The Modern Library e-newsletter
- A list of our current and upcoming titles and series
- Reading Group Guides and exclusive author spotlights
- Special features with information on the classics and other paperback series
- Excerpts from new releases and other titles
- A list of our e-books and information on where to buy them
- The Modern Library Editorial Board's 100 Best Novels and 100 Best Nonfiction Books of the Twentieth Century written in the English language
- News and announcements

Questions? E-mail us at **modernlibrary@randomhouse.com**.
For questions about examination or desk copies, please visit
the Random House Academic Resources site at
www.randomhouse.com/acmart